ANDRE GONZALEZ

Dirty Money

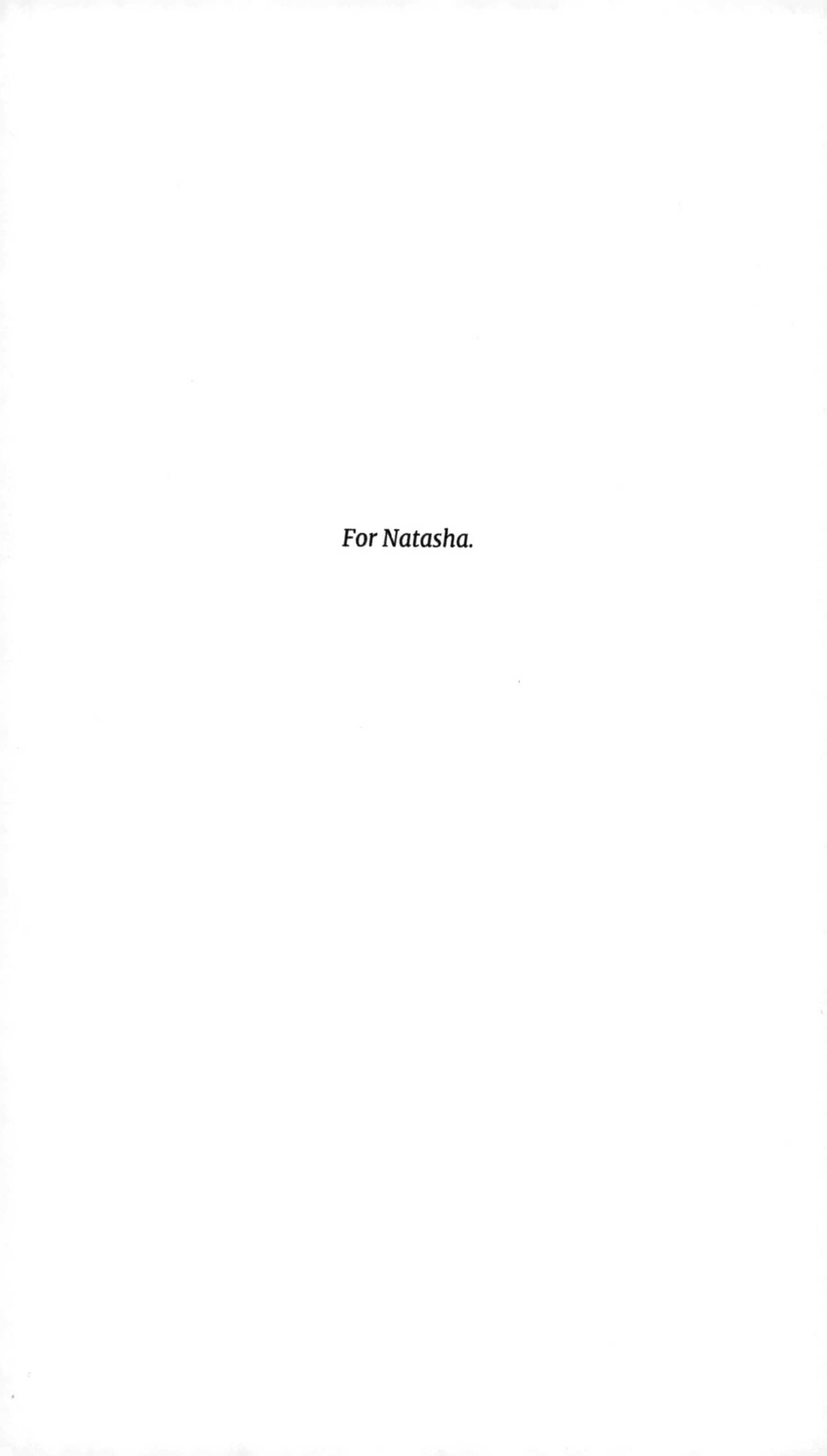

For Natasha.

"Greed makes man blind and foolish, and makes him an easy prey for
death."

—Rumi

Contents

GET EXCLUSIVE BONUS STORIES!

Connecting with readers is the best part of this job. Releasing a book into the world is a truly frightening moment every time it happens! Hearing your feedback, whether good or bad, goes a long way in shaping future projects and helping me grow as a writer. I also like to take readers behind the scenes on occasion and share what is happening in my wild world of writing. If you're interested, please consider joining my mailing list. If you do, I'll send you four FREE novellas as a thank you!

You can get your content **for free,** by signing up at www.andregonzalez.net

Chapter 1

July 22, 2017

The bold-lettered headline jumped off the cover of the *Seattle Times*: MOTHER KILLS TWO CHILDREN IN MURDER-SUICIDE.

Adam Marshall thought it was a twisted prank when he received the newspaper in his prison cell in Herlong, California, over six hundred miles from his hometown of Seattle.

The photo accompanying the article was a recent family picture of the mother and two children. Grins wide, teeth pearly-white, and no obvious concern about their father rotting away in a prison cell for a crime he never committed.

It was no prank—the newspaper was as real as the concrete walls around him. Hot tears rolled down Adam's face and splashed onto the page as he mentally inserted himself into the family portrait. Where he *should* have been.

Ten minutes passed before emotions got the best of Adam, prompting him to expel the contents of his stomach into his cell's metallic toilet.

"You okay in there, Marshall?" a voice called from the other side of the wall. It was his neighbor, PJ Phillips, serving a ten-year sentence for tax evasion.

"I'm fine!" Adam replied quickly, wiping the puke from his lips with a square of toilet paper before flushing it all away.

Adam was far from fine. Being falsely sentenced and imprisoned had taken its toll on his mental health, but reading the news that had broken out of Seattle sent his mind into a deranged tailspin. Would the headline exist if none of this bullshit had happened? Adam had been an involved father, there every day for his children. Never missing a baseball game or dance recital. Never too busy with work to cower behind the excuse so many parents used to get out of such events.

Rage intertwined with an overwhelming grief he'd never experienced before. If he could just lower his head and plow through the wall like a wild rhinoceros (and take out that cocksucking Warden Burke in the process), he might find some peace of mind.

Instead, he sat helpless on the ground, back against the wall while his hands trembled the newspaper. He was never getting out of this hell. Even at thirty-two years old, with eighteen years remaining in his twenty-year sentence, the duration seemed an eternity.

Adam *needed* to be home. He could close his eyes and smell the coffee brewing in the kitchen before heading out for work, Emily finishing up the dishes after feeding the kids breakfast. Jaxson's school was on his way to work, so he dropped him off every morning, leaving his son at the door with words of encouragement and a kiss on the forehead. He could still imagine that youthful scent between his lips if he tried hard enough.

That lifetime, though only three years in the past, had seemed another century entirely. Sometimes Adam wondered if it had ever been real. How could he go from having his dream job, house, and family to sitting in a six-by-nine prison cell, counting down every single day of a twenty-year sentence? Most people didn't know how many days were in twenty years, but Adam knew the precise answer: 7,305.

The only shining light was knowing he'd see his family a couple times during the kids' summer break, and that they'd be waiting for him after all of those days had passed. Emily had believed him when he explained himself, and she still had. Or else she wouldn't have kept visiting every summer. She knew the man he was, and couldn't connect the dots that tied him to the money laundering accusation. Adam had never even fully understood what money laundering *was*, let alone how to commit the crime.

Now Adam had none of that to look forward to. What would his life look like when he took his first step back into freedom as a 49-year-old man in 2035? He'd be utterly alone. His parents might have passed on by then—they were already in their mid-sixties. His three siblings had disowned him after the guilty verdict and hadn't so much as sent a letter during his first few years in prison. Friendships had already started dissipating once he had kids, and the few that remained surely wouldn't survive a two-decade absence.

Adam had these thoughts swirling in his mind as he read the article over and over, hoping by some miracle there was fine print deeming it a fake story.

Emily had shot each child in the head while they slept before turning the gun on herself, the reporter explained. Jaxson was their oldest, a seven-year-old boy who loved sports and playing with his little sister, Tegan. She was five and loved to dance and sing all over the house.

And Emily was the love of his life. A caring wife and mother who always put everyone else before herself.

Adam struggled to piece the story together. Where did Emily get a gun from? They had never kept one in the house. Who showed her how to use it? Did they know what she had planned on doing? Was it even a plan at all, or a crime in the heat of the moment?

He figured she would have gotten a gun since she served as the sole protector of the house. But they lived in a safe neighborhood. The worst crimes around were teenagers shoplifting from the mall. Did something happen that would have sparked her desire to have extra protection at home? He'd never know.

Adam brushed his thumb over Emily's face in the newspaper. "What happened?" he whispered. "What drove you to this?"

A lump bubbled in Adam's throat as a fresh wave of tears overtook him. He tried to put himself in his wife's shoes and imagine how awful life must have become for her to end it for all of them. It had to be tied to Adam's absence, and the thought sent sharp pangs of guilt throughout his body. Guilt for something he *didn't* do.

Adam imagined the night of the deaths in his mind, his fists balled up, fingernails drawing blood from his palms as he imagined his wife murdering their children in their sleep.

He never understood how miserable it must have been for his family. Emily had mentioned nothing on their visits—only talking about the good things happening in their lives. He never considered his family just might have it worse in their struggle to continue their life together without Adam in it.

His life was straightforward. Swallow watered-down eggs

for breakfast. Scrub the prison floors. Receive a two-minute shower. Sit in his cell for two hours before having another shitty meal for lunch. An hour outside. An hour inside reading. Scrubbing the floors again. More time in the cell. Another shitty meal for dinner. Back to the cell for the rest of the night.

It was the same monotonous routine every single day. He had been told of new chores after a few years, but none had come yet. They planned out his life until his release. Emily and the kids had to scramble to establish a new routine while being shackled to the story of their father caught in one of the biggest money laundering schemes in recorded history.

They had it much worse than Adam.

He closed his eyes, and everything that led to this came flooding back to his mind.

He saw himself applying for the job at WonderHome. Interviewing with the CEO and other executives. Receiving an offer letter. His first day on the job as a full-time personal assistant with a major salary. He remembered how on top of the world he had felt through it all. He *was* happy, in the truest sense of the word. All until the day the FBI barged into their offices and went straight to his desk. He could see the agent who had spoken to him, hiding behind a pair of sunglasses while two other agents yanked Adam's arms behind his back to arrest him.

The panic and confusion that had consumed him in that moment still hadn't left to this day. He saw the jail cell. The hours of interrogation by so many attorneys and legal experts. He remembered the courtroom. The jury. The district attorney and his team who were so hell-bent on sending Adam to prison. And the judge. The *fucking* judge who never allowed an objection from Adam's defense team, but always did for the opposition. He remembered the smug look the judge gave him while reading the twenty-year sentence aloud, and the way he waved his hand to dismiss him from the courtroom like he was nothing but a nuisance who had wasted tax dollars and time.

Adam opened his eyes. His family was gone. That was the reality of where this fucked-up road had led him. He'd remain stuck for the next eighteen years in prison, wishing he could just go back and stop it all from happening.

Chapter 2

Present day

Arielle Lucila tipped back the final remains of her second glass of wine.

She sat at a table for two in a dimly lit corner of one of Denver's finest restaurants, the Palace Arms. She had agreed to a date night with Javonte Morris, a running back for the Denver Broncos, who had been pursuing a night out with the top-ranked Angel ever since they met at a nightclub he partially owned.

They had already enjoyed a lavish dinner with the finest cuts of steaks, lobster, and a banana mousse dessert that she would surely think about long after they left.

The temptation remained for a third glass of wine. Conversation had flowed smoothly, especially for her first real date since college. Following the end of her long-term relationship, Arielle had given little consideration to jumping back into the dating world, and dove all the way into her career as an assassin for the time-traveling society known as the Road Runners.

Men had approached her plenty of times over the years, but none had ever caught her attention like Javonte. He had a quiet confidence, and despite his face being broadcast across the country every Sunday during football season, Javonte admitted to preferring a low-key lifestyle away from the cameras and glamour most superstar athletes flocked to.

"So, what did you think about dinner?" Javonte asked, cracking a childish grin as he leaned back and crossed his arms. Even in the poor lighting, his diamond-encrusted necklace and bracelet sparkled blindingly. Arielle estimated the two pieces were worth around $75,000. But athletes had their salaries publicized and debated by all those who cared. And Javonte was currently on year three of a $30 million contract.

That was something else that drew Arielle to him. They both had virtually unlimited funds, yet neither of them acted like the rich snobs sitting at the other tables in the restaurant.

Arielle smiled, poking around the remaining mousse on her plate. "I'll admit I had a great time tonight."

Javonte clapped his hands, drawing attention from the other diners. Some scoffed at the abrupt loud noise, while others gawked in amazement that they were sitting in the same room as a future Broncos legend. "I told you we'd have a good time. All I wanted was a chance."

"Yes, I know," Arielle replied, face breaking out into a full grin. "You were right."

"It doesn't have to stop, either. Do you want to go to my club? We have one of the best DJs in Denver spinning tonight."

Part of Arielle wanted to—the spontaneity of the wine made her feel laid-back for once.

"I wish, but I promised my friend I'd meet her for drinks after our date."

Javonte raised both hands, gesturing to her to say no more. "You gotta talk with your girl about how the date went. I get it.

If you two are looking for something to do later, you should still stop by. If not, when can I see you again?"

Arielle had been bracing for this question all night. It had become inevitable that they were connecting and their relationship wouldn't end after one date.

"I'll have to let you know," Arielle said. "Work is about to get pretty busy—I'm talking long hours around the clock. We don't all get to spend our days running around with a ball."

"Oh, hell no!" Javonte howled, clutching his gut. "Shots fired!"

Arielle had told him she worked in the district attorney's office. It was her go-to occupation of choice when she had to lie, seeing as the job could require upward of eighty hours per week and leave her the opportunity for abrupt phone calls that would "call" her into the office. And she had read enough Grisham novels to feel confident in bullshitting her way through a conversation about the law, if required.

"Okay," Javonte said, leaning forward. "You know where I'll be. Hit me up when you're ready to go out again. Now let's get you out of here."

He rose from his seat, and Arielle couldn't help but admire her date. Six feet tall, two hundred and fifteen pounds of pure muscle wrapped inside an Armani suit.

Damn, she thought, wishing she hadn't confirmed the plans with Selena.

Arielle joined his side, and now that the running back was standing—and towering above the room—everyone took notice and gazed while the couple strolled out of the restaurant, arms intertwined.

"So, where are you off to?" Javonte asked.

"Not sure yet," Arielle said. "Selena hasn't let me know

where. I need to call her."

"You sure like to live on the edge. Wandering downtown without a plan in the world. I don't think I could ever do that—I need some structure in my day."

Arielle giggled. "I'm the same way, actually, but Selena couldn't be any more opposite. Knowing her, she's dancing on top of a bar right now, gathering a crowd, and that's why she hasn't let me know where to meet yet."

Javonte laughed. "Sounds like a fun friend. I suppose we all need one in our life, right? Well, whatever you end up doing, I hope you have a good time. I'll be waiting for your call."

He released his arm from Arielle's, his fingers brushing over forearm in a subtle gesture that sent goosebumps up her back.

"Thank you for tonight," she said. "I really needed that."

"The pleasure was all mine. Now go have a fun night with Selena."

Javonte offered one last grin as he turned and started down the sidewalk.

Selena was at the bar across the street from the restaurant they had just left, probably on her second margarita. Arielle knew this, but didn't want Javonte to think they were being watched on their date—not that they were. Arielle had suggested the bar for Selena for the sake of having as short of a walk as possible after the date.

She waited for Javonte to disappear before crossing the street and stepping into La Loma, an upscale Mexican eatery that touted over one hundred tequila choices. Arielle pushed her way through the crowded lobby and found Selena sitting at the bar, her purse saving the open seat next to her.

Selena sat half-facing the bar and entryway, grinning and

waving as Arielle approached.

"Well, you look like you had a nice time," Selena said, the two hugging before Arielle took her seat. "I don't think I've ever seen such a big smile on your face."

Arielle nodded, pleased to find a frozen strawberry margarita already waiting for her. "It went way better than I was expecting. He really is a nice guy, not into the fame and all that."

Selena squealed before taking a long sip of her drink. "Tell me all about it."

Arielle spent the next ten minutes recapping the date, Selena eager for every detail, devouring an entire basket of chips and salsa while she listened.

"So, when's the next date?" Selena asked.

"You sound just like him," Arielle said with a light chuckle. "I don't know yet. We're about to start that mission, so probably after that. Depends if I go visit my grandma after the mission—I haven't decided yet."

"Well, don't make him wait too long. He may be humble and all that, but he *is* an NFL player and nightclub owner. It's not exactly a struggle for him to find other women if he never hears from you."

"I know that, but why does there have to be so much pressure? What does a second date mean? At what point does it transition from dating into an exclusive relationship? I enjoyed the night out with Javonte, but this is the part I was dreading. Why does dating have to be so complicated?"

Selena reached out and placed her hand on top of Arielle's. "It's only as complicated as you make it. Be upfront from the beginning. Tell Javonte how slow or fast you want things to go. If he can't accept your requests, you can try to compromise or just move on."

"But I don't even know what I want. I'm not opposed to being in a serious relationship—I was ready to marry Kevin, after all—but at this point in my life, I honestly don't understand where a boyfriend even fits into my schedule."

Selena had ordered two tequila shots that the bartender now placed in front of them. She grabbed one and held it up. "Arielle, you need to get out of your head. Not every aspect of your life has to be planned to the finest detail. Sometimes you just need to jump into the deep end, start swimming, and see where you end up. Some things in life can't be planned. You don't think Javonte has a busy schedule? He's a professional athlete. He has practice, workouts, trainings, film sessions, charity events, and tons of travel. Plus, he's a business owner. He's just as busy as you, but look, you both cut time out of your schedules to have dinner tonight."

"That was just dinner, though. I can make meal plans any time. Being in a relationship is a lot more than having dinner together. He'd want me at his games, probably even some of the road ones. He'll want me to join him at some of those charity events. I can't be that type of girlfriend."

"Did he tell you that's what he's looking for?" Selena asked. Arielle grabbed her shot glass reluctantly and tapped it against Selena's before they both downed the tequila.

"Well, no, but—"

"But nothing. *Talk to him.* You're playing mind games with yourself because you don't actually know what he wants. You're making assumptions. He might be totally fine with you having a busy schedule and only seeing you every couple of days. That's just how some relationships are. Do you think Beyonce sits around at home all day waiting for Jay-Z to come home, dinner cooked and served on the table? Hell no! They are both busy individuals, and they make it work, even if that means going weeks without seeing each other. Just stop trying to plan everything, and *talk to Javonte.*"

Arielle rubbed her forehead. The margarita and tequila shot were mixing with all the wine to give her a headache. "Okay. I'll talk to him and see where he stands with things."

Selena clapped her hands together. "Thank you. Now that I've helped you sort out your love life, have you heard anything about the next mission?"

"Not yet. I only ever get a list of the potential missions we can go on—usually twenty or so—but I don't find out until we meet with Commander Briar. He has the final say on what's assigned to us."

"Well, I can't wait for Monday morning to find out. I'm still riding a high from the last one. I still can't believe how that all went down."

"Believe it. You won that mission for us. *You* were the hero."

"And you made sure everyone knows about it—thank you for that. It was nuts seeing my name in the rankings. Top 300, sure, but it's not something I ever thought would happen. Top-ranked actress is still mine, but we're never expected to crack the overall rankings—that's for Angels like you."

"There was a time when a woman would never be considered for a chance of ranking. Now there are four of us in the top ten alone, and I don't know how many others in the top 300. Expectations are just other people drawing their boundaries for you. Who gives a shit what they say? Just go out there and do your best. That's all we can do."

Selena nodded. "Then I guess we'll keep climbing the ranks." She raised her glass, and Arielle clinked hers against it before they finished their drinks.

"Have you heard from Felix at all?" Arielle asked.

"I know he's alive and well," Selena said with a chuckle. "You know how he is. Been at home since the last mission ended. Pretty sure he locks himself in his basement to play his video games and watch sports—assuming he isn't going out to the games in person."

Arielle laughed. "We all have our ways of unwinding. I had promised him a trip to see his parents before we start the next mission. I'm not sure if he remembers that, but I'm still going to do it. We'll take my jet if you want to come with us a couple days before the mission starts. If not, you can just meet us wherever we end up going."

"You think we're finally leaving Colorado for a mission?"

"Oh, I insisted on it. We need a change of scenery every now and then. We're supposed to cover all of North America. I requested tropical locations in Costa Rica and Guatemala, but I'm sure we'll end up nowhere near there."

"Well, that would be a fun time!"

"Exactly. I think that's why they usually send Angels over the age of forty to handle the missions down there. I guess they don't fully trust us rowdy twenty-somethings to get the job done with all the temptation in places like that."

"Sounds like ageism to me."

"You can take that up with Commander Briar, if you'd like. Don't expect to make any progress."

Arielle stood up from the bar, swaying so slightly.

"You're ready to leave already?" Selena asked, an offense taken in her voice.

"Yes. I've had way too much to drink. You forget I don't do this often...it just hit me. I really need to lie down."

Selena giggled as she stood to join Arielle. "See, they can send you to Miami in the middle of spring break. What are they afraid is going to happen? You'll have a rager on the beach and pass out by eight o'clock?"

Arielle howled laughter, the booze exaggerating the humor in everything. "I just need to get to bed. I'll see you on Monday?"

"Can't wait."

Chapter 3

By Monday morning, Arielle felt like herself again. She wouldn't call Sunday a hangover day—she didn't have a headache or nausea—but she hadn't quite felt like herself, opting to spend the day in her pajamas to binge-watch game shows.

She couldn't remember the last time she had a lazy day like that, and was understanding the benefits of relaxation in between missions. It had only been a month since the recent shift to more work-life balance. She had grown so used to feeding a constant urge to do something, that a day of true leisure (she couldn't even recall if she brushed her teeth in the morning) seemed like a betrayal to her inner workaholic.

When she sprung out of bed on Monday, however, she had never felt so mentally or physically ready to start a new mission. It had only been a week since they returned from the last one, but her mind was so *clear*. Focused.

She had become used to transitioning from one mission to the next, sometimes with mere hours in between. Now, she had time to actually decompress from the last mission and start the next one with a clean palette.

Their meeting was set with Commander Briar for 10 A.M. While getting dressed, Arielle thought back to how skeptical they had all been before their first mission together. It was a new process for all of them having to work with the same dedicated team, and while Arielle knew she wouldn't have issues with her direct mission work, she had doubts on how the team dynamics would play out, especially with a loose cannon like Selena Nicole.

Two missions later, she and Selena were practically best friends, and Felix fit in perfectly when the trio were together. That initial angst had given way to excitement as they stared down their third mission together. Everyone understood each other's strengths and weaknesses, and how to make it all gel together.

By the time she arrived downtown, parking her BMW in front of the familiar marketing firm that housed the Road Runners' headquarters in its basement, Arielle stepped onto the sidewalk feeling like a new era had arrived in her career.

The calendar had flipped to August, and they only had a few weeks left of the blistering heat before autumn took hold. Arielle stood on the sunny sidewalk, drawing in a deep breath of the crisp morning air. She was still on top of her game and didn't even consider herself close to reaching her prime. She had more room to grow as an Angel, and now she had a team eager to rise with her.

Commander Briar had been right. These new teams were truly for the best. They would need to prove themselves on more missions, but Arielle already believed they could handle a mission of any magnitude thrown their way. No matter what the commander assigned them today, they'd take the files, make a plan, and execute it. Then it was back to another week off.

"Arielle!" Felix shouted from down the sidewalk, jogging

toward her with a wide grin smacked across his face. They embraced, and Arielle immediately noticed a similar wave of energy emitting from Felix. The last mission had taken an intense toll on him, and Arielle wondered if that had driven Felix into hiding upon their return home. Whatever he had done worked, apparently.

"How are you doing?" Arielle asked.

"Never been better." Optimism clung to each word. "I wasn't quite ready to come here today, at least last night. But when I woke up today, I was a little excited. Is this how it's always felt for you doing missions, being the best and all?"

Arielle laughed. "Being the best doesn't make any of this more or less fun. If anything, it has made it more routine. Trust me, I've had plenty of missions where I needed to drag myself to come here. I think the time off played a huge factor in how we're all feeling. Me and Selena were just talking the other night how we're excited to start this next mission, too."

"Well, if we're already on the same page, I'd hate to be the poor soul on the other end of this mission. You ready to go in?"

"Let's do it."

They climbed the short flight of steps and entered the marketing office, the place abuzz with agents on the phone and the *click-clack* of fingers banging on keyboards. The employees were all part of the Road Runners organization, their lone job being to operate a legitimate marketing firm. The last Arielle had heard, Commander Briar had implemented new leadership to make the company a reliable source of income for the organization.

The vibes were plenty different from the prior times Arielle had strolled through, back when they were simply going through the motions to keep the company afloat.

No one even paid them any attention as Arielle and Felix strolled to the manager's office in the back. When they stepped in, they found the typically forgotten office space completely remodeled with updated furniture, motivational artwork, and a fancy coffee machine in the corner.

Before, the room had been more like a closet, considering its rear door led down to the basement where the headquarters lay hidden.

"Like what I've done with the place?" a woman asked from behind, startling Arielle and Felix as they admired the new office.

They spun around to a short, pudgy woman, likely in her mid-thirties with reddish-brown hair brushed as straight as the bristles on a brand-new broom. She smiled at the two Angels, looking back and forth between them. Her eyes lit up when she realized who was standing in her office.

"Arielle Lucila and Felix Francisco?!" she squealed. The professional tone she had just used gave way to one of a teenage girl giddy to meet her crush from her favorite boy band. "They told me you'd be here at some point. Obviously, Denver is your home base. I'm just so . . . honored."

"It's nice to meet you," Arielle said, sticking out a hand. "What's your name?"

"I'm so sorry," the woman gasped, her cheeks flushing red. "I'm Jackie Monaghan, and I run this office now."

"I'm impressed, Jackie," Arielle said. "You did all this in a week? It's a whole new mood out there. Not to mention in here."

Jackie grinned, her face still red. "Why, thank you. A week in real time, maybe. Commander Briar hired me and asked for immediate results and an overhaul. So, naturally, I took our staff into the past where I could train them for a month, and brought them back the following day ready to hit the ground running. I might have scheduled all the contractors to come in while I was in the past, too." She grinned, satisfied with her recap of events.

Felix nodded. "That's actually really efficient."

"I suppose that's why Commander Briar picked me. Why waste my precious time on Earth doing any task in the present when I can go back a week and do it then, and only miss ten minutes in the present? I don't see why more people don't think this way."

"What did you do before taking over this role?"

"I was in the accounting department for the Road Runners. My efficiency was through the roof, and that gained me some attention." Jackie shrugged, her face finally returning to its normal pale tone. "I'd leave most days by lunchtime, sometimes earlier, with all of my work done for the day."

"Doesn't that get exhausting?" Felix asked. "And confusing?"

"Not at all. Hard to be exhausted when I get to take a nap every single day. One perk of being done so early. As for confusing—no. I keep tons of spreadsheets and checklists. It might seem intense to an outsider, but it's all very organized when I look at it."

"We just might have to get you on our team," Felix joked.

Jackie's eyes bulged, completely missing the sarcasm in Felix's statement.

"Don't listen to him," Arielle said, smacking Felix on the arm. "We don't have any openings right now—not that it's even up to us."

"Well, if that time ever comes, you know where to find me."

"Yeah, wandering around last week," Felix said, sparking a round of laughter.

"It was a pleasure meeting you, Jackie," Arielle said. "But we really need to be heading down to meet with the commander now. If you'll excuse us."

"Of course. Don't mind me. Best of luck to you on your next mission."

Arielle and Felix made their way past Jackie's desk and pulled open the door to welcome the usual mustiness that accompanied the dim, somewhat creepy stairwell that led downstairs.

When they started down and the door closed behind them, Felix said, "Well, she was interesting."

"I liked her. She has a ton of confidence, but a strange way of expressing it. Seems like she's already made an impact, so I'm sure the commander loves her already."

They reached the bottom landing and pushed open the door, Arielle bracing for what other changes they might have made in the short week since she'd last been down in the headquarters.

To her delight, nothing had changed. The bullpen bustled with chaos, always reminding her of how movies portrayed the stock exchange, with everyone shouting over each other, although not *as* loud.

This small corner of the world, buried beneath downtown Denver, ran operations affecting hundreds of millions of lives across North America. It was both intimidating and peaceful to Arielle, and she could never help but smile when she felt the energy the headquarters provided. Commander Briar wouldn't remain in his position forever, and she only hoped the next commander opted to keep the organization's main office in Denver.

"Good morning, you two," said a man sitting to their left at the corner desk, directly across from Commander Briar's office. It was Elijah Ward, the commander's assistant.

Chairs stood against the wall across from Elijah, giving the commander's office an official waiting area for visitors.

"Good morning, Elijah," Arielle said. "How are things?"

"Better now that you're here, darling."

Elijah rose from his seat and came around to give Arielle a hug. The two had gotten to know each other over the years. Elijah had left his home in Toronto after a messy divorce with his ex-husband, and ended up in Denver, where he took the first job he could find at the Road Runners office before it had become the headquarters. Commander Briar promoted Elijah to be his assistant shortly after the war against the Revolution ended.

"I like what you've done with the place," Arielle said. "Both down here and upstairs."

"Isn't Jackie just the best? She's made my life much easier, which has allowed me to do more of the things I've been putting off down here. HQ is about to get a massive overhaul as well, but we can only do it in small portions, obviously."

"Well, I look forward to it. Is the commander ready for us?"

"Give him about five minutes, and he'll see you. Hi, Felix." Elijah shot a wink at Felix before pivoting and returning to his desk, making Felix blush.

Arielle took a seat against the wall, Felix joining her. He leaned over and whispered, "Does he know I don't swing that way? He's always winking at me."

Arielle grinned, shaking her head. "I don't think he cares," she whispered back. "If he thinks you're cute, that's all there is to it. He's a real jokester, too, so it's impossible for me to know if he's being serious or just messing with you."

Felix shook his head, smiling to himself, when Commander Briar's door swung open, their leader strolling out with complete casualness. He grinned upon seeing Arielle and Felix, the two of them promptly standing up to greet him.

"Nice work on that last mission," Commander Briar said, shaking hands with both. "Selena isn't here yet?"

"I'm here!" Selena called out from behind, the entrance door closing behind her as she shuffled down the short hallway to meet them.

"Great, you're all here," Commander Briar said. "I have a pretty loaded morning, so I'd love to get started. Let's head into my office."

The commander spun around and returned to his office, the three Angels trailing behind him. Three chairs were positioned in front of his oversized desk, the commander taking his seat behind a thick file stuffed with papers.

"Before we discuss the next mission," he said, interlocking his fingers beneath his chin. "I want to hear your concerns about the last one. I know you got the job done, but it wasn't the cleanest of missions. What were some issues you ran into?"

Felix and Selena both looked to Arielle, happy to defer. They may have all been on the same team, but neither of them had reached a level of comfort in having these types of conversations with the leader of their organization. Arielle expected as much, and cleared her throat before speaking.

"I think the biggest issue we ran into was the setup of the entire mission. We understand there will always be some level of investigating that needs to be done, but this one seemed like we had to figure out the whole story. It made it difficult for us to really set a plan, and it felt like we were constantly chasing a moving target. We're not detectives, but the mission felt like one that should have had one. We don't know how to follow clues and build a case."

Commander Briar raised his hand, nodding. "I knew I'd hear all about this, eventually. From the day I assigned this mission to you. You have all the skills a good detective has. The only difference is that you've been used to using those skills to navigate around the past. Sure, we can line up a ton of missions with everything laid out. You'll just need to show up and know how to carry out the assassination without the past interfering. That alone is detective work—identifying problems and inconsistencies, opportunities for failure, your target's schedule and whereabouts.

"What we've found through recent studies is that there is less resistance from the past when our Angels go into missions having to figure things out on their own. The past knows everything, so it knows when you arrive with a plan, no matter how well you've masked your intentions. What it doesn't know is what you will figure out when starting from a virtually clean slate upon your arrival."

"So you're going to deliberately withhold information from us?" Arielle asked. "To make the mission easier?"

"Not easier," the commander replied firmly. "*Safer*. See, we've already had a few dozen missions done with this new team structure. And while they have successfully completed most, we've had an increase in concerns from the Angels. What you're telling me about your last mission is on par with what we've been hearing. It has elevated the danger since we launched these teams."

Arielle's stomach sunk. The Road Runners loved to experiment with many matters. An increased risk to any member would typically end an experiment. They didn't gamble with their members' lives, and she feared the new team structure might vanish as quickly as it had formed.

Commander Briar must have sensed her unease, saying, "But never fear, we're making adjustments. When I read Felix had been bitten by a snake in your post-mission report, I knew something was wrong. Granted, that could have been a total fluke occurrence, but I think we all know better. Especially considering *when* it happened during the mission."

"So our missions are going to become more *difficult?*" Selena asked. Felix had let his eyes wander into space, likely thinking back to the traumatizing night he had to deal with the snakebite.

Commander Briar lowered his hands to his desk and leaned forward. "I can't make a blanket statement like all missions will be more difficult. Some might be. Some might be easier. We can't really judge that yet. But our top priority is your safety, so I can say all missions should have less risk involved. More work once you're in the past, but not necessarily harder to complete our objectives."

He leaned back as the office fell silent, Arielle noticing the fatigue swimming behind the commander's eyes. An exhaustion she hadn't seen on him since the last days of the war.

"What do you guys think?" Selena asked her fellow Angels.

Felix shrugged. "I suppose it's like anything else. We just have to go out and see how it all plays out. You know less danger is okay in my book, even if it requires we have to worry about more details once we arrive. I think we'll manage."

All eyes in the room turned to Arielle, who had remained silent during the commander's explanation. She wasn't fond of the idea of having more to do after arriving in the past, but knew an argument over safety would be one she'd never win.

"Let's try it," she said. "I am curious, though—what will happen to the Advance Team that does all the research ahead of time?"

"Nothing different for them," Commander Briar said. "They will conduct the preliminary research ahead of time. The only difference is that you may see less information in your reports from them. Expect them to be a lot more high-level than the tons of details you're used to."

"So they'll be withholding information that could be beneficial."

"That is correct, Ms. Lucila. My team members, with the help of the Lieutenant Commander, have been working to find the sweet spot for how much information to give, and how it affects the risk associated with each mission. They believe they have found the breakeven point, and that's why I'm coming to you with all of this today. We would never test these things on our best-performing team—your missions are already risky enough. But they have enough of a sample size to feel confident in your next mission and what is provided to you in the Advance Team's report."

Arielle pursed her lips. She could recall only a handful of times where the commander had called her *Ms. Lucila*. The two had a strong relationship, but the formality of this address reminded everyone in the room who was in charge.

She nodded. "Okay. We'll report back with any concerns after the mission. Now, can we talk about what our next mission is?"

Chapter 4

The tension had grown heavy in Commander Briar's office, and he promptly called for a quick five-minute break before they jumped into the details for their upcoming mission.

The commander stepped out and disappeared to the kitchen.

"Are you okay?" Selena asked Arielle.

"Yep," Arielle said, her jaw clenching. She knew they wired the office with listening devices and wouldn't dare peep another word about her disgust concerning the recent changes. She already had her frustrations with playing detective on the last mission, having insisted she would speak with Commander Briar about never receiving missions like it again. Instead, this was going to become the new normal.

The thought of going into a mission with less information made Arielle's blood boil. She had grown accustomed to absorbing as many details as possible before taking a trip through time. The uncertainty she had felt during multiple points on the last mission was nothing she wanted to experience again. Now she didn't have a choice.

Felix and Selena took Arielle's one-word response as the obvious clue she didn't want to discuss the matter. They sat in silence until the commander returned and closed the door behind him.

"All right," he said as he settled into his seat, acting as if everything was fine. He opened the file that had been on his desk since they arrived and turned it around to face the three Angels.

They saw a newspaper clipping from a July 2017 edition of the *Seattle Times*. The headline read: MOTHER KILLS TWO CHILDREN IN MURDER-SUICIDE. A portrait below showed a woman with a young boy and girl.

"Meet the Marshall family," Commander Briar said, pushing the clipping forward. "The mother is Emily. Son is Jaxson. Daughter is Tegan. As you can see, these three had a night from hell a few years ago. Our goal is to stop this tragedy from happening. However, we strongly believe stopping it has nothing to do with interfering directly with the family."

The commander ruffled through the stack of papers to fish out a mug shot of a man in his early thirties. He dropped it on top of the newspaper clipping, the man's green eyes staring at all three Angels with a desperation swimming behind them.

"This is the father, Adam Marshall. The murder-suicide occurred in May 2017. Before that, the FBI arrested Adam in 2014 for suspicion of money laundering. They sentenced him to twenty years in prison in June 2015. Adam has insisted on his innocence to this day, and many believe him. All the money laundering was through the company he worked for, WonderHome, Inc."

"The real estate site?" Arielle asked. "Why didn't we hear about this? They're the biggest online real estate marketplace in the country."

"Exactly," Commander Briar said. "That's where it doesn't add up. The laundering scheme was all done within Wonder-

Home's infrastructure, but everything was only under Adam's name."

"So they framed him," Selena said, always eager to jump to a conclusion.

"Not exactly. It's entirely possible that he pulled this off on his own, and that he is indeed guilty. He worked directly for the company's CEO, so he had access to nearly every aspect of the company. His name is on all documents related to the laundering. No one else. His trial was a mess of pointing fingers. He said the company set him up. The company said they had no knowledge of what he was doing—which could be true since he only had one person, the CEO, overlooking his work. And we know a CEO won't spend their time monitoring their assistant."

"So why do the Road Runners think he's innocent?" Arielle asked.

"As our Advance Team dug deeper into this tragedy's past, they came across deposition interviews with Mr. Marshall. Several on our team believe he didn't understand what money laundering even was, let alone how to pull off a scheme of this magnitude."

"And that never came up in court?"

"Of course, but the prosecution just powered through, saying he was playing dumb. And why not? They had all the evidence they needed to put him away. It was a slam-dunk case, and they won with no issues. It was definitely an inside job, but it seems too big for one person to handle. He had to have someone helping him. I find it impossible that he didn't. We're talking *millions* of dollars. It could have been someone higher up in the company that kept their hands clean. Or maybe a colleague. A fellow assistant from another department. What we don't know is how happy Mr. Marshall was at his place of employment. Did something happen that could have sparked a thirst for revenge? That's what we'll need you to find out."

Commander Briar sat back and crossed his arms, waiting for one of the Angels to speak.

"If I may be honest, Commander," Arielle said. "The Mason Gregory mission had a lot of happenings inside his employer's offices, but we didn't have any way in. I wasted so many hours sitting in my car and staring at the outside of the office building."

The commander opened his mouth to speak, but Felix cut him off. "That won't happen again. Whoever needs to get inside the office will get inside. I'll see to it."

Felix spoke with a tinge of disdain, clearly still displeased with himself for the error he had made on the team's first mission together.

"This doesn't sound like a two-week mission," Arielle said.

"It's not. You'll be traveling back to mid-2013 in Seattle and staying for at least eight months. The goal is to get at least one of you employed by the company before they hire Mr. Marshall. It can even be all of you—that part is up to you to figure out, along with what might be the best position to fill to keep a close eye on Mr. Marshall. He was only with the company for six months before his arrest."

"I am *not* cleaning toilets again," Selena said, earning a light chuckle from Felix.

"I wouldn't worry about that, Ms. Nicole," Commander Briar said. "This will be a focus on the other end of the corporate ladder. The executives. The suits. Whatever you kids like to call them these days."

"Heartless sharks," Arielle muttered under her breath. "Eight months, though. Seems excessive."

Commander Briar raised a steady hand. "Missions will get longer, but it's lightening the workload. We've heard loud and clear from several Angels that the constant grind of going two or three weeks straight is taking its toll. I understand the simple necessities in life, like eating and sleeping, come at a premium during your missions. Just because you're in the past and not aging doesn't mean these things have no effect on you. You're still a human, and I'd like to apologize for the lifestyle you've had to endure."

"It's honestly never bothered me," Arielle said.

"Speak for yourself, *numero uno*," Selena said. "I, for one, am grateful, Commander. So thank you. When you say the missions will run longer, are you implying we'll have actual free time during the trips into the past?"

"That is the intent, but your schedule is ultimately up to Arielle. There shouldn't be a need to follow around your target every waking moment of the day. Especially on this mission, since most of the action is going to occur at the workplace, Monday through Friday. You might have to use a couple of weekends to get some matters sorted, or do additional tailing, but only if you suspect someone. Live in Seattle. Enjoy your time there, and you'll be mentally ready for the work as it comes."

"Why does it seem like there are so many changes?" Arielle asked. "Don't get me wrong, they seem for the better, mostly, but there are so many things in motion."

"We're in a time of peace, and it's my priority to make the lives easier for every Road Runner. I want to take advantage of that luxury. We're time travelers. There's no reason for us to rush through anything, or ever feel crunched for time. So what, live eight months in the past? You're still only losing ten minutes from today. We are running a mission per week for each team of Angels. In real time, you are losing ten minutes per week for working a mission. The teams in Europe are doing one mission each month, and their success rate is virtually perfect."

"One a month?" Selena gasped. "I could chase my Hollywood dreams on that schedule."

"Exactly. And my goal is for us to reach that level, but that's a matter of having more Angels recruited and trained, because we'll still need to cover the same amount of missions. Having more teams affords everyone more flexibility. I don't know if that will happen during my term as commander, but I will certainly get the ball rolling before I leave. As an organization, we owe it to our members for sticking through that war. It was all-hands-on-deck for too many years. Extreme levels of stress. Loss of family and friends. I want to reward our members by giving them their lives back—it's the least we can do."

"It definitely feels like the general mood is shifting across the Road Runners," Arielle said. "So whatever you guys are doing is working."

Commander Briar stood up and closed the file, pushing it into Arielle's lap. "I never wanted to be the commander. They forced this whole candidacy onto me because I could resist the freezing of time. But now that I look back, the Road Runners saved me from myself. Before any of this time travel business, I was in a dark place. I had been battling depression for two decades. Burying my pain in booze, pills, and junk food. I had even stuck a pistol in my mouth every year on the anniversary of my sweet Izzy's disappearance. Sure, I had my issues at the beginning, being recruited by Chris Speidel. Then his daughter was playing mind with games with me. But it was the Road Runners who ultimately brought me in and turned my life around. And this was *during* the war. We all deserve sunshine after the darkness, and I want to leave that opportunity as my legacy long after I'm gone. I want the Road Runners to be fun again, if they ever were."

Tears welled in Arielle's eyes. She had lived through the darkest points in the war. As the commander had just mentioned, she had lost friends at the hands of the Revolution. Even during her climb to the organization's top-ranked Angel, the life of a Road Runner constantly orbited around stress. The good had finally arrived out of the mess, and she could now clearly see what was driving Commander Briar as he stared down the final year of his term.

Arielle rose to her feet, Felix and Selena following suit. She stuck her hand across the commander's desk, and he grabbed it to shake. "I don't know if you hear this enough," Arielle said, "But thank you for risking your life to save us all."

He offered a tight-lipped grin, gulping down what Arielle believed was the urge to cry.

"Now," she continued. "If you'll excuse us. We have a mission to do."

Chapter 5

The trio agreed to depart Wednesday morning, leaving the rest of Monday and all of Tuesday to pack and prepare. Since they were traveling not too far into the past, the Road Runners had already worked many logistics out, and the three Angels simply needed to show up.

Arielle kept a three-week rotation of clothes she packed for every mission. For this one, she packed and an extra week's worth, limiting her having to do laundry to once a month while on the mission.

She packed within an hour of arriving back home from headquarters and promptly left for the cemetery across town where her family had been laid to rest. She tried to visit their graves once a month to keep the flowers and display tidy.

When she reached the site—three graves belonging to her mother, father, and brother all next to each other—she sat on the grass in front of the middle gravestone, her mother's.

"Hi, guys," she said, staring at all three graves. A towering oak tree showered her with shade on a hot, sunny day. Birds chirped from high up, while a trio of squirrels chased each other up the tree trunk. Arielle realized in this moment just how far out of touch she had fallen from nature.

She kicked off her flip-flops, letting the blades of grass

caress her feet, and drew in a deep breath of air. It had been weeks—hell, years—of being constantly in motion. Never having a moment to sit down and enjoy the little pleasures of the world. Though she was surrounded by the deceased, she felt the calming presence of the cemetery and its beauty. Perfect landscaping, bright flowers as far as she could see, and even a maintenance worker stopping to eat his lunch at a table in the distance. Life was happening all around her, yet Arielle felt like a stranger. A misfit. Wasn't she supposed to be doing something besides killing a few minutes sitting in the grass?

"I don't remember who I am," she finally said to her family. "Ever since I lost the three of you, I've kept myself constantly busy. It started as a way of coping with the loss. A way to distract myself from feeling the pain. But over the years, I'm afraid I got used to it. If I'm ever not in motion, I just feel . . . empty."

The three gravestones stared back, silent. Arielle felt her family's presence. She had lost her faith in any sort of religion after the incident that took her family, but she still believed in the afterlife. It wasn't a stretch for her to believe the spirits of her parents and brother visited her at this moment.

Normally, she had to fight off tears when speaking to the gravestones. Today, however, was different. She felt warmth within her soul. She felt connected to everything around her.

"I'm going to have a lot more free time soon," she continued. "And I don't know what I'm supposed to do with it. Maybe I'll finally get the time to properly grieve losing you three. I've been thinking about it a lot lately. Many people believe we're supposed to power through grief and not let it slow down our lives. Bury our pain with work or hobbies. But that does nothing. It's been seven years since you've been gone, and the pain is still here. The grief is still waiting. It doesn't just go away with time. It waits until you stare it down and confront it. That's the only way to truly get *through* it. I'm going to have some dark days ahead as I come to terms with all of this, but I suppose I need it."

Tears welled in Arielle's eyes, but not from sorrow. She still felt plenty of peace within. Her tears came from a place of fear of the unknowing. She had never confronted these emotions swirling around her family's death. Sure, they'd creep up from time to time and she'd have a good cry in the shower. But she'd never tried to work through them. Whether that meant locking herself in a dark bedroom for a week, eating gallons of ice cream, or just *feeling* the emotions to their core.

Her schedule had been deliberately jam-packed since she buried the three people she loved the most. She wasn't even tired after seven years of a constant grind, but knew that was all changing beyond her control. Improved mental health was clearly at the top of Commander Briar's agenda, and perhaps he was on to something.

Arielle would face her demons within the next year, whether or not she liked it. And while it would be torturous to go through, it could only leave her in a better mental state at the end.

Her cell phone rang, causing Arielle to jump from the ground. She had fallen so deep into herself that the obnoxious chime coming from her pocket had startled her back to reality.

She had no plans of answering until she saw *Abuela* on the caller ID.

"Hello?" she answered.

"Mi hita, how are you?" her grandmother replied, the worry

evident in her voice. "Is everything okay?"

"Yes, Abuela, why do you ask?"

"I don't know. Sometimes I get strange feelings. I thought I should reach out to make sure you're okay."

Chills broke out across Arielle's back. Her grandmother had always had an ability to sense different things about the family—either good or bad. The morning of the mall shooting, she had called to make sure everything was okay. At the time, it was. Little did any of them know what would unfold later that afternoon. Arielle often thought back to that phone call and wondered how it all worked. Did her grandma sense things that weren't quite clear? Was it like reading something in a language she couldn't understand? She was the complete opposite of Arielle, someone in total sync with the universe and its ways. Arielle often wondered if her abuela knew about the time-traveling life she lived, but kept quiet.

"What are you up to, mi amor?"

Arielle gulped. It was impossible to lie to her grandmother for a multitude of reasons. "I'm . . . at the cemetery."

"Ay, gracias a Dios," she replied, instant relief flooding through the phone line. "No wonder I felt something. You're all together right now."

Hearing her grandmother say this with such confidence opened the floodgates. She hadn't been wrong about feeling her family's presence. If her grandma could sense it 600 miles away, then it wasn't some part of her imagination.

"I'm having a hard time right now, Abuela," Arielle said through intense sobbing. She rose to her feet, blood rushing to her head and making her dizzy. "Some days I just can't handle it. I *need* them here with me. I want to share my life with them. They were always there, and one day that just stopped."

"I miss them too, hita. And there is nothing wrong with having these feelings. Your abuelo has been gone for twelve years now, and I still have days like this. We can't erase the memories or the connection we had with our loved ones. It's just impossible."

Arielle couldn't speak, and started crying harder. It felt like the world was pouring sorrow on her. She missed her grandfather, too. Missed the family trips to New Mexico to visit her grandparents when they were the happiest couple she had known. She missed her life the way it had been.

Arielle had never felt so far from being the top-ranked Angel than she did right now. None of her status or achievements mattered, because she had no one to share them with. Celebrating with yourself got old real quick.

"How are *you*?" Arielle asked, when the tears subsided. "Have things been going okay since I last visited?"

"Nothing has changed here. Same routine. You don't have to worry about me. It's you I worry about."

"I'm fine—I promise. I'm just a little . . . at a crossroads, I guess."

"Are you finally leaving this job that takes all your time?"

Arielle let out a laugh, grateful for a different sound than the heavy crying. "No, Abuela, I love my job. It's probably the only steady thing in my life."

"It's the *only* thing in your life. You need to go out and have more fun."

"That's exactly what's coming, and I don't know what to do for fun. I can definitely travel the world, but I already do a lot of that for work."

"I don't know what to tell you, but I'm sure you'll figure it out. I know you don't want to go to church, but do you pray?"

Arielle remained silent. She couldn't recall the last time she said a prayer, and knew her grandmother would scold her if that was her response. Her silence said enough.

"Well, hita, you need to pray again. Just try it. That's all I ask."

"I can do that. I need to try *something*."

"If it works, great. If not, then at least you tried."

"Thank you, Abuela. I didn't know I needed this phone call, but I'm glad it happened."

"Don't you ever hesitate to call me. It doesn't need to be for any reason."

"I know. I have to get going, but we'll talk again soon. I love you."

They hung up, and Arielle left the cemetery, eager for the mission to begin.

Chapter 6

On Wednesday morning, Felix sprung out of bed and dressed within minutes. He hadn't expected Arielle to follow through on her promise to take him to visit his parents before starting their next mission. People as busy as Arielle said a lot of things, and while their intentions were pure, something always seemed to come up in their schedules. Especially Arielle. She was always in demand. Needed at some meeting at headquarters. Or called on to write a report.

But when she called late Tuesday night to confirm the next morning's flight details, he understood nothing could change that. Arielle had looped in the trip to San Francisco as part of the mission, meaning on paper, the mission had officially begun and they could distract none of the three Angels to tend to something else.

He had been antsy about his parents meeting Arielle and Selena, not sure how to best explain his relationship with the two attractive women. Surely his mom would have lots of questions, while his dad would sneak in a suggestive wink at every opportunity, figuring his son had found himself in a love triangle worthy of the gods.

Felix would explain the situation for what it was—a work trip with colleagues—but his parents would still jump to their own conclusions. They couldn't help themselves. Regardless of what they believed, he knew they would welcome his new friends into the Francisco household with the warmness that always filled his childhood home.

Felix pushed these thoughts aside as he pulled into the hangar where Arielle's personal jet awaited. The top-ranked Angel had their own jet to use for personal or Road Runner business. With this being their first mission out of town, it was Felix's first time riding on the luxurious airliner.

He parked in the lot and stepped out to a row of at least a dozen different jets, all different sizes. He saw Arielle and Selena walking together, stopping in the middle of the row where a mobile flight of steps had been set up to reach a medium-sized white jet's entrance. "A1" decorated the jet's tail, presumably to signify the top-ranked Angel.

The two turned around and waved at him, waiting for Felix to catch up. They had their suitcases, two each, while Felix pulled his lone one behind him.

"Good morning, Felix," Arielle said once he had finally approached them at the base of the stairs. "Excited for the trip?"

"More than you know." They each took turns giving him a hug when the jet's pilot appeared from the open doorway. He was a muscular, middle-aged gentleman with a chiseled jawline and a perfect balance of gray hairs streaked into what was once all black.

"Peter!" Arielle greeted him as he descended the steps, throwing her arms around him.

Peter was in complete pilot's attire, and Felix appreciated the professional touch. He'd ridden on the commander's jet a few times, and the pilots had always looked like some random shmuck off the street, despite their credentials.

"Meet my friends and new teammates," Arielle said. "We'll be doing all missions together from now on. This is Felix Francisco and Selena Nicole."

"A pleasure to meet you both," Peter replied, taking off his hat to greet them, and offering a firm handshake to Felix.

"This is Captain Peter Holland," Arielle continued the introduction. "He was a fighter pilot in the United States Air Force for fifteen years. There is no one better to fly us around North America."

The captain smiled. "It's true. This jet might not be equipped to fight off enemies, but if something ever arises, I know how to get us to safety. Not that it's an issue anymore, since the war ended." He pulled up his sleeve to check a shiny Rolex. "We should get ready for takeoff. Can get you there a few minutes earlier than planned."

The pilot offered a grin that reminded Felix a bit too much of George Clooney, before he spun around to grab both of Arielle's bags and starting up the stairs.

"You get your own luggage service?" Selena asked, putting her hands on her hips. "Don't they know you can kill anyone with your bare hands? You hardly need—"

Arielle shot up her hand. "That's enough. He'll come back for all of our bags. No need to get all fired up about my perks."

Felix thought it odd that the pilot of a private jet would be the one to load luggage. But he was a Road Runner, and probably made an exorbitant amount of money to do just that. Within one minute, Peter hustled back down the stairs, grabbed Selena's two bags, and took them up.

Arielle led them up the stairs, where Felix had insisted he'd carry his own suitcase. When they reached the top and entered the jet, Selena cried out, "Are you kidding me?!"

Felix was the last to enter and immediately understood Selena's surprise. The inside looked something out of a Hollywood movie.

Four regular airline seats were behind the cockpit, all facing the front. Behind those, however, were two couches lining the opposite sides of the walls, centered around a long glass table with a lounge chair on each end. Everything was decorated a simple black and white, minus the light gray carpet. Toward the back of the jet was a fully stocked bar with trays of appetizers placed on the counter. A woman dressed in a flight attendant uniform had just finished putting the final touches on a plate of bruschetta.

"Welcome aboard," she greeted, coming around the bar. "How are you today, Arielle?"

"Good to see you again, Octavia. I'm doing wonderful. I'd like for you to meet Felix and Selena. The three of us are working as a team on all missions going forward, so you'll be seeing them around a lot more."

"A pleasure meeting you," Octavia said, offering a hand to each of them. After the pleasantries were out of the way, she snapped back into focus. "It looks like a three-hour flight today. Appetizers are all served on the bar. Lunch will be a prime rib coupled with fresh asparagus, mashed potatoes, and garlic butter mushrooms. I will serve it thirty minutes after takeoff. If any of you would like a drink from the bar, just let me know, and I can bring that out to you."

She offered a soft grin before disappearing through a door behind the bar.

"What's back there?" Selena asked.

"A small kitchen," Arielle said. "A closet with cleaning

supplies. And maybe a bedroom.”

Selena slapped her leg. “You have a bed on your own private jet? Get out!”

Arielle shrugged. This had been her norm for the past couple of years. “Flights are the one place I can get reliable sleep.”

“Apparently,” Selena said. “Private chef cooking prime rib and serving it to you all before nap time. Why have you never mentioned any of this to us?”

“It’s not that big of a deal,” Arielle said. “I don’t need to flaunt all this stuff. Honestly, it’s kind of embarrassing, but this is what they gave me when I reached the top spot. This is how I get around to each mission.”

Selena shook her head. “You know my dad is rich. I’ve been on yachts off the coast of France, and a couple of private charters, but I’ve never seen anything like this. You’re up here living like a Bond villain.”

“I don’t know,” Felix said. “I think a Bond villain would be incredibly jealous of this jet.”

They all shared a laugh before Arielle rose from her seat and led the way to the bar to make a plate of appetizers. Felix followed suit, both starving and eager to see what kind of fine dining they served on this luxurious airliner. Besides the bruschetta, he found a tray of shrimp, another with at least a dozen fresh cheeses, and bacon-wrapped figs. He grabbed two of each before returning to his seat.

After ten minutes passed with them ordering a round of drinks and starting on their appetizers, the jet had taken off. Once they reached a cruising elevation and things had settled down while Octavia prepared their table for lunch, Arielle said, “I want to brainstorm for this mission. Nothing formal. Let’s just talk out some ideas for how to best approach this one."

"Before we do," Selena said. "I have to admit, I don't fully understand what money laundering is. It has to do with hiding money, is that right?"

"I wouldn't call it hiding money," Felix said. "It's more like disguising money. Basically when criminals get their hands on money illegally, they will funnel it through a legitimate means to make it appear legal."

"How on Earth do you make it *appear* legal?"

"There are a few ways. Some run the money through businesses, either fake or real. They'll use the dirty to 'buy' goods, funneling that money to the business without ever receiving the goods they supposedly purchased. It's even more common with cash-heavy businesses. Think of car washes or strip clubs, places that deposit a lot of cash every day. Banks have no way of knowing if that cash is legal or not. This is the way the mob used to operate out of the back of restaurants before everyone started paying with credit cards. It was just another front to funnel money through."

"So we're getting involved with some pretty high-level criminal activity?"

"Absolutely. Money laundering is probably the most serious white-collar crime. Just based on what we know about the company we're dealing with, I'm willing to bet they laundered the money through real estate transactions. This is done when real estate is purchased with cash—the dirty money—then quickly sold. It's my understanding that WonderHome launched a new division of their business that deals specifically with purchasing and reselling property all around the country. They positioned themselves as the real estate experts in the nation, and no one ever questioned it. Say if you or I started flipping houses every other week, the feds would target us. But if a billion-dollar company is flipping dozens of houses every day, well, that's just part of their business, right?"

"It's always the corporations who can get away with whatever they want," Arielle said. "As long as they keep raking in the billions, no one ever thinks of questioning *why* they're earning so much money. Instead, they just get glorified by society, especially the poor, yet most of the time there are plenty of shady dealings behind the scenes. It doesn't make sense."

"And we're sure we have to deal with this money laundering and not the murder-suicide directly?" Selena asked. "I'm sure there are other opportunities where we could intervene to prevent the tragedy from happening. I mean, who would you rather take a risk with? A stressed-out mother with a gun, or a billionaire with their entire livelihood on the line? Who do you think has the resources to make a problem disappear with a quick signature on a check?"

"I've read through the initial report," Arielle said. "The issue with stopping the murders from happening is that we don't know if that will just delay them from occurring at a later time. Removing the *cause* of them is a guaranteed way to ensure neither of those children ever turns up dead."

"And what if we find out Adam Marshall really was guilty?" Selena asked. "Are we supposed to just let him free so his family never suffers? He still needs to face his own justice."

Arielle nodded. "That's something we'll have to deal with it as it comes up. But I don't think they would have ever assigned this mission if they didn't have a sound reason to believe he was innocent. Now, let's talk strategy. We need to infiltrate this company and pose as employees. Thoughts?"

Felix smiled, a certain dark satisfaction swimming behind it. "Easy. I can craft some resumes to get you both jobs in the company. Which departments do you think would be best?"

"Definitely HR," Arielle said. "They'll have the most oversight into all the departments and happenings. And those people love to gossip. Maybe we get Selena in there to start, then she can help get me hired in a different department. I don't see a reason for you to work for the company, Felix. We'll need someone on the outside still."

"Definitely," Felix said. "What if you took a job with IT or the software engineers? That would help me have easier access to hack into the company's system. We'll be able to see emails, authorized users, and really anything we want. That's probably our best play. Do you think you can pull that off?"

Arielle shrugged. "Acting has never been something I've needed to do on missions. But I guess there is a first time for everything. I don't have IT knowledge, though, so I'm not sure how I can exactly fake my way through this."

"Even easier," Felix said, his smile widening. He was growing pleased with his ability to mold this mission to his vision, and Arielle seemed to go along with it. "I can give you a small earpiece to speak to you. I can walk you through any sort of IT issue that may arise. We even have special glasses and necklaces equipped with hidden cameras, so I can know exactly what you're looking at. And it's all very easy to turn on and off, so you can only use when needed throughout the day."

Arielle put her elbow on the table and propped up her chin with a fist, staring into the distance. Felix recognized the look as her deep thought, something they had all gotten familiar with in such a short time.

"You know," she said. "It's just possible that between having us in HR and IT, we might prevent Adam from ever being hired by WonderHome. We can manipulate things like his application, interview schedule, whatever we need to make him seem like a poor candidate. If it works, it saves us a ton of work, and we can be out of there in less than a month."

Selena laughed. "You know it's never that easy."

"Oh, I'm aware it's unlikely to work. Pulling that off would drastically change Adam's timeline. But it's still worth trying."

"I agree," Felix said. "There is a lot we can try to prevent him from getting that job. All it takes is one action for him to get rejected, and we're in the clear. And we'll have time. It's not like you're both going to get hired and jump right into your roles. You'll have orientation and training to go through. A couple weeks, at least, until you're both on your own. During that time, I can see how we can make Adam look like a terrible candidate."

"Sabotage," Selena said with a crooked grin. "Makes us seem like the criminals."

"I don't think the Marshall family would agree with that statement if this all works out," Arielle said.

Octavia returned from the kitchen with a tray full of their lunch plates.

"Lunch is served," she said.

"I like what we've come up with," Arielle said. "We can flesh it out some more once we get to Seattle. But first, let's eat and get ready to meet the Francisco family."

Chapter 7

They landed in San Francisco two hours later, stomachs full and satisfied.

"Beautiful day," Arielle said once they descended the steps from the jet. "I've always loved the weather in San Fran. It's usually just the right temperature."

As with anything else on a mission, a town car had been arranged to take them from the hangar to the Francisco house, driven by a Road Runner who barely spoke to the three Angels riding in the back seat.

"I've never been here," Selena said, eyes glued out the window. "Are we going to do any touristy things?"

"That's up to Felix's family," Arielle said. "If they want to, sure. If they want some alone time with Felix, you and I can go sightseeing."

"I want to see the famous Golden Gate Bridge. And ride on a trolley. And visit Alcatraz."

Felix giggled. "So many things to do in this city, and you want to go where all the other people spend their time."

"I didn't grow up here, asshole," Selena said, reaching across Arielle to smack Felix on his arm. "I want to see those things. Maybe if you invited us out here more, we could go do more stuff that you locals love."

"You two need to relax," Arielle cut in. "We're here for two days, and the priority is for Felix to spend time with his family. If seeing these things is that important to you, Selena, we'll make it happen. Can we try to have two days without bickering before the mission? Please."

They drove through downtown San Francisco and made their way to the neighborhood of Nob Hill.

"What kind of neighborhood is this?" Arielle asked. "Half the buildings look modern and almost luxurious, and the other half are covered in graffiti."

"It used to be a really shady neighborhood," Felix said. "But over the past five years, it's gone through a lot of changes. It's actually becoming more of an affluent neighborhood. Think of it like Five Points in Denver. In a couple more years, people will have no idea these blocks used to be filled with drug dealers and murderers. I know because we lived in this area when I was a kid. Was never allowed to be outside past sunset. My parents have since moved to a different block and are in a much nicer apartment now."

"I'll say," Selena said when the car pulled over in front of a tri-level apartment building painted a light shade of blue with white trim around the curved windows. People jogged up and down the sloped sidewalks, parents pushed their babies in strollers, while couples walked their dogs.

It was a crowded intersection on California Street and Leavenworth, but one that felt entirely safe from its troubled past.

They gathered their luggage on the sidewalk and waited for Felix to guide them into the building, punching in a code on a keypad to jolt the door unlocked.

"We have to go up to the third floor," he said, barreling

down the hallway toward the elevator at the opposite end. Arielle hardly had a moment to admire the artwork hanging on the main level's walls. Paintings of San Francisco landmarks like Fisherman's Wharf, Golden Gate Park, and a massive one that overlooked the bay.

The elevator doors parted immediately after Felix pushed the button, and they crammed into it with their bags.

"Tight squeeze, I know," he said. "The buildings may have been remodeled, but they couldn't make them any bigger."

They reached the third floor, and the doors opened to a mini hallway, one door on each side, marked 301 and 302. Felix strolled up to 301 and knocked with a heavy fist.

His parents must have been waiting by the door because it opened within three seconds, his mother appearing in the doorway with the widest grin smacked across her face.

"Oh, Felix!" she cried, stepping into the hallway and throwing her arms around her son. She planted multiple kisses on his cheeks, his face promptly flushing red. "How I've missed you. How *we've* missed you. Please come in, all of you. And you two must be Arielle and Selena?" She released Felix from her grasp and stuck out a hand to Selena.

"I'm Selena. A pleasure to meet you, Mrs. Francisco."

"Call me Elise—I insist."

Elise had wavy brown hair that ran just past her shoulders, a slightly overweight frame, and was at least six inches shorter than her six-foot son. Her face had minimal signs of aging to go along with the warm smile she couldn't erase.

"And you must be Arielle," she said, moving her attention after Selena slipped into the apartment behind Felix.

"Yes, ma'am, it's so great to finally meet you. Felix has told us so much about your family."

Elise looked over her shoulder to confirm Felix was out of range, and whispered to Arielle. "He doesn't know it, but his sisters are on their way right now. It will be the first time we're all together, outside of Christmas, in years."

Arielle heard the pure joy emanating from Felix's mother, and it struck a sharp pain in her heart. She had heard that same tone plenty of times from her own mother whenever they had family visit from out of town. A glee that couldn't be matched by anything else in the world. The unconditional love for family.

Elise guided Arielle into the apartment where her husband stood behind the island-style kitchen counter, slicing up a watermelon, while Felix threw an arm around him and showed a rare, joyous grin.

"Selena," Elise said. "Arielle. This is my husband, Benji."

"My goodness," Benji said, looking Arielle and Selena up and down. "Fantastic work, son!"

Felix flushed again.

Elise hurried around the counter and smacked her husband on the chest. "Those are his coworkers, you dirty man!"

Benji howled with laughter, grabbing his gut that had seen its share of beer over the years. "I know, my love. I just can't pass up a chance to poke fun."

Elise rolled her eyes as she slung her arm around Benji's back. "Forgive my husband. His sense of humor has no limits. You'll get used to it."

"I mean no disrespect," Benji said, coming around the counter to shake hands with Arielle and Selena. "I've been the class clown my whole life. It's a role I've earned, and love to own it. That said, if I ever say something offensive, just call me out. You kids these days have so many rules—I can't keep up. I'd hate to be a comedian the way everyone gets offended by everything. Ooh, would you ladies like to go to a comedy club while you're here?"

"Enough," Elise said. "Let them settle in. My goodness, they still have their suitcases. Come, let me show you to your room."

The kitchen had white granite counters running in a U-shape around the island in the middle, stainless steel appliances, and at least a dozen cupboards and cabinets to keep everything perfectly organized. The kitchen opened up to the living room, where a TV mounted on the wall took up every inch of space above a fireplace. Behind the L-shaped couch facing the TV was a long wooden dining table that seated sixteen, with an elevated view of the window overlooking the peaceful neighborhood below.

On the other side of the entrance was a hallway that stretched down to the master bedroom at the end, a bathroom next to it.

"This place has two floors?" Arielle asked.

A stairwell ran down from the hallway across from the bathroom door.

"Yes," Elise said. "And that's where you'll be staying. Downstairs there are two more bedrooms and a bathroom. Come!"

Arielle and Selena grabbed their suitcases and followed Elise down the stairs where a smaller living room separated the two bedrooms.

"You two don't mind sharing a room?" Elise asked. "Otherwise Felix will have to sleep on the couch in the living room."

"Not at all," Arielle said. "Are your daughters not going to need a place to stay?"

Selena's head whipped around to Arielle at the mention of Felix's sisters, and she gave a satisfied grin. They were both anxious to dig deeper into the mystery known as Felix Francisco, and who better to give insight than his siblings?

"Oh, no, they live just outside of town and will drive back home." Elise led them into the bedroom with a queen-sized bed positioned in the corner and closed the door behind her. "I need to ask you both something," she said, just above a whisper. "You work with Felix pretty regularly? You know him well?"

Arielle and Selena looked at each other, unsure where the conversation was going.

"Yeah," Selena said. "The three of us spend a lot of time together. Our job requires a ton of teamwork and travel."

"I'd say we know him as much as he lets us," Arielle added. "We've gotten to know him pretty decently, but I feel there is still so much we don't know."

Elise nodded, sitting on the foot of the bed as she stared at the floor. "Does he seem emotionally stable, would you say?"

Selena shrugged. "Well, he rarely shows emotion, and we have a pretty stressful job. He stays calm under pressure. But I don't know if that's stability or if he's just hiding his true feelings. He's impossible to read sometimes."

"That's my Felix. He's always been so focused. He has tunnel vision with the things he cares about in life. Rarely gets distracted by outside matters. We had him seen by behavioral experts when he was a teenager. We worried something was wrong because he never showed emotion. He gets excited about baseball and whatever projects he works on, but that's really it. But everyone we spoke with said he is completely normal. Does he have friends? Does he go on dates?"

Now Arielle shrugged. "He doesn't mention friends to us, but we have no idea what he does during his time away from work. He's gone out with us a couple of times outside of work, and he always seems to enjoy himself. As far as his romantic life, I have no idea. He's never mentioned anyone. Has he to you, Selena?"

Selena shook her head. "No. I actually went to a baseball game with him when we first met. He told me many things about his life, but he never mentioned a girlfriend or anything like that."

"Keep in mind," Arielle said. "The people in our line of work spend a lot of their time on the job. I just went on my first date in years the other day, in fact."

It occurred to Arielle that she had no clue what Felix had told his parents he did for work. Every Angel had a lie they told to their loved ones, needing to keep the truth concealed. If Elise prodded into that, Arielle wasn't sure how they'd pivot out of the conversation.

"Okay, that's good," Elisa said. "As long as he's fine. I always worry about him. We're going to deliver some big news later once his sisters get here. It might shake him up because I know how much he hates change."

"Oh," Arielle said. "Do you need me and Selena to leave? Totally understand if you need some private family time."

"Not at all." Elise stood from the bed. "No one is dying—nothing that serious. But I know it will bother Felix, even if he doesn't show it. I'll let you two get settled in for now. Come back upstairs whenever you're ready. I think Benji is going to make some margaritas soon."

"Now we're talking," Selena said with a wide smile.

Elise grinned back before she left the bedroom, leaving

Arielle and Selena to worry about the Francisco family's impending news.

Chapter 8

They returned upstairs fifteen minutes later to find Benji back at the kitchen island, this time with a blender, a bucket of ice, three bottles of tequila, orange juice, lime juice, and a gallon of margarita mix.

A platter with crackers and cheeses sat on the front ledge of the island, where Felix and his mother had gathered around.

"Hope you ladies like margaritas," Benji said as he combined the ingredients in the blender. "I may or may not make them a *little* stronger than what you get at the bars."

"I can vouch for that," Felix said. "And yes, we all drink margaritas at our favorite spot in Denver after we finish our . . . projects."

"We love a good marg," Arielle said. "Felix, can we speak with you really quickly? It's about work."

Felix looked at them with a puzzled stare. "Okay?"

He shoved a cheese cube into his mouth before leading them to the balcony outside. The space had a patio table, a cornhole setup, a tall smoker, and a barbecue grill. All with a majestic view overlooking downtown San Francisco.

"Is something wrong?" Felix asked.

"No," Arielle said. "We just need to know what you've told your parents you do for work. Your mom was asking questions when she took us to our room. She didn't ask any specifics, but it would have gotten messy if she did."

"I didn't even think of that," Felix said, shaking his head. "All they know is that I work as a software consultant for top businesses in Denver. They don't even fully understand what that means, so I doubt you'll get specific questions about our work."

"Okay, good," Arielle said. "That's all we needed to know."

"What do you think about my parents?"

"They're awesome," Selena said. "So chill and fun. And your dad makes homemade margaritas. I can stay here as long as we need."

Arielle saw the apartment's front door open, two women who closely resembled Felix stepping in with their hands tossed in the air as they skipped into the kitchen.

"Looks like everyone is here now," she said, nodding toward the scene unfolding behind Felix's back.

He scrunched his brow in confusion before turning around. "Holy shit!" His jaw hung open while his sisters barged through the sliding patio door, howling like loons as they smothered their brother with hugs.

"I thought you both weren't going to make it," Felix said.

"That was a lie," said the older sister. "We just said that so we could surprise you. We wouldn't miss this for the world. So, who are your friends?"

The two sisters pivoted around to face Arielle and Selena, looking them each up and down.

"This is Arielle and Selena," Felix said. "My friends and coworkers. We're heading to Seattle to work on a project in a couple of days."

"Well, it's nice to meet you," the older sister said, stepping forward and hugging Arielle. "I'm Clara."

The younger sister did the same thing. "And I'm Sarah. It's nice meeting you."

They took a step back and the three Francisco siblings stood together, their resemblances to one another clear as day in the afternoon sunshine.

Clara was a few inches shorter than Felix, her sandy hair tied into a long, swaying ponytail. Sarah stood even shorter than Clara, with much darker hair cut to shoulder-length.

All three shared the same light brown eyes.

"So you're only here until tomorrow?" Sarah asked Felix.

He nodded. "We leave tomorrow night. We have the company jet, so we can leave whenever we want."

"Well, aren't you fancy," Clara said. "A private company jet. Look at you, little bro, doing big things."

It had been obvious to Arielle that Felix and his sisters had grown up in a humble environment. Felix had mentioned his mother's fashion boutique being highly lucrative and successful. Yet, outside of a beautiful apartment, they showed little signs of a family sitting on a fortune.

The patio door slid open again, and Benji popped out to announce that all margaritas had been served.

They retreated inside, where seven margarita glasses waited on the kitchen island.

"I'd like to make a toast," Benji said once everyone had grabbed their drink. He raised his glass in the air. "To family. We are so blessed to have everyone under the same roof. It's a treat that your mother and I never take for granted. And to Felix's new friends. We welcome you to our home and our family. *Salud!*"

Everyone raised their glasses, clinking them against one

another before taking their first sips.

"Mr. Francisco," Selena said. "These are incredible. What is your secret?"

"Why, thank you. I add a little more orange juice than normal, and less margarita mix. And double the tequila." He cackled as he said this, taking a long drink from his glass.

Elise slipped in beside Benji and wrapped her arm around his back. "Your father is right. Days like this are the ones I'll remember forever." Tears welled in her eyes.

"Mom, what's wrong?" Clara asked, her face shifting from a wide grin into a concerned frown within seconds.

"It's nothing," Elise said, shaking her head. She looked at Benji. "I don't think I can do this."

Benji rubbed his hand up and down her back. "It's okay, my love." He turned to the rest of the room, focusing on his three children standing next to each other. "Your mother and I have an announcement to make. It's her announcement, so I'm going to let her tell you. But I want you to know it is something we both discussed together. This was not her decision—it's both of ours. You may like it, you may not. But I'm incredibly proud of your mother and would do anything to support her. I hope you can do the same, because this was not easy."

Arielle looked to her left to see the three siblings swaying in nervous anticipation. To her right, Selena was doing the same thing, as if she had been a part of the family her whole life.

"What is it, Mom?" Sarah asked. "Tell us."

Elise stepped forward, taking a deep breath. "Your father and I are moving to New York City. My fashion business is doing so well, and I've come into an opportunity to open a boutique in New York. Our plan is to get it going and run it for at least five years. We figure that will be enough to allow us to step back and retire."

The apartment fell completely silent as tears welled in Elise's eyes.

"It's not forever," Benji reiterated. "Your mother is still being humble. She has made it to the top. It's not just the boutique. They have invited her to New York Fashion Week, Paris Fashion Week, and Milan Fashion Week."

"Mom, that's fantastic news!" Sarah said, running around the island to hug her mother. "Why would you be so worried about telling us this?"

"Because San Francisco is our home," Elise said, hugging Benji and Sarah at the same time. "Our dreams became a reality here. Our life is here. When we moved to this country from Colombia, we chose San Francisco because we thought the opportunities would be best. It's hard to just leave it all behind."

Felix shook his head, tears streaming down his face as he joined his little sister hugging his mother. "It hurts. I can't lie. But you made it, Mom. You were right when you chose San Francisco. The opportunities here are exactly what have led to this moment. Now you get to grow even more. The entire world is going to know your name. I'll miss coming here for the holidays, but I'm so, so proud of you."

Felix buried his face into his mom's chest and let out uncontrollable sobs.

Clara remained silent as tears streamed down her face, her arms crossed to hug herself. Benji shuffled over to embrace her and wiped the tears off her cheeks.

"It's going to be okay," he whispered.

Arielle and Selena exchanged glances before taking silent steps backward. Arielle wanted to drop and crawl all the way downstairs to hide in the bedroom, but that would only make the situation more awkward.

Instead, they stood like mannequins, refusing to move another inch to not draw any attention. After everyone had hugged and wiped their tears away, Elise faced Arielle and Selena. "I'm sorry to have done this in front of you. We wanted to tell everyone at the beginning of our gathering rather than waiting until the end. I'm sorry if it was weird for you both."

"Not at all," Arielle lied. "Congratulations on your new opportunity—it sounds like a lot of fun."

"Yes, congratulations," Selena said. "If you're up to it, I can connect you with my parents. My mom lives in New York, and my dad lives in Paris. They can definitely show you around."

"That would be fantastic!" Elise cried, strolling around the island to give Selena a hug. "I've been to New York a few times, but know nothing about living there."

"I can vouch for it. It's a wonderful place to live, especially since you're used to living in a big city. You'll have no problems adjusting. There's just a lot more people and places, but you'll learn your way around in no time."

"See," Benji said, both daughters now in his embrace. "Everything is going to be fine. And we have every intent on returning here to retire. In fact, we're not even going to sell this apartment. We'll rent it out, or leave it available for any of you three to use should you wish."

"I love you all so much," Elise said. "Your father is right. We've made it. And I couldn't have done it without all of you. I've never forgotten all the help you kids did in the first days of opening my boutique here."

The family all huddled around Elise, hugging her as the last tears made their rounds. Arielle watched Felix, worried the drastic change would distract him from his work on the upcoming mission.

Chapter 9

Friday morning saw the Angels return to Arielle's private jet. They had agreed to stay Thursday night at the Francisco house instead of catching a flight in the late hours.

The rest of their stay with Felix's family passed rather quickly. They ended up finishing the two pitchers of margaritas Benji had made before going out for dinner downtown, followed by a visit to their favorite ice cream shop, Wicked Scoops.

On Thursday, Arielle insisted on taking Selena out to all the touristy sightseeing she had wanted to do. This left the Francisco family alone with each other on Felix's last day in town. They visited Alcatraz, the Golden Gate Bridge, Fisherman's Wharf, and even stopped by the Mrs. Doubtfire house, where Robin Williams had once hosted a birthday party for the ages.

It left the two of them drained, part of the reason they opted to go to sleep later that evening instead of hustling back across town to catch a flight.

For now, they soared high above the coast, making their way to the Pacific Northwest.

"How are you feeling?" Arielle asked Felix once they had taken off and settled into the flight.

"I'm okay," he replied. "It was tough news to hear at first, and I'm obviously not thrilled about it. But they seem pretty set on returning home after a few years. I just hope that stays true."

"It sounds like your sisters are going to run the apartment as a vacation rental," Arielle said. "I overheard them talking in the next room when I was trying to fall asleep last night."

Felix nodded. "It should do really well. I guess we'll have a place to stay if we're ever back in town. It'll be weird. I associate San Fran with my parents and childhood. I remember when I was young, my mom didn't even know what she wanted to do with her life. All she did was work random jobs to keep food on the table. So did my dad. But it wasn't until she got a job cleaning up a local fashion boutique that something awoke within her. The owner let her take the scrap materials home, and she'd sit at the kitchen table of our cramped little apartment, trying new things with the materials. And the rest is history. My sisters and I have had all the success, and I know that's all our parents wanted when they moved to the States. As much as the change hurts, I'm just happy to see my mom accomplish something for herself."

"And not just anything," Arielle added. "Something *major*."

"I noticed your older sister didn't have much to say," Selena said.

"She's taking it the hardest," Felix said. "She got engaged last year, and is planning on having kids soon. My parents ranted and raved about how they'll get to be involved grandparents, since they don't live too far. That all just changed with the announcement. Clara won't move to New York, and I'm sure she's feeling a little abandoned by all of this. She'll be okay, though. Her fiancé has family in town, and by the time they get married and start having kids, there won't be much time left before my parents plan on returning."

Arielle sensed through his tone that Felix really was fine. His parents had softened the blow of the news with their promises to return. Benji refused to die in New York, and said he would crawl back through broken glass to San Francisco if it was the last thing he ever did.

"That's great. Are we feeling ready for this mission?" she asked both of them.

"I'm very ready," Felix said to Arielle's delight. "I have so many missteps from the last one that I want to redeem. This one will go much smoother. I actually spent an hour getting things started last night."

"Way to pull an Arielle," Selena said with a laugh.

"Wasn't much," Felix said. "Just started on your resumes so you can get hired sooner than later. The first thing I want to do when we get there is send in your job applications. Is there a particular date we are trying to go back to, and is there a reason? I ask, because I've been experimenting with the best approach. If we're putting Selena in the HR Department, it could be as simple as having her delete Adam's application from the system as soon as it comes in. Or would it make more sense if she was still a new hire in her ramp-up period, or someone more seasoned with a few months of work under her belt?"

"I see where you're coming from," Arielle said. "But I don't want to spend an extra six months, or even three months, on top of what has already been scheduled. It's just not efficient because you and I would have nothing to do for all that time until Adam even applies. We wouldn't make much progress trying to intervene with him so early. Even if we found a way, the past will still work to correct itself if given enough time. Because I've also thought about going back way before any of this is happening, finding a management role at some other company, and hiring Adam before he ever applies at WonderHome. There are just too many factors at play to ensure that would even work, and I'd hate to waste our time. Let's focus on what we can with WonderHome. Besides, if he really is innocent, we want to take them down. Because if it's not Adam, it will just be someone else later on, and who knows how *that* will all play out?"

"Do we have a backup plan in case I get fired?" Selena asked. "I mean, we are planning on doing some pretty questionable things within the company. It'd be foolish to just assume we don't get caught."

"You'll be doing that dirty work," Arielle said. "So you will be at the highest risk. But honestly, I'm not worried about it. Companies don't fire someone for making a mistake or two, and that's why it's important that we frame everything as a mistake on your end. The accidental deletion of Adam's application, or whatever else we come up with. I'll be in the company and blending more into the background. Even if you end up getting fired, or our plans simply don't work, I'll still be there. I'd love to get a bug planted in the CEO's office, but that is something incredibly risky and grounds for immediate termination if we get caught. We'll get a feel for things once we're hired, so we'll see."

"Only need two minutes to plant a bug," Felix said. "And putting one underneath a desk is very easy. You can probably do it in thirty seconds, actually. All you have to do is make sure no one sees you enter the office, and you'll be done. I'd say I'll do it, but if I were to get caught, well that's a legit crime. Trespassing. If one of you does it as an employee, you can at least make up something on the spot for why you're in there. Might face some discipline and questioning, but nothing that should land you in handcuffs."

"Gee," Selena said. "Thanks for really selling us on doing this part of the job."

They shared a quick laugh.

"We're almost there," Felix said, nodding toward the open window behind the couch.

Below the jet, the clouds formed a white sheet as far as they could see. Protruding through the clouds, however, was the snow-capped top of Mount Rainier. Its sheer size made the summit appear like a palace atop the clouds, a final destination at the end of an epic journey.

And it was.

Arielle loved to hike the challenging mountains in Colorado and other states. Mount Rainier had killed plenty of people who had tried to reach its top, but that didn't stop her from fantasizing about the accomplishment.

She had gone on plenty of hikes with her family as a child, though her parents and brother lost interest in the hobby. But not Arielle. She viewed hiking as the ultimate workout, as it challenged her mind, body, and soul all at the same time. Nothing else provided her with the same type of physical and mental therapy as climbing to the top of a mountain and reaping the reward of a sublime view of nature available only to those willing to make the sacrifice.

"So what touristy things are you going to make us do, Selena?" Felix asked, a grin spreading across his face.

Selena rolled her eyes. "I'm a world traveler. I'm sorry if

you can't handle that I like to see everything I can, even if that includes touristy things. But since you asked, I want to go to the original Starbucks, the Space Needle, and Pike's Place Market. And let me guess, you want to go to a baseball game?"

Felix nodded. "Of course. I've been out here a couple of times during the offseason, so haven't been able to catch a Mariners game, but it looks like I'll finally get the chance. And to be fair, I'd also like to go to the Space Needle. I've been to it, but have never gone to the top. Pike's Place is a really cool spot, and the Starbucks is just another Starbucks. Nothing special about it."

Arielle laughed. "I was afraid this might happen working on a longer mission. Let's set some ground rules. Just because we're going to be together for six months on this mission doesn't mean we have to spend every waking moment together. If Felix wants to go to a baseball game by himself, he can. If Selena wants to parade through Pike's Place and catch the fish out of the air, she can. We'll still do lots of things together, but don't feel like you're bonded to the mission. There will be lots of downtime. On the flip side, when it's time to work, I expect no distractions. All business from there on out. Are we clear?"

"Yes, *Mother*," Selena said, earning a shake of the head from Arielle.

They shared a laugh before Peter announced the jet's descent would begin in approximately twenty minutes.

Chapter 10

Selena didn't get the same excitement about starting new missions as the other two. Even as a Road Runner who had earned a most luxurious lifestyle, missions still felt like work. Something she *needed* to do, rather than wanted to do. Arielle and Felix identified their work as part of themselves, while Selena still dreamed of a career in Hollywood.

The recent changes to their time off between missions had rekindled her hopes. Weeks, possibly months, between missions would allow her to chase her dreams, and she planned to pursue them with the same ferocity she had while attending Julliard.

For now, the dream would have to wait for another day.

At least I don't lose time once we travel back, she thought, grateful she could do all this work for the Angels and hardly have any days pass in her real life.

When they touched down in Seattle, Selena felt the first rush of being on this trip. She had never spent time in the Emerald City and looked forward to exploring everything it offered. And with actual free time built into their schedule, she had a vacation sensation as they jammed into the town car that would take them to their new home during the mission.

"So, I didn't get to have any seafood while in San Fran,"

Selena said. "We need to make that happen tonight. I've already looked it up and there are a couple of fine dining spots overlooking the beach."

"You'll need to see if they exist in 2013," Arielle said. "When we get to the house, I want to jump back from there. No reason not to."

She spoke while scrolling through a block of text on her cell phone, not even looking up. It was the mission report, and Selena assumed she was confirming the exact date they were to jump back to in 2013.

"Good idea," Selena said. "Our phones should still work when we jump back, right? Thank God for a mission where I get to keep my phone."

"We may need to get new phones while we're here," Felix said. "The same cell towers might not exist. It's fifty-fifty, I'd say, based on other missions I've gone on."

The thought of spending her first couple hours in a new city and year at a cell phone store made Selena queasy. She just wanted to get out into the world and not worry about all the logistics.

"Well, let's hope it works."

"Okay," Arielle said. "We'll be going back to October 16, 2013. Adam applies for the job on November 17. That leaves us one month to apply, interview, and get accepted into our new roles. Felix, do you think that's enough time?"

"It should be. I'm going to make your resumes strong enough to grab their attention right away." He pulled up an image of the 2013 calendar he had already saved on his cell phone. "That's a Wednesday. We can submit the applications the same day we arrive, and I'll bet we get a call back before the weekend. I've worked with a lot of tech companies, and they usually move pretty fast. They'll probably book an interview for the following week, potentially a second one the week after that, and you'll be hired before November. Your first days will probably be on November 4 or 11, which still leaves us plenty of time before Adam applies on Sunday, November 17. Might not get to prevent his application from being seen, but we don't know for sure how long training will even be."

"I would think a job in HR is less time in the classroom and more hands-on," Arielle said.

"Not necessarily. HR deals with a lot of legal matters. Labor laws, insurance policies, hiring practices. It could very well be as much time in a classroom as any other."

They turned away from the skyscrapers of downtown and headed east, where cedar and maple trees lined the residential blocks.

"We're not staying in downtown?" Selena asked.

"Afraid it's not ideal for this mission," Felix said. "The only places we own are apartments in the big buildings. We need to get in and out quickly if needed, and waiting for an elevator to run twenty levels up and down isn't the way to do that. We're close to downtown, though, maybe a ten-minute drive. And I've spoken with the team who maintains our properties, and asked if they could leave us two cars. I may have accidentally launched a new initiative, as the Road Runners are now in the business of buying cars to keep at each property we own."

"One less thing for us to worry about," Arielle said. "It's really smart, actually. Sounds like something Commander Briar would have approved in a heartbeat."

Selena saw the GPS tracker standing on the dashboard, showing they had two minutes until their destination.

Not too far at all, she thought. Selena would have downtime and wanted nothing more than to explore Seattle's night life. A quick drive downtown would make that task much easier.

"Besides," Felix said. "Look at this neighborhood. The trees literally run the entire length of the blocks. So much privacy. Our house is on a big corner lot, but you can hardly see any of it passing by. And the house is incredible."

"Who maintains these homes all over the continent?" Arielle asked. "I guess I'm not familiar with that process at all."

"The Road Runners have an entire property management department. They hire contractors, cleaners, whatever is needed to update the properties as needed, depending on the year the mission will take place. It's almost like being a set designer in Hollywood. They can make any property fit its surroundings. If we were traveling back a century, they would make the house looked like it belonged in that era. It's all quite fascinating how they go about it."

"Sounds like it takes a lot of time."

"It does. I'd bet this mission we're on has been on the Commander's desk for at least the last six months while details get sorted out. It's also why we have multiple properties in each city, because there will always be at least one going under renovation."

"I'd bet Jackie's method of traveling back a week to get all the work done will become the new norm for everyone across the organization. Even I've been thinking of ways we can implement that practice."

Felix nodded. "Keep an eye on her. I hear her name come up all the time in different meetings. She's going to advance through the ranks real quick."

The town car turned onto a neighborhood block and immediately stopped in front of the first house on their right.

"We have arrived, folks," the driver said. She had remained silent ever since they left the airport. They instructed drivers to do just that when transporting Angels to the official start of a mission. The rule had been in place as long as Selena could remember, meant to allow time for mission discussion without distraction.

The driver opened her door and hurried around to the trunk, where she pulled out their luggage and lined up their bags on the sidewalk.

The three Angels joined her outside, finding the street narrow as cars lined both sides in makeshift parking spots. Only a handful of the properties had driveways. A Nissan Altima and a Toyota Camry, both gray, were parked in front of their house.

"I believe these are our cars for the mission," Felix said, studying them.

Arielle tipped and thanked the driver before she left them alone.

Slanted rays of sunshine fought through the trees towering over the neighborhood.

"You really can't see much," Arielle said.

"Only about half of each house," Felix said. "If that."

They grabbed their luggage and turned around to face their home for the next several months. Two droopy cedar trees stood across from each other, a walkway running up the center from the sidewalk to a flight of a dozen steps toward the front entrance.

"Everything is so *green*," Selena said.

Bushes, landscaping rocks, and flowers filled the small hills on each side of the stairs. A half dozen of plotted pants decorated the steps that led up to a busy front patio filled with three tables, six chairs, and a swinging bench. Two white pillars towered from the ground to the house's roof two levels above.

"Why do we have to spend all the winter here?" Selena cried. "I bet hanging out on this patio is absolutely stunning in the summer. Well, it *is*—look at it now."

Birds sung their late-morning tunes from high in the trees. Squirrels played on the branches. And despite being less than two miles from the bustling downtown, the area had a serenity matched by being alone in the wilderness.

"Let's go inside," Felix said, starting up the stairs, lugging his heavy suitcase behind.

He reached the front door and pushed it open. They followed him into a foyer complete with a coat closet, a staircase that led upstairs, and a long hallway running to the back of the house. To the right was a family room, complete with a mounted TV, coffee table, a couch, and three lounge chairs. To the left was a living room with two couches centered around another coffee table, this one with a pile of board games. A full bookshelf stood in the corner, two landscape paintings serving as the decoration.

"All of the bedrooms are upstairs," Felix said. "Let's check out the rest of the place."

He started down the hallway, passing by a door that concealed the main level's bathroom, and ended in a kitchen and dining area that spanned the entire width of the house. A dining table was on their left, leaving the rest of the space open for a kitchen that would make a chef drool.

That's exactly what they found Felix doing, his mouth hanging open as he looked around a shiny kitchen made almost entirely of marble. The floor, countertops, and cabinets all glimmered as they blended seamlessly into one another. A sliding glass door revealed a back patio overlooking an even more lush backyard, complete with a grill and a firepit.

"Okay," Selena said. "This place really is amazing. I'll have no problem calling it home for the next eight months, even if most of our time here is in the winter."

"I don't mean to burst your bubble," Arielle said, shuffling into the kitchen. "But the house is probably not going to look like this in 2013 when we go back. This is what it looks like today. Should we head into the living room to do this?"

"Let's go."

Chapter 11

October 16, 2013

They gathered in the living room, having wheeled their luggage with them to ensure it traveled into the past after they took their Juice.

Arielle and Selena took opposite ends of one couch, while Felix took the other to himself.

"This mission is going to be very different," Arielle said, rummaging in her suitcase for her flask of Juice. The other two did the same. "We've obviously done the whole roommate thing on past missions, but those have only been for two weeks at a time. And we were in Colorado for both. This time we're going to learn a lot more about each other, especially with all the downtime we'll have between mission work."

"What are you getting at?" Selena asked.

"I don't want us to lose sight of our cohesiveness as a team. We really are great together, and I'd hate to see anything break up that chemistry. Eight months is a long time. By the end of the mission, we just might become more of a family. And that doesn't mean it's all glamorous. Families fight with each other. They grow resentful. It is possible to spend too much time with the same people, that you get sick of each other, and that can spiral into hatred. Possibly to the point of never speaking to each other. I've seen it happen within my family, and others' families. Maintaining our team dynamic might be the most difficult part of this mission."

"I'm not worried about it," Felix said. "You laid out the perfect ground rules during the flight. If anyone needs their alone time, they are welcome to it. Personally, that's how I recharge: locked in my room, playing some video games or watching TV. Selena likes to go out and party to recharge. Two very different approaches, but it's what works for us."

"And what about you, Arielle?" Selena asked. "What do you do to unwind?"

Arielle rolled her head to look at the young actress who had once made her life a living hell, but had now become like a little sister. She shrugged. "I wish I knew. Usually I travel between missions, but it's been such a long time since I've had a mission with actual downtime during it. I'm so behind on TV shows—I don't even know what's out these days. And there are so many streaming platforms. How the hell does anyone keep up? I used to read for pleasure. Maybe I'll get some books. I also like hiking, and I'm sure there are some good trails further out from the city, if any of you'd like to join."

"I'll pass on the hike," Selena said. "I love the outdoors, but climbing up a mountain? Ugh, just shoot me now!"

They all broke into laughter.

"I'll go on a hike with you," Felix said. "I've never done one before. I suppose it wouldn't hurt to try."

"Well, thank you. I'd appreciate the company."

"Let's go back already," Selena cried. "The anticipation is killing me. Do you guys still get butterflies before taking a sip?"

Felix let out a nervous laugh. "Always."

No one quite understood how the Juice worked. All they knew was that the Road Runners had obtained the official formula to make the liquid from the Book of Time after the war. The secrets in the potion were passed down centuries, dating back to Chronos, and were altered over the years to achieve a seamless, time travel perfection.

There had never been a case of the Juice not working, or having a malfunction of any sorts, but any Road Runner who took that fateful sip always had a gnawing doubt in the back of their mind that it would all go haywire, leaving them trapped in the past—or future—forever. It was no different from riding an airplane. Sure, the odds were nearly non-existent of being on a plane that crashes, but the possibility always looms in the back of your mind. And when those wheels touch down at the destination city, the relief always floods over your system. Another successful trip.

"The nerves never go away," Arielle said. "Now let's get down to business."

All Angels traveled with a small flask of their Juice, each with a larger bottle kept at their home or office.

"To October 16, 2013," Arielle said, raising her flask as if proposing a toast.

The others raised theirs and repeated the date, and all three took a sip no more than a standard wine sampling, and screwed the lids back onto their flasks.

"Everyone, touch your luggage," Arielle said. Anything that was in contact with a time traveler during the transition through time would come with them.

The transition felt like a light intoxication. Arielle grew

lightheaded, and saw Felix and Selena bobbing their heads slowly from side to side, as if they were listening to a smooth jazz record.

After the lightheadedness passed, she fell asleep, but not unconscious, unable to physically open her eyelids. She could only trust Selena and Felix had reached the same stage, but it didn't really matter. They would all end up at the same place within seconds of each other.

Arielle swam in the void. Darkness consuming her entirety as her mind and soul blasted through the realms of time. She always thought of this stage as what it must feel like to die and assumed that was why everyone had the nerves they did after taking the sip of Juice. Silence complemented the blackness, regardless of what was happening in the world outside of her body. She floated through time and space—though not able to confirm this—a wandering soul looking for its host in whatever dimension they had been destined to go to.

The Juice truly was a miracle. A potion that bent reality in every sense. It was always during the suspenseful minute between two timelines that she felt genuine appreciation for the life she had.

The end of the transition concluded with what felt like a slap on the chest, as if someone had grabbed hold of her soul and was trying to smack it back into her body.

Her eyes shot open to see the same living room they were just sitting in from nine years into the future.

She had arrived in 2013.

Selena and Felix both stirred back awake, happy to once again have arrived safely.

The furniture in the living room remained the same, likely done intentionally as most Road Runners opted to drink their

Juice from a particular, safe area.

"We made it," Selena said, rolling her neck in circles as if she had just woken from an uncomfortable plane ride instead of bounding through the dimensions of time.

"Welcome to 2013," Arielle said, standing up and wheeling her suitcase back toward the stairs. "Doesn't look like much changed around here."

The aesthetics were all different. The kitchen had granite instead of marble, downgraded appliances, but it remained large and plentiful with all the equipment.

"Dammit," Felix said. "Cell phones aren't working. I'll need to buy some burner phones today if we plan on applying for your jobs. We *need* to do all that before anything. Do we still have cars outside?"

He rose from the couch and hurried to the window, sliding the curtain aside. Selena followed, bringing her suitcase with her.

"There are two cars still," Felix said. "I think they're the same ones—they're just brand-new in 2013, because they look a lot shinier than what we just left."

"Keys are supposed to be in the master bedroom night-stand," Arielle said, recalling this specific instruction from the briefing. "Let's take fifteen minutes to get settled into our bedrooms, then I want to have a quick meeting to discuss a tentative schedule for the mission before you leave for the store, Felix."

* * *

They gathered at the dining room table where Arielle laid out the mission files, along with her planner and calendar.

"Everything good in your rooms?" she asked.

"One of the bigger rooms I've had on a mission," Selena said. "Can't complain, especially for how long we'll be here."

"I have an incredible view of all the trees in the neighborhood," Felix said with a laugh. "If I didn't know better, I might think we were living in the jungle."

"This is definitely different from the last two missions," Arielle said. "To be fair, I've done a mission in the jungle before, and I don't recommend it. Lots of creatures to worry about, on top of the past. It wasn't fun in the least bit. But, I'm glad to hear everything is good here. I want to spend the rest of the day just getting familiar with the area. Maybe we can drive the route to the WonderHome office. First, I want a general schedule. And I'm sure it will change since we can't quite predict when WonderHome will call us for interviews."

She shuffled through the papers until finding a list of important dates for the mission and flipped open her 2013 planner to October.

"All right, we are here on Wednesday, October 16," she said, circling the date. "Selena and I are going to submit our applications to WonderHome today. And you think it will be a couple of days until they reach out to us, Felix?"

Felix nodded. "I've made your resumes so strong that you should both move to the top of their lists. I'd be surprised if they sit on your application beyond the weekend. But what do I know about recruiting for a major corporation?"

"Let's say Monday at the latest," Arielle continued, circling the twenty-first on the calendar. "They'll call us by then to set up an interview either later next week, or the week after. For the sake of our planning, let's assume everything falls later.

That way it's easier to move things up instead of pushing them back."

Arielle had gained her organization skills from her mother, and couldn't help but feel her presence now that the calendar was open amid a scatter of documents. She remembered plenty of times seeing her mother doing the same thing at their kitchen table, whether it was planning for the annual family vacation, tax preparation, or something as simple as a trip to the grocery store. Her mother never left the house unprepared.

"We're not going in completely guessing," Felix said, leaning over Arielle's shoulder to view the list of critical dates. "We know Adam applies on November 17, and reports to the office for his first day of training on December 2. That's only two weeks from application to the first day. They move fast."

"True," Arielle agreed. "It's also for a higher priority position, so I don't want to base everything off that. But, yes, they can move through the hiring process at a brisk pace. All that said, our goal is to be in a position at the company where Selena can influence the recruiting process. Ideally, she'll be the one who receives the application on Monday morning of November 18 and can remove it from the system before anyone else sees it. And even if not, she can hopefully have some say over the interviewing process."

"We should still try to intervene on Adam's end," Felix said. "If you're able to get to a point where you're working on your own, Arielle, you might get me the info I need to hack into the company's system. We can change the date and time of the interview, change Adam's contact information. Anything to make him *not* receive communication from the company. It would be better if I did this and tried to make it look like a technical glitch. Because there won't be a valid reason if we were to have Selena update those details in the system, since they could likely trace that back to her."

"So I'm basically going in there and acting like a complete dumbass for my few first days, aren't I?" Selena asked.

"Precisely," Felix said. "But don't act too dumb. We still need you there for the long haul. Being in HR will get you access to all the happenings around the company. Since we don't know how wide this scheme is, we'll need ears open across all the departments."

"Yes," Arielle said. "Let's not get fired in the first month. We'll need to be ready to adjust our plans, too. If Selena gets caught, or ends up on some sort of probation, we need to plan around that so she doesn't lose her job. I can shoulder more of the responsibility, as much as I can from my role. We should focus on preventing Adam's hiring, or getting him terminated from the company as soon as possible. He gets arrested on May 23, 2014, so let's set a target date for the first of May to have him removed. If we can't by then, everything will be in motion and out of our control."

"Then it will be dangerous for everything we try," Selena said, leaning back in her seat across from Arielle.

She never read the full mission reports. Arielle knew this. But she also had a mind like a sponge. After two missions of working together, Arielle knew Selena was absorbing all the information being presented, even the dates, and wouldn't have to look any of it up again. It was a gift she admired, no different from the servers at restaurants who could memorize all the orders for a party of fifteen, including who didn't want onions on their burger.

"Exactly," Arielle said. "We have enough time. I'm going

to tail Adam for the next week. We'll see how interesting it is. I'm bailing if it means sitting outside of an office or house all day like the two last missions. But I mainly want to get a feel for the guy. Who does he spend time with during the week? Weekends? You never know where a helpful detail can come into play."

Selena and Felix clung to every word. Even after two missions working exclusively with Arielle, they still had a hunger to learn her thought processes behind every decision.

"And that's why I'm going to head over to his house right now," Arielle continued. "Selena, would you like to come?"

Chapter 12

Adam Marshall had just arrived home from work. At noon. On a Wednesday.

His usually green eyes were bloodshot red from the tears of rage he had cried during the drive from downtown back to his home in the suburbs. His oldest son, Jaxson, was away at his second month of preschool. But his wife, Emily, remained home with their one-year-old daughter, Tegan.

How he wished he could have come home to an empty house. Adam didn't want to cry in front of his daughter, even if she had no means of understanding the situation. He had already called Emily to inform her they had fired him from his job, the second time in as many years that a company had done so.

The last time was a matter of the company moving to Montana. Adam didn't beat himself up too much over that job loss, because who the fuck wanted to live in Montana?

This time, however, his blood boiled at the mere thought of how things unfolded. He pulled into his driveway, killed the engine, then returned his death grip to the steering wheel, knuckles turning the color of freshly fallen snow.

Fired for doing a good deed, he thought, teeth gritted while he stared at the front of his house. They had packed his box of belongings while he sat in a conference room with his manager and a Human Resources representative as they delivered the final blow. The box now sat on the passenger seat, an apron, name tag, and various family pictures spilling over the edge.

"Those motherfuckers," he said, finally stepping out of the car, leaving the box behind. He could get it later. He didn't want to look like too much of a loser when he entered the house.

Adam followed the pathway from his car to the front door, passing the lawn covered in a fresh blanket of brown and yellow leaves, crunching the few that hadn't been swept off the concrete. They decorated their front yard for Halloween, an inflatable vampire and Frankenstein monster facing off in front of the maple tree that stood guard within their picket fence.

They had moved into this new house in the months before Tegan was born, excited at the opportunity to live in a better neighborhood with better schools thanks to Adam's new, higher-paying job as a grocery store manager at the local chain, Emerald Grocery. They hired him to run the chain's busiest store in downtown Seattle, a twenty-minute drive from his new home in Bellevue.

The tire swing dangling from the maple tree provided the daily reminder that Adam had achieved life's greatest dream of becoming a middle-class father. Every day was damn near the same thing. Wake up to get himself and Jaxson fed and dressed. Start the coffee for Emily—he didn't drink that caffeinated shit. Kiss his wife and daughter goodbye before leaving to drop Jaxson off at preschool, to then drive across two bridges full of traffic to make it downtown before nine o'clock.

And that had only been the last two months since Jaxson started at the Loving Hands Preschool and Child Care Center, where the other parents stuck their noses in the air at the thought of their children having to mingle with the son of a grocer.

These thoughts zipped through his mind as he reached the front door and pushed it open, dragging himself through the doorway where he tossed his keys on top of the small table that collected junk mail and whatever sloppy art Jaxson brought home from school each day.

Adam heard the TV playing the Baby Channel, an odd-looking puppet counting to ten in its high-pitched voice.

A hallway ran from the front door to the living room straight ahead, the kitchen and dining rooms off to the left through their own entryway. Emily appeared at the end of the hall, her lips pursed into a frown as she shuffled down the hardwood toward Adam.

"I'm sorry, babe," she said, planting a kiss on his lips that he didn't bother returning. The shame phase was already taking hold. Emily worked so hard to keep the house clean and proper, all while taking care of Tegan. That was their agreement when they found out Emily was pregnant for the second time. Adam insisted they could make it work for Emily to continue her career as a dental hygienist. She didn't need to give it all up to be a stay-at-home mother.

But Emily had insisted. She wanted to spend her time with the kids and be present in their lives as much as possible before they were both in school. At that point, she planned to return to her career, or possibly look into something new.

Today felt like they were back at square one.

"Let's talk about it," she said, running a hand up and down his back, guiding him down the hallway where he stole a quick glance of Tegan bouncing wildly in her jungle-themed baby jumper, the puppet on the TV now reviewing the colors of the rainbow.

More shame pounded within Adam's chest upon seeing his little girl.

How could I let everyone in my life down with one stupid decision?

Emily sat down at the dining table, her yoga pants highlighting her curvy lower half. She had added a daily exercise routine into her schedule six months earlier, and the results had led to a definite increase in Adam's libido.

"What happened?" she asked in a hushed voice, as if Tegan were snooping on their conversation from the other room.

Adam shook his head, shoulders slouched as he settled in the chair next to Emily. "I'm still trying to understand that myself. You know how the store partners with different non-profits to take the extra food that gets close to expiring."

"Right. And they take it to different shelters and soup kitchens."

"Exactly. Well, two weeks ago, we had a *ton* of food that needed to go. Like, double the normal amount. I called up the usual companies we work with and told them to invite any others we don't work with to come and get some food. They did, but even after all that, there was still enough food left over to send to probably five different companies. But no more were coming. So at the end of that day, I told the staff to take whatever they'd like home. It was all piled up separately in the back, where it wouldn't get mixed up with anything new coming in. And that's why I was fired."

Adam leaned back, fists clenched underneath the table, as he shook his head some more. He could feel his face turning red. He'd punch a hole in the wall if it wouldn't be his problem to repair, and now regretted not doing just that on his way out of the store earlier this morning.

"What?!" Emily cried. "How is that even a fireable offense?"

Adam shrugged. "The word of me allowing this made its way up to corporate. They said I was supposed to throw the food out, and that by allowing the staff to take it home, they considered it theft. Like, I know the rules and that's what we normally do. But there were at least fifty boxes of cereal, hundreds of cans of food, fresh fruit, veggies. It could have fed us for five months, at least. I couldn't just throw all that in the dumpster."

"Of course not," Emily said, reaching for Adam's hand, which promptly uncurled and allowed the caress from his wife. "Is there anything you can do, legally?"

Adam shook his head, tears welled in his eyes. "It's a clear rule written out in our policies and procedures. I'd have no legal ground to stand on."

"Who do you think did it? Did someone have it out for you?"

Adam shrugged. "Doesn't matter. I suppose there is always someone who doesn't like the manager, if not multiple people. Honestly, I doubt it was even told to corporate by some malicious intent. I'm betting word just got out and reached someone higher up. The corporate suits—now those people are always looking for someone breaking a rule to make an example out of."

"Did you even get a chance to defend yourself?"

"Not much I could say in defense, because this was a clear

rule violation. All I told them before I left was 'Based on how this all played out, one of us is going to hell for how this is being handled, and it's not me.'"

Emily threw her head back and let out a laugh. "You really said that?!"

Adam cracked a smile, his first of the morning. "I did. I was, and am, so pissed off about all this. Like, can you even believe it? I got fired for giving food to my staff that makes twelve dollars an hour instead of throwing it all in a dumpster."

Adam needed to say this out loud to make it feel more real. He laughed, continuing to shake his head. "Like, are you kidding me? After all we've gone through with these stupid jobs, and this is how it ends. I'm thinking I'm just not cut out for a job in corporate America. But what the hell else can I do? We have kids to feed and put through this expensive preschool. The last box isn't even unpacked in our house. I can't just take on a loan to start a new business. Most take five years before you'll even see a profit. Plus, I'd never be home."

Adam was rambling, and this prompted Emily to stand up and hug him from behind his shoulders, kissing the top of his head. "Relax, babe. Everything is going to be okay. It's always worked out before. There are thousands of jobs out there. Maybe you just haven't found that right one yet."

"Clearly."

"Why don't we go out to lunch?" Emily asked. "Let's take your mind off of all this. You pick the spot. We'll go relax with Tegan and unwind the rest of the day. And tomorrow, you can start a search for the next job."

Adam stood up and turned around to face his wife, sliding his arms around her waist and pulling her in tight. "I love you. You're the best."

They kissed, oblivious to the car parked outside with two time travelers from the future.

Chapter 13

October 17, 2013

The next morning, the three Angels gathered in the kitchen for a late breakfast. No one had gone grocery shopping yet, so Selena ran out for a box of doughnuts from Mighty-O Donuts two blocks down.

Arielle and Selena had spent the rest of the prior day following Adam and his family as they went to lunch at a 60s-themed diner. They even went inside to have lunch for themselves and enjoy the food and atmosphere. After lunch, the Marshalls returned home for a couple hours before Adam returned outside to pick up their son from preschool. Once they returned, no one stepped out for the rest of the evening when Arielle called it a day at five o'clock.

Felix didn't return home until a few minutes after Arielle and Selena had arrived back. His day had comprised of a prolonged visit to the Seattle weapons warehouse where he stocked up on the three Angels' usual requests. What took him longer than normal was the extended discussion he had with the warehouse operator about the best equipment Felix would need for hacking into a database for a company as grand as WonderHome.

Felix didn't bring his own equipment because it was against the Road Runners' bylaws, and likely wouldn't work, anyway. Every mission in the past required him to figure out how to best perform his job with the equipment available in that year.

He then had to stop at the Road Runners' Seattle office to print documents he needed for the mission. After that, he went to buy three cell phones they could use for the next six months. That process took nearly three hours before Felix left the Sprint Wireless, cussing under his breath.

"Sorry about last night," Felix said. "I just had so much to do still and wasted all the day doing errands. I got our phones, but I'd love to hear about what you found out following Adam."

"Well, it just so happens yesterday was the day he got fired from his job," Arielle said. "Or at least that's what it sounded like. We were three tables down from them at the diner and could only pick up bits and pieces. It explains him arriving home in the middle of the morning and the box of belongings we saw in the passenger seat of his car."

"They seem to have a strong family life," Selena added. "Obviously, we only observed half a day, but everyone seemed happy with each other, especially considering he just lost his job."

"I want to go back this morning to confirm. If he's home all day, it'll be safe to assume he lost his job."

"Isn't it possible he's just on vacation?" Felix asked. "And maybe he brought a box home of stuff."

"It's possible, sure. But the box had things like family pictures, a stapler, a calculator...all the things you'd expect to see for someone having packed their desk in a hurry. And it was all just thrown in there."

They munched on their doughnuts and coffee, taking a moment to process their findings.

"Sooooo," Selena said. "You have a phone?"

Felix chuckled. "Yes, Selena, I got us smart phones to use for the rest of the mission. I was about to buy the burner phones, but already started hearing your voice in my head. Complaining about how they didn't have the internet, and *how on Earth* would you ever manage six months without social media."

"Hey," Selena snapped back. "It's 2013. Facebook is actually cool."

"Oh, jeez," Arielle said, joining the laughter.

"All jokes aside," Felix said. "We needed smart phones for this mission. Burners don't have cameras on them—I thought they did. It will make our work a lot easier if you're both able to take pictures on your phone and text them to me. Especially you, Arielle, since you'll be sending me things to help hack into WonderHome's system."

"Works for me," Selena said. "So, where are the phones?"

Felix cracked a sly grin and stood up to reach into his pockets, pulling out three different cell phones.

"You had them this whole time?!" Selena gasped, standing up to smack Felix.

He howled with amusement as he laid them out on the table.

"I couldn't resist seeing that look on your face," Felix said. "And it was worth it, even if my arm doesn't think so." He smiled as he rubbed where Selena had just whacked him. *She packs a mean punch.*

"It's so nice having a smart phone on a mission," Arielle said. "It's been a while since I've had a mission with one. Were you able to apply for those jobs last night?"

Felix nodded. "I was up later than I wanted to be, but it got done. I needed these phones first, because hopefully they'll call today. That would be most ideal."

"Less than twenty-four hours after applying?" Selena asked. "Dream on."

"Not for me to say," Felix replied. "I also created a shared drive for us to swap documents—and uploaded both of your resumes. I suggest you review those now, because you'll need to speak about it whenever they call. Which will hopefully be today."

He shot those final two words directly at Selena, who only grinned in response while she searched through her new phone for the faux resume.

"I have three years of experience as a software engineer with Twitter?" Arielle asked.

"It shows you have experience from one of the biggest tech companies in the world," Felix explained. "I thought all of this out. The timing puts you there during Twitter's biggest years of growth, and by now in 2013, it would perfectly explain why you're looking to leave your job. They've grown too much. A lot has changed with the company culture. It's not the same place as when you started. Honestly, we can plug in any of the big social media companies if you'd like, and it will be the same story. Facebook, Instagram, LinkedIn. You name it."

"No, Twitter is fine," Arielle said. "And thank you for such attention to detail. You've never even worked a corporate job. How do you know what all goes into this?"

Felix smiled. "I know you don't think anyone could do as much research as you, but I do. I love reading about these things because it's all foreign to me. And besides, if I want to create a billion dollar company one day, I'm going to need a full understanding of every aspect within a healthy functioning organization. I'm actually a little excited about this mission."

"You're such a nerd," Selena said. "And so am I, apparently. I have a master's degree in Human Resources Management? That sounds like the worst six years of life one could waste."

Felix laughed. "You're going to do great. I uploaded some material for you to read as well. So you can sound like you have that master's degree."

Selena shook her head and muttered under her breath, "At least it's not cleaning toilets again."

"And same for you, Arielle," Felix continued. "You'll see that you're proficient in JavaScript, TypeScript, HTML, and CSS, among a few other things. I sent you a cheat sheet to understand what all of that means."

"Are these the things that come up in regular conversation?" Arielle asked. "Like outside of work?"

"I'm afraid so. I found a message board run by software engineers, and even the off-topic threads always circle back to software stuff. If Selena thinks she's a nerd, then you're Urkel. It doesn't get any geekier than a room full of software engineers."

"If you need any acting lessons," Selena said, shifting her voice to become high-pitched and nasally. "Just let me know!" She pushed an imaginary pair of glasses up the bridge of her nose and snorted, earning raucous laughter from around the table.

"Wow," Arielle said. "So that's what they taught you at Julliard."

"What can I say? I can pull off any role," Selena replied, still laughing.

"Well, let's not do that voice in your interview and you should be fine," Felix said, still grinning. "Your resume shows you as educated but disciplined. You worked in the HR departments for both Wal-Mart and Shutterfly. This shows you have both tech-industry experience along with major corporation exposure. I read a lot of blogs about what qualifications recruiters look for in both of your positions. For HR in tech companies, it's that combo."

"You're setting us up for success," Arielle said. "It's like we're counting cards and flipping the script on the house."

"And I love that," Felix said. "I do know how to count cards, actually. Only used that gift to make a couple hundred dollars here and there. I don't want to do anything that will get noticed. Would hate to end up in a back alley getting my kneecaps bashed in."

Arielle and Selena looked at him, astonished. "Is that really what happens?" Selena asked.

"It's a serious offense. It's one of those things that isn't illegal, but highly frowned upon. Casinos don't actually have someone to break your knees if they catch you. They just ask you to leave. That's all they really can do, since there isn't a law."

"Good to know," Arielle said. "Don't ever sit down at a blackjack table with Felix."

He grinned proudly. "You should be so lucky. I think you're both set for the day, though. I have some things I need to get set up on my computer, then I'll be free in the afternoon. You should both read as much as possible from the documents I shared. We're in this for the long haul—it's important you know your jobs like you really have been doing them for the past few years."

"Sounds good," Arielle said. "I'm going to head back to the Marshall house, and will read while I wait for something to happen."

Chapter 14

October 21, 2013

They didn't receive the call from WonderHome before the weekend, like Felix had hoped. Arielle and Selena had to calm him down, as he grew antsy during Friday afternoon when no calls came through. He started to doubt the resumes he submitted, and was already thinking of the next steps to get them into that office building.

After they stressed that these things could take two weeks sometimes, they had a relaxing weekend of grocery shopping, a few dinners out downtown, and a rainy Sunday exploring the city.

Arielle had spent a couple of hours on Thursday and Friday morning outside of the Marshall house to find nothing of significance. She confirmed Adam had indeed lost his job after a closer examination of the box that remained in his passenger seat. She saw memos on the company letterhead for Emerald Grocery, plus the termination letter that had fallen to the car's floor.

Monday morning, however, the Angels relaxed until they had something to do. Following Adam was a waste of time so early, especially since they didn't have plans to bug his house.

Not yet.

Selena was the first to receive the phone call that sparked everything else. It was a few minutes past ten o'clock. Felix had loaded the dishwasher with their plates and glasses from breakfast. Arielle was up in her bedroom reading more about software engineering. Selena was sitting at the kitchen table, chatting with Felix in between dishes, when the phone rang.

His head immediately whipped over. No one else had their phone numbers aside from each other.

"It's them!" he gasped, shuffling over to confirm the 206 area code on the caller ID.

"Calm down," Selena said, raising a hand. "I can't do this if you're going to jump all over me."

She stood up and answered the call, glaring at Felix. "Hello?"

Selena couldn't remember the last time butterflies flapped around her stomach, but they returned in a hurry once she pressed the phone to her ear. She knew how to act, but could she truly bullshit her way past a corporate recruiter to land a job she had no experience in doing? Would Felix's resume actually work? There were too many factors out of her control, and she supposed that was why the insects did cartwheels within her stomach.

"Hello," a woman's voice replied. "I'm looking for Ms. Selena Nicole."

"This is her."

Felix stopped doing the dishes but remained at the sink, leaning against the counter as he observed Selena kick off their first task of the mission.

"Hi, Ms. Nicole. My name is Janina Victoria with Wonder-Home. I was wondering if you had a couple of minutes to chat about your application to work with our People Operations team."

"I sure do. Did you say People Operations?"

Selena pictured a room full of surgeons operating on several bodies, and almost laughed out loud.

"Yes, that is what we call what is traditionally known as *human resources.* You'll probably hear a lot of newer companies call their HR departments People Operations instead. POPS, for short."

"Interesting."

"I see you've worked with Shutterfly and Wal-Mart. They probably still used the HR label. We felt *human resources* was an antiquated term and wanted something more modern-ized."

Selena had to turn on her acting skills. The phone call was already starting to drag, so she let out a hearty laugh. "Well, thank you for explaining. I was wondering what job I applied for. Threw me for a curve there."

Janina laughed through the phone, and Selena figured she couldn't be more than a few years older than her, judging by her voice.

"No worries at all," Janina said, a new cheeriness slipping into her voice. "It will take a few years for POPS to become the new norm, so I guess we'll just have to keep explaining. Now, I'd love to talk about your background because it sounds like a perfect fit for the type of candidate we're looking to hire."

"Oh?" Selena played dumb, feeling in complete control now that she understood how to best reflect the recruiter on the other end of the line. Plus, she had actually taken a couple hours the night before—on a Sunday night!—to read the notes Felix had provided. He had even outlined some potential questions and answers for this very phone call she found herself on. "Well, I'm thrilled to hear that."

"As are we. So it looks like you've been able to gain a lot of experience in a short matter of time. You graduated college in 2008 and went straight into the HR department at Wal-Mart. What did you do for them, exactly?"

"A little of everything," Selena said, smirking because she felt like a student taking a test with the answer key hidden up her sleeve. "One of my professors had a connection with their main corporate office and got me a job with similar responsibilities as an intern, but with a full-time salary and benefits. I look back and credit my three years there as the real education. I worked with the benefits team, recruiting, analytics, talent development, and improving the workplace culture."

"Very impressive," Janina said, the distant clacking of a keyboard as she took notes. "And that led you to Shutterfly?"

"Yes. As much as I loved what I was doing at Wal-Mart, I couldn't handle living in Arkansas. I need interaction with people. Diversity. Things to do on the weekends besides town fairs and museums. I applied for several jobs in California, Florida, even New York. Shutterfly called first and offered me a job, so I was on my way."

"Well, Seattle is definitely going through some serious growth and changes. Lots of run-down places have been upgraded and are now bustling with young professionals. And it looks like you focused primarily on recruiting during your time at Shutterfly?"

"Yes. They had me start as a sales recruiter and eventually branched out as a senior recruiter for other departments."

"And why are you looking to leave, if you don't mind me

asking?"

Selena indeed didn't mind her asking, because Felix had already provided a response to this question. *How does he do it?*

"If I may be honest," Selena said, lowering her voice as if telling a secret. "I think I've hit my ceiling here. I'm still in the senior recruiter role and there doesn't look to be any opportunity to move up any time soon. The company isn't growing, and because of that I'm just kind of stuck behind my director, and she is stuck behind the VP. I believe my only opportunity for growth can come with a bigger company like WonderHome."

"That is certainly possible here," Janina said, her perkiness remaining high. "We don't do things the traditional way. If we were to hire you, you'd become familiar with all facets of our department before deciding where you might best fit. Recruiting is what we need, and clearly what you have the skill set for, but if something else were to catch your eye, we wouldn't stop you from pursuing that instead."

"That's great to know. I really have been enjoying my time as a recruiter. I find it incredibly challenging. Like, how do you really know if the candidate is going to be as good as they look on paper? Or even after the interviews? Sometimes it's a complete miss, but that's what I've come to understand. Some people are simply good at interviewing and suck at their job. And vice versa."

Janina laughed at this, and Selena took it as some sort of inside joke only HR workers understood. She laughed back, not sure what else to say.

"I'm really impressed," Janina said. "Hope you're not one of those candidates who is only good at interviewing." She cackled again, and Selena once more returned the sentiment.

"Not at all. I'm just as good in person." Selena couldn't resist throwing in some of her own personality now that it sounded like the call was going to lead to an interview.

"What do you think about us flying you out here for an interview?" Janina asked. "We'll cover your flight and stay for two nights. One day to interview and see our offices. And another to explore the city and see if it lives up to your standards."

"That would be fantastic. When would that be?"

Felix pumped a fist into the air and hurried to the stairs to call up for Arielle before returning to watch the rest of Selena's conversation like a proud coach.

"Would you be able to take this Thursday and Friday off from work? I can even see about adding a third night if you'd like to fly in Wednesday evening."

"That shouldn't be a problem. I have so much PTO."

"Fantastic. I'll send you an email right now. If you can let me know by this afternoon for sure that this week will work, and what day you'd like to fly out here, we can get everything booked for you."

"Thank you so much, Janina. I can't wait to meet you in person."

They hung up, and Selena looked at Felix with a tight-lipped grin. Arielle barged into the kitchen. "What's going on?" she asked, looking back and forth between the two of them.

Felix gestured toward Selena to explain.

"I have an interview with WonderHome this Thursday."

"That's great!" Arielle cried. "So they just called you, I take it?"

"Sure did. And the phone interview couldn't have gone any

better, thanks to Felix. Every question she asked me was on the list he made. I hope you studied yours."

"Of course."

"And if you get Janina on the phone, you'll need to be a bit more enthusiastic than your normal self."

Arielle scoffed while the other two broke into laughter. "I know how to sound enthusiastic."

"Yeah, about staying up until two in the morning to read mission reports. Janina is definitely one of those girls who keeps the energy up all day. Probably partied like crazy in college and joined a sorority."

"Way to stereotype," Arielle said, crossing her arms.

"I'll make you a bet. A hundred dollars. I'll get Janina out for drinks after we work there, and I'll get her to tell me all about her sorority days."

"I'm not making that bet."

They all knew Selena had an uncanny ability to read people, even through a brief conversation over the phone.

"That's what I thought."

"All that matters is the first step has finally fallen into place," Felix said.

"And now step two is," Arielle said, pulling her buzzing cell phone out of her pocket. "It's them."

Felix grinned. "Let's do it again. Good luck."

Chapter 15

October 24, 2013

Arielle and Selena each had their first in-person interviews scheduled for Thursday morning.

Arielle's call with Janina had gone just as smoothly as Selena's. Wanting to avoid appearing too similar to her colleague, Arielle had informed Janina that she had just moved to Seattle in pursuit of a new opportunity.

Meanwhile, Selena left them Wednesday night to check into her free hotel across from the skyscraper that housed the WonderHome corporate offices.

"Hotels are relaxing," she had explained to Felix, who asked why she'd leave when they had a perfectly suitable house. "Think about it, a hotel is a place where someone comes into your room, makes your bed, cleans your bathroom, and makes sure everything is fully stocked. Every day. Why would I pass that up? Plus, they gave me a daily stipend of one hundred dollars to feed myself."

Arielle left early Thursday morning to meet Selena at her hotel room so they could get ready together. Selena had all the knowledge on makeup and clothing, and had grabbed everything they needed while on a mini-shopping spree with the free money WonderHome had given her.

Arielle arrived at a hotel room that looked partly like a salon. Makeup brushes lay spread out on the counter next to the TV, jars of nail polish and mascara peppered in between containers of lipstick and powder. Hair brushes, clips, and a blow-dryer were all set up in the bathroom. And on the bed were two outfits complete with boxes of brand-new shoes beneath each.

"Wow, Selena," Arielle said, stuffing her keys into her pocket because she didn't want to lose them in the mess. "Do you think all of this is necessary? I mean, they think they flew you out here. I'd say they are more than interested in hiring you."

"That's a shocking question coming from you," Selena fired back. "Do you think we should risk not getting these jobs by just coasting through the interview?"

"Fair. But damn, this just seems like a lot of stuff."

"Not like I won't wear my makeup again. Can't speak for you, though."

Arielle ignored the cheap shot. "So what all do we have going on this morning?"

It was 8:30 when she arrived at the Seattle Union Hotel, a twenty-one-story building two blocks away from the office. Selena's room was on the fifteenth floor and had a breathtaking view overlooking Elliott Bay and the Seattle Great Wheel. Selena's interview was scheduled for ten o'clock sharp, with Arielle's following half an hour after that.

"We're going all-out for these interviews," Selena said. "We need to wow everyone we meet, leave an impression, and become truly unforgettable. Just playing the odds, I'm probably going to interview with mostly women, and you with mostly men. That's why I got you a pair of heels and an outfit that will show off those calves you work so hard on."

"Heels? I couldn't tell you the last time I've worn heels. I hope you didn't get them too tall. Would hate to fall on my face."

Selena laughed. "That will definitely accomplish our three objectives. You'll be fine—they're two-inch heels."

Arielle rarely dressed up. Her date with Javonte had been the most effort she had put into an outfit in years, and even that one didn't have heels. Walking down the sidewalks in a pair of heels just might be the most troublesome part of this mission for the top-ranked Angel, and the thought made her snicker.

"So I get to show skin, and you'll be in a pantsuit?" Arielle asked.

"God no," Selena snapped. "I would never do that to myself. I got a new blouse and skirt with a little slit on the knees. And of course new heels. But I don't need to make anyone drool."

"Neither do I."

"But it'll help. I've already looked up the people we're most likely going to meet today. The manager of the software engineers is a middle-aged man. How many women do you think even apply for this job to begin with? I'm sure these guys would love some eye candy."

"Pigs."

"I know they're pigs, but that's what we need to appeal to. This is corporate America. Anything that can make these old guys' days at the office more enjoyable. Combine your looks with your resume and smooth-talking. You're automatically in."

Arielle shook her head, but knew Selena was right. She'd

have to swallow her pride—taking down the patriarchy would have to wait another day. "Fine. Doll me up."

The words felt gross leaving her mouth, but she had never seen such a cunning smile spread across Selena's face. A crazed look like she had been waiting for this moment her entire life.

Selena pulled out the chair parked beneath the TV counter and spun it around. "Have a seat."

* * *

At 9:30, Arielle and Selena stepped outside the hotel, dressed and ready for their interviews. Selena had even gone as far as buying a purse for Arielle, a $500 purchase from the Coach store a few blocks down in the fashion district. Arielle never carried a purse on missions, so Selena justified the splurge, citing she wanted the purse back after the interviews if Arielle didn't want to keep it (she didn't).

A two-block stroll through downtown had never felt so long. Arielle had to concentrate on each step, wary of cracks her heel could slip into and cause a rolled ankle.

Selena walked with much more confidence and ease, smiling back at the few businessmen who couldn't help but admire the two women who looked ready to overthrow a CEO.

"See," Selena said. "We're already getting checked out. Corporate America is too predictable."

Despite feeling like a drunken baby learning how to take its first steps, Arielle breathed a sigh of relief when they reached the entrance to the Wilson Investments Center, a skyscraper spanning forty-two floors, home to nearly every financial firm in Seattle, plus other major corporations like WonderHome and Nordstrom.

They looked up the glass exterior, unable to see anywhere near the top of the building.

"Okay," Selena said. "From here, we need to go on our own. We don't want them to think we know each other."

One thing that all three Angels had agreed on was Arielle and Selena should avoid crossing paths as much as possible while at the office. They were going to be digging into highly illegal activity, and if things took a turn, it could be catastrophic if the company made a connection between the two of them.

"Of course," Arielle said. "Thirtieth floor, yeah?"

Selena nodded. "I'll head up first. You can probably head up in about twenty minutes, just to play it safe."

"Deal. Good luck."

They shared a brief hug before Selena continued into the building, leaving Arielle alone outside. There was a waiting area in the main lobby, complete with lounge chairs and coffee tables, but she didn't want to sit around. The anticipation was already growing heavily on her mind. She had been up past midnight studying her resume and all of Felix's notes. He really had done a masterful job in preparing them to land these jobs.

Instead, she found a Target across the street with a Starbucks logo plastered across the window. She'd spend the next half hour there until heading up for the interview, wondering how it was playing out for Selena.

Chapter 16

Thirty floors up, Selena stepped into the WonderHome lobby. The company logo filled up the entire wall behind the reception desk, its letters massive and bubbly, except for the H that was shaped like a house.

A young blond woman, likely fresh out of college, sat behind the desk, a man of similar age with spiky black hair leaning against the desk as he spoke close to her.

The woman noticed Selena and turned on her most welcoming smile. The man looked over his shoulder, gave the woman a pat on her shoulder as he mumbled something before disappearing down a long hallway.

"Hello," the woman said, standing up. "Are you here for an interview?"

Selena noticed the nameplate on the desk. Becca Faulkner.

"Yes. I believe I'm meeting with Janina Victoria."

"Oh, Nina? She's the best."

Selena immediately heard the Valley girl accent in Becca's speech. The slightly higher pitch with a hint of ditzy optimism toward everything in life. "She is *totally* the best," Selena said, immediately jumping into a mocking impression of the unsuspecting receptionist.

"Let me take you back," Becca said. "Do you need a drink

or snack? We have coffee, water, soda."

"Just water is good. Thank you."

Becca reached under her desk and pulled out a water bottle from a mini refrigerator. "This way." She turned and started down the long hallway with doors to five different conference rooms before opening up to a bigger space Selena couldn't quite see.

Becca turned into the middle door, a conference room with an oval-shaped table in the middle that seated at least six people. "Nina will be about five minutes. Let us know if you need anything else. And good luck."

"Thank you," Selena replied as Becca left the room and closed the door. *We'll be seeing plenty of each other soon enough.*

Selena had studied her notes late into the night as well, but she didn't require as many times through the documents as Arielle. She absorbed information quickly, and now played it all back in her mind. The phone interview was one thing, but she now had to keep up the in-person charm while recalling a faux background working in Human Resources. Plus, she needed to be ready to adjust her personality depending on who else walked through that door. Not everyone would be as cheery and positive as Janina.

Selena chugged her water while waiting, and a knock came at exactly the five-minute mark, the door swinging open to reveal a wide-grinning Janina.

"Selena?" she asked, chomping on a piece of gum.

"Yes." Selena rose and stuck out her hand. "It's so nice to finally meet you."

"You have no idea." Janina closed the door and pulled out the seat across from Selena, speaking in a hushed voice. "You are my godsend. I've been having the hardest time filling this role, but your application came through and I knew it was exactly what we've been looking for. Are you ready to interview?"

Selena's heart raced a little faster. She wasn't entirely thrilled at the idea of Janina having likely already talked her up to the others she would interview with this morning. She didn't know what expectations were already set based on these behind-the-scenes conversations. If they already had Selena on some sort of pedestal, it could only increase the chances of her bombing the interview before it even happened.

Instead of sharing these thoughts, she only smiled and nodded. "I'm very ready. What does the schedule look like?"

"You'll be interviewing with the manager of our POPS department, Susie Foster, and her boss, the Vice President of POPS, Amara Edwards. They are both incredible women and have made our department the best by far. I'll let them know you're here and ready. I have to go get another interview started, but I'll be back as soon as you're done chatting with them."

The other interview was Arielle, likely sitting in the lobby not knowing what to say to a girl like Becca. A light smile touched Selena's lips as she thought about it, holding in her laughter.

"Thank you for everything. I won't let you down." Selena said this more to build her own confidence. The WonderHome office had a more laid-back vibe than a typical corporate setting. This made her more relaxed than she had expected, and she needed to be on her game, ready to focus and adapt to whoever walked through the door next.

Janina left Selena alone for another five minutes, where

she stared at the wall to rush through her last moments of recalling her made-up resume.

When the next knock came on the door, Selena felt as if the floodlights lit up the stage she was about to perform on. *Let's do this.*

The door opened and two women stepped in, immediately causing a panic for Selena. She hadn't understood the schedule as meeting with both of them at the same time. This complicated her plans for adapting to her interviewer, but she appreciated the challenge just the same.

"Hello, Selena," the first woman through the door said, approaching the table with her arm extended for a handshake. She was in her forties, possibly early fifties, judging by the soft wrinkles touching her hazel eyes. Reddish-blond hair flowed beyond the boxy shoulder pads of her purple blazer. "I'm Susie Foster, manager of the People Operations team here at WonderHome. It's a pleasure to meet you."

"Likewise," Selena said, standing to shake both women's hands.

"And I'm Amara Edwards," said the other woman. "Vice President of People Operations."

Amara had an intimidating presence, and Selena couldn't quite pinpoint what it was. Perhaps she was already jumping to conclusions that Amara was involved in the money laundering scheme. They had figured it likely for any member of the executive team to have involvement, yet Amara didn't seem like one to take shit from anyone. She sat down and brushed back her long braids behind her ears, slipping on a pair of glasses as she studied a copy of Selena's resume.

"You have an impressive background," Susie said, taking the seat next to Amara, and opening a folder with a blank sheet of paper on one side, and the resume on the other. She clicked her pen and started writing on the blank paper. "And for such a young age, to have had these jobs."

Selena grinned, feeling for the mood. Both women were older than her, that much was obvious, but did that mean they were necessarily old-school in their thinking? They worked at WonderHome, and this place was very much setting the trends for future corporate America. "I've always been a bit of an old soul," Selena said, dipping her toe into this approach. "Before I even graduated, I started looking for jobs. But not just any entry-level job I could find. I wanted to find a company that could be home for a long time."

"Tell us what happened that caused you to leave both Wal-Mart and Shutterfly," Amara said, scratching down notes of her own.

"I hit a wall at both places. I'm a very driven person with a constant need for growth and improvement. Honestly, I think my age held me back at those two places. I reached a point where I was ready to step into roles with more responsibilities, but they never entertained the thought, no matter how much of a top-performer I proved to be. That's why I'm hoping to work with WonderHome. I understand the company is a lot more open to advancing the careers of those who deserve it, even if it means in a different department. You invest in your people, and that's all I want. I even heard you have a girl who is a director, and she's only twenty-six."

Amara and Susie looked at each other and smiled. "You've done your research," Susie said. "And yes, that is true. She is the director of our public relations department, and has been in the role for about six months."

Selena felt she was taking the correct approach, so sat

back, crossed her arms, and shook her head. "A 26-year-old *woman*. Director at a major corporation. That's all I need to know about this place."

"Now, Ms. Nicole," Amara said, shifting in her seat to cross one leg over the other. "You understand you won't be jumping into a higher role, right? I wouldn't exactly call this recruiting position an entry-level job, but it's just above that."

"Absolutely," Selena said, sitting forward. "Clearly, I don't have any type of leadership background because of the way I've been held back. I tried shopping around for managerial jobs, but it became obvious I'd have no chance without it on my resume. All I'm hoping for is an opportunity to prove myself and get that chance. And I know that can take time, but like I mentioned, I want a company I can be with for the long haul to do just that."

"Have you been to Seattle before?" Amara asked, leaning back. The question softened the tension that seemed to linger in the room during any type of interview.

"I've visited a bit," Selena said. "I really enjoy this city. So much to do and see."

"That's good. Some people think working downtown is a chore, but I believe if you love the city, then it provides a certain energy to your day."

"I couldn't agree more. I actually grew up in Manhattan, so I'm used to life in a big city. That's why Bentonville was a bit of a culture shock for me when I was working at Wal-Mart's corporate office."

"I'm sure it was," Susie said with a chuckle. She exchanged glances with Amara, who nodded silently as if they were having a telepathic conversation. "We think you're a great fit for this job, Selena. With that, we'd love to end this interview and have you sit with our team for a few hours, if you feel up to it."

"We know this isn't quite the norm," Amara said. "But we like to do things differently. So many candidates look good on paper, but that doesn't always translate to real life. We'd love to see how you fit in with our team."

"So, like job shadowing?" Selena asked.

"Exactly," Amara replied. "You'll gain some insight into what your day-to-day would look like. And while it's not a *major* factor in our decision, we listen to feedback from our existing team on what they think about the potential of working with you."

"Let's do it," Selena said, taking the lead by standing up.

A screeching, sharp blare sounded from the hallway, repeating three times. Five seconds of silence followed, then the trio of blares repeated.

Amara and Susie looked at each, brows furrowed.

"Fire alarm?" Susie asked. "We're not scheduled for a fire drill."

"No," Amara replied, rising slowly out of her seat, appearing unsure if she actually wanted to stand up. "Excuse me."

Amara left the conference room, the obvious scream of the fire alarm even louder for the moment the door was open. Selena saw the strobing light that accompanied the sound.

"I'm sure it's just a mistake," Susie said, offering a forced grin. "Gotta love a fire drill, right?"

Selena smiled in return, nodding her head. The sound screeched throughout the room, making it nearly impossible to hear Susie's words clearly.

A minute later, Amara threw open the door, a light haze appearing the hallway behind her. "We need to go. Smoke is coming from the kitchen."

Susie jumped out of her seat, and Selena followed them into the hallway, where several employees were starting their trek from the other side of the office.

Selena had been in plenty of fire drills, but never in a real scenario where everyone followed the protocol. It surprised her to find everyone walking calmly toward the stairwell in a single-file line. A few people had backpacks and purses slung over their shoulders, but no one else appeared concerned with grabbing personal items from their desks.

Wow, she thought. *All the training really becomes ingrained in our minds.*

She checked her watch to find the time was 10:40. Arielle should have been in her interview, but she didn't see her in the hall. Selena couldn't exactly ask Amara and Susie about her friend, either, and could only trust she was okay.

"Let's go, Selena," Susie said, tapping her on the arm to snap her out of her trance. "We have thirty flights of stairs to go down."

Chapter 17

Ten minutes later, they stepped outside the skyscraper, the sidewalks and streets flooded with the thousands of employees who had their days interrupted. Three firetrucks barricaded the street from traffic, allowing everyone room to gawk at the building, many looking up for any sign of a fire.

The building stood undisturbed, and if it weren't for the massive crowd outside, anyone passing by would have no idea of the chaos unfolding inside. People in bright orange vests scattered among the gathering, hoisting up signs with their company names or logos on them.

Selena had stayed with Susie and Amara, and followed them over to Janina, who was holding the WonderHome sign, their employees gathering around while a man stood on his tiptoes, checking off names on a clipboard as he matched their faces in the crowd.

At least seventy people had encircled Janina, and Selena couldn't find Arielle anywhere.

Knowing her, she went to stop the fire.

A tap on the shoulder proved otherwise, as Selena spun around to see her fellow Angel. She took a step back, Susie and Amara not noticing as they had become engulfed with helping make sure everything was going as it should.

"Were you in your interview?" Selena asked, just above a whisper.

Arielle nodded. "I think this happened because of us. The past knows. Were you thinking about the mission already?"

Selena was about to say no when she remembered she *had* thought of how Amara might be part of the scheme. "Nothing major. And it wasn't even for that long."

"Dammit, Selena," Arielle said through gritted teeth, like a mother trying to scold their child in public. "Come with me."

Arielle grabbed Selena by her forearm and pulled her through the crowd, not stopping until they reach an open space away from the WonderHome employees.

"What the *hell*?" Selena cried, ripping her arm free from Arielle's grip. "You can't just—"

"No!" Arielle barked. "We're on a mission. I can do whatever I need to make sure it doesn't get messed up before we even start."

Selena was plenty familiar with Arielle's tones, but had never heard this one with such harshness swimming behind each word.

"What were you thinking about?" Arielle demanded. "I need to know."

Selena looked over her shoulder to make sure her interviewers were not within ear's reach. "All I was wondering about was if the VP of People Ops had any involvement with the laundering. That's it. The thought left as quickly as it came because they started interviewing me. I swear."

Arielle's face softened at this. "Okay. That's not bad."

"That's not bad?! You make a scene, just to tell me *that's not bad*?! What the hell, Arielle? How do I know it wasn't *you* having thoughts about the mission?"

"Because I wasn't—"

"Bullshit! You can't help yourself. You probably asked to use the restroom and were already snooping around the office. I know how you are."

"I did that, sure, but my mind was clear."

Selena's jaw dropped. "Unbelievable. On second thought, no, it's completely believable. You're a junkie for this stuff. We can't just turn our brains off from the mission, no matter how good you think you are at doing it. *You* still have a subconscious, remember?" Selena balled a fist and knocked it on her head to prove her point.

"Selena, enough. You're the one making a scene. We still have these jobs in the bag. Be smart."

Selena pursed her lips tight enough to turn them white. She wished nothing more than to blast her fists through Arielle's face.

"I'm sorry I jumped to conclusions," Arielle said. "I just can't imagine it's a coincidence that this is happening the day we're here to interview. Maybe this really happened in the original timeline—we have no way of knowing for sure."

"Don't ever come at me like that again," Selena said, sure to emphasize the disgust in her voice. "If you do, I'm requesting a transfer to a new team."

"I said I'm sorry. My emotions got the best of me. If I can be honest, when I saw the smoke up there, I thought the entire mission was about to go to shit. What if the office burned down? I never know how strong the past will push back against our work."

Selena shook her head. She hadn't even considered the ramifications of a fire in WonderHome office, and how it could alter their mission before they even secured their jobs with the company. "That doesn't excuse the way you acted."

"I know. Never again. I promise."

They looked around, the crowd seeming to grow with each passing second.

"So, how was your interview going before this happened?" Arielle asked.

Plenty of distance was now between them and the WonderHome employees, the space having filled up with at least another hundred people.

"It was going so well," Selena said. "They were about to have me sit with the team. I know I haven't done many interviews in my life, but it really sounded like they were ready to offer me a job on the spot. Did your interview even get to begin?"

"Well, that's great news. And yes, mine was about fifteen minutes in with the manager of engineering. We started early since everyone was ready. It was going as well as I could have hoped. The terminology still feels foreign to me, but I talked my way through the questions well enough. I'm not sure how this fire drill is going to alter our plans for the rest of the week."

"Why don't we go check with our interviewers and see what they say? The hotel is only two blocks away. We can hang out there and wait for all of this to die down. Pike's Place is probably going to be overcrowded now because of this, *and* it's almost lunchtime."

They agreed and fought their way through the crowd.

* * *

"Do you really not feel any type of anxiety around all of this?" Arielle asked.

WonderHome had advised them both to remain on standby for the rest of the afternoon. They had no clue when the building would become available again, if at all. But if so, they wanted to resume the interviews as soon as possible.

Arielle and Selena returned to the hotel, where they ordered lunch to the room. Selena flipped through the channels before landing on reruns of a game show called *The Weakest Link*.

"Honestly," Selena said. "No. I like the pace of this mission. It hardly feels like work, and more like adjusting my life to a new routine. I'm loving all the free time."

"Sure it's nice. But we've already been here for more than a week, and it doesn't really feel like anything is in motion. And then today with the fire alarm... Maybe I'm being paranoid, but I feel like it's a bad omen."

"Omen?" Selena asked. "I never took you as someone who believed in omens. You're always spewing facts and science. Are you allowed to believe in something as supernatural as an omen?"

Arielle laughed. "Selena. We're time travelers. You need to give me some credit. I believe in a lot more than you might think. Now, would I base a critical decision on something as abstract as an omen? Of course not. But there's a time and a place for such discussions."

Selena studied Arielle. "If you say so. All I know is that we're going to get those jobs. If it takes an extra day because of this fire alarm, then so be it. We still have over a month until Adam Marshall submits his application, so I don't see what there is to even be worried about."

"I know. I just prefer knowing exactly what is going to

happen on each day of a mission. The typical two-week missions are perfect for scheduling everything out."

Selena had ordered a French dip sandwich and let it soak in the beef *jus* before taking a bite. Arielle poked at her tomato soup.

"If they ask, I'm voting for more missions like this," Selena said. "I haven't felt a single drop of stress since we've been here."

Arielle's phone buzzed, and she grabbed it out of her pocket. "It's them." She answered and listened attentively, nodding while someone spoke on the other end. "Okay, I can plan for that. Thank you, and I'll see you soon."

"Well?" Selena asked, not giving Arielle a second after hanging up the call.

"Interview is back on for this afternoon. Two o'clock, which gives us an hour—I'm assuming you'll get a call shortly. You won't believe what the cause of the fire was."

"Did it come from WonderHome?"

"Sure did. Someone left the foil over their plate and ran it in the microwave. I guess it started sparking, and the food caught on fire with the paper plate. An entire skyscraper had to empty in the middle of a workday because someone doesn't know the basics of reheating their food."

Selena snorted laughter, clutching her stomach. "I wish I could say I had more faith in humanity, but we've all seen the future."

Arielle shook her head. "Unreal. I'd say that was the past that made that happen, but now I don't know. Just plain old stupidity, I suppose."

Selena's phone rang. "I guess it was only a hiccup. Everything is falling right back into place. Let's seal the deal this afternoon."

Chapter 18

October 28, 2013

They had both finished their formal interviews on Thursday after much laughter about the aluminum-wrapped lunch plate heard 'round the world. Friday, they both returned for additional job shadowing, where the staff was still abuzz regarding the fire.

Someone named Mick had apparently started it. "Classic Mick," one engineer had joked.

"Mick's such a sweet guy," Janina had explained to Selena. "But he's so fucking dumb sometimes. Like, who breaks a vending machine by ordering too many things? Mick. No one else."

The mood was light around the office on that Friday, giving Arielle and Selena a truer sense of their future coworkers. Bottles of wine and cans of beer were cracked open later in the afternoon, all noted as part of the typical end-of-week routine before different cliques made their way downtown for happy hour.

As much as Selena had wanted to join, Arielle warned against it. No good would come from joining the alcohol-filled ramblings and gossip. Not until they were officially on the books as employees.

One thing at a time, Arielle repeated all throughout Friday in random text messages she had kept sending to Selena and Felix throughout the day. She had heard the rumblings of happy hour and after-hours gatherings early in the morning and knew she had to put out that flame right away. Even Felix was growing frustrated with the slow-moving pace of the mission. Arielle had no choice but to emphasize how long of a process this would be.

They survived the weekend.

Selena went out Friday and Saturday night, exploring the city. Felix locked himself in his room all day Saturday, and planted himself on the couch on Sunday, where he watched a full slate of football games. He could have already known the results, so Arielle wondered why he opted to waste a day in such a manner.

But with no mission work to complete, she had no say in the matter. Even Arielle enjoyed a quiet Saturday shopping at the local mall, grabbing a couple of books to read for the inevitable downtime that would come.

On Monday morning, Arielle and Selena woke early with eager anticipation for the phone calls that would land them coveted access to the WonderHome office as employees.

They still had nothing to actually *do.* No interview. No job shadowing. No mission documents to read. And it drove Arielle antsy.

"When are you expecting a call?" Felix asked. In a rare instance, he was last to arrive in the kitchen, helping himself to a cup of coffee.

"They said they wanted to finalize a decision Monday morning and inform the candidates immediately," Selena said.

Felix nodded. "Probably an hour for them to chat about it and come to an agreement. Then maybe another hour for the offer letters to be prepared. They won't jump right into a meeting first thing on a Monday morning. Maybe nine o'clock. I'd say you'll get the call around eleven."

Even after a weekend locked in his virtual cave, Felix came out of hibernation sharp and calculated as always.

"What's on tap for this week?" Selena asked.

"Until you start training at WonderHome," Felix said. "A lot of nothing."

"We can try to check in with Adam," Arielle said. "Not saying we need to spend all day sitting outside his house, but maybe find an opportunity to bump into him outside of home. Were you going to see about hacking into his home computer?"

Felix nodded. "Honestly, it shouldn't be that hard, but we want to be careful. Keep in mind, the FBI will investigate Adam sometime within the next seven months. The last thing we want is our fingerprints all over his cyber data. They would know someone was in there illegally, and could likely pinpoint it back to us—well, *me*. I'm not worried about the ramifications because we can just disappear, but it opens the possibility of the mission being cut short, interfered with, or drastically changing the timeline of events."

"Why didn't you tell me any of this sooner?" Arielle asked.

"Well, because we don't need to worry about hacking into his personal computer, assuming either of you land the job with WonderHome. That's where our focus needs to be. Nothing in his trial notes suggests any of his wrongdoing occurred from a personal computer. They tied everything to his work accounts. The only thing we might gain from hacking his home computer is trying to sabotage his application. The risk doesn't outweigh the reward."

Arielle nodded, stroking her chin. "Okay. We can put that on the back burner for now and fall back on it as a last resort. You really will have a quiet week."

"We all will. But I'm not done, either. You've both never had jobs in the fields you're about to undertake, so I've been drafting up more material for you to read and get familiar with. More of a deep dive into the basics of each job. You'll need to sound a little more versed once you actually start training."

"Oh, joy," Selena said in a monotone. "More dry reading. That's my favorite part of this job."

They all laughed, enjoying a quiet morning while they waited for the phone to ring.

* * *

Felix wasn't far off. WonderHome called Arielle first at 11:26, followed by another call to Selena ten minutes later. They offered both of them jobs, with a start date set for the following Monday, the fourth of November.

With that, the Angels found themselves eager to plot out the rest of the month's events. According to Janina, the first three days of training were an orientation for all new hires to attend together. Arielle and Selena would be together during this time. After that, everyone would be with their own departments for job-specific training for the rest of that first week, and all the second week.

They hung a calendar on the side of the cabinets nearest the dining table in the kitchen. They circled November 17 in a bright red marker, signifying the day Adam applied to WonderHome. Being a Sunday, this meant they would review his application on Monday the eighteenth.

"Selena, that has to be you," Arielle said.

They had converted the dining table into a temporary workspace. Papers lay scattered about the table, three laptops flipped open with more documents on their screens. A container of lemonade stood in the center of the table, each Angel with a full glass in front of them.

"It's impossible to know if I'll be doing actual work by then," Selena said.

"It doesn't matter. If you have to go in an hour early, then so be it. We need to find that application and remove it from the database before anyone realizes it was there. Training will be over by then—that much we know. You can play it off as just coming in early for your first official day on the job and wanting to get settled and sorted out. If anything, you'll just look even more impressive. All I'm saying is we can plan for this, but be ready to adjust on the fly."

"Okay, I can do that," Selena said.

"Now, let's assume this plan doesn't work out for us. We know Adam's first day of training is on December second. This tells us he's going to follow a similar schedule to what we just had. He'll have to interview during that week of the seventeenth—most likely toward the end, like us. Then he'll be notified that he received the job the following week, before Thanksgiving, so he can start the following Monday."

"Aww, we're going to celebrate Thanksgiving together,"

Selena said, a genuine smile spreading across her face.

"A Thanksgiving that already happened," Felix murmured, earning the usual smack from Selena.

"Yes, I know," Arielle said. "We'll have a few holidays we get to celebrate together, even if it's just a replay of the past. That will be a whole other discussion. Now, for those two weeks between the application being submitted and Adam starting at WonderHome, I want us to take an aggressive approach. If we can do anything to prevent him from starting, we can call this mission good and go home. Leave it for the Futures team to figure out how everything unfolds from there."

"Remind us what the mission report says our objective is," Felix said.

Arielle pursed her lips. She knew Felix had the answer right in front of him, most likely, but wanted to hear her say it out loud. He had his little ways of keeping checks and balances on Arielle when her ambition could rise above what was actually necessary.

"Of course." Arielle shuffled through her papers to find the hard copy of the mission report assigned to them from Commander Briar. "The mission is to prevent the arrest and prosecution of Adam Marshall."

"Exactly," Felix snapped back. "There are no shortcuts on this mission. Even if we somehow stop him from getting this job, how do we know that stops him from being arrested? The past will still try to correct itself, so we have to stay until the day of his eventual arrest, regardless of what happens. That's the only way we can go back and say with confidence that we completed the mission. May 23, 2014. Buckle up because that's how long we'll be here for—no way around it."

Arielle grinned. She wasn't actually thinking of leaving the mission early, but planned to run the possibility by Commander Briar should they prevent Adam's hiring within the next month. Regardless, she said what she said, and Felix called her out.

"Thank you, Felix. How can we intervene with Adam during this two-week time frame? It sounds like hacking his computer won't be happening. Is there any way of intercepting communication between WonderHome and Adam? We can pose as a different company offering him a job with hopes of it leading to him declining the job offer from WonderHome. We can physically try to intervene with him on the days he's set to drive to the WonderHome office for his interviews."

"Those all sound like good ideas," Selena said. "If I'm not able to scrape him from the WonderHome database, I'll at least have access to the schedule for his interviews. Even his initial phone interview."

"It may be way out of your comfort zone," Arielle said. "But you need to be aggressive during that first week on the job. Possibly even towards the end of training. Insist that you get hands-on experience at every turn possible. Force the matter. Hell, see if you can be the one does the phone interview with Adam. We need to hit that two-week window with everything we can. I'll be doing the same in whatever capacity I can manage from my role, but mine is focused more on the long-term. You can make the most impact right out of the gate."

"Arielle's right," Felix said. "Even if we can throw things off in the slightest, maybe it can change the trajectory. A six-month mission is more like moving a cruise liner—one degree can make a world of difference, and you won't know until much later how much of a difference it was."

Selena leaned back in her seat, appearing to sulk in her stress as she stared at the floor below the table.

"We know you can do it," Arielle said. "And *you* should know that, too. After our last mission, how could you possibly have any doubt in yourself?"

Selena looked up, a seriousness swimming in her eyes Arielle had never seen. Gone were the childish antics and games she seemed to always play. Selena might never admit it, but Arielle knew their last mission had elevated Selena to new heights. New confidence. A stronger appreciation for their work. It was these characteristics that transformed an Angel Runner into a force to be reckoned with. If Selena would just lean into her new self, it would only be a matter of time until she climbed the rankings and would come knocking on Arielle's door in the top spot.

She looked Arielle directly in the eyes, and Arielle felt her presence expand within the kitchen. With just two words they all understood a new chapter was underway for Selena Nicole.

"I'm ready."

Chapter 19

November 4, 2013

The week passed in a blur. With Selena locked into her new role, Arielle encouraged her to use the past week to unwind. Clear the mind.

Once they both started work, their life in 2013 would change for the remainder of their stay. Even with weekends off from WonderHome, the mission would weigh heavy on their minds and consume their every waking moment.

Selena didn't believe this was entirely true, at least for herself. She knew how to turn her mind on and off from whatever it needed to focus on. If she had to grind through five days at the office to be rewarded with a relaxing weekend at the end, WonderHome and Adam Marshall would be the last things on her mind on Saturday mornings.

All three gathered in the kitchen before Arielle and Selena were set to leave for their first day of training at WonderHome.

"I forgot to ask," Felix said to Selena, "Aren't they under the impression that you were working and living in California at the time of your interview? How did you explain moving here so quickly?"

Selena ate a croissant with a glass of orange juice and

nodded while she finished the bite in her mouth. "They didn't ask anything about my living arrangements. And I don't think they can, aside from the address I'll need to provide them today. If it comes up, I'll just tell them I'm living with a relative for now, and that I packed up in a week—small apartment, not a lot of stuff. As for my job, I already told them I gave my two weeks' notice, and that Shutterfly told me to make the end of October my last day. From what I read, that's fairly common. A lot of these companies don't actually make you wait out those two weeks anymore."

"From what you read?" Felix sneered. "You keep saying that."

"And we love it," Arielle interjected, joining in on the fun by smacking Felix on his arm.

"What the hell?!" he gasped, rubbing the area. "I didn't sign up to be smacked around like I'm your little brother."

Arielle and Selena exchanged glances before bursting into laughter, Felix unable to resist and eventually joining them. "We just might keep it up until we get that dinner invite back in our real life," Selena said.

Felix sighed. "You act like we never have a meal together. All we do is have nearly every single meal together on missions. Six months of it coming up."

Selena shook her head vigorously. "The missions don't count. We want a dinner off the clock with you. At your place."

"I think Selena just wants to see where you live," Arielle said.

"I do. I have so many questions and theories."

Felix laughed and took a sip of coffee. "Theories, huh? Am I really that mysterious to you?"

"Well, duh," Selena said. "You fall off the map after our

missions and come out of the woodwork just in time for the next one. I can't even find you in the Road Runners database because all of your information is hidden."

Felix threw his head back and enjoyed a round of laughter to himself. "Impressive. You tried to look me up. Guess it was a good thing I blocked my data from appearing, or else I'd have Selena showing up on my doorstep with a bottle of vodka ready to party every weekend."

Arielle laughed, and that earned her a smack from Selena, making Arielle lose all control.

The mood was easygoing, and even Selena couldn't help but smile.

"Okay," Arielle said. "We can pick this up later. We need to get going for our first day of work."

They all stood from the table and made their way to the front door.

"Don't go sleeping all day now," Arielle said to Felix, who only responded with a shake of the head.

"Good luck!" he called out when they reached the car on the sidewalk. Arielle and Selena got into the car, Arielle behind the wheel.

"He really is like a little brother," Selena said. "He's older than me, but he still has that sort of way about him, you know?"

"I almost feel bad for him," Arielle said. "He grew up as the middle child between two sisters, only to end up working with us. I guess it's a dynamic in his life he just can't escape. He's a good guy, though. Obviously, he can get along with us well *because* of the siblings he grew up with."

"I really do just want to see his house. Don't you? He seems like a guy who has movie posters for decorations in all the rooms. And you know his gaming setup is *out of this world*. I'm just intrigued."

"There will be plenty of time for that when we get back. It's time to focus on today."

Always right back to business, Selena thought. Arielle couldn't help herself when it came to her work. She was someone who couldn't turn it off and on like Selena. Arielle was simply always *on*. Like that damn bunny from those battery commercials, Arielle would spend her entire day banging on a drum if that was what the mission called for.

"Of course," Selena said.

For a Monday morning, traffic was light beneath the gloomy skies. Rain had fallen overnight, leaving the roads shiny and full of puddles in the sporadic potholes.

"How do you think these two weeks of training will go?" Arielle asked. "What's your angle?"

Selena understood how deeply Arielle thought about her work. Before working with the top-ranked Angel, Selena jumped into missions with a set agenda. She understood the character she would portray and executed that performance with near perfection. And it had always been enough to succeed. But after doing it about fifty times, the routine grew repetitive. Selena would show up to go through the motions. And she was a fantastic actress, so no one ever realized how little passion she was putting into her work.

Working with Arielle had changed her outlook. Arielle drilled as deep as possible into the work ahead.

What's my angle?

Before, Selena would have said her angle was exactly what it said on the mission report: to portray a new employee at WonderHome and use her position on the recruiting team to interfere with Adam's application. Plain and simple.

That answer would never fly with Arielle, however, and she understood why. Succeeding at so many high-intensity missions required a deeper understanding. Selena had accidentally developed a relationship with Brian Dawkins on their last mission, but understood how to properly use that to their advantage when it came to the mission. How could she replicate that type of work on every mission going forward?

"I think my best angle is to befriend as many of my coworkers as possible," Selena said. "I need to develop trust with them, and that starts with the job. Show I'm reliable with my work and not some pushover, then people will be more open to trusting me outside of the office."

Arielle nodded. Selena had found her way onto the same train of thought as their leader. "And then what? How are you going to tie all of that together for the mission?"

She's challenging me? Teaching me?

Selena had to stop to think. Perhaps that was the point.

"I'm . . . not sure."

"And that's fine. But you'll need to consider it. I can't know for sure, but I have a feeling this mission is going to be won outside of the workplace. Someone in that building knows about the money laundering, even if it's ultimately not Adam. And because of that, people will *not* discuss the matter within the office walls. Maybe an occasional meeting in the CEO's office with a select few, but you won't be in there. Look for loose lips at a happy hour. Trust your coworkers who develop a healthy relationship with you. But always be wary of those who have something to gain by your failure—they'll always be your demise in the corporate world."

They reached downtown, traffic coming to a stop as the

next six blocks ahead were a row of red lights.

"How do you know so much about everything?" Selena asked, Arielle whipping her head around to look at her, eyebrows drawn in with confusion.

"I don't know everything."

"I didn't say you know everything. But you definitely know a bit *about* everything. Like you haven't had a corporate job, so how do you know how it all works with the happy hours, and who to trust or not trust?"

A light smile touched the corners of Arielle's mouth as she returned her attention to the road. "I've never told anyone this. Can you keep it a secret?"

Selena's stomach tightened like a wrung-out cloth. She was no gossip queen, but could she handle a secret from the great Arielle Lucila? Her curiosity throbbed like a stubbed toe, however. She *needed* to know. "Okay. I got you."

Arielle cleared her throat. "The tragedy with my family is the root of everything for me. After I officially became a Road Runner, I went through some really dark days. The grief never ends and can sneak up on you when you least expect. I thought I was doing myself a favor by joining this new organization, and couldn't believe all the opportunities that lay ahead with time travel.

"I was in the middle of training when a nasty bout of depression completely knocked my life off the rails. They don't mention this part of my story when they run articles or specials about my rise to the top, because I vehemently told them to never discuss this part of my life. I didn't leave my house for a week. I ate maybe five times total during that week. Didn't bathe, brush my teeth. Anything. I contemplated suicide, even went as far as preparing for it. Wrote a letter, bought a bottle of painkillers. Have you ever looked in the mirror and had no idea who was looking back? That can twist your mind into some really dark corners you don't even realize live within you."

Selena sat up, incredibly uncomfortable by Arielle's secret story. She didn't know what to say, and questioned Arielle's ability to tell it so calmly as they made their way through traffic.

"I never could bring myself to do it. Deep down, I knew the pain would last forever, but not the depression. Life would continue one day. And with those endless possibilities given to me by the Road Runners, why would I take the emergency exit before seeing what potential it all had? I think people take their own lives not so much out of disgust toward their current life, but out of hope that whatever happens next is better. It can't be worse, right? Just my thoughts. But for me, I didn't have to see what happened next. I had something so unique. I could live a different life in a different era, and so I did."

"Wait," Selena said. "So you used time travel as a sort of therapy?"

"I wouldn't call it therapy, per se. Therapy is working on and improving yourself. I absolutely hated my life, and wanted to immerse myself in someone else's life. I had a three-day stretch of time travel you wouldn't believe. If we only lose ten minutes in our real time for each trip into the past, then I'll let you do the math. I'd travel back, live a whole new life—I spent at least five years on each trip—then come back and immediately jump to another time to do it again. I'm talking mere seconds in between trips. There are 1,440 minutes in a day, and I did this for three straight days."

Selena looked at the car's ceiling and did the math in her head. "That's over 400 trips."

Arielle nodded. "I honestly lost count once I got into the triple digits, but I estimate I lived around 425 different lives during those three days. Name a job, and I've probably done it."

They pulled into the underground parking garage below the office building, Arielle wasting no time parking in the first open space she found, killing the engine.

"Looking back," Arielle continued. "Living all those lives is definitely the reason I've become who I am today, but that's not what I was ultimately seeking. I was just someone with no direction. And if you can't understand yourself—your true self to the core—then I suppose you'll just always wander through life. Lost. I had to live over 400 other lives to understand my life was unique. When I returned from what ended up being my last trip during those wild three days, it was that sort of feeling when you finish a good book. Like you're snapped back into reality and aren't sure what to do with yourself. It took me a few more days, but the most important lesson I learned was that no matter who you are, no matter your background, your family, your financial situation, or your job—everyone suffers through tragedy of some sort. It's universal. Sure, you might feel special, or that your tragedy is worse if it makes the national news, but that's not really the case. There were dozens of instances during those other lives where I read stories about entire families being lost in car accidents. Different method from my tragedy, but the same result."

"So you realizing that you're *not* unique . . . is what *makes* you unique?" Selena asked, not entirely following Arielle's logic of how it all tied together.

Arielle nodded, a long tear creating a stream down her cheek. "We're all unique in certain ways, but also the same in many others. This realization saved my life, and all I wanted to do was repay the Road Runners for the opportunity. It was at that moment I dedicated my life to the organization and helping in any capacity. I literally owe them my life. It's hard for us time travelers to think about our own deaths, because that can feel centuries away, but something in my gut tells me I'll lose mine defending the Road Runners." She paused and wiped away the tear. "And I wouldn't want it any other way."

The tension had grown as heavy as a boulder sitting on both of their shoulders. Selena could only shake her head, now having an even deeper understanding of what made Arielle tick. It was disturbing, but somehow beautiful when looking at it from the outside. She had so many questions she wanted to ask, but time was up on this conversation. They pulled into the office's parking garage.

"Gather yourself, Selena," Arielle said, unbuckling her seat belt. "We don't want to be late on our first day."

Chapter 20

The WonderHome office brimmed with excitement when Arielle and Selena entered the lobby. They had staggered their entries apart by a minute, still needing to keep their connection a private matter.

They had set a round table next to the reception desk, where Becca stood guard over plastic champagne flutes filled with mimosas. A dozen employees gathered in the lobby, most with the angst a child might feel on the first day of school. Nervous laughter, awkward smiles and handshakes, and attire to impress on their first day in a new environment.

Arielle knew by tomorrow they would all come in dressed casually.

"Welcome to your first day at WonderHome," Becca said, a wide grin as she handed mimosas to everyone in the lobby. "No, this is not how we'll greet you every day, but we wanted to make your first day special, especially since this is a larger new-hire class with fourteen of you."

Friendly laughter peppered across the room.

Arielle and Selena took opposite ends of the lobby and exchanged a hasty glance. Even after spilling her secret truth, Arielle fell right back into mission mode the second she had entered the elevator from the garage. It was freeing to share that dark part of her life that she hadn't even mentioned to her grandmother. Her therapist knew about the hundreds of trips throughout time, but still didn't have all the details—not that Arielle could remember the minuscule after hopping through so many worlds.

She shared this with Selena for both of their sakes. She hadn't realized the relief that swept over her. But her primary aim was to motivate Selena. She saw something in the actress she was certain Selena had yet to see in herself. The potential to be the best. Some people just needed a shove in the right direction to realize their full abilities, and with Selena getting a taste of success from their prior mission, Arielle saw this opportunity as paramount to capitalize on Selena's growth as a person *and* an Angel.

A lanky man made his way to the front of the room, standing next to Becca, where he took a long sip from his mimosa. He wore a button-up, baggy black jeans, and a solid blue baseball cap.

"I'd like to introduce you all to Kurt Brennan," Becca said. "Kurt has been our lead trainer for two years now. You'll be spending most of the next two weeks in a classroom with him and your fellow new hires. Kurt."

Becca stepped back, and Kurt gave her a cordial nod before facing the crowd. "I'd like to extend the welcome. You're all joining an absolutely booming company. We are number one in the industry and plan to stay that way for many years to come. Each of you will help lift WonderHome to the next level. If you're ready to jump into our training for today, please follow me down this hall to the conference room we'll call home for the next couple of weeks."

Just like that, the party had ended.

Time for business.

Arielle pulled out her cell phone, where she had created a new notes document to jot down any remarks throughout the day. She typed in Kurt's name and role. This early in the mission, anyone could be a suspect for the eventual fraud accusations that would fall upon Adam Marshall. She also put down Becca's name, but highly doubted she had any involvement.

The group of new hires formed a line to follow Kurt down the narrow hallway. They passed the conference rooms where they had attended interviews two weeks prior, and stopped in the kitchen area, home to the famous microwave fire that had halted everyone's life.

"This is our kitchen," Kurt said. "The fridges and cabinets are always stocked, and you're welcome to help yourself to anything you'd like."

The counters in the kitchen formed an L shape that connected with the wall that had four different refrigerators—one for drinks, one for beer, one for cold snacks like yogurt and cheese sticks, and one for general use by the employees to store their lunches brought from home. Toasters, mini-ovens, and coffee machines stood across the countertops, cupboards both above and below with a wide range of snacks and fruit.

One of the new employees gleefully took charge and stepped forward, helping himself to a bottled coffee from the fridge and a banana from one of the far cupboards.

"Don't be shy," Kurt reiterated. "I'll give you a couple of minutes before we head back to train."

Small chatter broke out as everyone studied the options. Arielle knew this sort of downtime was critical to building rapport with her fellow employees, but she didn't want to waste time on people who would have no relevance to their mission.

So she approached Kurt, who had been left alone while everyone else hunted for morning snacks. He leaned against the wall in the hallway, scrolling on his cell phone.

"Hello, Kurt," she said. "My name is Arielle."

He offered a polite grin before stuffing his phone into his pocket and shaking her hand. "Nice to meet you, Arielle. Software engineer, yeah?"

"That's correct. I'm so excited to be joining WonderHome. You've been here for two years?"

"I've actually been with the company for eight years and have bounced around so many departments, but I feel more at home doing orientation. I think that's why they asked me to train, because I've done a little bit of everything."

Kurt let out a chuckle. He stood a hefty six-four, and had a welcoming presence, like a man-sized teddy bear.

"Eight years," Arielle repeated. "That's impressive. Many people don't stay that long at tech companies."

"I know. I was here when you could still call us a start-up. It's truly bonkers to look back and see how much this place has grown. The entire company used to be on just this floor. Now we have four floors—looking to expand to five with the creation of our new real estate team."

Arielle's heart skipped a beat. The laundering scheme took place with real estate transactions, all of which were initially processed by the company's widely-touted real estate team.

"I've heard about that new department. How does that work, exactly?"

"We'll dive into all of that in training. Nine out of the

fourteen new hires are on the real estate team. The company is really pushing to get it going. They think it might even become the biggest part of the business."

The chatter from the group had slowed, so Kurt called for attention and continued down the hallway, everyone following where they saw the main bullpen to the left.

"This is our sales team," Kurt explained as he stopped in front of a door. "The heartbeat of the company. They make thousands of phone calls from here every single day to realtors around the country, hoping to earn their business. We have one new sales rep joining this new class, correct?"

A skinny woman raised her hand with an appreciative smile.

"Well, this will be your home after training, so buckle up."

The bullpen bustled with chaos. Nearly every visible employee was on the phone, speaking into their headsets as they either paced in circles or reclined in their seats, feet up on the desks. Arielle had gotten to know sales team members plenty of times throughout her trips through time, and appreciated the wide scale of personality types that succeeded in the cutthroat role.

"Let's head in," Kurt said, opening the door he had stopped in front of, holding it while the new hires made their way inside the conference room.

Four rows of tables spanned the length of the room. They set computers and name placards up at each seat.

"Please find your place and get settled in," Kurt said, closing the door behind him and strolling to a podium at the front corner of the room. He tapped on his computer, causing a projector to hum to life, blasting the white wall with a giant WonderHome logo. "Before we jump into training, I need to take a roll call. Just raise your hand when I call your name, please."

Everyone took a minute to find their spots. Arielle was at the end of the front row, Selena positioned in the row immediately behind her.

"Ben Burke. Real estate team."

A scrawny young man raised his hand with a crooked smile.

"Angeline Caldwell, real estate."

A middle-aged woman raised her hand and nodded at Kurt.

"Julia Ellis, sales."

The skinny woman from outside raised her hand.

"Rodney Perry, real estate."

"Present," Rodney said, booming loud and proud, earning a grin from Kurt.

"Oscar Harper, real estate."

An older man, seemingly of retirement age, raised his hand.

"Arielle, we just met," Kurt said, shooting a quick glance at her. "Daniel Mills, customer service."

Daniel looked fresh out of college and was the only one who cared to follow WonderHome casual dress code.

"Selena Nicole, recruiting."

Arielle turned around to act like Selena was a stranger, shooting over a sly grin.

"Amina Newman, real estate."

Amina looked exhausted, but raised her hand with the same excitement as everyone else.

"Ruby Osborne, customer service."

Ruby looked like the loving grandmother who kept snacks in her purse.

"I'm going to run down the last four on this list since they are all on the real estate team. Noah Pearson, Israel Pitts, Anna Roberts, and Leon Stone."

The four raised their hands in rapid succession. Arielle had written everyone's names and departments on her cell phone. The real estate team might be worth befriending, and that all started here in the training class.

"All right," Kurt continued. "There will be plenty of time to get to know each other, but I want to start with a brief history of the company and how we ended up where we are today."

The projection gave way to a picture of a man with two thumbs up in what appeared to be the kitchen area they had just left.

"This is our founder, Peter Howard. He started WonderHome in 2004 after struggling to find a home to buy after graduating from college. He felt there was too much disorganized, overwhelming information and envisioned a way of streamlining all that data to live in one place. That led to the birth of WonderHome. Since our founding we have worked with over 50,000 real estate agents and brokers and have contributed to hundreds of thousands of relationships between those realtors and homebuyers across the United States. We are a company on the verge of going public on the New York Stock Exchange, and that is very much the goal as we look to add a new stream of income with our new real estate team. Before I get into that, was anyone already familiar with Peter and the founding of this company?"

They all looked around at each other in silence.

"That's okay. I was just curious. Peter still serves on the board of directors, but has taken a much smaller role in the day-to-day operations to pursue other business ventures. Our leadership team has some of the best talent you can find and is well equipped to take us to that next level."

The screen changed to show the main five officers for WonderHome, complete with their portrait and names. Arielle gave up on the cell phone and started scribbling in the notebook provided to each employee. She'd get information written more swiftly this way, and wouldn't give off the appearance of disinterest by typing on her phone.

CEO, President, COO, CFO, CTO. One of these people definitely knows about the laundering, if not all of them.

Arielle had brushed up on corporate money laundering schemes throughout American history. Nearly every single case had people involved at the top. Lower-level employees couldn't pull off such matters on their own, plenty of checks and balances hanging over their heads. But who would check the CFO? The CEO, perhaps?

For money laundering to work, it seemed necessary for the Chief Financial Officer to be involved. They overlooked everything money related, so if the books needed some fudging, that would ultimately end up on their desk.

Landon Greene.

The portrait of the WonderHome CFO showed a smiling man of around fifty. Light brown wavy hair, a thick jaw at the bottom of a long, droopy face. Arielle stared into the dark brown eyes of his photo, trying to dig into his soul. She had seen it plenty of times throughout her career. The most innocent-looking people committed the worst crimes.

Are you our guy? Arielle wondered, the slide changing to give way to the WonderHome website's home page.

A knock came on the door before it swung open, a woman entering with a wide grin. Arielle's heart froze as she recognized the face from the screen they had just been looking at.

"Well, this is quite the surprise," Kurt said. "And what

timing. I was just showing our new class our leadership team. Everyone, please welcome our CEO, Michelle Garrison."

153

Chapter 21

Selena burned her gaze into the back of Arielle's head. While the CEO crossed the room, Arielle turned around, her eyes bulging as they locked with Selena's for a split second.

It didn't need to be said—they both understood the importance and suspicion of Michelle Garrison. All their strategies centered on the company's executive team, and it was natural to suspect the highest-ranking officer the most.

"Good morning, everyone," Michelle said, taking center stage at the front of the room. "Kurt, I hope you don't mind me stopping in. I just got in for the day and remembered we had a new class starting. Did they get you all mimosas and breakfast?"

Everyone nodded. The mood had shifted from the light playfulness Kurt had orchestrated to a much heavier one. Michelle had done nothing besides smile and speak in a soft tone since entering the room, yet her presence remained plenty intimidating.

"I wanted to extend a welcome on behalf of the entire company. We are entering a new era at WonderHome, and it should thrill you to join the team at such an explosive time."

Selena studied Michelle. They already knew she was forty-eight; however, not a single gray hair appeared in the sandy blond, and Selena wondered if she ever let her roots grow out enough for anyone to see the natural sign of aging. Michelle had plenty of money, over sixty million dollars, according to a 2010 article in Forbes highlighting the country's top female executives. And it showed.

She kept in great shape, curves highlighted by a gray Alexander McQueen suit. Pearls hung around her neck, two flashy rings on each hand, but none on the ring fingers. Freshly manicured nails and teeth that clearly had seen their fair share of artificial whitening.

Probably drives a Mercedes, Selena thought, suddenly wondering if they should have taken a different approach to get close to Michelle Garrison. The Road Runners had money, and any of the three Angels on this mission could have used that to their advantage. Michelle probably hung out at high-end restaurants with her fellow rich friends, where they all stuffed their faces and laughed about how great their lives were.

Arielle raised her hand, and Selena felt her stomach drop to her knees. Was asking a question not something that could alter the past? What kind of resistance could hit them again? Surely not another microwave fire.

Michelle pointed at Arielle. "Yes, ma'am, a question?"

"It's nice to meet you, Ms. Garrison," Arielle said. "I've heard a lot about the new real estate team WonderHome is putting together. Almost all of this class is working on that team. What can you tell us about it?"

"I'd be happy to." Michelle's grin widened as she paced softly. A couple steps to the left, a couple to the right. It reminded Selena of an attorney delivering closing remarks to a jury, the movement intentional to keep the audience engaged.

"We've been in this industry for a long time now. We have all the contacts, we know all the systems, we are essentially a database with all the knowledge. The wizards who crunch all of our numbers—shout-out to Accounting—came to me with an idea that I thought could revolutionize the company. We spend a lot of money trying to acquire real estate agents to market with WonderHome. And that will continue. It's still the forefront of our business and will be for several years to come. But where we have found opportunity is by entering the real estate arena directly.

"We can take some of the money from customer acquisition expenses, and instead use *that* to hire our realtors. We'll be hiring some who are already licensed, and others who are looking to earn their license. It's more cost-effective to hire a realtor directly than trying to get their business. And once we have a realtor, they can go out and make multiple transactions on behalf of WonderHome. We will be directly involved in buying and selling homes. Homeowners can hire WonderHome to sell their properties, and we take a cut of the closing costs. Our agents will keep an eye out for properties that can be flipped for a profit. It's going to open the floodgates on an additional stream of revenue."

"So WonderHome is becoming a broker?" Ben Burke asked from the back row.

"In a sense, yes."

"What do realtors think about this? Surely they will see you as competition instead of a partner in their business."

"RE/MAX has over 100,000 real estate agents. Our goal is to hire 10,000 across the country over the next two years. We're not cutting into anyone's opportunities. A RE/MAX agent doesn't go out into the world seeking properties to flip—unless they do that in their free time. They don't do it on behalf of their brokerage. We will pay our realtors a generous salary. They won't work on commission. They will scout the country for real estate opportunities that can bring in revenue for WonderHome. There is no brokerage that exists, at least on a large scale, that does what we do. This is only going to bring more traffic to our site. I say it will increase the opportunities for agents who market with us. If we have our own properties listed on the site, and an interested buyer comes along, they still need an agent to work with, and they can choose from the pool of agents who market with WonderHome. At the moment, we don't have plans to have our agents work with potential home buyers—*that* would create competition with other realtors. We want to remain in the background of these transactions as much as possible, and will deploy our realtors to buy properties to flip. Does that make sense?"

Michelle looked between Ben and Arielle, who both nodded back. She pulled up her sleeve to reveal a purple Cartier watch.

Selena shook her head. While everyone else in the office wore jeans and T-shirts, Michelle strolled in wearing at least $25,000 worth of clothes and accessories.

"I'm afraid that's all I have time for this morning," Michelle said. "I need to stop now, or I'll talk about our new real estate for the rest of the day."

I'm sure you would.

"Again, welcome to WonderHome, and I can't wait to work with you. Kurt, you can have your class back now."

This earned laughter across the room as Michelle made her way out the door, the stench of her perfume lingering well after the fact.

"Well, there you have it," Kurt said, standing at the front of the room with hands clasped in front of his belly. "That's our CEO. Michelle is a woman of grand passion and intensity. Once she believes in something, there is no stopping her. That's why we all believe so strongly in the direction the company is headed. Now, shall we get back into our training?"

Kurt continued with their originally planned material, but Selena's mind drifted away. She felt there was something with Michelle Garrison worth a deeper exploration. She couldn't wait to follow her.

Chapter 22

November 8, 2013

At the end of their first week of training, Arielle and Selena needed nothing more than to tend to their overworked minds. They had agreed to take the training as seriously as any other employee. They would be with the company for at least six months, and part of that responsibility was simply not getting fired for incompetence.

Despite sitting three feet apart all week, they communicated strictly via text messages, and rarely swapped words in the office. When Arielle asked Selena if she wanted to pick up dinner on the way home, it blindsided her when Selena wanted to keep working on the mission.

I want to follow Michelle, Selena's text message read. *I know there is SOMETHING tied to her. Want to know more.*

Arielle agreed to join her and sent a message to Felix, letting him know they would arrive later than originally planned. He had already been enjoying a quiet week at home, working on research and preparing for the later phases of the mission, and wouldn't mind a bit more time to himself.

They staggered to the garage, where Arielle arrived at the car first, Selena a couple of minutes behind as she waited for the next elevator.

The week had been nothing short of mentally exhausting. They knew more than any reasonable person needed to know about the history of WonderHome.

Selena arrived at the car and opened the door, tossing her bag onto the passenger seat, but remaining outside. "C'mon. Let's go."

"Oh? Where are we going?"

"Where are *you* going?" Selena asked. "I said we need to follow Michelle. She's still in the office."

"And how do you plan on following her? You can't just sit outside her office and wait for her to leave."

Selena sat down in the car and closed the door, tossing her bag into the back seat. "This has been eating at me all week—"

"So, more secrets you've been keeping to yourself? We've talked about this."

"No secrets. I don't have any information—just a feeling that we need to follow her. We talked about her passion for this new real estate team on Monday night. I know you sense her involvement."

"Of course. And I don't mind following her around, but we need to have a plan. We can't just wing it on a mission like this. What will you say if you get too close and she recognizes you?"

"That's why you're here. Those things never happen to you. Sneaky little ninja."

Arielle laughed. They were both slaphappy after the long week.

"And why did you wait until today? We could have been following her all week."

"I know you're into that boring stuff of watching people eat their dinner and wash their dishes. But I want something of actual substance. It's Friday. She's a filthy rich, single executive. She's not going home after work—she's going out to blow off some steam. We'll be able to see where she hangs out, who she's with, what kind of *activities* she's into."

Selena tapped her finger to her nose, prompting an eye roll from Arielle. "I've told you, not every executive does cocaine."

"We'll just have to see for ourselves."

As much as Selena's theories could seem incredibly off-the-wall, Arielle knew this was right up her alley of expertise. Raucous nightlife, chaotic clubs, swanky bars, lavish gatherings. You name it, Selena loved all that shit and would see things Arielle simply couldn't. It was her love language.

Always ready to cover all the bases, Arielle wanted to ask Selena about the possibility of Michelle staying in the office late. She had seen plenty of executives keep bottles of booze in a desk drawer—or even out in the open in a fancy canteen—all to enjoy a happy hour with their inner-circle before leaving for home.

But Selena had determination in her eyes, and it was obvious she was sensing *something*. Perhaps it was good to have someone on the team who followed their gut.

"Okay," Arielle said. "If you want my opinion, I think we should split up. We don't know if she's going out here by the office, or driving somewhere else. The weather is a factor, and today is pretty cold, so I wouldn't be surprised if she opts to drive where she's going instead of walking four or five blocks through downtown. As you mentioned, she's loaded—probably pays for valet wherever she goes."

"How does it work if we're split? If she drives off, I can't get back to the car in time if you need to follow her."

"I know. I'll follow, in that case, and let you know where we end up. You can catch a Lyft to meet me. That said, I think you should go back into the office. Try to follow her from there. There's a bathroom outside the elevator lobby on the thirty-fourth floor—that's where her office is. If you wait outside that bathroom door, you'll be able to spot Michelle once she exits her office further down the hallway. It's a long hall, so I doubt she'd even notice you at the far end. That gives you a moment to slip into the bathroom, wait about twenty seconds, and step back out to catch an elevator at the same time as her. You'll know from there if she's going to the garage or street level."

"Brilliant. Okay, I'm going in. Will text you."

Chapter 23

Training had ended at four o'clock that afternoon, and to Arielle's delight, Selena had texted her at 4:55 that Michelle was heading out for the day. She passed the hour listening to the spotty radio reception from the garage. Pharrell Williams sang about getting lucky when the messages started pouring in from Selena:

On her way.

In the bathroom.

She's in the bathroom. I'm hiding in stall.

Two minutes passed until the next message.

In the elevator with her.

STREET LEVEL!

The texts stopped for two minutes—it could sometimes take an entire five minutes to ride the elevator thirty floors down, especially around this time when everyone in the building was heading out.

Street level meant Michelle was indeed going to brave the cold weather and trek through downtown, so Arielle hopped out of the car and used the stairs to reach the building's main lobby where dozens of people bustled on their way out.

Arielle headed outside, waiting under an overhang until Selena texted her again.

Heading outside. Staying behind her.

Arielle turned her back from the building's main entrance. She had spoken to Michelle in the training class and couldn't risk being recognized. It wasn't raining for the first time all week, but she wished terribly to have an umbrella right about now. She was left no choice but to look over her shoulder every couple of seconds.

Michelle stepped out, a long black wool coat concealing what was surely another expensive outfit underneath. She was talking on her cell phone, a relief to Arielle. Michelle looked right in Arielle's direction before turning the opposite way down the sidewalk with the rest of the professionals stampeding to happy hour.

Selena bolted out of the building just as Arielle had started to follow. They nearly crashed into each other, both having kept their eyes glued to their target.

"Did she see you?" Selena asked.

"No. How was the elevator ride?"

"Fine. I'm not sure she even saw me. Six other people were all crammed into it."

"Perfect."

Michelle walked at a brisk pace. Arielle and Selena had both worn jeans, and the cold autumn air whipped at their ankles as they hurried down the sidewalk to keep up. They passed Pike's Place Market, where hordes of people stood in the street. Fortunately, downtown was pretty crowded as far as they could see, even after going two blocks, where Michelle gained speed on a downhill slope.

"My God," Selena gasped. "I've never seen someone put their head down and just power walk through a city like this."

They were passing multiple people trying to keep up with

the speedy CEO. Two more blocks later, they paused across the street from a bar called Red, a café and wine bar with a half-dozen people in business attire waiting in the short line outside.

Within a minute, the line dissipated as everyone made their way in.

"We're going in, right?" Selena asked.

"Of course. We just need to be careful. I highly doubt she'll recognize us, but you never know."

"Yeah, because *someone* just had to ask the CEO a question that sent her on a rant. Way to be."

"Hey, we learned a lot. Michelle is *clearly* involved with that department."

"No shit. Let's just go in, please. I can't stand out here all day. And doesn't a drink sound nice about now?"

Arielle rolled her eyes and started across the street, Selena eager to follow. They wasted no time stepping into the bar, Selena's eyes lighting up as they peered around.

"Holy shit," Selena muttered, eyes wide like a child who just woke up in the North Pole. "Their wine rack goes all the way to the ceiling."

Arielle followed the towering wine rack as it indeed had a dozen shelves that touched the ceiling. A staircase spiraled around the rack for easy access. Selena squealed beside her.

"Calm down before they kick us out," Arielle said under her breath, throwing an elbow into Selena's side. "Act like you belong."

The bar was definitely for the wealthy professional demographic, ranging in all ages. Mostly everyone wore fine attire, businessmen with their ties loosened as they blew off steam and business women with their blazers unbuttoned.

"Do you even see her?" Arielle asked, craning her neck. They were still in line to check in for a table.

People packed into the bar, not an open seat visible from where they stood. A bar top circled around the great tower of wine, tables and booths filling the rest of the space as far back as they could see.

"She's upstairs." Selena nodded toward the second level, across the back wall.

Arielle spotted Michelle sitting at a round table with a group of other people.

They reached the host stand where a young man with frosted pink hair greeted them. "Just the two of you queens today?" he asked.

"Yes," Arielle said. "Any chance we can sit upstairs?"

He leaned forward on the stand and whispered, "I'm not supposed to let anyone sit up there who isn't one of our high-roller regulars." He rolled his eyes. "But if you promise to not bother any of those people, I can find you ladies a table."

"You're the best," Selena said.

"Girl, I know it," the host said, batting his eyebrows at them. "And if anyone asks why you're sitting up there, you can tell them that Rolando sent you—and Rolando doesn't give a shit!" Rolando chuckled at himself, causing Arielle and Selena to break into laughter. "Y'all follow me now."

They followed Rolando around the bar, where they climbed a flight of stairs to the bar's exclusive second level. He looked back as they weaved through a couple of tables and rolled his eyes again. He put them at a table along the rail overlooking the rest of the bar below, sliding two menus onto the table.

"You ladies enjoy your drinks," he said, grinning as he spun around and disappearing before Arielle or Selena could thank him.

They sat in the center of the upstairs area, and Michelle Garrison was only two tables down, ordering from a server. Arielle faced her table, Selena with her back to it.

Selena looked down at the menu and asked, "Who's all sitting with her?"

Arielle had a much better view of Michelle's company at the table, but scrunched her brow as she tried to recognize any faces. "I honestly don't see anyone with her from WonderHome. At least not from the executive team."

"I guess that makes sense. If she was coming with someone from work, they would have walked over here together."

"It's a weird mix at her table. Six total people. Her plus two guys that look to be in their twenties or early thirties. A man and woman who look around her same age. And a younger woman who might have come with the other two guys."

Selena looked over her shoulder, trying to play it cool, whipping her head back around to Arielle. "I don't recognize anyone there, either. But we're in the VIP section. They could all have developed some sort of friendship at this bar. The host said up here is for the high-roller regulars."

"They certainly look comfortable, like they've known each other for a while."

Arielle watched as everyone at Michelle's table raised a shot glass in the air, toasting to the weekend ahead. They down their shots and returned to their conversation, occasional laughter rippling around the group.

"Can you take pictures of them?" Selena asked. "Here. Take a picture of me." She grabbed her glass of water and raised it.

Arielle nodded and rummaged through her small purse for

her cell phone, pulling it out and promptly snapping pictures of Michelle's table in the background while Selena pretended to pose. "Okay, we're good. I can see all of them except for the young woman. Her back is to us."

"Good. Let's just keep an eye and be ready. We need to follow Michelle's every move."

They ordered wine, Arielle stopping after the first glass while Selena opted for a second. They mimicked whatever happened at Michelle's table, so when that group ordered a round of appetizers, so did Arielle and Selena.

Two hours passed where they kept ordering appetizers, eventually becoming too full to keep eating. Arielle had let Felix know they wouldn't be home for dinner and he shouldn't wait up. He responded with a thumbs-up emoji.

Seven o'clock passed when Michelle's table finally threw in the towel and asked for their check. Arielle paid her and Selena's tab without even seeing the bill, needing to be ready to get up and leave as soon as Michelle did.

Michelle slipped into her jacket and stood up with the rest of the group. They all shared hugs before departing. Michelle stayed at the back of the line with one of the young men. Selena watched the group descend the stairs.

"What's happening?" Selena whispered, tipping back her glass of wine to kill off the final remains.

Arielle shrugged, her eyes glued to the impromptu private conversation. Michelle reached her hand up and stroked the man on his cheek before starting down the stairs, leaving the man a few steps behind.

"Act natural," Arielle said.

They rose and put on their jackets before Michelle had reached the bottom landing. They hurried through the crowded dining area and nearly ran down the steps, fighting through one more herd when Michelle stepped outside of the bar.

Arielle and Selena stepped outside and saw Michelle crossing the street. Arielle kept her gaze on the man who chased after Michelle. She reached out and grabbed Selena's arm. "Wait."

"Michelle!" the man shouted, dashing across the street toward her. "Michelle!"

"What the hell?" Selena asked as they started taking a couple of steps toward the unfolding scene.

Michelle stopped and turned around, remaining in place as she waited for the man to reach her. When he did, he crouched to plant his hands on his knees while catching his breath.

After a few seconds, he stood up and started speaking with Michelle again. She had her arms crossed to keep warm. She nodded, then the man threw his arms around Michelle and pulled her in close, where they shoved their tongues down each other's throats.

"Oh my God!" Selena cried. "What the fuck is *happening*?!"

"Uhhhh," was all Arielle could muster, unable to look away from the powerhouse CEO making out with a man at least twenty years her junior.

Selena started laughing. "This is great!"

Her words fell on deaf ears for Arielle as she kept watching them. The two kept their mouths interlocked for at least thirty seconds, the man running his hand up and down the small of Michelle's back. They finally broke apart and promptly grabbed each other's hands, continuing down the sidewalk.

Selena was still laughing. Louder, with an odd sense of joy.

"What the hell is wrong with you?" Arielle asked. "Do we

need to keep following them?"

"I think we've seen enough. I can't believe my eyes. All I had was a feeling, and it was right!"

"About *what*?!" Arielle asked, growing frustrated.

"That she was in to younger guys. I originally thought maybe it was rich men, but it's *young* men. Of course."

This was all coming out of nowhere. Selena had shared none of these thoughts before, and Arielle still didn't understand the relevance. "What—"

"Don't worry about it. I know how we can easily get into Michelle's house."

Chapter 24

November 10, 2013

Selena had shared her idea with Arielle during their walk back to the car on Friday evening. While Arielle thought it was a stretch, she still agreed to it. They'd need cooperation from Felix, however, and didn't know how he'd respond to such a request.

Rather than giving him a full weekend to dwell on the matter, Arielle suggested they discuss it with Felix on Sunday night, leaving him a full week to prepare should he agree.

Arielle knew he wouldn't be open to the plan right off the bat, but believed they could convince him. They let him watch his football games all of Sunday, until dinnertime when Selena ordered takeout from a local Chinese restaurant.

"Week two on the job coming up," Felix said as they settled around the table. "What do you two have planned?"

"A few things," Arielle said, exchanging a quick glance with Selena. Neither of them expected the topic to come up so soon. "A week from tonight, Adam Marshall will apply to WonderHome. I'd still like to see what kind of interference is possible to prevent that from happening, but I understand it's a long shot."

"Do you think you'll be getting access to the WonderHome system?" Felix asked. "Because I came up with an idea. It's not guaranteed to work if we have to wait until next Monday, but if Selena works in the recruiting system this week, we might be able to stop the application from even happening."

Arielle had a particular way she wanted tonight's conversation to go, and it was already on a complete detour. She wanted to dictate the topics and present the grand idea. Instead, Felix had jumped right into mission-talk and now had his own ideas. She needed to reminder herself that her team was collaborative. And while she had the authority to make final decisions, Felix and Selena wouldn't accept such things without a discussion. Slowly, they had evolved into a singular unit. Anything that involved one of them on a mission now involved all.

"Okay, what is it?" Selena asked, stuffing a bite of chicken fried rice into her mouth.

"I'm thinking we apply for Adam. I can dumb down his resume and set up a dummy e-mail address for him to receive correspondence. And I can communicate directly back to the company *as* Adam. As of this week, they have no idea who he is. Ideally, they can reject his application, and that way when he applies on Sunday, it will look like he's being greedy, and possibly a liar, since they'll see a different resume."

"That's actually a fantastic idea," Arielle said. "Let's try it. But what is the relevance of Selena having access this week? It sounds like this can all take care of itself."

Felix laughed. "I thought you knew better than that, Arielle. We're dancing with the past. I've been trying to understand it at the level you do. I doubt I'm anywhere near that point, but I have some new confidence. This mission isn't about

WonderHome or Adam Marshall and his dead family. It's about the past. We have our objectives we want to accomplish, and we need to work around the past to achieve them. That's it, plain and simple."

Arielle nodded. The week off hadn't been a total waste for Felix. Quite the contrary. Much like Selena, he had grown. Elevated his skills and understanding of their work to the next level.

"But you're right," Felix continued. "It's not mandatory for Selena to have access for this to work, but if she does, I see it as one less possible barrier. We still don't know what happens when this application comes into recruiting. They might call him to ask questions about his resume. Maybe they'll think he's a good fit for another team. Who knows? If Selena can intercept the application and reject it right away, that would be ideal. That way, it's in the system that they already turned him down before his real application comes through on Sunday night. And Selena will have actual ground to stand on, saying Adam does not look like a good fit for the job."

Selena nodded along. "I see. I think it's a wonderful idea, too. All they told me on Friday was this next week will be more hands-on."

"Same for me," Arielle said. "However, I know I'll be working out of a sandbox version of our systems—all dummy accounts. If recruiting does the same thing, none of this will pan out how we want."

Felix shrugged. "All we can do is try and see what happens. Hopefully, it's a quick, automated rejection."

The conversation calmed down, and they ate in silence for the next minute.

"We have an idea, too," Arielle finally said to break the silence. On cue, Selena cracked open a can of beer and took a long swig.

"We?" Felix asked.

"The idea came to Selena after what we saw on Friday evening at the happy hour."

Felix stared back and forth between the two. "I thought you said it was a normal happy hour."

"Selena, please explain." Arielle stuffed food into her mouth, grinning across the table.

"All right, thanks Arielle," Selena said. "So, the happy hour was normal. What we didn't tell you was what happened after. Michelle was with a group of people inside the bar, and when they all left, a younger man chased her down outside and they started making out."

"And you left that out why?" Felix asked. "What does that have to do with anything?"

"Well, my idea came from seeing that, but I needed to check on some things over this weekend. If you didn't notice, I've been on my phone a lot."

"You're *always* on your phone." Felix would never resist a chance to call out Selena.

She glared at him, a smirk touching her mouth. "Anyway. My idea is for the long term, assuming we're not able to prevent Adam from getting hired on. We need to do anything we can to get close enough to Michelle to find out who really should go down for the crime. When I saw her with that guy, it made me curious. So I spent all weekend browsing about a hundred different dating apps and sites. I found Michelle on two of them. Cougar Love and Elite Bonding."

Felix started laughing. "She thinks of herself as a cougar.

Too funny!"

They all laughed. Arielle was relieved to hear Felix still in a light mood, and wondered if he really didn't see where this was going.

"Yes. So Cougar Love is exactly what it sounds like—older women looking for younger men. And then Elite Bonding is a dating app for executives and professionals. Or just rich people. Because of this, we know exactly what she is looking for. And we can deliver it to her on a silver platter."

Felix had been grinning and nodding along, even after Selena finished speaking, and left the three of them in an awkward silence. Both Arielle and Selena held steady gazes toward Felix, neither wanting to come out and say exactly what Selena's grand idea was.

Thirty seconds passed, and Felix's grin faded, a tinge of panic slipping into his eyes. "Wait," he said, then gulped. "No, no, no. I don't think so. You're nuts, no, out of your mind. That's it. You're out of your *fucking* mind if you think I'm doing this."

He let out a nervous laugh and swung his head around to Arielle.

"We only want to discuss it," Arielle said.

Felix smiled, a somewhat manic look as he realized the walls closing in around him. "Cool. I don't. So how about that? This is definitely not part of my job. Not in the slightest."

"Hold on now, Felix," Arielle said. "You don't even know what we're suggesting."

"Of course I do! You want to prop me up as some rich professional on these dating apps. Try to land a date and develop a relationship to spy on her. Right?"

Selena pursed her lips before saying, "More or less, yes."

"Exactly. And I'm not an actor like the talented Selena Nicole, so you know I'll just botch this. How can you even expect me to understand how to date an older woman? That's just . . . wrong. She's only a couple of years younger than my mom."

"Okay, just slow down," Arielle said, frustration slipping in her voice. "One thing at a time. Selena will prepare you for everything on the acting front, including your outfits."

Felix threw his head back and laughed. "I've seen how the rich people dress at my mom's boutique, remember? I don't need help on that front."

Arielle gritted her teeth. Felix was normally open-minded and willing to at least hear out someone's idea, but he now was being hostile and interrupting everything she said. He was acting like Selena, and it caught Arielle completely off guard.

"Okay, dress yourself," Arielle said. "Selena will still help with how you can approach this."

"The hell she will."

"What the fuck, Felix?!" Arielle shouted and slammed a fist on the table. After the brief rattle of their silverware and glasses, the room fell deathly silent. "Why are you being like this?"

Felix raised his eyebrows and let out an exaggerated laugh. "*Me?* You think *I'm* the one at fault? I'm just trying to stand up for myself. Like Arielle Lucila would. This shit is not my job. I stay behind the scenes. If you want me to break into her house and plant a bug, then just say so, but all of this is grossly unnecessary. I can do my job without having to speak to a single one of these people."

"I'm not trying to force you into anything. I was only trying to have a discussion. If you really don't want to, that's fine. We'll find another option, but hear me out. Okay?"

Felix rolled his eyes and crossed his arms, leaning back in his seat. "Whatever you say, Arielle. It's your world and we just live in it. I'm sure you have all the perfect words to convince me to do this. So let's hear it."

"First off, our roles are evolving on this team. I'm not one for acting, but here I am about to start a second week of pretending to be someone I'm not. This is not the way I wanted things, but it's what the mission calls for. The way it looks, more missions are going to look like this. We're all going to need to be more involved than our main roles. We have to really get into the mission and immerse ourselves in the world around our targets, all while keeping a safe distance to not piss off the past. And so far, I'd say we have it figured out. It was a smooth first week at WonderHome. Our presence hasn't altered anything."

"Okay," Felix said in a calmer tone. "But how is me dating Michelle Garrison not going to have an effect? Messing with someone's love life has always proven costly in this line of work. Just ask our dear commander."

"We're not expecting you to marry the woman. Just go on a couple of dates and see what happens. I don't expect you to do anything physically that you're not comfortable with. This would be strictly to see what kind of information you might pry from her. If it looks like there's nothing, then call off the relationship. No harm done. And if you don't want to do this, I can submit a request to the Road Runner offices here in Seattle for another actor who can help, but you'll miss out on what can be a big boost in your ranking."

Arielle knew Felix didn't care about the rankings—few of

those in his role did—but knew he wouldn't like the thought of having a third party come in to do what he was being asked. That wouldn't look good on the final mission report, which was read by several people across the organization, Commander Briar included.

"You would bring someone else in?" Felix asked, his tone now the complete opposite of the outburst he had moments ago.

"Yes, Felix. This is a brilliant idea that I'd like to see play out. It opens up so many possibilities for us to get close to who we believe is the brains behind the laundering. Besides, you'll get to pick the mind of a highly successful executive. You want to be a billionaire one day, so maybe she's worth talking to."

Selena cleared her throat after taking another drink of beer. "And I'll be here every step of the way. You'll be prepared for whatever comes up. Just trust me. Trust *us*. We know this is so far out of your comfort zone, but is that not the only way to grow? By doing something out of your norm. If either of us could do this, we would. But we're not young millionaire men."

Felix balled a fist and gently touched it to his lips, staring at the table with an intensity they were all feeling.

"You don't need to decide right at this moment," Arielle said. "Take a couple of days to think it over. All I really need is some notice if I need to bring another actor on or not. Deal?"

Felix drew a deep breath and took his time blowing it out of his mouth. He pursed his lips and shook his head. "I'll think about it."

Chapter 25

November 13, 2013

On Wednesday morning, Felix informed Arielle that he would do it. She responded to the news with a big hug and a promise that he wouldn't regret it.

Felix didn't really *want* to pretend to date Michelle, but he couldn't bear the thought of a fourth person coming to live with them so deep into the mission. He respected the dynamic of their trio. It worked. Everything ran smoothly the way it was. And with little work to do until Arielle could lend him access to WonderHome's systems, Felix would have to spend his free time brushing up on how to act like a young, rich executive to court one of the most successful women in the world.

If he viewed it as a challenge with certain levels of achievement, the whole thing became easier to swallow.

Felix spent Wednesday morning in his bedroom, working on a jigsaw puzzle of the Seattle skyline that he had purchased a couple of weeks ago.

He had spent Monday and Tuesday crafting and polishing a resume to submit on behalf of Adam Marshall. He pulled as much information as he could find online, which was plenty for this purpose. His education background and prior jobs were all listed in Adam's LinkedIn profile. Felix copied it all over and weakened a resume that was rather impressive. He wondered why Adam would settle for a job that was essentially Michelle's servant in the first place.

He sent Selena and Arielle a text message to inform them he'd submit the application later that afternoon. Everything was uploaded and filled out on WonderHome's hiring page—he just needed to click "submit".

Selena had believed she would be in front of her work computer during the entirety of Wednesday afternoon. What she'd have access to was still in question, but it was their best shot to push this attempt of sabotage through.

Until then, Felix did the unbearable and created profiles on the two dating apps where he planned to connect with Michelle. A big part of him was hoping her profiles were inactive. Perhaps she had accounts on these sites, but hadn't logged in to use them in months. That would throw a wrench in this absurd idea and get him off the hook.

Selena had prepared notes for him to create his profiles, including taking a couple of pictures using his phone to upload to the dating sites. She once again stressed the importance of creating a backstory for the character he would portray while on dates with Michelle.

A knot formed in Felix's stomach. He didn't want to do any of this. None of it fueled his passion like hacking into a computer system did. Even the mindless busywork that went into preparing for a mission—things like getting fake ID's and paperwork sorted out, drawing routes on maps and circling key locations—were more appealing than creating a dating profile where he would be hunted by what society referred to as cougars.

"So fucking weird and wrong," he whispered to himself.

His oldest sister, Clara, had once brought home a man fifteen years older than her, and that led to nothing but a dramatic outburst from both of his parents. One of which Felix and his younger sister, Sarah, enjoyed watching. Clara had always been the golden child. Never in trouble, never even *suspected* of wrongdoing. Felix couldn't recall a time they had ever grounded Clara, and truly believed if she wasn't an adult at the time of this incident, their father would have sent her to her bedroom to "think about what she had done."

The thought made Felix giggle to this day, and eased his mind as he re-focused on the disturbing task before him. It took him half an hour to get his profile up and verified on Elite Bonding, positioning himself as a corporate executive currently working for Starbucks. They were a large enough company that if Michelle tried to look up their employee roster online, she'd get nowhere quickly. He listed his title as the Head of Research and Development.

Selena had brought home a suit and tie for Felix to wear for his profile picture, eventually snapping a portrait that could serve as a professional headshot. She encouraged Felix to upload the picture and create a fake profile on LinkedIn because "any executive worth their weight is on that site."

That much was true, and to make things appear legitimate, Felix called in a favor to his colleagues to create fake corporate Starbucks employee accounts to connect with on the platform. He had done all this on Tuesday when he had secretly moved forward with Arielle's plan before informing her.

All he had left to do was upload his new portrait, and everything would be in motion.

The morning had passed, which meant Felix could finally submit the application left open on his computer for Adam Marshall. Deep down, he knew this plan had little chance of working, but for his own sake of not having to pursue a date with Michelle, he prayed it would.

"I guess there's only one way to find out," he said, and clicked on *SUBMIT*.

Chapter 26

November 17, 2013

"I have news!" Emily Marshall said as she entered the kitchen on Sunday evening. The Marshalls had finished a dinner of grilled cheese sandwiches and tomato soup, where Adam remained to clean up the aftermath, a mountain of dishes piling out of the sink.

The kids were off to their rooms to get ready for bedtime.

"What kind of news?" Adam asked, picking at a piece of melted cheese stuck on one plate.

"I've been putting out some feelers for jobs you might be interested in," Emily said, leaning against the counter next to Adam, cell phone in hand.

"I have a friend who knows the CEO for WonderHome. They have lots of jobs posted, but there's one they're having trouble filling: an administrative assistant."

Adam laughed. "An *assistant*? Em, I was just a store manager for a major grocery store. I think I can find something a little more within my qualifications."

"I knew you'd say that, but hear me out." Emily turned her attention to read from her phone. "They're looking for someone who has great organizational skills, understands complex problem-solving, and can make quick and difficult decisions on the fly. Doesn't managing a store require all of that? I'd say you qualify based on that alone."

"Well, sure, but that doesn't mean I *want* to be someone's assistant. I've gotten used to calling the shots at work. I can't imagine it any other way."

"I get that, but this isn't just being anyone's assistant. It's the *CEO's* assistant. You don't think you'll have some pull for that reason alone?"

"I guess, but where is the opportunity for growth? Not like I can get promoted to CEO."

"Babe, have you really become this close-minded since you lost your job? Think bigger. No, you won't get promoted to CEO, but put in a couple years as her assistant, and you'll have every door in the company open to you. You'll literally have the most important person in the company to vouch for you. Do you think some hiring manager will just ignore their own CEO recommending you for a job? Not at all."

"But I've never done anything remotely close to being an assistant. So I'll handle paperwork and fetch this lady's coffee every day? Like, I get the opportunity is more than it seems, but I can't see myself committing to this type of work."

"What if I told you it pays more than you were making before?"

Adam laughed again, turning off the sink and turning his full attention to his wife. "Then I'd say you're high. No way in hell an assistant job pays more."

"*CEO's* assistant. You know this lady is worth hundreds of millions of dollars, right?"

"You know I don't follow all that stuff. So what does it pay?"

"Well, for the right candidate, the pay will start at $100,000 and could go as high as $125,000."

"Uh, what the fuck? Excuse me?" A giddy smile spread across Emily's face as she looked up from her phone. "You're joking."

"I'm not. This is very real. Look!"

Emily held up her phone, the job application on the screen.

"You think I have a chance at this job?" Adam asked. "Which friend has this connection?"

"Emma, from the Pilates studio. She said she'll put in a good word for you. And from what it sounds like, she goes back a long way with Michelle Garrison."

Emily let the moment hang in the air between them, and she watched as Adam looked up at the ceiling, then down to the floor as the gears in his mind twisted into motion.

I can't just become this lady's assistant, he thought. *For that much money, she's definitely looking for someone specific.*

"Well?" Emily asked, her eyes bulging. She had surely recognized the look on his face as his acceptance. Spend enough of your life with someone, and they'll know what you're thinking before even you do.

"This is an interesting opportunity. But am I a sellout? Because I promise you, if it paid the same as my old job, there is no way in hell I'd be doing this."

Now Emily let out a laugh. "A sellout? Adam, it's a good-paying job at a top-tier company that will open up so many opportunities for your future. How is showing interest in that being a sellout? You would work directly with a multi-millionaire. We'll get invited to her house, meet her friends and family, and build connections that way. The opportunities from this go way beyond the walls of WonderHome. And that money is just the salary. Emma told me Michelle gave her last assistant a $25,000 Christmas bonus, plus an all-expenses-paid trip to the Caribbean for their family. You can stand there and wrestle with some moral decision that doesn't really exist. Or you can apply for this job that can change our lives."

She was right. If Adam applied for this job, their lives would be unrecognizable this time next year. Thanksgiving was less than two weeks away, which meant Adam's in-laws were heading to Seattle in the next ten days, a thought that deserved its own throbbing headache. They would cram into this house that didn't have enough space. They would dirty the place with their inability to discipline the kids in the slightest, letting them run wild and overriding whatever Adam and Emily said.

Between his mother-in-law's nonsensical opinions about everything and his father-in-law hogging the remote—*who the fuck pauses live sports?!*—it was no wonder Adam drank himself into oblivion at Thanksgiving dinner.

But with an alternative lifestyle driven by a fatter bank account, that could all change. They could be the ones taking the trip to visit the in-laws in Oregon. They could book hotel rooms and not have to be around the in-laws every waking second of the day. And just maybe, Adam could watch Thanksgiving football games in peace without the nagging about how violent a sport it was from his mother-in-law.

Maybe we just take a cruise next year and deal with none of it.

The thought sent a flutter into Adam's chest.

"I suppose there is a lot we could get done with that kind of money," he said.

Emily nodded. "We've been talking about finishing the basement, remodeling the kitchen, and building that shed in the backyard. We'd finally get to look at all of that."

Adam could sense the angst radiating from his wife. She desperately wanted him to apply for this job. He drew a deep breath for dramatics. It was a rare occasion for Adam to hold so much influence over his wife, and he wanted to drag the moment out as long as he could, returning his stare to the ceiling as he blew out the air.

"Oh my, God, Adam!" She finally caved. "Apply for this job before I do."

Adam broke into howling laughter, clenching his stomach. "Okay, okay. One question though—will you still love me when I'm an administrative assistant?"

Emily bit her bottom lip and punched him playfully on the arm. Adam had known Emily equally well, and knew that lip bite signified a moment of fierce attraction. Send in this job application tonight and he'd almost certainly get lucky after the kids were asleep.

He couldn't pass up a slam dunk of an opportunity. "Okay. I'll apply right now if you finish the dishes."

Emily squealed and clapped her hands, jumping like a teenage girl who just met her boy band crush. "Deal."

She planted a wet kiss on his lips and slipped into the space between him and the sink, her ass brushing against his crotch.

It's so on, Adam thought, running his hands down her sides before he pulled away. "Okay. Can you send me that link to apply?"

"Already did five minutes ago," she said with a chuckle.

"Ahh, so this was all an act. You already knew I was going to apply."

"Maybe." She threw a grin over her shoulder. "Now go get it done."

Adam obliged, shuffling out of the kitchen and down the hallway where they kept a room that was half office, half guest space with a futon and a nightstand crammed next to the computer desk and bookshelf.

Seeing that futon just reminded Adam that his in-laws were coming, and it was indeed urgent he apply for and get this job.

"Okay, let's do this," Adam said, turning on his computer and waiting for it to load. The older models were nowhere near as fast as the computers he had the privilege of using at his grocery store office.

After a couple of minutes, all was set. He opened the application and read through it, finding his past job experience somehow aligned perfectly with the role. He'd been applying to multiple jobs over the past week, never feeling truly inspired by any of the companies he had been researching.

But they knew WonderHome around Seattle as the ultimate company one could work for. With his resume already updated and ready to go, he attached it to the application, filled out his information, and submitted.

He leaned back and smiled, staring at the screen with the most hope he had felt in weeks. "I have a good feeling about this."

Chapter 27

November 20, 2013

By Wednesday morning, they were certain they had pulled off the impossible. The week prior, Selena had found her way into the recruiting system and marked Adam's fake application as rejected because of substandard qualifications. On Monday morning, she had done the same thing with Adam's actual application.

She removed both applications from the shared recruiting inbox, placed into the vast folder where tens of thousands of rejected applications fell victim during the year.

Arielle had made plans for them to potentially leave the mission early, assuming Adam never received contact from WonderHome through the end of 2013. They would spot check the next six months to see that Adam remained away from the company to pursue other opportunities. If so, that should have been enough to clear him from the illegal activity that would eventually befall him and lead to the death of his family.

Selena rode high on cloud nine, believing she had once again done the dirty work behind the scenes to close out another successful mission. Felix was the lone skeptic, urging them to at least wait out the week before planning a victory lap.

When Selena's manager, Susie, called her into her office just before lunch on Wednesday, all of Felix's doubt and warnings immediately rushed to the front of Selena's mind.

Shit, she thought.

The training class had ended last Friday, and all the new hires got a couple of hours that afternoon to set up their new desks and finally mingle with their department colleagues. Recruiting was a small team of five, and all five of Selena's coworkers exchanged glances when Susie had stuck her head out of her office door across the hall, adding to Selena's paranoia.

Shit, shit, shit. Play it cool. You're new. It was an honest mistake.

The fluids in her stomach drained and seemed to pool in her wobbly knees as she stood from her desk and grabbed her water bottle.

It could just be a check-in. I am new, after all. Not everything has to be doom and gloom when your boss asks to speak with you in private.

Selena entered Susie's office, where her manager had returned to the seat behind her desk.

"Please close the door behind you and have a seat," Susie said.

Shiiiit.

Selena could immediately tell from Susie's tone a serious conversation was underway. Susie kept a lone goldfish in a round glass tank on the ledge of the window behind her. Selena watched it swim laps around a miniature castle, then looked out to the window to the skyscrapers of Seattle.

"How have your first couple of weeks been?" Susie asked, leaning back and softening her tone. "You getting settled in?"

"Yes," Selena said. "I've loved every minute so far. I'm definitely happy and see myself being with WonderHome for a very long time."

Susie smiled, looking at the empty space on her desk before making eye contact with her new employee. "That's great. We always love to hear that. And I'll say, you are quite popular already with your new teammates. They've had nothing but praise for how fast of a learner you are. Same from Kurt—thinks you'll go very far here."

But? Selena wanted to ask. Susie trailed off and let them sit in uncomfortable silence for a fifteen second period that felt more like five minutes.

"Well, that's great," Selena finally said. "I like them all, too. Great group on this team. One of the best I've worked with."

"Glad to hear it. Part of being new is obviously having your work spot-checked for quality purposes. We came across something that caught our attention."

The room started spinning around Selena. This wasn't even her real job. She was playing make believe. Why did she feel so nauseous all the sudden?

I can't get fired, right? It's not that serious of an offense.

"Oh?" Selena said, fighting with every cell in her body to sound in control of her emotions. "Did I make a mistake on something?"

"Yes. Does the name Adam Marshall ring a bell?"

Fuck. It's okay, play it off. Talk your way out of this.

Selena looked up to feign deep thought and avoid eye contact with Susie, who was staring her down.

"Adam Marshall," she said to herself. The name tasted dirty in her mouth, like speaking it while in the past would somehow unravel the very fabric of reality. "Oh! The guy who submitted his application twice and changed all the information. Yes, what was the matter?"

"It appears you marked his initial application as rejected, then quickly rejected the second one that came in without giving due diligence. That isn't something you should even do yet. You'll need more time getting familiar with the team's processes now that you're out of training. Probably another couple of weeks. Did someone tell you to mark those as rejected?"

Selena couldn't lie. Throwing out someone else's name would only make this situation messier. "No, it was all me. I'm sorry if I got ahead of myself. That application came in and I clearly saw it wasn't a good fit. A grocery store worker as the assistant to Michelle seemed like a stretch, so I marked it as rejected. Then the second application came through again from the same guy, but his resume was completely different. I've seen that old trick before and knew he was certainly lying about the details on the new one."

"Okay. And I can agree with him not being qualified based on the first application, but he's actually a direct referral from someone Michelle trusts very much. Because of that, we had to dig around to find his application and that's when we saw it in the rejected folder. We also called the candidate, and he said he never sent two applications. We told him about the first one that came in, and he swore up and down it was not him. A coincidence, he said, because the email address provided wasn't even his, and that's all appeared true so far."

"I see," Selena said, genuine worry spreading across her face. This failed plan dealt too closely with Michelle. *Fly too close to the sun and get your wings burned off.*

"I can excuse the mistake because I understand your thought process behind it. But you still shouldn't even be clicking on anything in our applications queue. Look around it to get familiar, sure, but this could have been a costly mistake that Michelle would have seen through directly. Fortunately, she had only emailed inquiring about the applicant's status, and we could get it all corrected without her knowing."

"I'm so sorry, Susie. I won't do anything like that again."

Susie raised a hand. "Nothing to apologize for. Just wanted to bring this to your attention. And honestly, if this candidate wasn't a direct referral from the CEO, this wouldn't have even been an issue. One thing you'll learn is that we don't have a ton of involvement with recruiting for the executive team. They will ultimately hire who they want. They interview their candidates directly. We set up the scheduling and initial communication for these roles. The executives take care of the rest."

"I guess that makes sense. What can we possibly know about being Michelle's personal assistant, right?"

Susie rolled her eyes. "Sounds like a nightmare, if you ask me. Not because Michelle is hard to work for, but it can be some serious pressure to work that closely with the CEO. It's more demanding than people might realize."

"I'm sure it is."

Susie leaned forward. "Between you and me, I'd bet my entire salary that this Adam Marshall guy gets the job."

Hearing this from the manager of recruiting sent a nasty jolt throughout Selena's body. After all that, Adam still emerged as the favorite to land the coveted job that would change his family's life forever. The past really didn't care what came its way—it would always preserve itself.

"How can you be so sure?"

"We have had this job listed for two months. We've received lots of qualified applications, but Michelle has brushed them all aside, claiming she's looking for someone who can shake things up. I don't know what that means exactly, but this Adam guy is the first direct referral from Michelle. That she reached out to us tells me he's already her favorite. Besides, he's a man younger than Michelle. Her last two assistants have been younger men—she's just into that, I suppose. I think she gets some sort of kick out of the reversal of the gender stereotypes by having a male assistant. And they're always so handsome, I'll give her that. Michelle gets credit for a lot of things, but she doesn't get enough love for the giant middle finger she throws up to the patriarchy."

Susie laughed, and Selena joined her, sensing the drastic shift of the mood in the room.

"What did this Adam guy do to you, anyway?" Susie asked, the question catching Selena off guard.

"Excuse me?"

"Well, his is the only application you did anything to in the system. If I didn't know any better, I'd think you were trying to make sure he didn't get hired here."

"Ha!" The sound escaped Selena's throat, and she wasn't sure if it was real or not. "No, of course not."

"Well good. Because he's most likely going to work here, and he'll have some serious pull. Would hate to be off to a weird start with the big boss's number two."

Selena forced a wide smile. "No, we can't have that."

Chapter 28

November 25, 2013

"They're officially hiring him," Selena said.

The three Angels gathered for dinner on Monday night. Felix spent the weekend preparing for this possibility, expanding his profiles on the two dating apps to position himself as appealing as possible to Michelle.

Arielle and Selena had spent a portion of Saturday tailing Michelle, finding nothing of significance. The CEO spent her morning at the gym, followed by a trip to the spa and a solo lunch at a local barbecue restaurant called Flamin' Dave's. When she returned home after lunch and didn't reappear for an hour, they called it a day.

On Sunday, they followed the Marshall family around, hoping to hear any insight about his potential job. WonderHome hadn't made a final decision until Monday morning, so the status was still up in the air while Arielle and Selena followed them. Their morning started with an early mass, where the two Angels sat in the back pew. Being in church for an hour caused Arielle plenty of guilt, but she could finally tell her abuelita she had finally gone to mass—she didn't need to know that it was actually for work.

After mass, they went down the street to a Denny's, where the family devoured pancakes, eggs, and bacon. A trip to the grocery store followed, the Marshalls seeming to genuinely enjoy each other's company while they loaded their cart with groceries for the week ahead, the two kids sitting in the cart and making up games to pass the boredom. Arielle grew sickened imagining how this family's fate would play out if they weren't able to stop Adam from getting involved in the messy world of money laundering.

They never heard Adam mention a peep about the WonderHome job to his wife, and once more gave up on the cause when the Marshalls returned home for a lazy Sunday afternoon lounging around the house, the wind howling outside all day, blowing red and yellow leaves in violent swirls around the neighborhood.

By the time the three Angels convened for dinner on Monday night, Adam had received his offer letter from WonderHome, and they had officially failed to prevent his hiring. A solemn mood hung over the dining room where Felix had served a dinner of baked chicken, mashed potatoes, and asparagus.

"Well, we weren't entirely positive we were going to stop him from getting hired," Felix said. "Too many moving parts. Maybe if we have arrived earlier, we could have had more influence on that part of the process."

"I don't think it matters," Arielle said. "It was always going to be a tall task. Adam getting hired has such a long ripple effect on several other things that happen over the next six months. Things we're not even aware of yet. We're going to have to chip away at it like always."

"Were you involved in any of the hiring process?" Felix asked Selena.

She shook her head. "Nope. I think after my blunder with his application, they really might have suspected me of something. They let me nowhere near his application after I cleared my name."

"Again, nothing I'm worried about," Arielle said. "He's hired, starting on December second, after the Thanksgiving break. Everything is right on schedule, and we both have our jobs. I should have some free rein after the break as well, and we can really get into the thick of WonderHome and hopefully figure out what's going on behind the scenes. For now, we need to look at the next steps. Felix, your profiles are ready?"

Felix nodded. "Sure are. I analyzed some of the more appealing accounts and mimicked them."

"Perfect. Now is probably the time to engage on the app until you connect with Michelle. If you can get a date lined up before the new year, that would be ideal. If you can get into a somewhat regular schedule of dates with her by February or March, that will give us our best shot of at least trying to get some information out of her."

Felix nodded quietly as he took a bite of potatoes.

"Think this is going down to the wire again?" Selena asked.

"I hope not, but we have to plan for it, just in case. While Felix works on Michelle, you'll need to keep your ears open for any happenings involving the executive team. And I'll be trying to monitor their emails and phone calls as best I can. I'm still not sure what checks and balances exist in my department. I don't know if anyone will watch what I'm doing, so I'll be playing it carefully in the beginning. As for Adam, I want to be ready to pounce on any mistake he makes. We need to get him written up for as many things as we can humanly justify. Make his file look like a disaster and make his life hell.

Just maybe we can drive him to quit."

"Be careful if you're getting involved in that personally," Felix said. "Who do you think the CEO is going to trust more, her handpicked assistant, or the recruiter who 'accidentally' deleted Adam's application?"

"That's a good point," Arielle said. "We all need to be more diligent than usual. As Felix mentioned, when we first started brainstorming, the FBI will be in the WonderHome system at some point. We can't leave any virtual fingerprints that show our involvement. That would force us to dip out of this mission before having time to execute our work. We just need to take everything one day at a time."

"Should be easy," Selena said. "My team is getting Wednesday off, so that's a long five-day weekend for me starting tomorrow night. Might go out and find a ladies' night somewhere after work if either of you wants to join me."

Arielle had come a long way since their first mission of working together. Before, she would have lost her mind at such a prospect. Now she understood this was just part of Selena. She worked hard and played harder. But it all made her function at her best level when it came down to mission work.

"We'll see about that," Arielle said with a grin. "Some of us work for a living around here."

They all howled with amusement and finished dinner, unaware of the obstacles that lay ahead.

Chapter 29

December 2, 2013

The following Monday, the calendar flipped to the second day of December. Arielle was up earlier than normal, as was Selena. It was the biggest day of the mission so far—Adam's first day at WonderHome.

The two were out the door fifteen minutes earlier than normal, eager to arrive at the office. Arielle earned more freedom within her role and planned to see what all she could get for Felix to hack into the company's internal systems.

Felix had connected with Michelle on the Elite Bonding app, swapping multiple messages with her over the Thanksgiving weekend. Their first date was scheduled for December 14, a moment Felix was already dreading, yet preparing for in his usual professional manner.

Overall, Arielle was pleased with their current standing on the mission and hoped the week would bring further momentum. She let her team know this during their Sunday night dinner, which was the Thanksgiving leftovers they had ordered for the holiday.

When they arrived at the quiet office, Selena and Arielle parted ways as they had been doing since their interviews.

As far as anyone was concerned, Arielle and Selena were complete strangers, despite being in the same training class.

They had already set the main lobby up to welcome yet another new hire class. Becca was finishing her preparations for the mimosas, silently minding her business with a pair of headphones strapped over her head.

Selena arrived at her desk to find Janina already at work. She sat on the endcap where she could easily be reached by anyone on the team.

"Good morning, Selena, how was your Thanksgiving?" Janina asked, leaning back in her seat.

"It was good and relaxing, can't complain. How was yours?"

"Oh, flew down to San Diego to spend the weekend with my family. It was a good time. Plenty of food and drink. I still feel full from that Thursday night dinner."

Janina laughed, much too early for Selena's liking.

"I hear that," Selena said. "Hard to come back to such a busy week."

"Ugh, I know. Most companies get to relax between Thanksgiving and Christmas. But not us. It's all because of this new real estate team. We're going to be pretty steady with new hires until next summer. I'll need your help with some things today—time to show you the ropes for new hire classes, anyway."

"Oh?" Selena replied, her anticipation promptly shooting through the roof. She just might get to dip her toes back into the lake that was the Adam Marshall mystery. "What all does that entail?"

"Essentially processing them as employees within the system. They should have all submitted their important documents to us—driver's license, social security cards, et cetera—but after Kurt takes roll call later this morning, he'll give us the list of everyone who actually showed up, and we can begin processing once we know they're actually here."

"Do people really accept a job and not show up for it?" Selena asked, genuinely puzzled at such a sentiment.

"It happens more than you might think. Not *too* often at WonderHome, but I'd say maybe one person out of every three hiring classes will just go MIA and never show. We don't like to assume the worst about people and do our diligence in trying to get in touch. I think some people find a job they like better and don't have the courtesy to let us know. I have a feeling it might start happening a little more with all these realtors we're hiring. Real estate, in general, is a competitive job market with lots of bouncing around to different brokerages."

"That's nuts. I couldn't imagine just blowing off a job, especially at a place like this."

Janina laughed. "Oh yeah. Us in the world of recruiting like to think there's a special place in hell for these people. But what can you do? Life is too short to get hung up on the negative, don't you think?"

"Indeed it is."

"Do you want to get started? There are supposed to be eight new employees showing up today, so what I like to do is get a head start and get all of their profiles open."

"I'd love to!" Selena said, certain her early morning enthusiasm came across in a positive light for her team lead. In reality, she was just excited to dig deeper into Adam Marshall's file and understand what she might manipulate further down the road.

Janina rolled her chair into the aisle of desks and parked it next to Selena. For the next five minutes, she directed her through the system where they converted applicants to employees. They poked around the database, Janina showing her the different tools and options available, along with brief explanations when each might be used.

After the impromptu training session, they made their way down the list of the new hires who would stroll into the lobby in mere minutes. Each profile had a checklist on the side for any outstanding documents. All new hires still needed their pictures taken for their work badges, something Janina said she would handle later in the morning.

"Is that not something I can do?" Selena asked.

"One thing at a time," Janina said with a laugh. "I'm sure you can handle taking a picture, but that's not the issue. I just don't like to throw too many things out to the newbies on my team. I'll take the pictures and let you upload them. By the new year, you'll be comfortable enough where I'll let you take care of the whole process."

It seemed trivial, but that was also why Selena needed to let it go. All she really wanted was a chance to speak to Adam Marshall.

I'll get my chance, she told herself. *Just stay patient. It's only his first day.*

Patience, however, was far from her strong suit.

"Do we go out there to meet the new class once they arrive?" she asked.

A crooked grin spread across Janina's face. "You just want a mimosa, don't you? No need to lie about meeting the new hires. You work in POPs—you can get a mimosa without asking."

Selena let out a hearty laugh. "Guilty," she said, suddenly giddy. She would absolutely wander out to the lobby for the morning celebration. And she would meet Adam Marshall.

"They should actually start arriving in the next ten minutes," Janina said, standing up from her chair and rolling it back to her desk. "Keep getting those profiles ready so we can just click 'enter' once we know they've shown up."

"Will do."

Selena focused on her work, saving Adam's profile last.

* * *

At five minutes to eight, Selena locked her computer screen after jotting down all of Adam's information she could fit onto both sides of a sticky note. She had his prior work experience, address, emergency contacts, social security number, and both his cell phone and home phone numbers. It was a virtual gold mine that she wasn't even sure Felix could do anything with. But in the name of sabotage to save an innocent family, all was fair game.

The POPs department sat down the hallway in the opposite direction from the training room and the rowdy sales floor. Even from there, in the glorious silence, the noise level carried down the hall and sent a flutter into Selena's stomach.

She sent a text message to Arielle: *New hires in the lobby. I'm going to say hello. Not sure if you can?*

She didn't expect Arielle to join her. No one else from any other department outside of POPS was even told of the morning event. A software engineer showing up for a mimosa would certainly look out of place, but it was still worth a shot.

A couple other of Selena's teammates had shown up and were getting settled in for the morning. Selena took advantage and bolted away before they could suck her into the usual morning chitchat.

She hurried down the hall and found the small crowd gathering around Becca's desk just as they had on Arielle and Selena's first day. This time, there were boxes of doughnuts and croissants to complement the table filled with mimosas. For a class of only eight new hires, there were already a dozen people gathered in the lobby, a handful of faces Selena didn't recognize.

But she saw the only one that mattered. The face she could close her eyes and see thanks to his mugshot being drilled into her head like a piercing migraine.

Adam Marshall stood nearest the drink table, mimosa in hand as he engaged in conversation with another new hire. He had dressed for success, as they say in the tech world. A navy blue suit jacket, unbuttoned to show an eggshell dress shirt underneath. Dark blue jeans and a laptop bag slung over one shoulder completed his ensemble.

He's kinda good-looking, Selena thought, her only other reference being his raggedy, shocked and surprised mugshot.

Adam wore his hair in short messy spikes, a new look from what they had seen in their prior days following him.

New haircut for a new job, Selena thought, now taking slow steps toward the mimosa table. She studied him, then looked away, not wanting him to sense her gawking.

When she reached the mimosas, she grabbed one, keeping her back to Adam and the other man he was speaking with. From what she could gather, they were talking about the Seahawks game that was scheduled for Monday Night Football later that evening. The other man was bragging about how he had scored some tickets to the game, convinced the team was going to win the Super Bowl (which they would).

Selena spun around, taking a sip, but getting their attention and stopping their conversation. They stared at her, saw her badge dangling from her waistband, and knew she was not part of the new class.

"Hello, guys," Selena said, immediately trying to get a feel for how she should act. Friendly and open was the safest bet for the current situation. "Welcome to WonderHome. Are you both part of the new class starting today?"

"Yes," the man said, sticking out a hand to Selena. "My name is Shane Lawrence."

"Nice to meet you, Shane," Selena replied, shaking his hand.

"And I'm Adam Marshall." He offered a charming grin, and Selena immediately thought back to the prior mission and how she had caught feelings for Brian Dawkins while working in the past. Then she remembered how fucked-up that all turned out and erased any budding attraction.

"Adam, nice to meet you," she said, shaking his hand. When they touched, she felt that sensation of destiny looking over them. As of this moment, she could look him in the eye and tell him exactly how his future would play out. Of course, he'd laugh at her and probably report her to the authorities for some type of mental illness. "And what role are you gentlemen taking on at WonderHome?"

Gentlemen? Who the fuck am I?

"I'm merely a new sales rep," Shane said. "I guess we can't all hit the big time right out of the gate like Adam."

"Oh?" Selena said, playing dumb and turning her attention to Adam.

He blushed and stuffed his free hand deep into his pocket, where he was surely fidgeting with his fingers.

"I'm going to be the assistant to Michelle Garrison," he said, promptly taking a long swig from his mimosa to avoid saying anything further.

"That's right!" Selena cried, hoping to ease his tension. "I forgot we were expecting her new assistant this week. How exciting!"

He grinned, and she couldn't read if he was truly embarrassed or simply holding back his joy.

"So what do you do?" Shane asked Selena, crossing his arms and shifting his weight back on his heel.

"Apologies. My name is Selena Nicole, and I work in recruiting. I just started here last month, so I'm still pretty new myself."

"Selena? I don't believe we spoke throughout any of the hiring process," Shane replied.

It had become clear Adam was happy to let his colleague take on the brunt of the speaking. Every new class had that one yapper who just needed to make their presence known.

Fucking kiss-ass, Selena thought.

"No, you probably would've spoken with my lead, Janina. I've been working on things more behind the scenes. Processing applications, scheduling interviews. Things like that."

"Ahh, that's right. Janina is who I spoke with on the phone."

A moment of silence hung between them, and Selena took the chance to change the subject.

"So Adam, how do you know Michelle? It's my understanding not just anyone can score an interview with her, let alone get hired on."

"It's crazy," he said, adjusting the strap on his shoulder. "I had never met her until the day of my interview. My wife has a friend who is good friends with Michelle. She heard I was looking for work and threw my name into the hat. I honestly can't believe how fast it all came together."

"Classic friend-of-a-friend situation, am I right?" Shane said, chuckling and bumping his elbow into Adam's arm.

I'd love to punch this guy square in the jaw, Selena thought, knowing she could make him cry. *Classic douchebag-on-the-floor situation, am I right?*

Selena saw Susie and Amara enter the lobby together and knew this conversation had seconds remaining.

"Well," she said. "It was nice meeting you both. I need to make my rounds, but I look forward to seeing you guys around the office."

Not so much you, Shane, she thought, grinning as she shook both of their hands once more.

"Likewise," Adam said. "Looking forward to it."

Chapter 30

December 14, 2013

Over the following two weeks, Adam Marshall settled in the new routine of his life, reporting every morning to the office at eight o'clock sharp, and leaving around five in the afternoon.

For Arielle and Selena, they found tailing Adam at the office wasn't as simple as they had hoped. With Selena on the thirty-first floor, Arielle on the thirty-second, and Michelle and Adam up on the thirty-fourth, the logistics complicated matters beyond their control.

Arielle never had business on the executive floor. And Selena could only justify a trip up there once a week. That did little to allow them insight into Adam and Michelle's world.

Arielle had gradually brought home information to Felix with hopes of hacking into the WonderHome systems. One issue, however, was Arielle's security clearance. She had access to most facets of the company, but not all. She could mainly deal with day-to-day operations that affected employees across the company. This would only help to an extent. What they really wanted was the access to read emails, private chat messages, and bank account information. Not even Arielle's direct manager had access to these things, and it was her understanding that only the Chief Technology Officer had the coveted blanket clearance for all tech matters, with a handful of others having a variety of levels of access in between.

Felix spent many nights of those first two weeks of December trying to break ground, running into one obstacle after another. It neither fazed nor surprised him. This was a company worth just over four billion dollars, and they had obviously not spared a penny in the cybersecurity budget.

Arielle had even requested access to work from home, citing the need in case issues arrived in the middle of the night or over weekends. Besides, most others in her department had similar access. She was approved by her manager, but the final approval needed to make its way up to the CTO, who could take weeks, possibly months to get around to such a trivial request.

Felix believed having that VPN access at home would open more possibilities for him, but he would continue forward just the same until then.

Today, however, none of that mattered.

Felix had a Saturday night dinner date with Michelle Garrison, and all worries about hacking came to a screeching halt. He understood algorithms well enough to manipulate the dating app to finally show him Michelle after hours of mindless swiping. He had sent her the initial default message of interest when she popped up on his screen over Thanksgiving weekend. And by Sunday morning, Michelle replied with *Hello there ;)*

Seeing the message made him want to vomit. A winky face? From a middle-aged woman? Felix had dealt with enough emojis and what he considered childish games throughout college, to the point he gave up on even trying to date.

Most of the women he went to classes with were wise beyond their years. Strong, independent, brilliant, and often fierce. Yet, for some reason, in the name of dating, those same women resorted to the same antics of playing mind games and refusing to be straightforward with their intentions.

Felix figured no matter how intelligent a person was, they couldn't outrun their age. He has planned to wait until his thirties to start his search for a life partner, but the reply from the WonderHome CEO gave him second thoughts about that as well.

Michelle advertised herself on the executive app as a hard-working CEO looking for someone who could "appreciate" her lifestyle. Her portrait looked like a professional headshot, the kind she might put on the company's online directory. She listed her city as Medina.

Medina was home to the wealthiest residents of Seattle. Bill Gates, Jeff Bezos, and a handful of athletes called Medina home. An eight-figure salary was basically the minimum requirement to live in the lavish city overlooking Lake Washington.

Felix felt incredibly in way over his head.

"Do I try to go back to her place tonight?" Felix asked, the question tasting like dogshit on his tongue. Arielle and Selena had posted up in his bedroom to help him get dressed for the date, making sure the outfit would precisely portray him as a young, rich executive.

"Slow down, cowboy," Selena said, working on Felix's necktie. She had taken full control over all wardrobe decisions and dressed Felix in an all-white suit from Armani, shoes from Dolce & Gabbana, and even the necktie was over two hundred dollars from Gucci. When Felix had asked Selena why it was necessary to buy such excessive clothing, she explained that Michelle would expect nothing less. *We're in this to win it,* she had said. *If you want to get a suit from the mall, then this date will be the last. If we want to infiltrate this woman's life, you need to play the game by her rules.*

Arielle laughed. "Going back to her place tonight is entirely up to her. If it does, you need to make it clear you're not interested in sex, yet still be receptive to the invitation. Does that make sense?"

"Of course it doesn't make sense," Felix said. "I don't play these mind games. I just say how I feel."

"Oh, we know," Selena said. "So whenever you're with Michelle during these coming months, you need to be less Felix and more of a rich asshole."

"How do you know she likes assholes?" Felix snapped. "Not all rich people are assholes. Hell, I'm rich and I'm not an asshole."

Selena smiled. "Because I looked up that guy she was out with when we followed her. Sergios Vascou. Moved to Seattle after working on Wall Street for three years. Still in finance, and still a piece of shit. You should see this guy's social media. Different women every weekend. Always at a nightclub popping bottles. Even saw a picture where he forgot to wipe the coke off his nose. Young, rich, and stupid. Doesn't know what to do with all that money, so he tries giving it away to strippers and bartenders."

"Look at you," Arielle said. "Doing the snooping work Felix usually handles."

Selena laughed. "Anyone can look up an account on Facebook. Don't patronize me. The point is, Felix, Michelle likes rich men."

"Clearly. We're having dinner at Birelis. I looked at their menu and read reviews. Dinner for two comes out to a thousand dollars on average. Why in the world do people live like this?"

"Because they can," Selena said. "And it's fun to do on occasion. And choosing Birelis is just a test. I've done some more reading—what can I say, I have at least two hours of downtime during my workday—and something people do on this Elite Bonding app is choose the expensive restaurants to make sure their match is legit. Apparently some people can fake their way onto the app and show up to the first date in a beat-up car, wearing jeans and a T-shirt."

Felix couldn't help but laugh. "That actually sounds like a fantastic prank to pull on the elite class."

Selena shook her head. "Well, these people don't think so. As you can guess, some of their users got together and did what any rich American does when they don't get their way. They filed a lawsuit against Elite Bonding."

Felix and Arielle both burst into raucous laughter.

"Naturally," Selena continued. "That failed. So the users have sort of adopted this method on their own. It was typically men who were pulling this prank, so the women will make the reservations and arrive at the restaurant first. They'll instruct the host as to who they are expecting, and only if they are dressed the part will the host bring them back to the table, and the date can officially begin."

"What?!" Arielle cried, sitting on the foot of Felix's bed and grabbing her stomach as she continued laughing. "Is this for real? Or is this just something one person has done and wrote an article about?"

"Oh, it's very real. There are message boards and Facebook pages dedicated to this particular demographic, and this method is used by nearly everyone. Even the men understand this is the norm if they are serious about advancing to the actual date."

Felix shook his head. "Only you and your love for this kind of gossip could have figured all this out. I guess we owe you some thanks."

Selena stepped back from Felix, brushing his shoulders as she looked him up and down. "Please. I'm only getting you through the door. It's *your* job to take it from there."

Arielle rose from the bed and stood next to Selena. "Wow, you do good work. Felix, you look like you could get any woman in the world right now, if you really wanted."

Felix immediately blushed. He wasn't used to compliments like that. When he looked in the mirror, he was always satisfied with who he saw. Not ugly. Not sexy. Just a normal guy. But that was only his perception, and he understood how other people saw him was beyond his control. Arielle's compliment was intimidating. Because for the first time in his post-college life, he looked in the mirror and couldn't believe his eyes.

He looked ready to go head-to-head with James Bond, and the sensation was overwhelming.

"Thank you," he whispered under his breath. Selena and Arielle exchanged wide grins. "As long as this helps with Michelle, I guess it's okay."

Selena clapped him on the back. "This is more than okay. You, sir, could walk into a *GQ* photoshoot right now and no one would think any differently."

Felix pulled at his lapel to tighten the suit jacket more

snugly around his shoulders. "Okay, let's get this date over with."

Chapter 31

The three Angels had more money than they knew what to do with. They knew better than to blow it all on cheap entertainment. For this portion of the mission, they found it extremely unlikely the Road Runners would reimburse them for a limo for Felix's date, so Arielle picked up the tab.

Before the limousine had arrived, Arielle stressed the importance of the evening ahead. Under no circumstance was Felix to bring Michelle back to their house. She would take one look at their middle-class neighborhood and leave back to her castle in Medina.

Selena had coached Felix as much as she could about how to proceed through the date, covering topics like best appetizers, wines, entrees, and desserts. Plus topics of conversation to avoid, which ones to dive deeper into, and how to best use his posture and body language to portray interest in Michelle.

By the time Felix fell into the silence of the limo, promptly trying to make sense of why anyone in the world would pay for a limo for a solo ride to a dinner date, his head spun with a clutter of reminders that he hoped to deploy during dinner.

The limo had a soft purple glow from a hidden light tucked somewhere along the edges of the ceiling. A bucket of ice with a bottle of champagne sat unattended on the rear seat, so

Felix kicked back, put his feet up on the empty, stretched-out bench in front of him, and poured himself a glass.

The driver kept the glass divider up, something Felix was grateful for. He had enough on his mind and couldn't possibly bear the awkward small talk. Perhaps the driver was equally uncomfortable, surely not having driven solo passengers frequently.

Felix spent the twenty-minute drive across town, mentally running down the list Selena had jammed into his mind. She had offered to use his bugging equipment to guide him through the date, but he dismissed that notion immediately. He may have not had the most experience dating rich women, but he was confident to execute this plan without a hitch. The champagne helped soothe his nerves, so he poured a second glass, knowing it would be his last. A bottle of wine was surely in the cards for dinner, and he needed to pace himself. Getting sloppy was the last thing this mission needed, but he also had to push aside what Selena had called his *inner Felix.*

"How do you stop being yourself?" he asked the empty limo, leaning his head back to relax, the champagne bubbles still exploding in his throat. "There is no such thing as hiding from yourself. We are who we are, to the core."

Felix understood this just fine, but further appreciated the stakes that lie ahead. His job with the Angels had always been to make life easier for the lead Angel assigned to a mission. This staged date with Michelle was no different. If it went poorly, they'd have to dig elsewhere to find the truth about who was responsible for the laundering scheme. Even Felix believed Michelle had involvement. But to what extent?

While the topic wouldn't come up on a first date, Felix planned to poke around as best he could to pull information out of the CEO.

The limo came to a last stop, the glow from a nearby street lamp shining over the vehicle, resting in front of Birelis.

The restaurant was hidden behind lush foliage, sitting atop a hill overlooking the west coast of Lake Union. The surrounding area felt like they had entered a forbidden forest, tucked away somewhere off the map where you could only find if you knew the exact route.

The limo's door opened, a man in a tuxedo and white-gloved hands standing guard outside. He was not the limo driver.

Felix slid over, letting his feet lead the way out, and when his shoes touched the pavement the man said, "Welcome to Birelis, sir. We hope you have a most pleasant dining experience this evening."

"Thank you," Felix said, reaching into his jacket to produce a twenty-dollar bill he slid into the man's gloved hand. Selena had explained how any person who helped in even the slightest way, such as opening his door and greeting him, expected a tip.

Twenty bucks for opening a door and saying hello, Felix thought. *I've clearly been in the wrong profession.*

Once outside, Felix realized it wasn't a street lamp they parked under, but a covered entryway for the restaurant. There were no street lights as far as he could see from their perch on the hill. A couple of boats had their lights beaming out on the lake, but were far enough to not disrupt the secluded ambiance of Birelis.

It feels like we're all alone in the world, Felix thought. The surroundings were pitch-black thanks to the towering trees. And completely silent, the subtle putter from the limo's exhaust providing the only audible sound within a half-mile radius.

The man stuck out his arm toward a red velvet carpet running from the limo to the restaurant's entrance. Classical music played somewhere from a hidden speaker. Two valet workers stood off to the side, speaking to a customer at the podium. Felix walked on the carpet where another tux-wearing man opened the door for him.

I'm not giving him a twenty, Felix thought, heart drumming in his chest as he passed by and nodded a thank you.

He stepped into the waiting area, where a smiling college-aged woman stood behind the host stand. "Good evening, sir," she said warmly. "Do you have a reservation tonight?"

Felix looked around, blown away by the interior layout. Chandeliers hung from the ceiling, each spaced ten feet apart, dimly lit. They looked to be made of pure crystal. The dining room was crowded, yet the usual bustle of chatter was non-existent.

People were still talking, yet it seemed like they were all whispering. It reminded Felix more of those few minutes in church right before mass starts. *Where the hell am I?*

The room was so dim, he couldn't clearly see where it ended. It just gradually got darker, despite the chandeliers glowing gently above.

"Sir?" the young woman asked.

Felix snapped back to the reality before him. His palms immediately started sweating, and he could feel the moisture forming in his underarms. Selena had been sure to stuff a handkerchief into Felix's suit pocket, and he promptly whipped it out to wipe the sweat from his brow.

"I'm sorry," he said, just now realizing the beauty of the

woman trying to get his attention. If he didn't feel like he was about to faint, he just might have talked to her about what she liked to do in her free time. "First time here." He let out an awkward laugh as he stuffed the handkerchief back into its place.

The woman maintained her charming smile throughout the entire exchange. "I understand, sir. We have a beautiful dining room. Breathtaking, some might say. Did you have a reservation?"

"Not me personally, but I am meeting someone. Michelle Garrison."

The hostess looked Felix up and down, gave a nod of approval, and said, "Please follow me. Ms. Garrison is already seated."

That was it, Felix thought. *The nod meant I pass the test. I'm dressed well enough.*

While everything about this evening, and the process leading up to it, seemed like utter bullshit to Felix, Selena had once again proven she knew her stuff. Perhaps better than anyone else.

Felix gulped as he followed the woman through the dining room, wiping his hands on his pants to get them as dry as possible. The last thing he needed was to greet Michelle with his nervous sweat.

All tables had small fishbowls as their centerpieces, candles somehow floating on the surface while little betta fish swam laps underneath. Their table for the night was positioned along the wall at the centerpoint of the restaurant. Far from the kitchen. Far from the entrance where the chilly breeze would whip across them each time the door opened.

There sat Michelle Garrison, hands folded on the table, a

glass of red wine directly in front of her.

"Ms. Garrison," the hostess said. "Your company."

She bowed out without another word, leaving Felix standing there like a dumbstruck buffoon trying to figure out what to do next.

"Felix?" Michelle asked, standing up. She wore a form-fitting black dress that sparkled even in the dim light, flowing loosely at her ankles, an opening that revealed a teasing sliver of her tanned left leg.

"Michelle," he replied, stretching out his hand. She shook it and pulled him in to plant a soft kiss on his cheek.

"I'm so glad we could get together tonight," she said, returning to her seat.

Felix hurried across the table to help push her chair in.

"Oh," she said. "Such a gentleman. Not many like you these days."

Felix was struggling to flip the mental switch and become someone else he had no interest in being. He pressed through and gave it his best shot.

"Thank you," he said, immediately regretting his response. *What the hell am I thanking her for?*

Michelle giggled as Felix got himself situated across the table. "I've ordered us a bottle of Chateau Margaux. Would you like a glass now?"

Felix had no idea what that meant. "Sounds perfect. Thank you."

Michelle raised a hand and pointed to Felix, nodding to someone off in the distance. Felix was becoming hyper-aware of his surroundings, his mind racing just beyond his grasp of control.

"So Michelle," he said, hoping his acting could distract his panicking thoughts. "Are you *the* Michelle Garrison?"

Fuck, that was a stupid question.

But she didn't seem to mind, laughing it off and taking a sip from her wineglass. Felix noticed the red lipstick stains stuck on the brim of the glass, something that had always grossed him out.

"You're funny," she said. "But if you're being serious, then yes, I am Michelle Garrison, CEO of WonderHome."

Felix had played out how this date would unfold at least a dozen times. He assumed Michelle would be an intense personality. Even Arielle and Selena agreed with this sentiment, as was the word around the office. But outside of that skyscraper, Felix was seeing Michelle in a different light. And it made sense. She had a persona to maintain while at work. She was the big boss no one could push around. Her employees could never see the way her bottom lip quivered when she was attracted to a man. Or the way her foot bounced underneath the table as she fought the same nerves as Felix—albeit for much different reasons.

"That's incredible," Felix said. "How are you liking it?"

Michelle studied Felix with a gaze of intense curiosity, and he didn't know how to interpret it. Was he saying something out of the ordinary? Did people at this particular level of employment—and society, for that matter—*not* discuss their jobs? Felix found it unlikely, and Selena had mentioned nothing of the sorts. Chatting about work was perhaps the most universal of conversation starters after the weather.

"I like it a lot," Michelle said. "It's an incredibly stressful role, but so rewarding at the same time. I have a wonderful team and it trickles all the way down to our most entry-level positions. Have you ever done anything in a leadership type of role? What is it you do exactly for Starbucks?"

"I'm a senior director in our communications department. I have a small team that reports to me, but we mainly overlook press releases and social media response. I enjoy it. Starbucks takes good care of us."

"Do you work much with Howard?"

Howard? Felix thought, soon realizing she must have meant the CEO, Howard Schultz.

"Not really, honestly. I'm two levels below him. I report directly to the VP of communications, who works with Howard."

"I'll have to mention your name to him the next time I see him."

Felix's heart returned to its violent thumping. He *hated* living this lie. Of course all the CEO's in Seattle knew each other. Michelle probably had Bill Gates' number stored in her phone, and that thought was all he needed to keep pushing through. If he could actually stretch this date into them regularly seeing each other, it was only a matter of time before he found himself with an opportunity to meet one of his idols.

"That's not necessary," Felix said with a chuckle, sounding more nervous than he intended.

"Enough about our work life," Michelle said excitedly. "I want to know about you as a person."

Felix noticed her finger running along the brim of her wineglass in slow, steady circles. She kept biting her bottom lip and her foot beneath the table wouldn't stop bouncing. He could feel the subtle motion inches away from his own feet.

She's actually into me, he thought, feeling both relief and dread at the idea.

And stress.

Chapter 32

December 20, 2013

"We have to capitalize on tonight," Arielle said, driving her and Selena across town for the WonderHome holiday party. "We didn't even know about this party during our planning. It feels like a gift being dropped into our lap."

It was the Friday evening before WonderHome would shut down for the entire week following the Christmas holiday. Felix was still struggling to hack into the company's system, but he remained persistent, confident a breakthrough loomed around the corner.

Tonight, however, was the holiday party set to take place at the Washington State Convention Center, where they would welcome over 1,000 guests. The company flew in their employees from all around the country for the celebration, and plus-ones were welcome.

"And if we have some fun along the way, that'll be fine, too," Selena said. She had unsurprisingly volunteered to get the outfits for the occasion, giddy to have a night out in a fancy dress. "It has an open bar."

"Just work your magic," Arielle said. "You're going to have an easier time than me. No one outside of my department even knows who I am. We don't work directly with too many others. But you seem to know everyone, so you need to play that card and get a conversation going with Adam."

"We can figure that out. It's a big party, lots of people and movement. I feel like I can strike up a conversation with anyone there tonight, even Michelle."

"Did you find it weird that she wants to see Felix again, but didn't ask him to be her date for the party?"

"Not at all. Someone of Michelle's status won't bring a date unless it's serious. Now, if she shows up with someone else, then we'll have some issues to address. But I would bet she's going to arrive solo and leave that way. No CEO wants to take any chance of a potential scandal or rumors. She's smart—she knows how to play this game."

"True. I think we need to strike up a conversation with Adam's wife. She might relay valuable information without even realizing it."

They had agreed tonight would be appropriate to be seen together in front of their coworkers. Few people would recognize Arielle thanks to her low-profile job, and most would assume she was simply Selena's friend.

"Don't you think this is weird? We're going to mingle with our subject and his wife. Like, we know this woman is going to kill her kids one day. Does that not bother you?"

"Well, no, not really. Because we're going to stop all that from happening. One thing I've learned in this line of work is that people aren't purely evil. I've seen my share of evil and those who hurt others for sheer amusement, but ninety percent of the rest are just good people being pulled into bad situations. I guarantee you when we meet Adam's wife, she will probably be someone you'll want to be friends with. The demons that plague her in the future don't even exist yet."

Selena nodded. "We're here."

They pulled into the convention center's parking garage, where they got into line for the valet parking, another tab picked up by WonderHome. The company spent just under three million dollars on the holiday party, not sparing a dime to provide the ultimate evening as a thank-you for the employees' hard work during the year.

Five minutes later, Arielle and Selena rode the elevator up from the garage, the doors opening to an obnoxiously elegant showcase of holiday festivities.

"Are those real people?" Selena asked as they stepped out of the elevator and started toward the long line forming at the check-in table. She nodded upward, where three people dressed as angels were hanging from the ceiling, floating with the grace of acrobats.

"What the hell?" Arielle replied. "Yeah, those are definitely real people."

Selena laughed, shaking her head. "Well, I'm glad we decided to not bring Felix as a date. He'd have a heart attack if he saw this."

They stood in line, mesmerized by the angels twirling their arms and legs in such slow, smooth motions that Arielle kept second-guessing if they really were humans or some sort of advanced mechanical robot. By the time they reached the check-in desk ten minutes later, they looked back to see the line wrapping around a corner, out of sight.

"Oh. My. God!" Becca cried. She had been manning the line at the check-in, eyes lighting up. "Selena and Arielle, you two are *fucking* hot! You look like supermodels. I've always known you're both pretty, but you know, it's at work. Arielle, look at your calves. Holy shit! Selena, you go on with your bad little body."

Arielle laughed, blushing. She had been hit on by plenty of men, but couldn't recall having ever received such an aggressive compliment from a woman. Plus, Becca was clearly beyond the point of tipsy, booze radiating from her breath.

"Why, thank you," Arielle said. "You look gorgeous tonight, too."

Becca batted her eyes at them before turning her attention to the list of names in front of her, crossing off Arielle and Selena. "You two are all set. We have an open bar, dance floor, silent disco, and games. Enjoy yourselves tonight. We also have free Ubers at the end of the party if you need transportation getting home safely."

"Thanks, Becca, we'll see you in there."

They continued beyond the check-in, handing their jackets off to a young man running a coat check station, and stepped into the grand ballroom.

There was a circular bar in the center of the room, a dozen bartenders hustling to serve the long lines forming. Against the wall nearest the entrance stood a photobooth station with two thirty-foot tall snowflakes on either side of equally massive letters that spelled out WonderHome. A replica of Santa Claus in his sleigh hung from the ceiling, being pulled by all the mythical reindeer. The dance floor far was along the back wall, where the booming of music and flashing lights lit up the otherwise dim ballroom.

To the left was the silent disco, a dance floor full of people wearing headphones with flashing lights. Beside them was a pool table, ping-pong, giant Jenga, and a miniature bowling alley.

"Seriously," Selena said. "Where are we? I feel like a little kid walking into Chuck E. Cheese for the first time."

Arielle laughed. "I don't know, but I think we're going to have some fun tonight. Look, our guy is here."

She nodded toward the bar where Adam and his wife were standing with Michelle and a small group from the executive team. They all had a shot glass in hand and were toasting before slamming them back.

Selena grinned. "When the CEO is doing shots, it's about to get rowdy up in here. Let's go."

Selena marched toward the bar, pulling Arielle by the wrist.

"Selena, what are you doing?" Arielle muttered under her breath.

"Just trust me, okay?"

Selena took them straight to the huddle formed around Michelle.

"Are we already doing shots?!" Selena asked, planting herself next to Adam. He shuffled aside to allow room for Arielle to join the circle.

"Selena!" Amara, the vice president of POPS cried out, reaching across the circle to hug her department's newest hire. "You look incredible. Everyone, Selena Nicole is the newest addition to our recruiting team. She has hit the ground running in her role, and we couldn't be any more excited to have her on the team. I think she has a long career ahead with WonderHome."

Arielle remained by Selena's side, feeling invisible, but not completely caring as she scanned the surrounding faces.

Michelle Garrison, CEO. Landon Greene, CFO, plus his wife. Raj Kalan, President of WonderHome, plus his wife. Mila Bachman, CMO, plus her wife. Adam and Emily Marshall.

"Well good," Landon said. "Maybe she can work her way up and take your job, Amara, so you can finally take that vacation."

They all burst into laughter, except for Arielle and Selena, who had clearly missed the inside joke.

The executives kept laughing and carried on a separate conversation. Arielle turned to Adam on her right. "You guys been here a while already?" she asked.

"No, just a few minutes, actually," Adam said. "We had a little too much fun at dinner before, though. When the CEO tells you to order whatever you want, what else can you do?"

He let out a nervous chuckle.

"Very true," Arielle replied, forcing a grin, pleased to know Adam was already being invited to such social events with his new boss. "I'm sorry, but I don't believe we've met before. I'm Arielle Lucila, and I work in software engineering."

"Oh!" Adam cried, sticking out his hand. "I'm Adam. I was just hired as Michelle's assistant."

"Congratulations."

"Thank you. And this is my wife, Emily." Adam half turned and pulled Emily by the waist to be at his side. She offered a polite smile before sticking out her hand.

"Nice to meet you," she said. "This is quite the party!"

"I'll say." Arielle looked over her shoulder to see Selena chatting with her VP, and couldn't help but feel a sense of pride in how confident the young actress had been in forcing this situation. No dancing around the subject, just walk up and start. Arielle felt relaxation spread over her, knowing she was in the driver's seat with the Marshalls now only speaking with her. "So you're new to WonderHome, but are you new to Seattle?"

"Far from it," Adam said. "I'm a Seattle native, and Emily has lived here since she was six, so practically a native, too."

"Oh, how cool! And how long have you been married?"

"Five years in April," Emily said proudly.

"That's great. Do you have any kids?" Arielle knew the usual checklist of topics people asked upon first meeting.

"A three-year-old boy and an eighteen-month-old girl," Emily said.

"She's one," Adam cut in, grinning. "Eighteen months is one and a half."

Emily laughed and playfully smacked Adam on his chest.

Arielle thought they were very much in love. They each kept a hand on one another, whether it was holding hands, an arm around the waist, or a caress on the back. They were in constant physical contact.

Arielle's heart ached. She hoped this hadn't been the case, as if them hating each other would somehow lessen the mounting pressure to complete their mission. But here they stood, just five months until they would arrest Adam and throw their life into shambles.

"Excuse me," Adam said. "I'm gonna get another drink. Do you ladies want anything? It's on the house."

He laughed, delighted with himself, and clearly tipsy.

"Oh, stop it, babe," Emily said, finally releasing her grip from Adam's back. "I'll have another vodka cranberry."

"I'll do the same," Arielle said. "Thank you."

Adam nodded before disappearing to the growing lines at the bar. Arielle saw Selena still consumed in the tight huddle of executives.

Now, Arielle had Emily Marshall alone, not another soul in the universe to speak with.

"So, Emily, how is Adam liking the new job? Honestly."

Emily looked around. "What do you mean? Every day he comes home and raves about working for WonderHome."

"Sure, the company is great. But what about his actual role? I've heard some horror stories about working directly for Michelle. She's intense. Cutthroat."

"You know, he's mentioned that he's seen that side of her, but never directed toward him. I suppose that's because he's getting his work done on time and correctly."

"Well, that's good. As long as Michelle is happy, then I suppose he'll be happy, too."

"Indeed. I think what he's enjoyed the most is he's doing meaningful work. He thought being the assistant would be more like a paid internship—getting coffee, booking appointments, that sort of stuff. But so far, the work has been whatever they need help with. He feels like the position is more of a tryout for a consistent role doing something else. But so far, he's enjoying dipping his toe in all the different departments."

Arielle could sense the excitement radiating from Emily. She was a proud wife who absolutely adored her husband. Thanks to her research, Arielle had already known about the struggles Adam had run into holding down various jobs. With his wife now in front of her, she heard the relief in her voice, like Adam had finally found that job and company he could spend the rest of his life with.

Adam had reached the bar and was ordering their drinks. She needed to speed this conversation up before he returned and veered their discussion in another direction.

"That's good to know," Arielle said. "I'll have to keep an eye out for him. Do you know if he does anything with the new real estate team?"

She felt this was the best opportunity to ask, and braced for the answer, the room seeming to fall silent as she shifted all of her focus to Emily's response.

"The real estate team? My goodness, that's been the main part of his job since he started."

Chapter 33

December 31, 2013

"Oh, my God," Felix cried out from the living room couch. "I'm in!"

It took until the last day of 2013, but Felix had finally broken through WonderHome's security.

The holiday party ended up a bust for Arielle and Selena. Shortly after Adam had returned with drinks, the group of executives had excused themselves from the small gathering, and disappeared through a door that Arielle assumed was a private meeting room for the upper echelon of the company to mingle in privacy, away from the noise and annoying lower-level employees.

Arielle's conversation with Emily Marshall had been the last of their interaction with that group.

"We know he's working on the real estate matters," Arielle had said during their ride back home after the party ended. "It wasn't a complete waste of time—we still learned something."

With the party landing on Friday evening, and the company closing their offices for the following week for Christmas, Arielle and Selena had gone a full ten days without going to work.

Felix, meanwhile, insisted Arielle take over the duties he normally handled while they were at work—cleaning, cooking, grocery shopping, and whatever else needed to be done around the house. Felix was close. He had known it. Sifting through thousands of lines of coding, trying tens of thousands of different passwords, and just wishing on a prayer to get into the system had pushed him to the brink of near madness.

Never mind the looming second date he had coming up with Michelle after the new year on Saturday.

"What?!" Arielle cried out, jumping up from her seat in the dining room. Selena lazed on the love seat in the living room, mesmerized by an all-day countdown of 2013's top music videos on the TV.

"I am *in!*" Felix shouted, now getting Selena's attention as she stirred back to reality and joined Arielle in front of Felix.

A smile stretched over his face with a look of complete shock that he had achieved this goal. His eyes were bloodshot from late nights staring at the screen, chugging caffeine to keep going. Arielle had warned him to take a break a week earlier, on Christmas night, but he hadn't.

He had worked straight through, insisting he had already celebrated 2013 Christmas in his Original Time, back when he was seventeen years old.

Now he could rest, satisfied with the work he had accomplished.

"I can see everything," he said, eyes refusing to break away from the laptop screen. "Internal chat messages, emails, HR reports on different departments."

"We're called *POPS*," Selena corrected him, her words

falling on deaf ears.

"Look," Felix said, raising his hand, showing them how much it was trembling.

"*Felix*," Arielle said in a disappointed motherly tone. "You need to go to sleep. I can't have you killing yourself on this mission."

He shook his head. "I'm not shaking because I'm exhausted—which I am. I'm shaking because I'm nervous . . . excited. I don't know. But we're in. We can find any communication that has taken place within WonderHome. Look."

He spun his laptop around to show the email inbox for Michelle Garrison.

"Holy shit!" Selena said. "Felix, you've just changed this mission. Do you know if you're going to stay in this, or is there a chance you somehow get kicked out?"

"There is always a chance of getting kicked out. But it's not likely. WonderHome keeps a running log of all activity happening on their VPN. Every single computer that logs into the VPN, all of their activity gets tracked. So yes, technically someone with the company *could* look over these logs and see I'm a non-employee with access."

"Well, that doesn't sound too promising," Arielle said, crossing her arms. "This will be fairly short-lived, then."

Felix raised a finger, spinning the computer back around to face him. "Not so fast. I'm logged in with full access, which means I can view this log and what happens within it. It appears to get checked every two weeks. This is fairly common because there are hundreds of thousands of line items on this log. Keep in mind, it spans the entire company, and not just the Seattle office. WonderHome has remote workers all over the country who sign in to this VPN at strange hours of the day. Most likely they make sure nothing looks out of the ordinary—say a mysterious login from a foreign country, or repeated attempts to log in to the company's bank portal. Things like that. My activity, while logged in, will look no different from a sales rep checking their email on the weekend. It will get lost in the shuffle with everything else, as long as we work out of it during business hours. We can do a couple of things on weekends and after hours, but I'd advise we only do that for urgent matters."

"Should we even be looking at anything right now?" Arielle asked. "The office closed at noon, and is off tomorrow for New Year's Day."

Felix looked at her, balled a fist, and pursed his lips so tightly they turned white. "No, you're right. We probably shouldn't. Dammit! We probably should wait until Thursday now."

Arielle reached out and grabbed Felix by his trembling arms. "Felix, breathe," she demanded. "We've been here two months without this access. I think we can wait two more days."

Felix's face soured. He despised this feeling. "I know, but it's right *here*." He jammed his finger into the laptop's screen, his voice coming out above a defeated whimper.

"Does the duration we're on a particular screen account for anything?" Selena asked.

Felix stared blankly at his laptop, Arielle releasing her grip from his arms.

"Felix?" Arielle asked.

"It shows up on the log," he said. "But I doubt that's something they even look for."

"Good," Selena said. "So instead of calling this feat a waste, we can at least examine Michelle's inbox. See what we can find out from there."

Felix grinned. His mind was wandering. He felt like he had just run a marathon, only to be told at the finish line that he actually had two more miles to go. Emotions rarely got the best of him, but he suddenly felt the urge to run through a brick wall.

He slammed the laptop shut, causing both Arielle and Selena to jolt back.

"Felix, really?" Arielle said, crossing her arms.

He stood up, hands elevated, all ten fingers spread wide apart. "No. You're right—I need to take a step back. I've been swimming in this mess long enough. I accomplished what we needed, but now we have to wait two days. Looking at those email subject lines will only drive us crazy and crank up the temptation. It's New Year's Eve. Let's celebrate with the rest of the world, and tomorrow we can find something else to do." He pointed a firm finger at the laptop. "Because if I flip that open one more time before Thursday, I cannot control what I do. So what do you say?"

Arielle checked her watch. "It's almost six o'clock. Why don't we go see a movie? Then we can grab a late dinner somewhere and decide what we want to do for the rest of the night."

"Deal," Felix snapped, his reply cutting off Selena, who had parted her lips.

"Okay then," Arielle said. "Let's head out. I believe one of the *Hunger Games* movies is showing right now."

Within five minutes, they had gathered what they needed, Felix looking over his shoulder on the way out, the laptop remaining on the couch.

Chapter 34

January 2, 2014

On the second day of the new year, Felix woke up at six o'clock in the morning to dig through everything he could find within WonderHome's system. Arielle and Selena had returned to the office, and hurried home at four o'clock that afternoon to see what all Felix had found.

Arielle had sent him a couple of text messages through-out the day hoping to learn something new. But he never responded.

When they strolled through the front door at 4:22, they found Felix still dressed in his pajamas, eyes sunken while he sat at the dining room table with his laptop open, papers scattered to cover nearly every inch of the table.

His work entranced him, eyes scanning up and down, before grabbing his pen to scrawl notes on a piece of paper. He repeated this action three times, paying no attention to Arielle and Selena, who had shuffled into the dining room.

"Felix?" Arielle called out.

He dropped his pen and jumped out of his seat. "Christ! Is it already four o'clock?!" He swiveled around to find the clock and smacked his forehead. "Oh, my God. I haven't eaten today. I haven't even brushed my teeth."

"You're nasty," Selena said, Felix blowing off her words and her friendly giggle.

"Felix, this isn't healthy," Arielle said. "We can't ask you to keep working if you're not taking care of yourself."

Felix shook his head, his hair a raggedy mess. "I know what you're saying, but I promise this wasn't intentional. I just . . . lost track of time."

"For *ten* hours?! Felix, c'mon. This is truly unacceptable."

"I know, and I won't do it again. And do you know what I have found after looking through hundreds—no, thousands—of emails today?! Go head, take a guess!"

He looked at them with crazed eyes and a somewhat terrifying smile.

"Not a single fucking thing!" he cried, slamming a fist on the table, sending a couple sheets of paper flying off the edge. He tossed his hands in the air. "I've read emails between Michelle and every executive in the company. Between her and the software development teams responsible for launching the real estate portion of the website. The legal department outlining the best way to launch this program free of lawsuits. Executives from the other national brokerages, some threatening her with those same lawsuits. All I could find was that Michelle Garrison doesn't give a damn what anyone has to say about her launching this new real estate team."

"So Michelle isn't responsible for the money laundering?" Arielle asked.

Felix shrugged. "Hell if I know. Let's talk about our guy, Adam Marshall. This dude gets hired and his first email is a list of responsibilities from Michelle. They're all over the place. Helping with the social media team, checking in with customer service on recurring issues. So many items, but nothing I could find regarding the real estate team. This is suspicious because his own wife admitted to Arielle at the holiday party that Adam was working a ton on the real estate matter. So why isn't there a single trace of it?"

"Felix, relax. We will figure this out together."

He laughed. Not at Arielle, but at the thought of there being an explanation to the mystery.

"I'm not sure what else we can do to figure it out. I looked through the inboxes of everyone on the executive team. All I could find was that this whole real estate thing was the CFO's idea, but even he had little involvement in getting it launched, aside from approving budgets for hiring and development."

"Okay," Arielle said, speaking forcefully to take control of the conversation. "Let's take a step back and consider all of this. We're just too early. And that's fine. This tells us they didn't launch the real estate program with the intent of money laundering. It started out as a legitimate stream of income. If we can't find anything connecting Michelle or Adam, or any of the executives, to the laundering scheme, then it has to mean it hasn't happened yet."

Felix nodded. "Okay. So I'll monitor things every day until we see something. But something is drastically off if Adam said he's working with the real estate team and nothing is showing up. How do you explain that?"

"Keep in mind it wasn't Adam who said that. It was his wife. We'll never understand how she's interpreting what Adam is telling her each night when he comes home. For all we know, Emily Marshall understands WonderHome is a real estate company her husband works for. We can't put too much weight on her words."

Felix crossed his arms, unsatisfied with such an explanation.

"Okay," he said. "So let's assume nothing has happened yet—I still don't buy it. What do we do next?"

"Selena and I will crank up our efforts at the office. Mainly to see what people are gossiping about. Perhaps we can start a rumor about Adam. Something that will look bad on him, and force Michelle to have a conversation with him. As of now, this might be our best play until new information comes through."

Selena smiled. "That's a good idea. And being in the POPS department, I'll get the inside scoop on how it all plays out."

"Perfect. We can plan to get that in motion tomorrow. What a better time to start a rumor than on a Friday. People will go out to happy hour after work and definitely let the gossip fly. Let them bask in it over the weekend, so when they come back on Monday, they'll have convinced themselves the rumor is true."

"What's our angle?" Selena asked. "Sexual harassment? Racism?"

Arielle shook her head. "I don't want to do anything like sexual harassment that could get the actual authorities involved. Too messy. Do you still have access to that first application Felix submitted under Adam's name?"

"We should."

"That's our play. We'll start a rumor that he sent in a fake resume. Make his entire presence at the company feel like a big lie. If we can get this rumor started tomorrow, maybe Felix can start planting the seed in Michelle's mind on their date on Saturday."

"That's already this Saturday?!" Felix gasped. He ran his fingers through his hair, making it stand up in messy spikes like he had just woken up. "I really have been so far out of the loop. I can't believe I have to go on another date with her."

"You do," Arielle said. "And it's going to be productive. If we can't find anything through the WonderHome system, then maybe we need to shift our focus to these executives' personal email accounts and phone lines."

Felix scoffed. "Oh, so now you just want me to do it all over again. For how many people? Forget the last two months I've spent trying to get into this damn system, right?"

Arielle pointed at Felix, anger rising to her surface. "That's not what I'm saying. I'm not even suggesting we do it, just throwing it out there as another option. Of course, we're going to exhaust everything we can before that point, which includes capitalizing on your next date. That said, I'm ordering you to not do any work tomorrow or Saturday morning. I need you to wash yourself up and get ready to play your role as her executive love interest. Because if we sent you out like this right now, she'll be sending you right back."

"What?! I don't think—"

"It's an *order*," Arielle snapped. "Not up for debate. Thank you."

The air left the room in a hurry. Even Selena's jaw hung open.

Felix balled a fist as he stared down Arielle, and she thought he might actually take a swing at her.

But he didn't.

"Look, Felix," she said. "Don't take this personally. You've done fantastic work, but I think you're overcompensating for all the downtime you had when we first got here. Look at you. You're still in your pajamas. I know you enjoy that your work is mostly from home, but this is a first for you. You look like someone who hasn't slept in a month. And *you* admitted to not even eating today. Are you hearing these words? Are they processing in your mind, or are you still stuck in the WonderHome system? Does any of this sound healthy or reasonable to you?"

His fist uncurled, but his burning glare remained fixed on Arielle. She could tell he was biting the inside of his mouth.

"She's right," Selena said, Felix swinging his head around to look at her. "We're just looking out for you. We all know you can get so deep and lost in your work. This time is bad, and you need to be pulled out. When's the last time you took a shower?"

Selena put her hands on her hips as she cocked an eyebrow to Felix. He licked his lips before shaking his head.

"I honestly don't know. I . . .I feel so dead inside."

Arielle noticed his bottom lip quivering and rushed to his side, throwing an embrace around him. He broke into intense tears, their moisture seeping through Arielle's shirt as Felix buried his face into her shoulder. Selena joined them, running a hand up and down Felix's back.

"Felix," Selena said. "Our work is important, but you don't have to take it to this extreme. It's okay to take a break and go for a walk. Breathe some fresh air. It will be better for your work in the long run. You *need* to take care of yourself, or else you become this...zombie."

Felix pulled away from Arielle, wiping his tears away as he stood to face his friends. "I don't know how to be any different," he said through a hoarse throat, prompting him to clear it. "I've always been this way. Since elementary school. If I'm working on something, and it requires any sort of problem-solving, I can't step away until I've solved it."

Selena grabbed Felix by the shoulders, and Arielle took a step back, knowing Selena had a more personal relationship with Felix than she did. Selena knew how to get through to him. "Dude, this is a seven-month mission. Don't you remember us talking about all the free time we'd get because the mission is so long? You can take weekends off. You can work normal hours and enjoy your evenings. We still have over five months until Adam gets arrested. You're not going to solve this mission overnight or on your own. Set a schedule and stick to it. Pace this out."

Felix nodded. "I'm too hard on myself. Part of me still believes we can finish this mission sooner than planned if we can just crack the code. But it won't be that simple."

"If it was," Arielle said. "We'd have no jobs."

Felix laughed. "Okay. Thank you both."

"I mean it, Felix," Arielle said. "Take tomorrow off, and the entire weekend—beside your date with Michelle. Go do something fun to clear your mind. And jump back in Monday morning refreshed. I bet you'll look at that WonderHome system with a whole new perspective."

Felix nodded. "Okay. I'll do that. Now, what exactly do I need to prepare for this date with Michelle?"

Chapter 35

January 4, 2014

After a day off, where Felix spent the morning walking around Pike Place Market and the afternoon at Mount Rainier National Park, Felix not only felt like a new person, but empowered to take control of his role.

What Selena had said was true. They had five months left until the authorities would barge into the WonderHome offices and take Adam Marshall away. Five months meant it wasn't time to panic, but to focus and use time efficiently.

The opportunity in front of Felix was uniquely his. He had access to Michelle Garrison's work inbox and was currently driving to his next date with her. If he could nail down the intricacies of a faux romance and truly get Michelle interested in him, there was no telling how he could leverage all the information he would gain.

The first date had gone well enough, considering he had been a nervous wreck. Now, on the second date, he could finally appreciate this as part of the mission and something he was being entrusted to handle for the sake of the team. Gaining Michelle's trust was simply another puzzle he needed to figure out. Her desire for a second date proved she had some sort of interest in him.

Felix pulled up to a sports bar called My Oh My in the Pioneer Square neighborhood. With their first date at an obnoxiously formal restaurant, Michelle asked Felix what he would like to do on their second date. He suggested they grab a quick dinner downtown before going on one of the underground city tours offered all around town. He expected Michelle to push back and was pleasantly surprised when she agreed with much enthusiasm.

"I've never done one of those tours but have always wanted to!" she said over their brief phone call to make arrangements.

Felix had suggested the date idea not just to avoid the lights and glamour of the filthy rich. Getting Michelle out of that scene would loosen up her personality. She would get to be a regular person on a normal date. Maybe they'd even get ice cream at the end of the night.

He parked and entered the bar, finding it crowded with people watching the Saturday slate of NFL playoff games. The local Seahawks were in the playoffs as a big favorite to win the Super Bowl (they would), but they were on a bye week, leaving everyone to watch who they would match up with the following weekend.

Much to Felix's delight, he found Michelle seated at a booth for two along the outer perimeter, away from the drunken, howling fans. He pushed his way through the crowd, admiring the decorations on the walls celebrating the Seahawks, Sounders, and Mariners.

"Well, this is fun!" Michelle said with a big smile, standing up to hug Felix before he sat down. She pulled him in a little tighter than he expected.

"I know it's not a fancy place," Felix said. "But what do you think?"

Michelle looked around. A table of five men doing shots. A couple trying to find the back of each other's throats with their tongues. Waitresses somehow navigating through it all with wide trays of drinks that never spilled.

"I love it," Michelle said. "I never come to places like this."

"Why not?" Felix asked, his focus kicked into the absolute highest gear. If conversation veered into a random void, he'd guide it back to something relevant, even if just getting to know Michelle better as a person. Felix had learned from his last mission that the better you understood your subject, the better you could anticipate their next actions. And that ability only came from knowing someone as deeply as possible.

Michelle drummed her fingers on the table. "Not to sound like a total snob, but when you reach a certain level of wealth, your circle of friends changes. It's nothing malicious or intentional. I guess lifestyles and interests change. I don't exactly have friends these days who would invite me out for beer and a burger at a sports bar, even though I totally enjoy it."

"You like sports?" Felix salivated at the opportunity of having something they could actually bond over. No acting needed.

"I grew up in a small town where Friday night football games were as important as going to church on Sunday. I've never gotten into other sports, but I love me some football. I'm so excited for the Seahawks right now. I really think they can win it all."

"I have a hunch they will," Felix said, offering a sly grin. "They'll cruise to victory. Do you ever get to go to the games?"

"I go to a few each season. I'm good friends with Jody . . . the owner's sister."

Of course you are, Felix thought, actually doing cartwheels inside. The woman sitting across from him knew Bill Gates, so naturally she knew his co-founder of Microsoft, Paul Allen, and his sister. *Five minutes in, and not one mention of work.*

"That's really cool," Felix said. "So how has work been for you?"

He hoped the question didn't come out as dismissive of what they had been talking about.

"Oh," she said. "It's been good. Always exciting to have a new year ahead."

Felix nodded. "I know what you mean. How was the holiday party? Last time we went out, I think you said it was the following night."

Michelle smiled, reminiscing. "It was spectacular. My team really went all-out. It was more of a production than a party. I'd say everyone left with a big smile on their face. How was the Starbucks party? I assume they had one."

Felix froze. If Starbucks had a holiday party, he had no idea where it was, or what day it had fallen on. And it was entirely possible Michelle knew these details, considering she was connected to everyone in Seattle.

"It was good, from what I can remember," Felix said with a laugh.

"Ahhh, one of those nights? Can't blame you. You're young, though—you can handle it."

Michelle bit her bottom lip, and Felix could sense the lust radiating from across the table. He had never been so grateful for a mob of people to holler like they did when a running back for the New Orleans Saints broke free for a sixty-yard touchdown run. The distraction made it impossible to hear anything else, forcing their conversation into a brief hiatus.

"Lots of Saints fans here tonight," Michelle said once the noise returned to a more bearable level.

"I'll say."

A server stopped by their table to take their order. Michelle ordered a beer and wings, impressing Felix, who ordered the same thing.

"I heard something interesting last night about an employee at your company," Felix said.

"Oh, gossip? This should be good. What was it?"

Michelle seemed genuinely unconcerned, as if she heard this type of statement at least twice a week.

"Well, the word is someone named Adam—I forget his last name—applied with a fake resume and still landed a job. An important job, by the sounds of it. The details weren't too clear."

Michelle sat frozen, her eyes reading Felix, trying to figure if this was a joke. "How did you hear about this?"

Felix's stomach flipped in a violent cartwheel. He struck a nerve and had no clue how it would all play out. She could storm out of the bar right now, and he would forever beat himself up for ruining the mission. Self-doubt immediately crept back into his mind for the first time on this date. Had he gotten too greedy?

"I, uh, I was at a happy hour last night. Lots of execs from all around Seattle. I don't even remember who I heard it from, but people were talking about it."

"Fuck," Michelle muttered under her breath, shaking her head. "Not good. How the hell do people already know about this? Do people have no lives in this city?"

Felix sensed rage from across the table, but didn't feel it directed toward him. "So it's true?" he asked in a soft voice that could barely be heard.

Their server returned and placed two steins of beer on the table, along with a basket of French fries. Michelle immediately stuffed four into her mouth and washed them down with an exaggerated swig of the beer.

"I don't even know the details yet. They literally alerted me of this yesterday, but honestly, it's not as big of a deal as everyone might think."

"How do you figure?"

Felix leaned forward in his seat, elbows planted on the table, the beer the furthest thing from his mind.

"The employee in question is my assistant, Adam. He started about a month ago, and has been exemplary in his work."

"How does something like this even happen?" Felix asked, needing to test the waters and make sure nothing was being tied back to Arielle or Selena.

Michelle shrugged. "Word of mouth. We could try to trace it back to the source, but with over 500 employees in the building, that would be nothing but a pointless witch hunt. I have my recruiting team looking into the matter, and they should have something for me on Monday."

"Have you asked Adam about it?"

"No. I had sent him home a couple of hours early yesterday. We're still a little slow to start the new year, so I always try to make life easier for my assistants when I can. That way, I can grind them to dust when it gets busy again." She let out a laugh and took another long drink from her stein. Felix finally did the same.

"You know, I think you should take this a little more seriously. Regardless of what you find, people might think they can fake their way into WonderHome, especially if they hear this happened, *and* the employee remains with the company. In a time where so many people would love to work for a company like yours, you need to show you take this allegation serious. Or else you'll be bombarded with fake applications."

"Is that what people are saying they'll do?" Michelle asked in a near gasp.

"No, no, no. Nothing like that was said. I just know how people in my generation act, so I'm imaging how it can all play out if you do nothing. Worst-case scenario, of course."

"I can talk to Adam, but would he admit this so freely?"

Felix shrugged. "I don't know the guy. You'll have to be the one who reads him. Maybe wait until you see him in person."

"I have a hard time believing it. Adam is an incredibly focused worker and a good family man."

"Good people can do bad things when they're desperate. How well did you know him before hiring him?"

"One of my close friends had suggested I interview him. They said they knew Adam, his family, and vouched for him. I have no reason to think my friend would be in on some sort of scheme. Then again, he had a guaranteed interview because of the mutual connection. He had no reason to lie because I was going to interview him regardless of what his resume said. He used to manage a grocery store—not exactly the qualifications we look for when hiring an administrative assistant. What do you think? Have you ever heard of something like this happening?"

Felix drew a deep breath and looked around to feign deep

thought. Inside, he was dancing. Boogeying. Michelle had complete trust in Felix for even entertaining this conversation.

"I think you need to take a step back and look at the big picture. As of now, this is just a rumor. So someone started it, completely made up, intending to harm Adam's career. Does he have any haters at the office? Anyone who can gain something by him losing his job? Or on the flip side, it is true, and Adam bragged about it to someone, setting in motion the rumors himself. Because if it's true, who else would know about it besides Adam?"

Michelle leaned back and rubbed her fingers frustratingly on her temples. "I don't know what to think. I don't want to deal with either of those scenarios. Damn it all."

Felix reached across the table and caressed Michelle's arm. "Look, maybe it's not a big deal like you think, but you need to do *something*. Brushing it under the rug is the absolute wrong choice."

The move startled Michelle in a good way. Her eyes fell to Felix's hand, then moved back to him. She leaned back and grabbed his hand.

"Thank you," she said. "I'll have to deal with this on Monday. I need to know how widespread this rumor is. Do I need to address the entire company, or is it much smaller than that? This is not how I was planning to start the new year."

"If you give it proper attention, this whole matter can be behind you before next weekend, and you can get back to your regularly scheduled plans."

The server returned, this time with two baskets of chicken wings. Michelle's mood had gone through a whirlwind in the last ten minutes. Felix almost felt bad about it, but this was business, after all. And business was good today.

Then it got even better.

"Say," Michelle said. "Would you like to join me at the Seahawks playoff game next weekend?"

Chapter 36

January 8, 2014

On Wednesday, Arielle and Selena arrived home after work, Selena steaming with fury. Felix was in the kitchen, tending to a boiling pot of chicken noodle soup he had prepared for dinner.

Selena tossed her purse and car keys on the counter and immediately poured herself a glass of wine.

"What's wrong?" Felix asked, looking at Arielle for guidance, only to receive a tight-lipped grin.

"Your girlfriend is letting him off the hook," Selena said, taking a sip from the wineglass as she leaned back against the counter, staring at the ceiling in disbelief. "You know, it would be one thing for her to actually acknowledge what happened and address it. Share her thoughts on the matter. But *no*, she wants to leave us all out in the dark."

"Selena," Felix said. "I have no idea what you're talking about. Would you mind explaining?"

"We've had this investigation open since the first thing Monday morning. It was supposed to be perfect, because I was directly involved, especially since I was the one who 'accidentally' deleted the application from Adam that is now in question. This was supposed to help our mission. I spent all of Monday and yesterday digging up the details, and writing a report to make it look like Adam definitely submitted a fake application. I spoke with everyone involved in his hiring. My team lead even asked me questions and helped me write this report—I'm so pissed! We *had* him right where we wanted."

Selena took another sip of wine and paced frenzied circles around the kitchen, looking like a college professor so deep in her lecture that she wouldn't hear anyone's question.

"Yesterday afternoon, we sent the report with our findings to my manager. She read it, agreed that Adam had applied with a fake resume, and sent it further up the chain to our VP. Within thirty minutes myself, my team lead, and my manager were called into the VP's office. She thanked us for our work and basically double-checked everything we mentioned in the report. 'These are serious allegations,' she told us. 'Adam will probably lose his job. Michelle isn't going to like it, but that's where we are after reading this.' Do you have any idea how excited I was? I wanted to break open the window in her office and shout it to all of Seattle. We had done it. Somehow, some way, we framed Adam Marshall for this silly offense and he was going to be fired. Mission complete. Let's go home."

"I take it that's not what happened," Felix said, earning the most intimidating glare from Selena.

"I take it you haven't checked Michelle's sent messages this afternoon," Selena replied, mocking Felix's voice.

"I haven't since about three o'clock. That's when I started on this soup."

Selena pointed to Felix's laptop, still sitting on the kitchen table. "Why don't you turn that on and pull open the email she sent to the four of us who put this report together?"

Felix turned the dial down on the stove before crossing the kitchen and taking a seat behind his laptop. He flipped it open and punched in his password, then logged in through the back-channel VPN he spent months figuring out.

"Okay, I got it," Felix said.

"Read it out loud," Selena said, crossing her arms as she finally stopped walking in circles. She returned to the counter where she had left the bottle of wine and poured a second glass.

"From Michelle Garrison to Susie Foster, Amara Edwards, Janina Victoria, and Selena Nicole. This one, right?"

"Mmhmm."

"Hello team," Felix said, eyes glued to the screen as he read the email. "Thank you so much for your hard work in preparing this report. Me and the executive team have reviewed the details and have decided, at this time, to disregard the incident as a misunderstanding. Mr. Marshall will remain employed with WonderHome. Thank you."

Selena shuddered. Felix thought her head might fly off the hinges of her neck.

"The past," Arielle said. "Always protecting itself. This one is impressive. I wonder what was said that allowed this to happen."

"Let's see if we can find anything," Felix said, clicking out of the email and searching through the rest of Michelle's inbox.

"I'm just in so much shock," Selena said. "This was a slam dunk for us. I don't understand."

"How did your bosses take it?" Felix asked.

"I don't know about Susie, but I'm pretty sure Amara threw a stapler at the wall. She was in her office with the door closed when this email came into our inboxes, and we all heard a loud bang. All we could see was her standing over her desk, huffing and puffing. She's always so gentle, despite my intimidating first impression of her. I've never seen her so pissed off; I could only assume it was because of that email."

"Well, we can likely eliminate her as a suspect. Why would she get involved with the other execs after something like this?"

"Not necessarily," Arielle said. "If anything, I'd say this makes her a bigger suspect. We're trusting the laundering scheme is coming from somewhere in the executive team. What if Amara comes up with the idea of framing Adam to get her own personal revenge for this? I don't think it's likely, but we should see how things play out in the coming weeks."

"I don't get it," Felix said, rubbing his forehead. "There are no emails between Michelle and anyone else regarding this matter. Not even an initial one that brought it to her attention. Do people in the company not email her? Do they just stop in her office to share information like this?"

"Did you check Adam's email?" Arielle asked. "He might field everything for her before deciding what she actually needs to deal with."

"I did, and still nothing. Obviously, they wouldn't include him in anything about this. I checked all the executives' inboxes and none mentioned this. Michelle claims to have met with the executive team, but did she really?"

"We need to bug her office," Arielle said. "I wanted to avoid it because of the risk, but we have no choice. How can we go about it? There are security cameras in the hallway outside of her office pointing right at her door. It records anyone who goes in and out."

"Do you know how closely those are watched?" Felix asked. "What if you tried after hours?"

"I'm honestly not sure. It's my understanding that both WonderHome and the building security have access to the feed. Do you know, Selena?"

She nodded. "They're watched and reviewed pretty regularly."

"Does Michelle ever have groups meet in her office?" Felix asked, running down a mental checklist of possibilities to get into the coveted office.

"As far as I know, only with the executive team," Selena said. "I can't imagine a scenario that would get me or Arielle into her office on official business. Even if we had a concern for the CEO, we'd get told to run it through Amara."

"Same for me," Arielle said. "We don't even know what the inside of her office looks like, either. Say we got in somehow, we'd have to figure out where to plant the bug, and how to do it without getting seen by anyone else in the room. All on the spot."

"For an office," Felix said. "Under the desk is always best. It's the one area that gets completely neglected, even by the cleaners—they don't dust the underside of a desk."

"What about tapping her phone line?" Selena asked.

Felix shook his head. "Way too risky. Especially if the feds will investigate her in a few months. They'll find the wiretap, and who knows what kind of mess that would cause."

The room fell silent as they all grew discouraged at the prospect ahead of them. After a minute, Felix cleared his throat and said, "I have an idea that just may work, but it all depends how my date with her this weekend goes."

Chapter 37

January 11, 2014

A chilly wind slashed across Felix's cheeks as he stepped out of the car. Arielle had just dropped him off outside of CenturyLink Field, home to the Seattle Seahawks and their playoff game against the New Orleans Saints that would begin in less than an hour.

The energy outside the stadium hummed unlike anything Felix had experienced at a sporting event. Swarms of fans wearing navy blue and neon green crowded the sidewalks and streets as they made their way into the game. People poured out of the several neighboring bars, marching toward the stadium.

Felix needed to fit in, especially if he was going to be in a private suite for friends of the owner. It was the one shopping trip he had wanted to make, going out to buy a Russell Wilson jersey and a Seahawks beanie hat to match. He looked and *felt* like he belonged as he pushed through the crowd toward the exclusive VIP entrance that had a line of only two other fans getting wanded by security.

Michelle had left his ticket at will call on Friday, and he picked it up that same day to avoid the long lines before the game. The mission aside, Felix couldn't believe he was actually going to experience a playoff game from the comfort of a luxury suite. Sure, he already knew the outcome of the game, but the energy was about to boil over inside the stadium that had become known as the loudest and most difficult to play in for visiting teams.

Felix checked in at security, a chipper guard patting him down before running the metal-detecting wand across his body. After being cleared, Felix stepped into a world he had never seen before. Even with all the money and connections he had through the Road Runners, he had never watched a game from a suite. Front row was his preferred location, but he was already seeing how the closest seats lacked the amenities of a suite ticket.

Instead of walking on the typical dusty concrete floor most outdoor stadiums had, he strolled along a carpet decorated with the Seahawks logo in a dizzying pattern. The entryway turned into a hallway with a concession stand, merchandise shop, and private elevators.

Felix took the elevator up to the suite level, where he found himself on a concourse that seemed much too quiet for a playoff game. It was a fairly even mix of fans dressed in Seahawks attire and others in suits and dresses. The suite concourse welcomed luxury. A massive sculpture of a flock of twelve hawks flying hung from the ceiling. There were fondue and carving stations, a handful of bars serving top-shelf liquor, a dessert tower, and an array of concession stands serving everything from sushi to hot dogs and the typical stadium grub.

These people know how to take in a game, Felix thought, suddenly wondering what he had been missing out on his whole life. *I wonder if I can buy a suite at Coors Field or Ball Arena when I get back.*

Overwhelmed, Felix checked his ticket for his suite number and made his way through the concourse, scanning the ticket outside the door of suite number four to unlock it. He pushed open the door to a suite full of at least thirty people, surveying the room for Michelle.

He found her at the suite's own private carving station; the chef preparing top sirloin. Through the window, Felix saw they were right around midfield, and was delighted that the view seemed closer to the field than he had always imagined.

"Why, hello there," Felix said, sliding next to Michelle.

"Oh, my goodness!" Michelle cried, throwing her hands in the air and wrapping them around Felix's shoulders. "I'm so glad you made it. You got in no problem?"

She released him and took a step back, Felix relieved to see her dressed in a Seahawks hoodie and jeans to match his casual outfit.

"I wouldn't miss this for the world. This has already been an incredible experience, and the game hasn't even started."

"First time in a suite?" Michelle asked.

"Yes, actually. I didn't even realize it was my first time until I stepped into the private entrance. I'm hooked!"

"Well, that's good. Let me introduce you to my friend."

Michelle grabbed Felix by the wrist and pulled him through the crowded suite, where huddles formed with the different cliques present.

They reached a standing table near the window overlooking the field where both teams were finishing their warm-ups. A woman wearing a Seahawks jersey with the name "Allen" on the back was enjoying a plate of lobster when Michelle reached out to touch her shoulder.

She turned around, brushing back her short reddish-blond hair.

"Jody," Michelle said. "This is my good friend Felix. Felix, this is Jody."

Felix's eyes bulged as he reached out a shaky hand. "It's such an honor to meet you, Ms. Allen. I'm a big fan of you and your brother's work."

Jody smiled and shook his hand. "Why thank you, sir. I'd like to say Paul will make it to our suite today, but he's dealing with some business on the other side of the field. Besides, he likes to wander down to the sidelines a couple times during the game. I'm glad you're here. Make yourself at home and let Benny know if you need anything."

"I still need to show him around and introduce him to Benny," Michelle said, running a hand up and down Felix's back. He was too awestruck with everything to even realize it.

"Of course. Hopefully, we'll have some champagne to celebrate a win at the end of the game."

"We'll win tonight," Felix said. "We actually won't lose again for the rest of this season."

"Now that's what I like to hear," Jody said. "I like this guy, Michelle. You bring him back next week if we win. I'm sorry, *when* we win."

Felix looked over and saw Michelle blushing, snapping him back to the reality that he was on a date with the CEO of WonderHome to learn who was responsible for the money laundering that sent Adam Marshall to prison.

"*When* we win, of course," Michelle replied.

"You two have a fun time. I gotta check on a couple of things, but I'll be popping in and out during the game." Jody grabbed her plate and vanished through the crowd on a mission.

"She's not Bill Gates," Michelle said to Felix. "But what did you think of Jody Allen? It's not every day you get to meet the owner of a sports franchise."

"She's a lot more down-to-earth than I would have thought."

Michelle nodded. "She's always been that way. The money never changed her. She believes in her work and the causes their foundation supports."

"That's admirable. I hope to be a billionaire one day. It's sort of a life goal of mine."

"Well, if that's your goal, you're in the right room. Obviously, not everyone here is a billionaire, but there are several worth nine figures. Strike up conversations, pick their minds. It's honestly the only way to get anywhere near that sort of status."

Michelle's response caught Felix off guard. Normally when he shared this dream—often to others his age—people would laugh it aside, not taking it seriously. But Michelle didn't so much as flinch, and even encouraged him. Presumably, everyone packed into this suite wanted to become a billionaire one day, and that was simply what everyone was talking about, from what Felix could hear from the surrounding conversations.

Minutes before a playoff game was about to start and not a single discussion of how the Seahawks would beat the Saints. Stocks, investment accounts, business ventures, risks, failures, success stories. Rich people talked about money almost exclusively, and Felix was taking notes.

He also felt bad for them. For Felix, becoming a billionaire wasn't a matter to elevate his status in society. It wasn't even to afford himself a better life—he could earn unlimited funds through the Road Runners. He wanted the challenge of earning such an astronomical amount of money through his own work and ideas. And when he reached it, all that money would go right back into the community to lift others to the next level in their lives.

"Well, I appreciate you bringing me today," Felix said. "I'm honored."

"You're a good guy, Felix. I can tell that much already, and I see nothing but bright things in your future."

"Thank you. Can I get you anything else before the game starts?"

"No, I'm good for now."

The mood had lightened, and Felix was ready to attack. "Say, I've been wondering since we saw each other last. Whatever happened to that employee at your company?"

Michelle rolled her eyes. "A false alarm. There was definitely cause for concern, but it looks like there was another applicant who had the same name as my assistant. They applied a few days before my assistant did, which caused all of this suspicion. It was a brief hiccup, but everything is back to normal now. And thank goodness, because Adam has been an absolute lifesaver. I invited him to join us here today, but he wasn't able to make it. He'll be free next weekend, if there's a game."

"Well, I look forward to meeting him."

Felix was content to let the conversation drift wherever it needed for the rest of the evening, for a new opportunity had come into play. There *would* be a game next weekend, this he already knew, and he'd get his chance to question Adam Marshall.

Chapter 38

January 19, 2014

The next week flew by for all three Angels. Arielle and Selena had put in another routine week at the WonderHome offices, where Arielle continued to fake her way through her job. She considered leaving the job in the coming weeks to dedicate more time with Felix in trying to resolve their mission from behind the scenes. Her colleagues rarely carried on meaningful conversations, let alone shared gossip from around the office. She was finding her time at the office a headache and a waste of time. Felix was still figuring out the logistics of keeping their access to the WonderHome system without Arielle's VPN connection.

Selena had received an Employee of the Month award for her efforts in December, for not only ramping up so quickly after her training, but hitting the ground running. The perks of the award came with a wooden plaque, an extra day of paid time off, and a fifty-dollar gift card to spend on Amazon.

Sometimes Selena seemed to veer off into her own world, and they wondered if she forgot she was working on a mission and not actually an employee for WonderHome.

None of that mattered on the following Sunday evening,

when the Seahawks were to square off against the San Francisco 49ers for a chance to advance to Super Bowl XLVIII.

Felix was indeed invited back. Michelle had been out of town all week for a conference in Texas, so Felix had no opportunity to execute his plan to get into her office and plant a bug. He'd have to navigate one more successful date to keep those hopes alive.

By the time he arrived at the stadium, dressed in the same attire as the prior week, he strolled through the VIP entrance with an extra hop in his step. His confidence soared after last weekend, and knowing he'd have the chance to meet Adam Marshall today had carried him through the week.

By the end of the first quarter, when Adam had yet to appear, Felix asked Michelle where he was.

"Adam isn't going to make it," she explained. "I guess his in-laws are in town and he couldn't make it work."

"But it's the NFC championship," Felix said, as a genuinely concerned citizen of sports fandom.

Michelle shrugged. "I suppose that's one reason to not get married."

She cackled at this, and Felix joined.

He had rarely given thought to marriage, considering he rarely even went on dates. But if missing a hot ticket item like the NFC championship was at risk, then maybe marriage would forever remain off the table. Sweat dripped down his back just thinking about such an atrocity.

So they sat through the game, carrying on the usual small talk with Michelle, high-fiving at the opportune moments. Despair hung in the stadium at the start of the fourth quarter when the Seahawks were trailing by four and looking out of sorts. After a long touchdown pass to take their first lead of the game, the building erupted with the energy it was known for, staying that way while the team closed out their rival and punched their ticket to face the Denver Broncos in the Super Bowl two weeks later.

Champagne bottles popped in the suite, some for drinking, some for spraying around to celebrate. Felix was glad to have remained in the outdoor seating on the other side of the glass when this happened, but appreciated the sentiment just the same.

Michelle tapped him on the shoulder while they watched the team gather on the field to receive their NFC championship trophy. "Would you like to come over to my place and have a drink?" she asked, the question instantly removing Felix from the excitement on the field and spinning his stomach into the tightest knots he could remember having ever felt.

He gulped, leery of how Michelle envisioned the night would go.

I can't bail right now, he thought. *I haven't even bugged her office yet. If I don't go, she could get upset. She's not afraid to jump around to different men, and I can't get left out of the picture.*

"Sure," Felix said, trying to sound remotely interested.

A grin spread across Michelle's face. "Let's go."

They spent a couple minutes telling people goodbye as they made their way out of the suite. Everyone had been too drunk or too distracted by the celebration to pay them any attention.

"Do you need a ride, or did you drive here?" Michelle asked when they reached the street level.

"I drove."

"Great. You can follow me. Do you know how to get to Medina?"

"Yes."

They walked one block to the parking garage that had a VIP section on the main level, an added perk to having a suite ticket. Felix walked Michelle to her car.

"Race you there," she said, winking at him as she closed the door.

His stomach dropped more. *This old lady wants to sleep with me.*

Felix tried to erase the image from his mind. He had never tried to get out of sex before, and wasn't even sure where to begin. Headache? Stomachache? He could take a bunch of shots of alcohol when they arrived and give himself whiskey dick. He even considered being honest with Michelle by explaining he wasn't ready to get physical.

Michelle, however, was a wild card. It had been four dates, and he couldn't get a solid read on the things that bothered her, or the things that brought her pleasure.

You are the pleasure she wants, Felix thought, gagging at the thought. *You and your young, tight body.*

"Fuck," Felix cried out as he found his car and got behind the wheel.

He backed out and saw Michelle waiting ahead at the garage exit. Since everyone was still inside the stadium celebrating, traffic was at a minimum. Part of him had hoped it would take too long to leave the premises, and he could make up an excuse that he had to go home and get ready for work in the morning.

But it was only 7:30, and the city of Seattle was rocking with their Super Bowl ambitions.

Because there was no traffic, it only took them twenty minutes to arrive at Michelle's home.

It wasn't the castle they had all expected, but it was still a stunning two-story home with a perfectly manicured front lawn. Michelle pulled into the driveway and parked in the garage. Felix stopped behind and stepped out of the car with hundreds of different things he could say to throw off the scent of attraction.

"Do you mind if I use your restroom?" he asked as he entered the garage, Michelle promptly closing the door behind him. "I'm not sure those nachos are sitting too well with me."

"My goodness, are you okay?" she asked.

"I think so. Just need a minute."

"Absolutely. Let's head in."

She hurried out of her car, a silver Mercedes sedan with a license plate of *WONDER*.

When she opened the side door, they entered a dark foyer until she flicked on a light to reveal a laundry room complete with a coat rack and a small bench, where she slipped out of her shoes and tucked them into a basket.

"If you don't mind, please take off your shoes here," she said, pulling out a second basket from under the bench.

Felix obliged.

The foyer opened to a hallway connecting the living room to a family room, a spiral staircase in the middle that led upstairs.

"I'm sorry, Michelle, but where is that bathroom?" Felix asked, trying to make his words sound urgent. He hoped Selena would approve of his acting skills.

"Yes, second door on your right." She gestured down the hallway, where the door stood ajar across from the staircase.

Felix let himself in and raised the toilet seat with an audible *clank!* for dramatic effect.

Okay, how the hell do I get out of here? Felix asked himself, standing over the sink and studying himself in the mirror. He took off his Seahawks beanie to find his hair a frazzled mess. He debated cleaning it up, but left it to look as unappealing as possible. *How long can I stay in here until she comes knocking?*

Felix didn't know the rules of etiquette that most of society played by, and wondered if this was even a thing. Surely, common courtesy called for a host to check on their guest if they were in the bathroom for over five minutes. Ten, maybe?

His face flushed a light shade of red, so he turned on the sink to splash some water on cheeks.

"Dammit," he muttered under his breath. Felix always kept a backpack with tools he might need, and he'd love to bug Michelle's house in as many places as possible. But the backpack was on the passenger seat of his car.

Just don't ruin the night. She likes you, and you need to leverage that until you can at least bug her office at WonderHome.

Felix grew nauseous and wondered if he hung over the toilet for a minute, if he could force his body to vomit. Then he wouldn't have to pretend to be sick to leave.

He shook his head and froze at the sound of footsteps approaching from the hallway outside.

"Felix?" Michelle called out. "Everything okay?"

It had been five minutes, and Felix knew he had overstayed his welcome in the bathroom.

"Yes," he shouted back. "I'll be right out."

"Would you like a drink?"

"Yes, please. Whiskey or scotch."

"Okay. I'll meet you in the kitchen."

Felix had no idea where the kitchen was, nor did he care. He figured he had one last minute before needing to step out.

He flushed the toilet and blasted the sink. "Okay," he said

to himself. "One drink and we're out of here." His reflection nodded back in understanding.

Felix killed the flowing water and drew a deep breath before spinning around to open the door.

The hallway was abandoned, but the lights were on everywhere in the house. Music carried from down the hallway, some sort of smooth jazz, so he followed it towards what he presumed was the kitchen.

"Jesus Christ," he whispered to himself as he stepped in. Sure, the kitchen was state-of-the-art and would have normally earned all of his attention, but what had really caught him off guard was Michelle.

She stood along one counter, pouring two glasses of whiskey, dressed in lingerie. Navy blue panties and bra, and a neon green see-through robe that stopped at her upper thighs, opened at her chest to reveal her cleavage while a bow tied the rest of it snugly around her waist.

Michelle hummed along to the music, grinning while she screwed the top back onto the bottle of whiskey.

"Did someone ask for a drink?" she asked, grabbing the glasses and gliding across the floor toward Felix.

His heart drummed madly in his head, adrenaline slipping into his veins as sheer panic settled in. He had mentally prepared for this moment—granted, not so soon.

Michelle stopped in front of him and extended a glass, which he grabbed and promptly took a sip. As much as he had dreaded this, he couldn't resist looking her up and down. Her body was tight and chiseled, but what Felix was now finding the most attractive was her confidence that seemed to seep through every crack in the house.

"What do you think?" Michelle asked, swaying her hips

side to side to ensure Felix saw every curve of her body. "It's Seahawks colors. Don't you want to keep celebrating?"

Discipline was a universal trait across all members of the Angel Runners. When altering the past, temptation was practically guaranteed on any mission, whether emotional, mental, or, in this case, physical.

Michelle reached out with her free hand and ran a finger down the center of Felix's chest, not stopping until she reached his waistband. Heat pulsed in his crotch, and he knew it was time to make a move.

He threw his head back and gulped the remaining whiskey. "I'm sorry, Michelle," he said, keeping his voice soft and his eyes on her face for a reaction. "I'm not feeling too well right now."

"Oh?" Michelle took a step back and placed her glass on the counter. "Is there something wrong with me?"

"Whoa, no, not at all. My God, it's my *stomach*, not you. You're . . . incredible."

A tender smile touched her lips at this compliment.

"I really think something from the game is not settling well with me," Felix continued, running his hand in a circle over his stomach. "I thought the shot of whiskey might help, but I'm not feeling any better yet."

Felix wondered how many other men his age had found themselves in this same predicament in Michelle's house. They probably raced to take their clothes off, of course, not find an emergency exit out.

"Do you want to lie down?" Michelle offered, now hugging herself to keep her lacy robe closed over her body.

"I think I should get home, actually. Would hate for me to get worse and have to drive home any later. I think I can make it right now, and will probably dive straight into bed."

"Oh," Michelle said to herself, disappointment tangible in the air. "Okay. If that's what you need to do. I hope you feel better soon."

Felix's heart hadn't stopped pounding away, apparently looking for its own exit. He needed to ensure this wasn't the last time he'd see Michelle, because he understood a debacle like this could very well cancel his next invitation for a date.

He took a big step forward, reaching out to grab Michelle by her hips and pulling her in toward him. Their faces hovered inches apart for five seconds before Felix closed his eyes and pressed his lips against hers.

There was no resistance from Michelle, who promptly gave in, throwing her arms around Felix, where her nails scratched seductively along his back.

Felix pulled away right when he sensed Michelle about to open her mouth to challenge him to a game of tongue Twister.

"Don't take tonight to heart," Felix said. "I *really* want to see you again."

Michelle tasted like wine, and the flavor was stuck on his lips. She had three glasses during the game that were still making their way out of her pores, apparently.

She bit her bottom lip and nodded. "Me too. Now go home and get better, so we can try this again."

For good measure, he kissed her on the forehead. "I'll call you this week and we'll plan something."

Felix wasted no time leaving, relief flooding over him when he sat down behind the wheel of his car.

Crisis averted.

Chapter 39

January 22, 2014

Arielle and Selena couldn't help but bring up the story of Felix escaping Michelle's sexual advances every day since it happened. Arielle couldn't believe how quickly it had all escalated, and told Felix he could bail on this mission whenever he pleased. Selena simply liked to poke fun.

"Not until I've planted the bug in her office," he said. "Which will happen this week if all goes according to plan."

It was Wednesday, and Felix was beyond ready to execute his plan that he had kept to himself so far.

"Look at you, Felix," Selena said earlier that morning at the breakfast table. "Acting like Arielle with your mission secrets. You're going to pull this off, aren't you?"

He only smiled. "I've learned from the best. That's all."

Felix had joined them on their drive to the office, spending the morning hours wandering around downtown, stopping for a coffee around nine, and spending the rest of the freezing morning walking underground at Pike Place Market. When 11:30 rolled around, he sent a text message to Michelle.

Good morning! I'm off work today, but have some business downtown. Can I bring you lunch at your office?

It only took thirty seconds for a response. *Good morning, handsome. Yes! Floor 34. Excited to see you <3*

Felix shook his head. Was Michelle truly falling for him, or was the past trying to force the issue so he couldn't interfere with its plans for the Marshall family? It didn't matter to Felix either way. He needed to plant the bug this afternoon and get the hell out of whatever relationship was forming with the WonderHome CEO.

"Okay, I'm getting in the building," he said, finding a deli to stop at for two sandwiches. Once he had the sandwiches in hand, he patted his pockets to make sure the two bugs he had brought along were still secure. With that confirmation, he made his way out of the underground portion of the market, back up to street level, where the WonderHome office waited only two blocks away.

The sidewalks were filled with those who liked to take their lunch on the earlier side. Felix never understood how anyone could eat lunch before noon.

He strolled into the lobby of the Wilson Investments Center, confidence creeping back into his mind. *This* was the part of the job he thrived in. Sneaking around and planting bugs. There was no one better, and nothing else gave him the rush of getting away with it.

Felix entered the elevator and rode it up to the thirty-fourth floor, the doors parting to reveal a hallway that stretched far into the distance. It only ran in one direction, so he followed it, passing a bathroom and several conference rooms before he saw the first sign of life.

"Can I help you?" a woman with short, spiky hair asked. Felix immediately recognized her as Mila Bachman, the chief marketing officer.

"Yes, actually. I'm meeting with Michelle, but this is my first time here. Which way is her office?"

Mila looked him up and down and crossed her arms. "Fresh meat, huh?"

Felix stared back, not sure how to respond. Not even sure what the comment was supposed to mean.

Mila broke into howling laughter, stepping forward to clap Felix on the back. "I'm just messing with you. The big boss is at the end of the hall, corner office so she can hog all the space and have two views of the city. Good luck in there."

Mila didn't wait for Felix to respond and walked off, disappearing down the elevator he had just arrived in, still cackling to herself as the doors closed.

The floor seemed deserted, only a couple of other people appearing in the hallway as he made his way to the furthest end. A small group of employees huddled around a computer monitor in a miniature bullpen area.

The end of the hallway opened up, a desk sitting outside of Michelle's office.

There you are, Felix thought, seeing Adam Marshall for the first time in the flesh.

He was busy typing away on his computer when Felix approached, stopping when he saw him.

"Hello," Adam greeted him. "Are you Felix?"

"Yes. How did you know?"

"Michelle told me you were coming by for lunch. Feel free to go on in."

Adam gestured to the open door and returned to typing on his computer.

Their encounter was clearly not a big deal to Adam, nor should it have been. But Felix had so many questions he wanted to ask, not sure how, realizing he wasn't getting that opportunity today.

One thing at a time. Get this planted and so much more is going to open up.

"Thank you," Felix said, receiving no further acknowledgment from Adam.

He let himself through the door, finding Michelle in a similar position, typing from her desk.

"Felix!" she cried, jumping out of her seat and rounding her desk, which was oddly centered in the room, at least twenty feet away from the windows. She hugged him, and he hugged back. "This is such a pleasant surprise. Do you want to go eat on one of our balconies?"

"No. In here is fine. It's cold outside, anyway."

"Well, they have those outdoor heaters, but that's fine. We can eat in here."

Felix had only ever been in offices for high-ranking Road Runners, and Michelle's compared rather closely. She had her own refrigerator, a microwave, stovetop, sink, and a couch. Being the corner office, she had the dual view that overlooked both the bay and downtown Seattle. If anything, the view made her office even better than the Road Runner ones, since theirs were always underground without so much as a window.

Michelle shuffled to the door and closed it.

"I met Adam just now," Felix said. "A man of few words."

"Oh, don't mind him. He's had a ton of work this week. We sold a lot of homes over the weekend, and he's processing all of those contracts."

"I didn't realize he worked on the real estate side of things. I thought he handled more of your daily tasks."

"He does that, too. But the real estate program is off to a much better start than we expected, and there's been a backlog in contracts to process. He's just helping until we can get more people hired on that team. Besides, the entire program is an initiative from our CFO, so it's not exactly busywork."

"How important," Felix said, mentally tucking all of this information away for later.

"Look in the fridge and grab yourself a drink. I'll have a Sprite, please."

Michelle returned to her desk and cleared it free of papers, wheeling two seats around the corner of the desk so they could sit side by side.

Felix rummaged through the fridge, looking for a reason to get Michelle out of the room. He saw cans of Coke, Sprite, Diet Coke, Fanta, bottled water, and lemonade.

"Do you not have Pepsi?" Felix asked. "I prefer it."

Michelle gave him a look as if wondering if Felix was being serious or not. Could he really not find something to drink out of all the options?

"We have Pepsi in our kitchen. I'll get you one."

"Thank you so much, Michelle." Felix hadn't expected it to be so easy. Until it wasn't.

Michelle only moved to the center of her desk and laid her finger on her work phone's intercom button. "Adam, are you there?" she asked.

His voice crackled in response.

"Can you do me a favor and grab a Pepsi from the kitchen?"

"On it," he replied.

Well, shit, Felix thought, his confidence now wavering. How could he get Michelle out of her own office if she didn't *need* to leave it for anything?

He hurried back to the desk and unwrapped his sandwich, flipping up the top piece of bread. "Dammit! I asked for ranch and mustard, and they didn't put it on. Do you have any?"

Michelle was about to unwrap her sandwich and paused. "I think I only have ketchup in the fridge. We should have mustard and ranch in the main kitchen."

"The one Adam just left to? Of course."

"It's just down the hall if you want to go look."

"Could you?" Felix asked, fighting to make sure his voice didn't sound too desperate. "If you can go grab those for me, I'll finish setting up our little picnic here."

Michelle studied him for a couple of seconds before agreeing. "Okay. Anything else we might need?"

"Just the condiments and I'll be set."

"Okay, I'll be right back."

Michelle stood from her desk and started for the door, Felix's heart pounding away in angst. There was still a chance Adam would return and Michelle would send him right back. When she opened the door and stepped out, Felix stuffed his hand into his pocket and pulled out a microphone disguised as a functioning pen. He jumped out of his seat to round the desk and dropped the pen into a cup of a dozen others sitting on the far edge.

Felix had brought a few options for bugging the office and wanted to use one more besides the pen that only had a 50-hour battery life.

The supreme bugging device was burning a hole in his pocket, so he whipped out the USB flash drive that doubled as a recording device. The advantage of the flash drive was that it plugged directly into a computer to keep a constant charge. No concerns over the battery life. An added plus was that Felix already had access to Michelle's computer, so he'd be able to log in from home and access the recordings without an issue.

Footsteps echoed from down the hall, so Felix dropped to the floor, found the computer underneath, and stuck the flash drive into a port on the back side, out of sight from Michelle, who would never suspect a thing.

The footsteps grew louder, high heels clacking on their way to the office.

Felix lunged out from the desk and returned to his seat, where he hurried to unroll Michelle's sandwich and tossed some napkins around just as she entered the office with a can of Pepsi and bottles of mustard and ranch.

"Are you okay?" she asked. "Your face is super flushed."

Felix's heart rate and breathing had ramped up, and he fought to control at least his breathing, giving a slow nod. "Yeah, I'm okay. Just hungry, I suppose."

Michelle frowned at him while she returned to her seat. "Okay, silly. Let's eat."

And they did. Felix enjoyed his lunch, eager to get home to listen to Michelle's private conversations, and overjoyed he'd finally get to end his fake relationship with her.

Chapter 40

February 8, 2014

Two and a half weeks passed since Felix had planted the bug in Michelle's office, and they hadn't gained a single bit of valuable information. The bugging had worked as it should, and this finally gave Felix something to do throughout the day while Arielle and Selena continued working at WonderHome.

Felix had grown more suspicious since planting the bugs. If the real estate program truly was thriving as Michelle had mentioned, then why was there never a conversation about it? Or why in the hell did Adam Marshall not have a single email regarding the matter? He was supposedly taking on much of the work. Did it just magically fall on his desk? Did the company not keep any electronic records of the real estate transactions? That might make sense if they had planned out the money laundering from the start, but that had never appeared to be the case.

He even spent two days combing through the emails of everyone on the real estate team. It mostly consisted of back-and-forth messages with clients to schedule appointments, review contracts, and answer basic questions. But where were the contracts going to be completed and signed on behalf of

WonderHome?

It was like the entire process fell off the grid as soon as it was time to sign.

Felix couldn't find a trace anywhere in the WonderHome system.

The frustration was growing heavy on Felix. He felt like he kept running into one dead end after another. There was literally nothing further he could do than directly asking Michelle if she was laundering money through the company's real estate program.

But that conversation would never come, for it was time for Felix to end the relationship. He had confirmed all was running smoothly with his bugging efforts over the past couple of weeks, and felt confident about never having to step foot inside Michelle's office again. His relationship with her had served the mission's purpose, and he didn't need to waste any more of his free time dodging her sexual advances.

They actually hadn't seen each other since their lunch date in her office. He lied about having plans already that following weekend, and the weekend after that Michelle had gone to the Super Bowl with Jody to watch the Seahawks dismantle the Broncos and bring the first Lombardi trophy back to the Pacific Northwest.

She returned from that trip and had a busy week at work, asking about Felix's plans for the upcoming Saturday, February 8. He said he'd let her know that day if he'd be available that evening.

Snow fell outside while the three Angels gathered in the living room, Selena most eager to hear the phone call Felix was about to make.

"You know," she said. "It's much better to do this today

and not drag it out closer to Valentine's Day. That would be so fucked-up."

"The whole thing is fucked-up," Felix said. "I know this is going to hit her hard. I had to listen to some of her conversations with her therapist because they do some sessions over the phone, and this lady actually brings my name up. She's genuinely into me."

Selena laughed. "It's because you're playing hard to get. That woman has gone through life getting whatever she pleases, and you're probably the first man to be so difficult to get in the sack."

"You're sick."

"It's true. Just saying."

Arielle nodded. "Definitely true."

They all burst out laughing.

"Now, before I do this," Felix said. "Have we thought about the repercussions? This relationship didn't exist in the original timeline, which means we have no idea what the breakup might do."

"I've thought it through," Arielle said. "I can't speak to what it will mean for Michelle, but I can't imagine it having much of an impact on our mission. The sooner the better, so we don't get too close to the day of the arrest."

"And neither of you have heard anything around the office?" Felix asked.

"No," Arielle said. "No one is mentioning anything. I've tried to launch a new initiative with our accounting department in hopes of spending more time with them and getting to really dig into our bank accounts, but it's going nowhere fast. I've told you for a while now how I'm considering stepping away from this job, and I think that day is coming soon. My time is being wasted. Selena is thriving and gaining trust from people all around the company, so I think we'll be okay with having her there while I focus on other aspects of the mission."

"Are you asking for our permission?" Selena asked. "Because that's kind of what it sounds like. You've been thinking this for weeks and haven't done anything about it. That's not like you at all."

"No, I'm not asking for your permission, but I'd love your input. What do you think?"

"If we're not gaining anything by you being at the office every day, then you should absolutely leave the job and figure out what to do here with Felix. Surely he can't cover the entire company himself. There could easily be something slipping through the cracks."

Felix nodded. "We can make it work. As long as that flash drive stays plugged into Michelle's computer, I can get into the system no problem. If you can, maybe sneak a computer out of the office before you leave. I know IT always has some lying around that aren't accounted for. Take one of those, so we can have a backup in case Michelle gets a new computer or discovers the flash drive. I'd need about a week to get it configured to match your computer's setup, but after that, you'll be home free."

"Okay," Arielle said. "I'll grab a computer on Monday and we can get this in motion. I'll be out of this job by the end of the month."

"How long does it take the feds to investigate the laundering?" Selena asked. "Won't they be starting that soon if Adam gets arrested in May?"

"It can take a few months for them to sift through records

and trace it all to the responsible party," Felix said. "Forensic accountants get tasked with this sort of work, but a good laundering scheme can make their job incredibly difficult."

"Are they allowed to do this without the company's knowledge?"

"Yes. It's sort of a loophole when it comes to electronic data. If the feds need access to electronic data, they can go through the company's service providers to obtain it. All they need to do is present a case for their investigation to a judge to sign a warrant for such a request between the feds and WonderHome's internet and phone provider. That way they can investigate in the background while WonderHome has no idea what's going on. I'd imagine, if they haven't already, they'll be starting their investigation within the next month. We're getting a little off track, though. Can I make this phone call I've been dreading for weeks?"

"Why are you so nervous?" Selena asked. "It's not like you're in love with the woman."

"I'm just worried about what will happen. I want to get it over with and see."

"Go for it," Arielle said, prompting Felix to pull out his cell phone.

His fingers trembled as he clicked on Michelle's name and the phone started dialing.

"Why hello there, handsome," Michelle greeted in a cheerful voice. "I thought I'd never get to see you again."

Felix's stomach plunged. This would not be easy.

"Hey, Michelle. How are you doing? How was the week?"

"It was a busy, stressful week. But I'm doing better now that I can hear your voice."

Jesus Christ, Felix thought. *Is the past really going to make this so difficult?*

"Well, I'm glad to hear that. Do you have a minute?"

"Sure. Is everything okay?" The cheer left Michelle instantly, zapped with a sudden concern.

"Yes, I'm okay. I just need to talk to you about something?"

"Oooookay? What's going on?"

"It's about us. I don't think—"

"Are you breaking up with me?" Michelle snapped. "Are you kidding me right now?!"

Her voice elevated, and Felix felt the instantaneous rage radiating through the phone.

"Look," he said. "I've enjoyed the time we've spent together, but I just don't feel this is working out. We hardly get to see other. We're both so busy."

"Is this because I didn't take you to the Super Bowl? They only offered me one ticket—you know that."

"No, it's not the Super—"

"Am I just some ticket whore for you? You got a taste of the high life at the Seahawks games, and now that the season's over, you just toss me aside."

"Michelle, you're not letting me talk. I promise it has nothing to do with the Super Bowl. I can't speak for you, but I don't feel like I can dedicate the time to our relationship that it deserves."

Arielle and Selena both nodded, impressed with Felix's cool demeanor as he navigated through what was certainly unknown territory. He had to look away from them and paced in the other direction.

"This is *bullshit*, Felix," Michelle said, through what sounded like gritted teeth. "After all I've done for you. And you don't even have the balls to *fuck* me! You're such a chickenshit!"

"Michelle, that's enough."

"You fucking slimeball! I could have slept with a different guy every night while I was in New York, but I didn't! Because I thought we had something. You have some nerve. I'll give you that, you rotten piece of—"

Felix hung up the call, wheezing as the tension lingered.

He turned back around to face Arielle and Selena, who had settled on the couch, and watched him closely.

"So . . ." Selena said. "It's done?"

"She completely exploded," Felix said. "You'd have thought we were dating for years. I don't understand. Do people really fall this strongly for someone after such little time?"

"It happens more than you think," Selena said, standing from the couch to approach Felix. "Everyone is searching for love in some capacity, and when they get hopeful that they may have found it, the reality can catch them completely off guard. You can call yourself a heartbreaker now."

Felix chuckled. "I don't think that's something I'll be bragging about. That was the worst thing I've ever done. Thank God she doesn't know where I live, or I might be worried."

"So it's going to be a dark mood at the office on Monday," Selena said, laughing at herself. "I wonder how long until she gets back to her normal self."

"I don't know," Arielle said. "It can take some time to recover from the unmatched charm of Mr. Felix Francisco."

They all roared with amusement.

"I'm just glad it's finally over," Felix said. "That was *not* fun. I never want to be put in that kind of situation again, if you're taking requests, Arielle. In fact, I'll be fine if you don't even mention anything in the mission report about me doing that. The last thing I need is requests coming in for me to do it again."

"You did so good, though," Arielle said, Selena nodding in agreement. "Even if you don't realize it, what you did has made a major impact on this mission. We're officially set up for the home stretch."

Chapter 41

February 10, 2014

On Monday, Arielle had grown eager enough to finally step away from the job at WonderHome. Her department, though critical for helping Felix gain access to the company's system, lacked opportunity in all other ways. Her colleagues couldn't care less about the happenings outside of their individual projects.

The team was comprised of mostly middle-aged men. They'd gawk at Arielle occasionally, but were otherwise harmless. Before she could turn in her notice to leave, Arielle spent an hour hovering outside of the IT department's workspace, a counter with garage doors that opened up to the rest of the office on the thirty-second floor.

She took one of the open desks in the nearby bullpen, keeping an eye for whenever the rep inside the IT station would step away. Once he did, she stood up and rushed to the aisle, where she saw him disappear down the hallway and into the restroom.

Took long enough. Dude only drank a quarter gallon of water an hour ago.

The coast was clear, the IT station surrounded by only a

handful of quiet employees from the accounting team.

Arielle slipped into the IT station, already knowing the table along the back held stacks of laptops that were undergoing repair or being prepared to ship out to remote workers across the country.

Felix had known what he was talking about, as most of the computers on the back table were unassigned in limbo. A junkyard of sorts, with some in perfect shape and others on their final, technical limb.

Arielle snagged one that looked fairly new—she could tell because the charging cord plugged into was still wrapped in plastic, and there wasn't so much as a scuff on the laptop's surface.

She had brought her company backpack and slipped the computer and charger inside, vanishing from the IT station without a peep.

When she returned to her desk, Arielle jumped back into her side project of combing through different email inboxes from employees on the real estate team. She kept running into brick walls like Felix had, and expected as much, since she still had limited access compared to Felix at home. Within the confines of the WonderHome office, Arielle was still an entry-level software engineer and could get nowhere near bank account information or the private inboxes for upper-level management.

Shortly after her lunch break, which she spent hunkered over her computer, desperate to find something and continuing to come up short, when she received a text message from Felix:

Meeting in Michelle's office. 2pm w the execs. She sounds pissed.

Arielle checked her watch to find the time as 1:52 and responded: *Any chance you can share the feed with me? Slow day here.*

She waited for a response, knowing her team was losing hope on this mission. It was hitting Felix the hardest. He had put so much effort into setting matters up for success, yet answers continued to elude them. Arielle didn't waver, though. The money laundering was happening, or going to happen, and every day that passed was one closer to them finally learning the truth. Sometimes, no amount of effort or planning could yield the desired results. Sometimes you just had to wait and let the truth come out on its own.

Felix replied with a link for some sort of screen share to view and listen to his computer screen. Arielle opened it, gratified to find it worked. She saw his screen, showing the inbox of Michelle Garrison, along with another open window she presumed was the audio software connected to the bugged flash drive sitting in Michelle's computer.

He sent a follow up text: *No audio yet. It's voice-activated. We'll hear everything.*

Arielle sent back a thumbs up emoji, grabbed her laptop, and shuffled down the hall until finding a small conference room with only two seats and a desk. They didn't frost the windows to obstruct the view like the bigger conference rooms—these smaller ones were meant for quiet workspaces instead of actual meetings. With her laptop open in front of her to give the appearance of her working, she slid her cell phone on the desk next to it and plugged in a pair of headphones.

It occurred to Arielle that this was the first instance of a meeting in Michelle's office since Felix had bugged it. He had listened to plenty of phone conversations and small talk with Adam, none of which ever discussed the real estate department.

A gnawing suspicion grew in her gut. This meeting was the one to turn the corner on this mission. Why call for a sudden meeting with the executives with virtually no notice?

At 1:58, a hollow knocking sound came from the headphones, along with a static white noise as the flash drive kicked on.

"Come in!" Michelle's voice called out. "Landon, how are you doing?"

Arielle listened as the CFO and CEO caught up after the weekend. Michelle mentioned nothing about being dumped by Felix.

Over the next three minutes, Mila the CMO, and Raj the president trickled into Michelle's office, followed lastly by Adam Marshall.

"Are we expecting anyone else from the team?" Raj asked at 2:03.

"No," Michelle said. "I just wanted to meet with you four. We have an issue, and I'm not sure what we're supposed to do." Her tone shifted into one of intensity. "Landon, what the *fuck* is going on with this real estate project of yours?"

"I beg your pardon," Landon said, entirely surprised.

"We are *bleeding* money for this initiative of yours," Michelle said. "You told us it would only take a few months to get it up and running and bringing in serious money. Now, it didn't look too bad to end the year, but we have another seven weeks until we have to share our first quarter reports to the board, and as of right now, this real estate department has lost over half a million dollars. Are you trying to get us all fired?"

Michelle's tone was furious, accusatory. Arielle wished she could see inside that office.

"I know it looks bad, but lots of things are in motion. This can very well turn into a half a million dollar profit by the end of the next seven weeks."

"Is that true, Mila?" Michelle asked. "Because from what I've seen, there have been virtually no marketing efforts pushed behind this initiative. How are people supposed to buy and sell their houses through WonderHome if they don't know it's even possible?"

"I'm not here to point fingers," Mila said. "But Landon, you haven't submitted any requests to us. We have no idea what kind of language or material we should push publicly. And since we're the first in our industry to do something like this, we're not just going to make something up. I've worked with legal to understand the things we *can't* say, but I need something from your team to actually push out into the world."

"The new section is live on the website," Raj said. "It just released over the weekend. We had a team working all weekend to make sure it ran smoothly, so we really should start seeing some traction."

"That's too organic," Michelle fired back. "Sure, we get millions of visitors to the site every week, but how many go straight to the map or search bar to look for homes? No one is going to notice the new tab on the menu unless we tell them about it. My apologies for sounding like I'm attacking you, Landon. This is a team effort, but since this was your initiative, I expect you to take more control over it. I shouldn't be the one calling this meeting to demand answers—you should have done this yourself."

"I understand," Landon said. "And so you know where I'm coming from, I'm just not worried. I truly believe by the end of March, you'll be looking back at this meeting and will say how silly it was. The money will pour in soon enough. Mila, can we at least get an email and a social media campaign sent to our existing users about this new feature?"

"Done," Mila said. "I can have something out tomorrow."

"Why do I hear about all these contracts Adam has been working on and the bottom line doesn't reflect it?" Michelle asked.

"We've run into some issues," Landon explained. "Nearly every lender has been hesitant to work with us, but I'm working on that issue, too. It's taken some manual work on my part. I'm on the phone all day with different banks trying to explain our program."

"Are you shitting me?!" Michelle cried. "We launched this without having that part of the equation in place?! The actual financial logistics. Absolutely sloppy work."

"Michelle," Landon said. "I'm telling you, it's all under control."

"It'd better be. Because if we report this kind of loss at the end of the quarter, they're going to make us gut it, or worse. I've seen entire teams get fired for reporting losses much smaller than this. Maybe they'll give us the benefit of the doubt, but I don't want to find out. You may not be worried, but honestly, I'm freaking the fuck out. Turn it around, immediately."

"Yes, ma'am," Landon said, cool and confident.

"If you need my help on anything, just let me know. Thank you all for stopping in."

Chapter 42

Arielle rushed home with Selena after work, explaining what had happened.

They found Felix at the dining room table, buried in his laptop.

"Can you believe that meeting?" Arielle asked, pulling out a seat and sitting across from him. Selena joined them at the table, pouring a glass of water.

"Yes, that was really intense," Felix said. "I almost feel bad for Landon, but doesn't it kind of seem like he might be the one responsible? Michelle all but threatened their jobs if he can't get this turned around."

"My thoughts exactly, but how does laundering money help his cause? Isn't the purpose of laundering to *hide* illegal money?"

Felix nodded. "It is, but this is a golden opportunity to kill two birds with one stone. If we assume he's involved in some shady dealings, he can then dump that money into the real estate side of WonderHome by having moles purchase real estate. That gets money onto the books *and* it also masks the dirty money."

"You don't seem entirely convinced it's him," Arielle said. Felix was usually confident once he grabbed hold of an idea, yet that aura wasn't present.

"Don't get me wrong, I feel great after today. No matter how you look at it, this was a breakthrough for us. All signs point to Landon, but we can say with confidence the scheme is tied to anyone who was in Michelle's office for that meeting. I actually don't think Michelle is involved, based on the way she was speaking. She sounded like a pissed-off CEO demanding answers for a suffering portion of their business. Nothing more."

"I heard she was in quite the mood today," Selena said. "Word around the office this morning was to steer clear of Michelle. Someone saw her at the coffee machine. It was broken, and Michelle just started punching it over and over. Busted two of the side panels. Must have had a rough weekend."

Selena laughed at herself and rolled her eyes when no one else did.

"Not now, Selena," Arielle said. "We're on to something here. Felix, I know you started digging into Landon's stuff after that meeting. What did you find?"

"He placed multiple phone calls after that meeting—seven, to be exact. All were to masked phone numbers, so definitely suspicious. No internal calls, as you might think—all were outside of the company."

"Did you find it weird that Adam didn't speak during the meeting?"

"I did at first. It became obvious during that meeting that Adam is *not* the brains behind this scheme, or else he would have had a lot more to say. Michelle acknowledged his workload, but that was it. He's definitely a puppet in all of this, and I don't think he has a clue. We need to find out who is pulling the strings, and our search should obviously start with Landon. He has the most to lose, the pressure is on him, and he's the CFO overlooking all the funds for the company. What we need to find out first is where the illegal money is coming from."

"I can tail him," Arielle said. "In fact, I'd *love* to do that. Gives me something else to do besides rotting in the office. I'm gonna submit my notice tomorrow."

"Tomorrow? Did you even get the—"

"Right here," Arielle said, reaching into her backpack and pulling out the stolen laptop.

"Okay then. I can start setting it up tonight, and you can leave your job in peace."

"Thank you." Arielle sensed a fresh wave of optimism, even if it was just between her and Felix for the time being.

"So you're just gonna leave me to go to work by myself every day?" Selena asked.

"I'll still be there if I'm following Landon around. I'll just be spending most of my day outside the building waiting for him."

"I've got his address here," Felix said. "Looks like he lives in the Broadmoor neighborhood in northeastern Seattle, right by the bridge that crosses over to Medina. That's over fifteen minutes from here. Rich neighborhood. Not mansions, but large houses and yards. Lots of cars parked on the streets, so you should be able to do your usual stakeouts."

Those words had never sounded so sweet for Arielle. "It's crunch time," she said. "If the laundering hasn't started by now—which it doesn't sound like it—it's going to soon."

Chapter 43

February 11, 2014

The following morning, Arielle stopped by her manager's desk and asked him to speak in private. She told him something had come up in her life that wouldn't allow her to continue working at WonderHome. She needed to return home, and while she could wait out the next two weeks, it would be ideal, if possible, for her to step away today.

Her manager, Adrian Decker, folded his hands on the conference room table. "Is everything okay?" he asked. "If you don't mind me asking."

"Just a family matter," Arielle said. "Trust me when I tell you this was not a simple decision at all. I guess sometimes you just need to roll with the punches in life."

Arielle could dance around this matter until her feet fell off. She had mastered the craft of bullshitting and knew precisely how to use words to create sympathy from others. Here she was, making up a story about nothing, offering no details, yet Adrian leaned back with a concerned face.

"I think we'll be okay if you need to leave today," Adrian said, defeated. "Do you have plans for work wherever you're going?"

"Not yet. I just need to move and get settled before I worry about that."

"Understood. Well, if you need a recommendation from me, just let me know. I'd be more than happy to help however I can."

"Thank you so much." Arielle hadn't realized until this moment just how beneficial having Adrian as her manager had been. Sure, he provided nothing of substance for their mission, which is why she had long considered him useless in the grand scheme. But things could have played out drastically different if she had a different manager. Adrian never micromanaged. He could have easily questioned why Arielle needed a setup at home so soon, or browsed her online activity throughout the day and grilled her about how she spent her downtime. As long as her work got done on time, he stayed out of her way, and that alone brought its own value to the mission. "Thank you for everything. I'm gonna miss this place."

"The pleasure is all mine, Ms. Lucila," Adrian said, standing up and extending his hand. "And if life ever brings you back to Seattle, call me and you'll have a job in no time."

"I appreciate that. Thank you, again. So, do I just go pack up my desk now and leave? I've never done something like this before."

"Yep. I'll take care of everything with POPS. Take care of yourself, and good luck."

Arielle nodded before stepping out of the conference room and returning to her desk that would take only five minutes to pack into a small box.

* * *

When Arielle reached her car before nine o'clock, the whole day ahead of her, she sat behind the wheel in silence to plan her next move. Landon was in the office that she no longer had access to, but that didn't concern her. He was definitely tied up in the laundering, but it was unlikely that he conducted such illegal activity from within the building.

She had only made a handful of friends during her time at the FBI academy, and now was a time she wished she had paid more attention to those relationships. A quick phone call could answer a lot of questions and help point her in the right direction, but she hadn't spoken with any of those colleagues since she left several years ago. She didn't even know which of them still worked with the agency.

Arielle sent a text message to Felix and Selena, letting them know she had quit her job with WonderHome. Felix called her immediately.

"What's up?" Arielle answered.

"I've been diving into Landon's world. Still nothing concrete in his email inbox, but I found his calendar. He keeps everything fairly broad, but I have no idea if that's intentional or just his personality."

"How do you mean?"

"Like his work meetings are just marked as 'meeting' or 'meeting with accounting team', things like that. But I'm noticing a weekly meeting he has scheduled for every Thursday, after hours, titled 'Down by the bay.'"

"Down by the bay? Do you know if he has kids?"

"One sec. Let me check my notes." Arielle waited for a

minute while Felix fell silent, the only audible sound his frantic clicking as he rummaged through digital data. "He does not. Why?"

"'Down by the Bay' is a popular kids' song. I thought maybe the calendar event had something to do with a child. What time is the event scheduled for?"

"From six to eight. Every single Thursday."

"Is he married? Girlfriend?"

"Not married. Not sure about a girlfriend. His Facebook profile lists him as single."

"Well damn. It could mean anything. It could be a weekly dinner date, not necessarily romantic, either. Could be a session at a gym. Doctor, therapy."

"It doesn't help that we're in Seattle. There are five bays all within a quick driving distance."

"Exactly. It could even be a weekly fishing session, for all we know."

"I think we need to follow him and see what it's all about. And by we, I mean *you*."

Arielle laughed. "I'll plan for it this Thursday."

"Good. I wouldn't have called you about it if I didn't think it was suspicious. Nothing else on his calendar is labeled, except for that one recurring meeting."

"Thank you. I think you're right. Psychologically speaking, he may mark it different because it has an elevated importance in his mind. He wants it to stick out when he looks at the calendar. Has he made any noise today?"

"No. He's apparently in meetings until lunchtime, so you might not see him slip out of the building until then."

"Good to know. Back to my long days of staking out the bad guy. Beats sitting in front of a computer all day, I suppose.

No offense."

"Whatever floats your boat, Number One."

Arielle giggled. "Hey now, I thought we were past that kind of name-calling."

"We are. Just thought I'd remind you that you're the best. I think sometimes you forget it."

"Well, thank you, Felix."

"No problem. I gotta bounce. Gonna spend my day in front of the computer." Arielle could hear the sarcasm in his voice. "Just promise me you'll be careful out there. We're getting closer, and I have a feeling you might get mixed up with some bad people."

Chapter 44

February 13, 2014

Arielle had followed Landon home Tuesday after work. He stopped by a sandwich shop to grab dinner, which he took back to his vast house and didn't step foot outside for the rest of the evening.

On Wednesday, his regiment had included a stop at a gym for an hour, before grabbing food to-go from a local Italian restaurant just outside of his neighborhood. He stayed in the rest of the evening.

Arielle expected nothing less. It was the middle of the work week, after all. On Thursday, however, they were all expecting something of significance. Felix had dubbed it "Bay Day" and believed whatever the mysterious event on Landon's calendar was would lead to answers for the mission.

The three Angels had gathered on Wednesday night to discuss their ideas on the mission. Arielle liked to do this once a week, but had lost a regular cadence while they all fell into the grind of day-to-day jobs. Besides, nothing was changing during that time.

Confidence reached its peak in the belief that Adam Marshall had no direct involvement in the money laundering. This allowed them to shift their focus on saving Adam from the downfall awaiting him in just three months. They were even ready to cross Michelle Garrison off the list of suspects, but Felix fought against it.

"I don't think she's part of it, either," he had said. "But we need to understand the full picture. She is the CEO, after all, and she *could* be tied in at some capacity we don't understand yet."

They concluded Landon was most likely operating with help from someone else within the company. It could have been anyone on the executive board, or possibly a lower-level employee he could have bribed to help him cover his dirty tracks.

Arielle had found a parking spot in the garage around lunchtime, and took the place directly across the aisle from Landon's blue Corvette. She had backed in to make it easier to follow him on his way out.

Landon had left the office at five o'clock sharp on Tuesday and Wednesday.

He didn't reach his car until 5:35 on Thursday, and Arielle had grown plenty anxious by the time she saw him appear. He wore his usual suit and tie, a heavy briefcase in hand he tossed onto the passenger seat before pulling out of his spot and leaving the garage.

Arielle followed the Corvette, a tight grip around the steering wheel turning her knuckles white. They paused at the gate as Landon swiped his badge to get out. Selena had left her badge with Arielle after swiping herself out earlier to go home, so Arielle used it in the same fashion to get onto the road promptly behind Landon.

The heavy downtown traffic made it nearly impossible for

Arielle to lose sight of Landon as they were stop-and-go for the first few minutes rolling down First Avenue. Once they broke free into a clearing, Landon floored his Corvette to blast down westbound Elliott Avenue, eventually merging with Fifteenth Avenue that took them north.

They drove this way for ten minutes, hitting minimal red lights and making great time. When Landon exited at the Port of Seattle, Arielle's stomach fluttered.

"*Down by the bay* definitely meant something near the water," she said to her empty car. They drove through a neighborhood of businesses entirely dedicated to marine life. Boat repair and care. Terminals. Fishing Gear. Seafood restaurants.

They put the Port of Seattle behind them when Landon turned onto Twenty-First Avenue, a road that split civilization on the left, and the bay and piers on the right.

Landon slowed down to drive at a reasonable speed, thanks to the road being filled with cars parked along the sides, pedestrians filling the sidewalks. They reached the end of the road, and Arielle turned off her headlights. She had maintained a safe distance of about fifty yards since they had exited the highway, and it was becoming clear they were about to enter an area in the middle of nowhere.

Landon turned onto a side road labeled as "NW Dock" and honored the posted speed limit of eight miles per hour. The road stretched about a quarter mile, and Arielle found the mixture of boats peculiar as they made their way down the dock. They passed private yachts, fishing boats, and cargo boats. There was even one rather large cargo ship undergoing construction. Parked vehicles filled both sides of the roads. Landon reached the end of the dock and parked under a massive sign that read: *NO PARKING. FIRE LANE.*

A blue fishing boat was anchored around the tether at the end of the pier. A handful of people standing at the boat's entrance waved to Landon when he stepped out of his car.

Arielle found a tight parking spot along the side of the road, and sandwiched herself between a muddy pickup truck and a worn-down Crown Vic. She was roughly one hundred feet away from Landon's car and had a clear view of his illegal parking space.

Two white vans without windows were parked on either side of Landon's Corvette.

Arielle pulled out her binoculars for a closer view.

The people on the fishing boat looked to be all men, though it was difficult to tell since they were all bundled up from head to toe, thanks to the whipping wind that swirled the winter's most recent cold front.

The men stepped off the boat, each shuffling toward Landon, where they stopped and huddled in front of the Corvette. Landon sat on the hood of his car, reached into his suit jacket's interior pocket, and pulled out a packet of cigarettes.

After offering one to each of the men gathered around, he popped one into his mouth and lit it, taking a deep drag before blowing long clouds of smoke into the brisk air.

The men were all dressed in dark colors, and each wore a pair of gloves. One was carrying on the bulk of whatever conversation he and Landon were having, the CFO occasionally nodding and responding.

After three minutes of this back-and-forth, Landon stood up from his car and followed the men onto the boat. Arielle had paid little attention to the contents on the boat, but now saw the stacks of wooden crates lined around the deck's perimeter. The crates were each about five feet long, three feet tall, and two feet deep, all stacked in neat columns of three.

The group on the boat gathered around a crate while one man fiddled with the padlock hanging from it. They shared a round of laughter once the padlock was removed and tossed aside. He lifted the crate's lid and reached in, pulling out a gun nearly as big as his arm.

"Holy shit," Arielle whispered to herself.

Another man reached into the crate and pulled out a second gun, Arielle now able to tell they were both AR-15 rifles. Landon pushed through the huddle, stood on his tiptoes to see deep inside the crate, and reached in.

When he pulled out a bag full of white powder, all of the dots started connecting.

"Son of a bitch," Arielle said. "Cocaine and guns."

She pulled out her cell phone and started snapping pictures, most of them coming out grainy from having to zoom in too much, but still clear enough to tell what was happening.

Landon patted the bag of cocaine like a proud father might pat his child on the head. He tossed it back into the crate. The two men with guns followed by returning the weapons, and watched as the first man put the padlock back on.

Landon shook hands with all five men before one of them ran into the cockpit and returned with a black duffel bag. He dropped it on the floor at Landon's feet, who promptly bent down to unzip it and examine the contents.

Arielle couldn't see. The boat's exterior walls cut off her view of everyone just below their waists, but it was obvious Landon was most likely counting money.

"That money is going to appear in a WonderHome bank

account soon, isn't it?" she asked, shaking her head.

She had seen enough, and turned on her engine to get the hell out of there before anyone could spot her.

Chapter 45

"It's Landon," Arielle said, having just burst into the house, where Felix and Selena were watching *This is 40* in the living room.

Felix powered off the TV, vaulting off the couch. "What happened?!"

"His calendar event is a meeting, all right. He drove all the way to the docks at Salmon Bay for a drug and weapons deal."

"Jackpot," Felix said. "There's the source of the dirty money. So Landon is facilitating these deals and collecting enormous sums of money to launder through the real estate program. We did it, guys. This knowledge makes the mission pretty straightforward from here."

Arielle shook her head. "This is just important information. We still have to figure out what to do with it."

"Well, sure," Selena said, finally standing to join the conversation. "But do you honestly think we're not going to? All we've needed to know is who was behind this, and now we have our guy. The next step is just figuring how to tie the crime to Landon instead of Adam."

"Exactly," Arielle said. "This is where it gets dangerous. We don't know anything about those men on the boat tonight. I had no way of identifying them. We don't know what we're going up against."

"Why get involved with those guys?" Selena asked. "We shouldn't need to. For all we care, Landon can keep on having his weekly meetings and bring in the money. We just need to figure out the part of the equation that takes Adam Marshall out of the picture and leaves Landon as the lone target."

"I'm aware of all that, but we don't know how it's going to play out. We should still be prepared to deal with these drugs and weapons dealers because we don't know how the rest of this mission will play out. We're still going to follow Landon every time he steps out of the office, and that could mean getting close to these people he's dealing with. And I agree with Selena. We shouldn't interfere with Landon's illegal activities. Our job was to prevent the murder-suicide of the Marshall family, and that begins with painting Adam as innocent."

"How do we know Adam *isn't* involved?" Felix asked. "Sure, we know Landon is the one pulling the strings and not Michelle. But Adam's supposedly working on real estate matters on behalf of WonderHome, and we can't find any-thing that actually shows this as true. Something still isn't adding up."

"That's all a good point, and I'm sure it's just a matter of sorting out the moving parts," Arielle said. "I've actually been toying with the idea of us trying to sell this house to WonderHome, just to see what happens from our end. The laundering has to take place when WonderHome buys property from someone selling their home. I don't see another opportunity where such a thing can happen. But that opens up another question. If Landon is laundering his own money through the company, there is still a disconnect somewhere. He can't just show up to the bank and deposit duffel bags of cash into the company's account, can he?"

Felix nodded. "He actually can if he's an authorized user on the company checking account. And as the CFO, I'd imagine he definitely is. Even so, that wouldn't work. Companies this large have accounting teams dedicated entirely to making sure every cent is accounted for. If money comes in, they must notate a reason. Same when money goes out. They balance the books at least once a month, from what I've been able to find digging through the accounting team's work. And if there is even a single discrepancy, the accountants reach out to all parties involved on a particular transaction, demanding answers. This is literally how companies remain compliant and avoid money laundering."

"But he's the CFO," Arielle said. "Literally in charge of the entire accounting department and all money activity for the company. It wouldn't be a stretch for him to have fudged these cash deposits as something related to the business—especially with it being cash. All he'd really need is one or two people to be in on the scheme to pull this off."

"Or an entire team," Selena said. "Felix, have you reviewed the members of the real estate team?"

"Of course," Felix said. "Their activity looks completely normal. They negotiate contracts with home buyers and sellers. It's all pretty standard."

"I think Arielle may be on to something. We need to investigate the process, and what better way than to do it by selling our house?"

"Well, I don't think we can sell this house," Felix said. "It belongs to the Road Runners, and we can't just decide to do that for the sake of a mission. What I *can* do is check in with *our* real estate team and see if there is a property in the area they're willing to sell. If so, I can handle that transaction with WonderHome, and we can follow the paper trail from there. I'm not sold that WonderHome buying properties from sellers is when the laundering takes place. That's money going out. Laundering has to be when the money comes *in*."

"So, when WonderHome sells the property they've purchased," Arielle said. "That would mean the people buying the homes are part of the scheme. That doesn't seem possible. Aren't they selling hundreds of homes each day across the country?"

"I don't think it's as many as you think," Felix said. "It might grow to that now that Landon is getting desperate to save his job and his entire scheme. But their team doesn't have enough members to pull off that many transactions. I'll look through their recent contracts again, but nothing stood out in terms of suspicious deals. Maybe that's all about to start now after that heated meeting with Michelle."

"Do you know how many people are on that team, Selena?" Arielle asked.

Selena looked upward, thinking. "I can double-check when I'm in the office, but I would guess around forty."

"And I assume these realtors get paid on some sort of commission, yeah?"

"Definitely."

"Felix," Arielle said, turning to face him. "Would you be able to get into payroll's system and see what each individual realtor is making on commissions?"

"Yeah, I can do that," Felix replied. "Where are you going with this? I see your wheels turning."

Arielle's wheels were always turning. "I think we need to

have a talk with one of these realtors. Perhaps one who will talk to us about what really is going on. Selena, you have access in your department to see these realtors' personal information, right? Like their marriage status, children, things like that?"

"Absolutely," Selena said. "That's all standard information I can get easily."

"Tomorrow is Friday. I don't want to take this into the weekend. If we can get profiles completed for each realtor, we can narrow it down to who we want to approach."

"How do you plan on confronting whoever we choose?" Felix asked, brow furrowed in curiosity. "You worked there—someone might recognize you."

"I doubt it. We were on completely different floors. I don't recall seeing anyone from the real estate team after finishing training. So we can avoid anyone from my training class, and we should be fine. I'm not Ms. Popular over there." Arielle nodded at Selena, who responded with a satisfied laugh. "Depending who we select will determine my approach. I'd love for it to be a civil conversation—I don't even mind paying off one of these realtors to get the info we need. I also don't mind shaking one of them down. We need our answers."

"Well, well," Felix said, crossing arms and shooting a smile across the room. "Look who's back to being herself now that she's out of the office. It only took one night of following Landon when he actually did something, and you're firing on all cylinders. I wouldn't be surprised if we're going home next weekend at this rate."

Arielle grinned. "I've been here this whole time—just hasn't been much of an opportunity to do anything. Now that we have some action, it's time to get shit done. So, what do you both say? Let's get those profiles ready tonight. Tomorrow is going to change everything."

"I'll say," Selena said. "Felix, why don't you give me one of those spy pens?"

Chapter 46

February 14, 2014

On Friday morning, Arielle was ready for the day by seven o'clock, but not because she *needed* to. Felix was right. She was back on the ball since leaving her job behind at WonderHome.

She hadn't even realized how dead she had felt during that time, stuck inside the office like a fish in a glass bowl, unable to explore the town and dive deep to investigate suspects in this ever-changing mission.

Felix and Selena worked hard into the night, providing Arielle with a list of forty-three realtors employed by Wonder-Home, along with their commission averages, performance reviews, and familial situations.

Arielle had received the list shortly after 10 P.M. and reviewed it thoroughly until one o'clock in the morning, when she called it a night and selected who she would approach the following day: Owen Adams.

Owen had been working at WonderHome for six months, one of the original ten realtors hired at the launch of the company's new real estate program. Despite the experience in the role, Owen was currently on a performance improvement plan, also known as a PIP, because of lackluster results in the field. He averaged one closing per month, while many of his colleagues from the same class averaged one per week.

Owen's placement on a PIP meant he had ninety days to improve or risk losing his job. According to the metrics Felix could find, satisfactory performance meant at least two closings per month. It had been fifteen days, and he still had no closings in February.

What stuck out the most about Owen, besides his potential to lose his job, was he had married just over a year ago and had a two-month-old infant at home. Arielle needed someone vulnerable to approach about the shady dealings taking place at WonderHome, and who better than a fresh realtor—WonderHome had helped him get his license upon his hiring—who couldn't afford to lose his only stream of income.

He was twenty-six, eager to prove himself, and failing miserably.

Arielle had sent him an email through WonderHome's portal, asking to view a house the following morning. She stressed she was only available between eight and ten and wanted to see the property as soon as possible.

She didn't know if such a simple request would work to lure Owen, but it was his job, after all. When her phone rang at 7:30 from an unknown number in the Seattle area code, she knew it was him.

"Hello?"

"Yes, hi," Owen said. "Is this Arielle? My name is Owen—I'm calling in response to a request you sent last night to view a property."

He spoke fast, as if he had been used to getting hung up on

while delivering his spiel.

"Yes, Owen, good morning. Thank you for calling. Are you able to show the property today?"

"I sure can, and I can meet you there at eight, if that works."

"Can we make it eight-fifteen? I'm running just a few minutes behind."

"Absolutely." Owen's voice elevated to a higher pitch filled with glee and hope. She wondered if he treated every showing like this, only to have something go astray before a closing could happen and dampen his dreams.

"Perfect, I'll see you there."

Arielle hung up and left the house, stopping first at the bank where she had to wait until they opened at exactly eight o'clock. She had heard the desperation in Owen's voice, and figured two thousand dollars would be enough for him to share everything he knew. She didn't want to rattle the man, who sounded like he might jump away from his own shadow. It was no wonder he wasn't cutting it in real estate. Successful realtors had confidence. They could walk into a home and tell you everything right and wrong with the place with a quick fifteen-minute tour. They knew what they could squeeze out of the seller during negotiations and how to lower all the bullshit costs and fees that typically fell upon the buyer. Just hearing Owen over the phone, she figured he probably struggled to even get the front door unlocked.

At eight, Arielle was first in line at the bank, withdrew the cash, and was on her way. She had found a property listed on WonderHome's website just outside of her neighborhood, a short five-minute drive away.

She arrived at the property and found the one-level home a disaster. Shingles were missing from the roof. The main window had a wide crack webbing out from the center. The screen door hung crookedly off the hinges. And the lawn was nothing but a scatter of dirt and weeds, trash littered about.

Parked in the driveway was a Toyota Prius, so Arielle pulled up and parked behind it, ensuring Owen couldn't leave until Arielle was ready.

Owen got out of the Prius, and Arielle immediately recognized him. She had seen him around the office, if only in passing. He was tall with a messy mop of black hair, his face droopy. If Arielle hadn't known any different she would have figured he was the IT guy for some startup tech company operating out of the CEO's basement.

"Arielle?" he asked, sticking out a hand.

"Yes, you must be Owen."

The stench of coffee oozed from his breath. Dark bags clung to his bottom eyelids. He was clearly the parent of a newborn, dodging sleep at every opportunity.

"You're aware this is a home for flipping, correct?" Owen asked. "Just always like to make sure of that before we go in. It needs a *ton* of work."

"Yes, I figured as much," Arielle said, following Owen to the front door where a lockbox hung from the doorknob.

"Good. It's honestly the best way to get a killer price, assuming you know how to do a lot of the repairs on your own."

He fumbled with the combination lock on the box, cussing under his breath as he had to do it three times before the little door popped open to reveal the key.

I knew it, Arielle thought, fighting off a laugh. *This poor guy has no future in real estate. He needs to take the money I'm about to offer and run.*

Owen unlocked and pushed the door to find it stuck. After another failed attempt, he lowered his shoulder into the door with enough force to get the damned thing open.

A musty smell flooded their senses immediately as they stepped into the house.

Carpet covered the floor as far as they could see, frayed along the edges. The walls had holes and splatters of random paint colors.

"The kitchen has carpet?" Owen asked, more to himself, his face drawn in complete bafflement. "Who in the world would do such a thing?"

He let out a nervous laugh, probably assuming he was already losing his next opportunity at a sale.

"Well, there's no need to worry," Arielle said. "I'm not buying this house."

"Oh?" he replied, not sounding entirely surprised. "But we just got here."

"I know. But I was never buying this house. I needed to get you in private to speak with you, if you don't mind."

Owen's eyes focused on Arielle, and she could see his mind trying to figure out what the hell was going on.

"I'm sorry," she said. "I shouldn't have led with that. Owen, I'm a private investigator looking into the dealings of the new real estate team at WonderHome. Would you mind if I ask you a few questions? I understand you've been there for six months now, working in this same role, correct?"

Owen gulped, his fingers fidgeting .

"You have nothing to worry about," Arielle said. "This isn't about you directly. You're not in any sort of trouble. I can't just barge into your office and demand to speak with someone, so investigators like myself have to get creative. Hence, why

I've asked you here this morning."

"Okay," Owen said, unsure of himself. "I don't know if I can be of much help."

Arielle sensed the anxiety emanating from Owen, could almost smell it over the rotten stench of water damage that had never been treated. Somewhere inside these walls were pipes and framing devoured by mold.

"I can sweeten the pot for you," Arielle said, reaching into her coat pocket and pulling out the wad of cash. "I know you're not doing too well selling houses. Here is two thousand dollars to help you get by if you'll just answer some questions for me as honestly as you can."

Owen's eyes bulged, and she figured she could have gotten the same reaction with half the amount.

"Okay," Owen said. "What do you want to know?"

"Thank you. And seriously, relax. This has nothing to do with you."

Owen nodded, and she watched the tension leave from his hands as they stood awkwardly facing each other in this abandoned home.

"You've been on this team since it first launched, right?" Arielle asked.

"Yes. My training class was first."

"And the CFO, Landon Greene, created this entire team. Is that correct?"

"Yes."

"Did he have any involvement during your training?"

"Yes. He basically trained all of us himself."

"Interesting. Did you not find it odd that the CFO would take, what, two to three weeks out of his schedule to do training? Doesn't WonderHome have a team of dedicated trainers?"

"Well, sure, it was weird. But WonderHome isn't your typical company. They do things differently, so I didn't think anything of it. It was all his idea, and he had mentioned how no one on the training team had ever done real estate before, so there was no point in having them try to teach it."

"And who does the training now? I can't imagine Mr. Greene is still taking time out of his busy schedule to train new realtors."

"Our team takes the training directly after the new hires finish their orientation part of training. We have two managers who take the bulk of training, but sometimes us realtors get called on to help."

"And how often does your team hear from the CFO? Whether that's in-person meetings, or even an email to the team."

Owen scrunched his face, his lips crookedly pursed while he thought. "I'd say about once a week. He still sends out a lot of emails about our team's performance since we're still pretty new. He's always done that. I guess he likes to be transparent with our performance."

"And how has that performance been? What did he say in his most recent email?"

"He said our team is struggling to stay afloat, and that we need to close more deals, or else. He told us to keep doing the work, and we'll find the qualified buyers in no time. Stressed to not get desperate."

"And do you feel desperate?"

"I do, yes. This is my first job in the professional world and I don't want to lose it already. I feel like I'm just getting the hang of it."

"I see. And what can you tell me about the actual closing

process? How involved are you, as the realtor?"

"We help all the way until the actual closing. We do the showings, communicate with lenders on behalf of the buyers..."

"So you work with only buyers?"

"Personally, yes. But our team has other realtors who specialize in working with sellers, and they try to negotiate deals for them to sell their home directly to WonderHome."

"Aren't realtors typically present on the day of a closing? It's a big moment for everyone involved."

Owen shrugged. "I told you, this is my first professional job, so I don't know what the norm is. I just know with WonderHome, they take care of the contract and transaction, so I can move on to the next showing and hopefully find the next deal we can close on."

"And that's how it's always been, this part of the process?"

"Yes."

"Do you know who at the company handles the contracts? Someone *has* to put their signature on the form."

Owen shrugged. "No idea. When I come to an agreement with a buyer, I draft up the basic details and send it to my manager. He takes it from there, and I have no clue what happens."

"Do you ever deal with Adam Marshall?"

Owen stared at Arielle as if his mind were absent from this conversation.

"I don't know who that is. I think I've heard the name Eric mentioned around the closing part, but I don't even know an Eric at the office, so don't hold me to that."

The mention of Eric caught Arielle off guard. She wasn't familiar with the name either, which gave her hope that they were on to something new.

"You're doing great, and I thank you for that. I just have a few more questions and we can both be on our way. Let's pretend the person's name is indeed Eric. Once Eric signs the contracts, you get paid your commission, right?"

"Yes, five percent of the final closing amount. Gets paid out on the following paycheck."

"And you've never had an issue? They've always paid you on time?"

"No issues."

"And do all of your potential clients reach out to you how I did, or are there other ways?"

"There are lots of ways: an online form like you did, inbound phone call, and sometimes we get a list of home buyers sent to us. That's where I've had most of my luck."

"I see. Where does that list come from?"

"We get it from our manager. They assign everyone a list of clients to follow up with and see if they're still interested in buying properties. I think WonderHome uses some of their internal information, since they can see who is browsing the site, because most of these calls the people sound surprised to hear from us. But now and then, it's like we make the perfect connection and the buyer is ready at that moment to get a deal done."

"Interesting," Arielle said, more to herself. "And how often do you get this list?"

"About once a week. We were told yesterday we'll start getting more of these types of clients, and they're hoping to make them more qualified. But I haven't seen anything yet."

"I see. I think that's all of my questions. Are you okay if I reach out to you down the road if I think of anything else?"

"I guess," Owen said, eyeing the money that Arielle held in her hand during the entire questioning. She had no plans of ever speaking to this man again, and handed over the money.

Owen examined it like it couldn't possibly be real. Once he realized it was, he stuffed the wad of cash into his pocket. "Thank you. This actually helps me more than you know."

"No, thank you, Owen. You've been a tremendous help and made this process much easier than it usually is. If I can leave you with one piece of advice before we part ways. Leave your job at WonderHome. Just trust me on that. Start looking now, and get out as soon as you can."

She turned and left him dumbfounded in the house. When she reached her car, he still hadn't appeared outside. Poor guy was probably suffering an anxiety attack after everything that had just happened, but Arielle had to leave.

She understood what was happening, and how to bring the entire scheme down.

Chapter 47

February 17, 2014

Selena had taken one of Felix's microphone pens to work on Friday and planted it in Landon's pen cup with no detection. Only Michelle kept her door closed on the executive floor. Selena found a conference room along the hallway with a direct view of Landon's office. Once she saw him step away and enter the bathroom, she glided right in and planted the pen. The executive floor was known for being a ghost town, and it was even more abandoned so early on a Friday morning.

No one saw her, and she vanished without a trace.

Felix began listening immediately, and Friday ended with nothing of substance. Landon had even called it a day after the lunch hour and was gone for the weekend.

Arielle had followed him home, but he simply ventured into his house and hadn't come back out when Arielle decided she had wasted enough time and left at five o'clock.

Over the weekend, with not much else to do, Arielle demanded they unplug and take a step back to prepare for a chaotic week ahead.

"We're going to get aggressive starting next week," she had told them. "We have a basic understanding of what's going on and where the obvious opportunities are for the money laundering to occur. Let's apply some pressure on everyone involved and see if we can't cause a panic."

They agreed to spend their Sunday at the EMP Museum and its dozens of exhibits covering American pop culture throughout the years.

By the time they arrived home later that night, after a fun dinner out downtown, Arielle knew her idea for a laid-back weekend had worked. Felix and Selena were not only ready for Monday, but excited at the prospects of the new week.

On Monday morning, the breakfast table hummed with an anxious anticipation.

"All right, the weekend is over," Felix said. "You said you wouldn't talk about the mission until Monday, so let's hear it. What do you have up your sleeve for this week?"

Arielle took a bite of her Fruit Loops before answering. "I don't want to get our hopes up, but I think we can end this mission this week. If not, next week at the latest."

"Say what?!" Selena cried, jumping out of her seat.

Arielle raised her hand to silence the energetic Selena. "My ideas take time to marinate. I may have not discussed the mission, but trust me, it's all I thought about this weekend. The way I see things, Landon is playing two different roles at the same time. He's the CFO for WonderHome, and also the one behind these drug and weapons deals—who exactly he is in *that* whole scheme, I don't know. I also don't care. We're here to get Adam Marshall off the hook. If they want us to investigate Landon and his dealings separately, they can assign another mission for that."

"So, what are we doing?" Selena asked, urgency clinging to every word.

"There are a lot of moving parts, but I think we can cover all of them. Landon is desperate right now. His job is on the line, and if he loses it, he can kiss his laundering operation goodbye. Felix got us some snapshots of the company's bank accounts. They've spent a ton of money buying properties across the country. Properties that are not selling at the prices they're looking for. I don't think Landon has ever worked directly in real estate, because he didn't entirely think the program through. Their whole angle was to buy properties needing lots of work, to then resell at a higher cost. Now, I don't know if this was intentional, or if this somehow fell through massive cracks, but WonderHome has no way of improving these homes they're buying. It would have made sense for them to hire contractors directly to their payroll and deploy them to each home needing repairs. But that never happened, and it makes zero sense why not. Because of this, I believe it has always been Landon's intent to use the entire program for his laundering purposes."

"So, this has all been going on for months?" Felix asked.

"Not necessarily the laundering, but the plans for it. The real estate program was the framework to make it all possible. With it now fully in operation, Landon can start funneling the funds back into the company."

"I still don't understand how this gets Landon paid," Selena said.

"Felix, shed some light on that part, please," Arielle said.

"Yes," he replied. "I found the original email conversations from before the real estate program even launched. The CFO is to receive fifty percent of all profits from the real estate program, paid out monthly as a commission."

"Fifty percent?!" Selena gasped. "That's outrageous and

makes no sense. He's losing a lot of money by doing that."

Arielle nodded. "He is, but this is all being set up for the long term. If this runs smoothly, Landon can have a constant supply of bonus money coming his way, completely legal in the eyes of the government, all without ever having his name tied to anything illegal. On paper, the company makes money from this program, which keeps them happy with his employment, meanwhile he's pulling in half of whatever he's making off these drug deals without a worry in the world. It's actually kind of genius because it can literally last until he retires. And at thirty-six years old, that's a lot of money to be made. It makes sense why he didn't seem worried at all during that meeting with Michelle, and it's because he's pulling all the strings. I've done some more reading on major laundering schemes over the years, and I'm fairly confident his next move is to pay off people to buy these worthless properties. We're ahead of him."

"How do you figure?" Selena asked.

"Because whatever money he's made from his illegal dealings hasn't made its way into WonderHome yet. Now, it's clear Landon is not some evil genius, or he would have covered more bases. I think the higher-earning realtors are in on the scheme, but Landon hasn't entrusted everyone on the team. Too many people involved opens up the possibilities of getting caught. Someone always gets too greedy and blackmails the ringleader. It's a tale as old as time. Now, Landon needs to turn things around quickly, and there is a simple way he can do that. He can bribe people to buy these properties for a certain amount of money. He can do this a couple of ways. Option one is by paying someone a flat rate to do it. He can offer, let's say, ten thousand dollars to call into WonderHome with an interest to buy one of their properties. He can have them claim they want to buy the property with cash, which eliminates the need for a lender and all of that paperwork. Since WonderHome owns the deed on the property, all they need to do is take the paperwork and sign it over to the pretend buyer's name. The buyer leaves with their ten thousand, and WonderHome can file the paperwork as a successful closing, all while depositing the cash from the alleged purchase. Boom, the drug money is now legally on the books for WonderHome.

"Option two would include Landon preying on those less fortunate. He can seek out the poor and make them the same offer, only instead of a cash payment, they can live in the house rent-free. He can literally offer this to the homeless and they'll agree to it. They won't *need* the running water or electricity, since they can't pay those bills, but it's a roof over their head. A lot of these properties are already in pretty run-down neighborhoods, so it's not like some trust fund family will have a homeless person moving in next door. *That* would cause many problems for Landon. But the way it's all set up now—intentionally, I'm sure—no one will bat an eye."

"So if he's thinking of the future, option one is probably the most likely route," Felix said. "Less opportunity for things to go awry."

"I agree," Selena said.

"As do I," Arielle added. "Now, where do we come in to this? I want to scare some of these hired home buyers. We will follow one of the top-earning realtors from WonderHome, and if we see them showing a run-down home to someone, we'll know that's exactly what's at play. There are only five real estate agents at WonderHome who are bringing in big money. Everyone else is struggling, like my friend Owen. The five have to be working directly with Landon while the rest get left out to dry, trying to sell homes that no one actually wants to buy. I think the new classes that keep coming in for the real estate team are intentionally big. It's all a numbers game. New hires come in, and Landon sorts through them to find even just one person who can join his small team on the scheme. They have to be trustworthy, in Landon's eyes, and if so, they all get to make tons of money together, sworn to carry this secret to their graves."

"Do you think he threatens them?" Selena asked. "I can always ask for a transfer to the real estate team."

"I'm sure he threatens them with reality. If any of them get caught, they're going to prison for a long time. It's simple. And if someone else gets caught, you keep your mouth shut. Now, after my meeting with Owen, I'm quite confident we can continue to play the role of a private investigator. I want to approach these fake home buyers and threaten them. I'm not interested in taking their money or anything like that, I just want them scared. If we scare enough, one of them will crack and reach back out to their WonderHome agent who crafted the deal. That agent will tell Landon what happened. And once Landon gets word that his real estate program is being watched, well, we sit back and watch the fireworks."

Felix laughed. "You wouldn't sit back. That's not the Arielle Lucila way. Once you smell that blood, we all know you're going to pounce like a lion on a wounded zebra."

Arielle smiled. "That's probably true. I want to go home, and I know you both do too. That's why I've already called in for you today, Selena, and for the rest of the week, in fact."

"What?! How did you—? When did you—?"

"I called this morning and said you had an unexpected

family emergency and won't be in for the rest of the week. The attendance line is just an answering machine. It wasn't too hard to sound like you." Felix burst into laughter. Arielle turned to him with a devilish grin. "And what's so funny over there, Mr. Francisco? I called out for Selena so you wouldn't have to join us today in acting like private investigators. Unless you'd like to, of course."

Felix's laughing and his grin halted immediately. "No. Thank you for doing that."

"Exactly. Selena, I have the names of the agents we're going to follow. These high-performers are collectively closing three deals a day, but I suspect that will start ramping up even more now that Landon has to show some big numbers coming into the company. Felix can access their schedules, so we'll know exactly where they're going. We won't be together this week so we can cover more ground, but our job is simple. Look for the transaction that makes no sense, then approach the pretend buyer once they're out of sight from the realtor. Tell them we're investigating real estate fraud and have some questions. Make up the questions, it doesn't matter, because by the time you've already said all that, they're going to be shitting their pants. Leave them in peace afterwards and tell Felix once you've done it. Felix, you'll need to keep a close eye on Landon's inbox and potential conversations in his office after these encounters."

"How do you figure this takes a week?" Felix said. "We have no idea if or when any of these people will reach out to their WonderHome agent."

"Exactly, that's why I said a two-week cushion," Arielle said. "Someone *will* talk. I'm confident about that. It's human nature to panic if you think you might go to prison, especially for something you just did, like we'll be doing with these fake buyers. It's even more natural to seek blame and point fingers, which is what will happen when they reach out to their agent. Then the dominoes fall, and we swoop in to complete the mission."

"This is honestly a brilliant plan," Selena said. "But what if it takes some time before someone calls back in? Then what?"

"Well," Arielle replied. "We can wait patiently. I have no issue with that. But we know where Landon will be every Thursday night. I don't mind sending him a little warning shot while he's there. Hell, I might do it either way. That warning shot can do a lot more damage if he already thinks he's being watched. Then he'll really unravel. Because if I've learned one thing about these types of criminals, and further confirmed through his lackluster planning of the real estate program, is that they never have plans for getting caught."

Felix nodded and stood up, prompting Arielle to do the same. "I'm ready to get to work. But I have one question. How does all this get tied back to Adam Marshall?"

Arielle walked her empty cereal bowl to the sink and turned around, crossing her arms. "I haven't been able to confirm this yet, but I'm pretty sure Adam is the one signing these real estate contracts on behalf of WonderHome. It's why we haven't been able to find anything—it's all physical paper contracts with his name in ink."

"But how does that responsibility fall to him?"

Arielle laughed. "Do you really not see it? Because that's what they hired him to do."

Chapter 48

Arielle and Selena each took a car and went their separate ways after the motivational breakfast. Felix hung back to monitor the surveillance activity set up in both Michelle's and Landon's offices.

Selena had yet to feel this level of optimism while on this mission, content to enjoy the ride as a popular new employee at WonderHome. Even that honeymoon was fizzling, the energy fading quickly as she got deeper into a routine at work, every day feeling like the same thing after another. She supposed that was natural, and a reason many in her generation hopped around from job to job.

Knowing she had a week off from going to the office (and potentially never returning), driving across town energized her in a way she hadn't realized she needed. She had no idea what awaited over the course of the day, no clue when she might return home, and no idea who she might meet today. Plus, she got to act in a different role when approaching these realtors.

According to their schedules for showings, Arielle and Selena would each confront two different realtors during the day.

Felix had shared the details with them about how Wonder-

Home managed these transactions, and where they would be best suited to intercept the fake buyers.

The transactions were unorthodox for real estate purchases, where the alleged buyer would meet the realtor at the property. They would enter and do a final walkthrough, and sign the paperwork there on the spot. Even for a cash transaction, this process seemed strange, but WonderHome touted same-day closings for cash buyers as a perk of their program.

How this wasn't seen as a red flag by whichever authorities monitored money laundering was beyond Selena. Or perhaps that was exactly what led to them being caught in the original timeline of events where everything was tied to Adam Marshall.

Selena's first target of the morning was Cody Hayes, the top-ranked realtor on the real estate for WonderHome. According to their records, Cody was closing at least three transactions per week for the last two months, most of which were run-down homes that sold for well above their value.

Arielle had insisted Selena take Cody, claiming she had earned the right.

That familiar sense of destiny worked its way through Selena's body as she entered the neighborhood. Vehicles with deflated tires, scratched paint jobs, and cracked windows lined the curbs. Nearly every business had bars over their windows, graffiti sprayed on the side of the buildings. Stray dogs roamed the streets, and not a single property kept a maintained front lawn. Most had more cars parked right on the patches of grass and weeds outside the front door.

The houses were in even worse shape, and Selena figured none of them could sell for more than one hundred thousand in 2014, if that.

I'm in the right place, Selena thought. *It's going down right here to start the day.*

The meeting between Cody and the buyer was scheduled for ten o'clock, and Selena arrived at 9:45, parking across the street and two houses down where she could have a clear view of the property in question. For a neighborhood that lacked any sort of colorful cheer, the bright green and yellow WonderHome "For Sale" sign stuck out like an orange in a batch of apples.

Selena parked and killed the engine, checking her surroundings. She had turned off the main road and found herself on a long block of ranch-style homes, trees providing plenty of overhead coverage.

She parked in front of a house that appeared abandoned, one of the few without cars stuffed into the driveway and lawn. Most of the homes on the block had their dumpsters rolled out to the curb for trash pickup. It was the middle of the morning when the kids would be at school and most people at work.

Selena watched as a shiny black car turned onto the block from the main road, rolling steadily down the street and stopping in front of the house for sale.

"There you are," Selena said, leaning forward for a better look, but unable to see anything through the blacked-out tinted windows. The car, an Audi of some sorts, was clearly out of place.

The door swung open and out stepped Cody Hayes, a tall and skinny kid with black hair slicked to the side. He wore a long gray peacoat and black gloves, and strutted to the house's front door with plenty of swagger and confidence.

"You slimy motherfucker," Selena said, shaking her head, wishing she could hop out and key this cocky dude's car.

While she had known plenty of rich and narcissistic people, she suspected none of them earned their money in such a fake way. Most had taken gambles in the stock market or risky business ventures that ended up paying out. And most donated money to charitable causes, even if only for a tax write-off.

How low could a person go for a quick buck? Selena was now finding out, and hoped all the realtors who took part in this scheme would go down in flames with Landon once it all collapsed around him.

Cody disappeared into the house without so much as a look over his shoulder. That told Selena that he had become comfortable in such settings, especially considering he hadn't even locked his Audi despite it being out on the curb.

"There is definitely a closing about to happen."

She only had to wait five more minutes until the next car appeared on the block, parking in the driveway.

A heavyset bald man stepped out of the Ford Focus and scratched his gray goatee before stretching. He was much bigger than Selena and could pose issues should he get physical when she encountered him. But there was no way he was fast on his feet, something she would play to her advantage if matters escalated to that point.

"Where do you even find people to do something like this?" she asked the empty car. Was there a network of regular folks looking for easy money to help money launderers?

None of that mattered, and when the bald man let himself into the house without knocking, she had one hundred percent confidence this was all part of the scheme.

The urge to disrupt the transaction from even happening swelled within Selena, but she knew better than to step into a situation where she'd be outnumbered. They still didn't understand exactly what *type* of people they were dealing with.

Fifteen minutes passed when Selena grew antsy, wondering what was taking so long. But it was only another five minutes after that when both men emerged from the house, a shit-eating grin smacked across Cody's face.

They made their way to the WonderHome sign standing tall near the sidewalk. Cody grabbed both sides and wiggled it out of the earth, tossing it into the next-door neighbor's dumpster.

The men laughed and shook hands, the fake buyer patting his pocket where an obvious wad of cash had been stuffed, appearing like a bulge of rocks in his pants.

Cody hopped into his car first and sped away with a quick wave out the window to his most recent buyer.

The man trudged down the driveway, moving gingerly as he strolled around his vehicle.

"I can take this guy," Selena said, slipping on a pair of sunglasses, stepping out of her car, and dashing across the street.

The man hadn't seen her yet. As she approached him, she shouted, "Hey! Excuse me!"

The man was getting ready to open his car door and had his back to Selena when he heard this. He stopped and spun around, a dumbstruck look on his face.

"Can I help you?" he asked, his voice deep and slow.

"You sure can. Start by telling me what happened in there."

The man's hand gradually inched toward his bulging pocket, and he covered it with his massive palm. "I don't know what you're talking about."

"Of course you do," she said. "This house has been up for sale. You went inside and came out, and now that sign is gone. Did you just buy this house?"

The man looked around the neighborhood, and Selena had no way of knowing if he was scared or planning to try something. Either way, she was prepared.

"Do you live on the block or something?" he asked. "You one of those nosy neighbors?"

Selena grinned and crossed her arms, glaring at the man from behind her sunglasses. She knew wearing them would intimidate him. The oldest trick in the book was to interrogate someone and not allow them to see your eyes.

"I'm not your neighbor," Selena said smoothly, growing confident the man wouldn't try to hurt her. "I'm a private investigator looking into WonderHome. Did you just buy this home from one of their real estate agents?"

The man gulped, looked up, looked down, all the while his fingers clenched the bulge in his pocket. "I, uh. Yes, I did. I bought this home."

"Really? Do you have any paperwork proving this?"

The man parted his lips and started looking in every direction *except* at Selena. "I, uh. No, I don't. My realtor just left here. He's going to finish the contract so I can sign it."

"Right," Selena said, taking one more step closer to the large man. "So, when do you close?"

Beads of sweat formed around the man's forehead, despite the morning being a cool forty degrees. "Next week," he said, continuing to avoid eye contact.

"I see. Are you aware that I know you're lying? I can see right through you. Standing here sweating like a Catholic in church. If you're going to be involved in such criminal activity, you should at least learn how to lie and remain calm under pressure, because people like you are the ones who always end up in jail."

"I didn't do nothing, lady," the man said.

Selena smiled. "Let's take a step back. What's your name?"

The man hesitated, not replying for twenty seconds.

"Well?" Selena asked.

"Ed," he said. "Ed Zimmerman."

"If you say so. Ed, let me start over and say that you're not in any sort of trouble. I'm not here to investigate *you*. I don't care about that cash in your pocket. You will walk away from this conversation with your money. If someone else wants to come after you later, then that's their business. I want to know what WonderHome is doing. How much did they pay you just now?"

Ed was squeezing his pocket so tightly his knuckles were a sheet of white. "Ten thousand dollars."

"Ten thousand?! Christ, I'm in the wrong line of work. And for what? All you had to do was sign a deed for the house, yeah?"

Ed nodded slowly.

"Again, I'm not coming after you, but I'm just curious. Are you aware that you're assisting WonderHome in a money laundering scheme?"

Ed nodded again, not speaking, still not making eye contact. Selena figured his throat had probably tensed completely shut.

"Are you aware of the punishment for aiding in such a crime?"

Ed shook his head.

"It's twenty years, Ed. Twenty years in prison. *And* you

have to pay back all the illegal money you received, *plus* some. If I were you, I'd think twice about doing such a thing again. You'll get caught eventually—I can promise you that. You signed your name on a legally binding form, after all. If WonderHome ever gets caught, the feds will investigate every single piece of property they've ever sold. It's only a matter of time before they find your name on that deed, which you don't even have in your possession. You signed it and let the bad guys take it with them. You, sir, are truly a fool."

"I'm sorry," Ed pleaded. "I have kids. I lost my job. My wife is sick and can't work. This money is all I have to keep us in our home for the rest of the year."

Selena tossed up her hands. "I'm not taking your money. It's yours. You've taken the risk and earned it. Just be ready for when the feds come knocking—they won't be as kind as me. Now get the hell out of here before I change my mind."

Ed nodded one last time before hurrying into his car, flying out of the driveway and zipping down the block.

Selena stood there, alone in the silent, eerie neighborhood, smiling. She had definitely gotten through to him, but was it enough to help their cause?

Chapter 49

February 18, 2014

Monday had passed with Arielle and Selena successfully approaching all of their targets. Three of the four encounters played out similar to Selena's with Ed Zimmerman. One man dashed away in a mad sprint that Arielle had no intent of chasing down. Her only goal was to scare these people, and clearly that had happened, judging by his record-breaking speed.

All of their work had turned up zero results by the end of the workday on Monday. No emails, calls, or direct meetings with Landon occurred around the topic. It was deflating, but Arielle assured them they just had their hopes too high. She gave a two-week cushion for a reason, though admittedly agreed she believed something would happen much sooner.

Tuesday morning, Arielle and Selena were back out in Seattle, following WonderHome's best realtors, and shaking down the fake buyers. Arielle commented how absurd it was that they weren't even trying to disguise what they were doing. They made no efforts to sprinkle in actual home buyers interested in legitimate properties.

"That's what the rest of the real estate team is for," Felix had said as he wished them a good day out the door.

And it was true. He had taken a deeper dive into the financials of the real estate team. Outside of the top performers, everyone else struggled and had much lower deals, on average.

Felix spent his Tuesday morning how he preferred, a hearty breakfast followed by a light jog around the neighborhood, then back home where he planted himself in front of his computer to get started for a fun day of work.

He still listened to Michelle's conversations, convinced she was involved in the scheme to a lesser degree. Surely a CFO couldn't pull all this off without the CEO knowing. She could have even caught wind of what was at play and turned a blind eye, giving that public shaming of Landon for appearances.

The morning passed with no drama. Landon had meetings from nine to eleven, then an open block where he returned to his office for an hour until lunch time. Michelle's schedule was similar, although her meetings took place in her office, leaving Felix to listen to a heated discussion around hiring more sales agents to further expand their market reach across the nation.

It wasn't until ten minutes after one o'clock when a knock banged on Landon's door and another voice immediately started speaking. "Hey, boss," a man said. "You have a minute?"

"Charles," Landon replied. "Come on in. Close the door and have a seat."

Felix looked over his list of WonderHome realtors and identified the man as Charles Hawkins, the team's second-highest performing agent.

After a few seconds, Landon spoke first. "How is everything

going out in the field? Looks like you've got more closings lined up."

"Yes, I can't complain," Charles replied, then lowered his voice. "I just got an interesting phone call I think you need to know about."

"Does it pertain to Eric?" Landon asked, followed by a silence Felix assumed was filled with Charles nodding his head. "I see. What was the call about?"

Charles continued just above a whisper, but Felix's pen microphone was plenty strong enough to pick up the discussion. "My buyer from my first closing this morning just called me. He sounded terrified. He said some lady in sunglasses walked up to him after we left the property, claimed to be a private investigator, and was asking all kinds of questions about the transaction."

"And what did the buyer say?"

"He said he made up some answers as best he could. The lady asked if he had received any money for signing the contract. Luckily he had it in his backpack and he told her he didn't know what she was talking about. But why would she ask such a specific question? Landon, is someone on to us?"

"Well, it certainly sounds like it," Landon said, not sounding too distraught. "That's a lot of details. I wonder if someone tipped off the feds. Who do you think it could be?"

"What do you mean? Like someone from our team? No one's crazy enough to do that—way too risky."

"Unless they were approached first. The feds could have figured it out some other way and started snooping around. If they got hold of one of our agents, they could offer immunity for the truth about what's going on. But let's slow down. I don't want to jump to conclusions."

"With all due respect, sir, I think jumping to conclusions is exactly what we need to do. This wasn't some chance encounter. Whoever this lady was, she knew exactly where to go, who to follow, and what to say. We're being watched."

"How did your buyer say this meeting ended?"

"He said the woman questioned him, and he gave made-up answers until she finally decided she heard enough and left."

"No threats?"

"Not that he mentioned. But I could hear the fear in his voice. He sounded on the verge of tears."

"Just shaken up, I'm sure. Easy money is never actually easy. Did anyone ever tell you that, Charles? Easy money still requires a lot of hard work. Some might classify what we're doing as easy money, but I don't see you sitting on the couch picking your nose all day. God no, you're out there busting your ass every single day, even if it's all rigged. You still gotta show up and put in the work."

"Yes, but none of that means a thing if we're in prison."

Landon laughed. "Prison. Slow your roll, young man. Nobody is going to prison, remember? This is all set up in a particular way, with certain checks and balances, to make sure no one on our team is ever held responsible. Is your name on the contract your buyer signed today?"

"No."

"Exactly. If shit were to hit the fan, we'll get questioned, sure, but nothing is falling to us. We're just a team of real estate agents out doing our jobs. Eric is the one pulling all these other strings for his own agenda. Don't forget that. Tell your buyer to not worry and to keep his mouth shut. Maybe we need to lie low for a bit, but we can't really afford to. Our entire department is on the chopping block unless we show more money coming in. For now, business as usual. Okay?"

"Yes, sir," Charles said. "Do you want me to bring this up to you if it happens again, or are we really going to keep pretending everything is fine?"

"Excuse you. Everything *is* fine. I have everything under control. Speak to me like that again and you'll find yourself unemployed. I don't appreciate the accusing tone you've had since you walked in here. Get back out there and do your job."

"Yes, sir, my apologies," Charles said, and left the office.

Once in silence, Felix listened as Landon let out a frustrated, "Fuck!" followed by frantic typing on the keyboard.

Everything was becoming clear, except for this Eric character. There wasn't a single Eric listed anywhere in the WonderHome database. It had to be a code name for someone, or perhaps something.

Once Landon's typing stopped, Felix watched closely for any outgoing email messages. After a few seconds, it popped up, and Felix's heart sank. Landon had just sent an email to Michelle, calling for an urgent off-site meeting in ten minutes.

Felix picked up his phone and called Arielle.

Chapter 50

Arielle was finishing a burrito bowl for lunch when Felix called in a panic, urging her to get back to the office as soon as possible.

Fortunately, she had been in the general vicinity after approaching the last fake buyer and demanding details they didn't have.

She didn't think she could make it in ten minutes, but would try. Selena was even further from the office, so it would all depend on traffic. Her GPS said she was exactly twelve minutes from the office, so she hopped in the car and sped off. If Landon and Michelle were to *meet* in ten minutes before heading out of the office, that would give Arielle just enough cushion time to make it to follow them.

The mission gods must have been looking over her because traffic was light, and she caught very few red lights and she raced across town, tight grip on the steering wheel while she pinched her tongue between her lips, weaving around cars going much too slow.

It had been 1:22 when Felix called, and she pulled up to the front entrance of the Wilson Investments Center at 1:33, screeching to a stop in the loading zone that only allowed fifteen minutes for parking.

"Shit!" Arielle cried, seeing Landon and Michelle step out from the building. She looked around, saw no metered parking available, and opted to leave her car in the loading zone.

Arielle jumped out and hurried around to the sidewalk, where plenty of people crowded the walkway. She set her eyes on Landon and Michelle, who strolled along at a leisurely pace, one block west, until they entered the Starbucks on the corner.

All three Angels had visited this Starbucks back when they first arrived in Seattle. It was famous for being the first and original location for the chain that would eventually rule the planet. Selena had wanted to see it, and insisted they stand in the ever-growing long line.

But in the middle of a workday afternoon, there was no line out the door like there was in the morning, so Arielle took cautious steps as she entered, delighted to see a decent amount of people sitting at the tables inside.

Landon and Michelle didn't even bother waiting in line for a drink. They headed straight back to the corner nearest the bathrooms, where they huddled together at a two-seater table. Landon planted his elbows on the table, both hands balled into fists that covered his mouth. He was speaking, and it was impossible to read his lips. His eyes were also scanning the Starbucks, as if expecting to see someone.

Michelle matched his positioning, the two looking like a baseball coach and pitcher convening on the mound, hiding their mouths so the cameras couldn't pick up what was being said.

Both of them kept scanning the room, causing Arielle to turn her back from them as she pretended to stand in line. It was too risky to get any closer, at least without something to conceal her face. An open table was three spaces over from them, and she might be able to sit there while keeping her back to them.

Arielle cocked her head downward and started walking toward the table, looking ashamed of herself. Just before she arrived, a couple pulled out of the seats and sat down, leaving Arielle stranded in the middle of the room, standing awkwardly among the patrons enjoying their afternoon treats.

She spun around and headed back toward the line, keeping her back to Landon and Michelle. Arielle grew paranoid about getting caught—that was too risky of a decision to get that close. If only she had one of Felix's recording pens, she could drop it next to their table without them even noticing.

But she only had herself, and remembered one of the key lessons she had learned during her rise as the top-ranked Angel: Never force a matter under any circumstance.

The line inched closer to the counter, bringing Arielle gradually closer toward the direction of her two targets. Standing in line was simply a way to blend in—she needed to get closer to actually hear their conversation.

Arielle stepped out of line a second time, this time pulling out her cell phone and holding it down by her waist. She shuffled into the narrow walkway that led to the bathroom and strolled confidently past the table where she could overhear Michelle saying, "You need to fix this."

Those five words tantalized Arielle as she slipped into the restroom, leaning on the door. She could spare thirty seconds before stepping back out and not appearing suspicious. And the way they were both looking around the café, she couldn't take a chance of them having already noticed her walk by.

Once the thirty seconds passed, Arielle stepped back out of the bathroom, the short hallway giving her just enough room to see Michelle sitting at the table, facing Landon. She pulled out her cell phone again and pretended to be texting as she walked by.

This second trip was a waste, with neither Michelle nor Landon speaking as Arielle wandered by their table.

Once Arielle was three steps past the table, Michelle's voice called out to her. "Hey!"

Arielle felt every muscle in her body tighten.

You forced the issue, and now you pay.

Arielle continued forward, calm and confident, not looking over her shoulder.

"Hey, you!" Michelle called out again, this time loud enough to earn the attention of others in the room.

Arielle was about fifteen feet away from the exit when she looked over her shoulder, still not stopping. Her eyes locked with Michelle's, who had stood up to face her.

"Stop!" Michelle snarled, but Arielle had already turned back around and bolted out of the Starbucks, breaking into a full sprint away from Pike Place Market and down the block toward the Wilson Investment Center, where she had left her car parked.

It had only been ten minutes, so she was still within the time restrictions for the loading zone. She didn't look back until she reached her car, gasping for air after the unplanned cardio workout. She saw nothing but crowded sidewalks. No Michelle. No Landon.

Stupid, she told herself, disgusted with her performance. *High-risk, no reward. That's all that was.*

Arielle didn't chalk up too many losses on missions, but this blunder would weigh on her mind for the rest of the day.

350

Chapter 51

The three Angels gathered at the dinner table Tuesday night, mentally battered, sitting in silence.

Arielle had just shared the story of being spotted by Michelle at the Starbucks.

"Better than spotting me," Felix said with a laugh that failed to lighten the mood.

"We're getting close," Selena said. "I had a situation arise today, as well. I'm pretty sure it's the past resisting *because* we're so close."

"What now?" Arielle asked.

"I got a call today from work."

"But you're off for the week."

"Exactly. It was my VP, Amara. . . she had some questions about why I was in Landon's office the other day when he had stepped out."

"What?!" Arielle cried.

"Shit," Felix said.

"Someone saw you?" Arielle asked. "I thought you said there wasn't anyone around."

"There wasn't," Selena said. "She said the surveillance cameras caught me. Apparently, Landon submitted a request to the security team to review footage of the outside of his office and to report anything out of the ordinary. Sure enough, there I am, seconds after he steps out."

"But they couldn't see *inside* his office, right?"

"Correct. All they saw was me go in. They didn't even mention anything about the pen, so I think we're in the clear."

"What did you tell Amara?" Felix asked.

"Told her I was looking for Landon to review some payroll questions. I have no idea if she bought it—I don't think so. She said I'm to meet with her, Landon, and a security rep when I get back on Monday. We need to finish this mission this week—we can't keep going at this rate. I'm pretty sure they're going to fire me if my story makes no sense."

"That's probably true," Felix said. "But you're absolutely right. We *are* close. We rattled Landon. That's why he called an immediate off-site meeting with Michelle. Unfortunately, we don't know what they said, but it's obvious—again—that Michelle at least knows about the laundering scheme. It doesn't seem she's actively taking part in it, but her knowledge will be enough to put her away. I suppose the biggest question now is, where do we go from here? We have Landon against the ropes."

"He thinks he's being watched," Arielle said. "The call to review the security footage. The way he was looking around Starbucks. That's the only reason I'm not outside his house tonight. He's probably sitting at his window waiting to see anything that looks remotely close to someone following him."

"But we have a slight advantage," Felix said. "He thinks the feds are watching him, not us. And why would he think any differently? It's not like he knows there's a team of time travelers coming to bring him down."

"Exactly," Arielle agreed. "We can do whatever we need to stop this entire scheme from getting pinned on Adam. Speaking of, does anyone know how he's doing?"

The other two shrugged. No one had kept an eye on Adam over the past couple of weeks. As far as Arielle was concerned, Adam didn't need to be stopped. He was just going about his job and minding his business.

How Michelle could stand by and watch him get taken to prison proved everything about her character. Adam did nothing to deserve such a brutally harsh life. He had a family and dreams for a bright future. Still, Felix questioned how they pinned everything on him without a trace going back to Landon.

"He was fine, last I heard," Selena said. "I never got to see him at the office, but the POPS team hears everything. Everyone wanted to talk about the secret boyfriend who dumped Michelle after she got back from the Super Bowl. It made the gossip start about Adam and if Michelle would try to make a move on him, as she had done with past assistants. Honestly, it's all gibberish. People talking out of their asses. Still, we need to do the right thing. Not just to save Adam and his family, but to make sure these evil people get what they deserve. Michelle and Landon are literally using people like pawns in a sick game of chess. I'm sorry, but I have no sympathy for people like that. They really don't need to exist in our world."

"I completely agree," Arielle said. "Which is why we're going to ramp up the pressure. I think we've done enough to send the entire executive team into a frenzy. Think we can get away with placing some threatening calls?"

Felix nodded. "We have some ways to do that without being

caught, yes."

"Good. I think we can end this Thursday night. Landon is going to be so paranoid by the time he meets with his drug mules. Who knows, he might even bail if he's scared enough. But I don't want it to get to that level. Not yet. We need evidence tying everything back to Landon. I'm going to take pictures of him at his next drug meeting. Tomorrow, I want pictures of the realtors and fake buyers making their make-believe transactions. And instead of approaching the buyers, let's approach the realtors in the same way. Once Landon gets wind of that, he'll have no choice but to call off the entire operation."

"Do you think that's safe?" Selena asked.

"Of course. Landon is the criminal—that's who we should avoid for our safety. These realtors are nothing more than realtors. They won't take a shot at us or anything like that. Some might get mouthy, but I'm not too concerned."

Selena nodded to herself, taking a sip from her nightly glass of wine. "We're gonna make these assholes sing our praises to Landon. And I can't wait."

Chapter 52

February 19, 2014

The following morning, Arielle and Selena followed their same routine. Arielle was to confront two of the real estate agents in the morning before heading back home, where she would call Landon's office. Selena would remain out during the afternoon to intimidate more realtors.

Arielle's goal, by the end of the day, was to have the walls closing around Landon. He probably still believed they would tie every trace of criminal activity to Adam. But the phone call to Landon would throw a wrench into that belief. He wouldn't get away with it, and she'd make sure he knew that.

Before any of that could happen, Arielle had business to tend to. She sat outside another beat up property. This one had missing pieces from the roof and didn't look like anyone had lived in it for at least ten years. It was an abandoned property that stood alone across the street from a business strip offering tires and auto repair work.

Cars zipped by on the main road, and this would work to Arielle's advantage. The realtor she was about to approach, Rodney Perry, had been in Arielle's training class. The two had never spoken, and she was counting on a simple pair of sunglasses to keep her unrecognizable when she strolled up to him.

She had watched Rodney and his fake client go into the battered house ten minutes earlier. Once she saw them step out, Arielle immediately hopped out of her car. She didn't care if both the realtor and buyer were present. If she could scare both at once, then it would be that much sweeter.

She had her pistol tucked into the rear of her waistband, just in case, and walked up to the house with her arms crossed.

"Excuse me," Rodney said. "Can I help you?"

"Yes," Arielle said. "I'd like to see the property."

Rodney frowned. "I'm sorry, ma'am, but we just closed on the property."

The buyer shuffled away to his car, hopping in and taking off in a hurry.

"Do you always pay your clients to buy a house?" Arielle asked. "I'd love to get in on that sort of deal."

"I don't know what you're talking about."

"Did you not just bring ten thousand dollars for that man to sign his name on the deed for this house?"

"Nope," Rodney replied, smug. He clutched a briefcase at this side.

"Kind of strange to close on a property *at* the property, isn't it? I've never heard of such a thing."

"Cash transactions can happen anywhere."

Rodney was a lot sharper than Arielle was expecting. Aside from the overly tight grip on the briefcase, he showed no signs of worry.

"I see. And you have the cash in the briefcase?" Arielle nodded to it.

"I don't need to speak to you, ma'am. I'm sorry, but this

property is no longer available."

"Then you should probably take down the 'for sale' sign, don't you think?"

"I'll do that as soon as you leave. This is private property. If you don't leave, I can call the police."

"Oh, that would be fun. Let's get the cops over here. Maybe they can take a peek inside your briefcase and all the cash I'm sure you just got. I saw this house listed on WonderHome for $250,000. Most estimates show it's valued at $80,000. That doesn't make sense. And now that I'm standing here, I suppose even the eighty is too high. How much will it cost to fix that roof?"

"Look. I sold that man this property. He wants to turn it into a restaurant. My job is to sell properties, not worry about what happens to them after the deal is done."

"I didn't see your buyer with any paperwork. Shouldn't he have had a copy of the deed? Especially with a cash purchase. No need for all the other paperwork those pesky lenders ask for. He gave you cash, so you should have given him the deed and the keys."

"I don't know what you're talking about."

Arielle sensed a growing frustration from Rodney. This was not the way he had planned his morning on going.

"Well, a deed is a piece of paper showing who owns—"

"I know what a deed is," Rodney snarled through gritted teeth.

"Oh, well then, why do you keep saying you don't know what I'm talking about?"

"Look, lady, just leave. There's nothing here for you. Okay?"

"I'm not here to make any trouble for you. Just answer some

questions and we can both be on our way. First question, are you aware of the money laundering taking place by Wonder-Home with these fake transactions you're processing?"

"Bullshit," Rodney said, continuing to his car.

"You'll go down as an accomplice when this all comes crashing and burning. And it will. I can promise you that."

"Have a good day."

Rodney got in his car and slammed the door. Arielle didn't think he actually wanted her to have a good day.

"Tell Landon hello for me!" she shouted from outside the car, an older Honda Civic.

Rodney threw up his middle finger before blazing out of the driveway, swerving onto the main road and narrowly missing contact with an oncoming vehicle.

Arielle pulled out her cell phone and called Felix. "Hey, stay tuned. This guy left extremely heated. I'd be surprised if he's not already on the phone with Landon. His name is Rodney Perry."

"Got it. You're still going to the second realtor on your schedule now?"

"Yes. I'll see you after that for my call to Landon. Probably another hour."

"I'll be ready."

* * *

Arielle arrived back at their house just before noon. Her second encounter was with Cody Hayes, the top-ranked performer on the real estate. Cody had already spoken with

Landon about someone being on to them.

He mentioned how he was "expecting" Arielle and had nothing to offer. He professed his rights as a free American, and without a warrant signed by a judge, she had no grounds to keep questioning him. Cody insisted he had committed no crime.

Arielle hounded him with another half-dozen questions, but he simply ignored her like a celebrity pushing through a crowd of paparazzi and reports.

The meeting did nothing to advance their cause, but gave Arielle all the assurance she needed to know they were making substantial strides.

"Your buddy Rodney called Landon like you said," Felix explained to Arielle as she joined him at the dining room table. "I could only hear Landon's half of the conversation, but it was obvious the discussion was about you. We're getting to them. He told Rodney to take the rest of the week off while he brainstorms ideas to get the feds off his back."

Arielle laughed. Landon really had no clue what was going on, and that couldn't have played any better to their advantage. "Let him brainstorm all he wants. Tomorrow night, I'm kicking the wheels all the way off. Are we ready to make this call?"

"Let's do it."

Felix handed Arielle a headset, and she slipped it on while he configured the computer to make the outbound call. "This software records the call and masks the number. When the feds eventually pull all the records, they'll see we placed this call with an untraceable number. And by that time in the investigation, they'll just assume it was another one of Landon's illegal dealings. Why else would he receive a call from an untraceable number?”

“Genius,” Arielle said, earning a grin from Felix.

“Okay, dialing now,” Felix said, clicking in rapid succession on his screen.

The phone rang in Arielle’s ear, and she waited patiently while it rang for fifteen seconds. She almost gave up when the familiar voice of the CFO spoke. “Landon Greene.”

“Hello, Mr. Greene,” Arielle said in her most professional voice. “This is Lucia Ariano, and I’m an agent with the Federal Bureau of Investigation. May I have a few minutes of your time?”

“Hello, Ms. Ariano,” Landon replied, calm. “I have a few minutes right now.”

“Thank you. My team is investigating a money laundering suspicion at WonderHome, and I’d like to ask you a few questions. First off, you are the company’s chief financial officer. Is that correct?”

“Yes.”

“Great, and are you familiar with the company’s real estate program? It’s my understanding it was just launched within the last few months.”

“Yes, we have a team dedicated to that.”

“And may I ask who is in charge of that team?”

“I’m not entirely sure. It’s not a department I work with.”

“But you just said you’re the CFO. Don’t you work with all departments?”

“Well, sure. I overlook all funds for the company. I know how well every department is performing financially.”

“Yet, you don’t know who you would reach out to if you needed to speak with someone on the real estate team. Hard to believe, Mr. Greene.”

"Look, Ms. Ariano, I don't know what this is about. And it sounds like it has nothing to do with me. And if you're with the FBI, shouldn't you be speaking to the company's legal department? I'm not sure what I'm even allowed to say on this phone call right now. You know, confidentiality and all that."

"I can respect that," Arielle said. "And I've attempted to contact the WonderHome legal team. No one has ever responded, so now we're going through your company directory for people who might be of interest. Naturally, since you're the CFO, you're at the top of our list. Now, I'm not accusing you. If anything, this phone call can help clear your name and help us narrow our search for whoever might be responsible."

"Okay? I'm not involved in anything illegal, so I'm not sure what you can even clear me of. You should speak with our legal team. I'm happy to go down there and find someone right now."

"That won't be necessary, Mr. Greene. I'll try them again after we speak. Since I have you on the line, I was hoping you could answer some questions about the real estate team, mainly about some properties that have been reported as sold through WonderHome."

Silence.

"Mr. Greene, are you there?"

"He hung up," Felix said. "He's probably running out of the office right now because I hear nothing on his office feed."

"This is a big deal. If he's really convinced he's being watched by the FBI right now, there's no saying what he might do. He could run. And if he does, then what are we supposed to do?"

"I wouldn't panic. That only opens another opportunity for

us. He'll be away from WonderHome. Him running might be the best option. We can have Selena plant the evidence after hours, and we can get out of here."

"We'll have to see how it plays out. If he still goes to his meeting at the docks tomorrow, I think we can bring this all down."

Chapter 53

February 20, 2014

Thursday morning arrived after a long night of the three Angels debating their next move. Arielle had driven to Landon's house half an hour after he had hung up on her. She sat there for six hours before leaving.

He never showed up.

Arielle had driven through Michelle's neighborhood, just to see if Landon was maybe hiding there. But the house was also abandoned.

Selena frightened one more realtor on Wednesday afternoon, and with that, Arielle ordered they remain home on Thursday.

Selena argued against it, believing they should continue to follow the realtors until they broke down and stopped showing up at their fake closings. Felix urged Arielle to make additional calls to the WonderHome office. Why not dig deeper and call other members of the executive team or random employees? Combine some rumors with Landon presumably not showing up to the office, and it just might guarantee the employees at WonderHome would jump to their own conclusions about their CFO's guilt.

Arielle listened to their proposals and offered reasons for her rejection. First, Landon was right where Arielle wanted him. As long as he showed up at the meeting at the docks, then he hadn't abandoned all hopes for his scheme. They could live with him not showing his face at the office. Arielle expected as much. Wherever Landon was hiding, he was surely plotting his next steps. She had seen enough greedy criminals to know he wouldn't pull the plug on the operation. If anything, he was fielding different ideas for how to launder the money without using WonderHome.

They didn't need to approach any more realtors. Calling other employees could backfire. They still didn't have a full understanding of who was all involved. Contacting anyone else could risk others to cover up on behalf of Landon. Because if he went down, they were all going with him.

Selena and Felix understood Arielle's perspective on the matter, and braced for an eventful Thursday ahead.

Arielle made plans for the evening when Landon was to meet with his drug runners at the dock. They had no way of confirming if Landon had actually called out for the day. Felix listened to the bug in Landon's office and didn't hear a single peep all morning. Emails came into Landon's inbox and remained unread. Selena floated the idea of stopping by the office, but Arielle shot that down as unnecessarily risky. With Landon about to be in the spotlight for highly illegal activity, and Selena already on the radar for having snuck into his office, conclusions could be drawn, and they did not need any more targets on Selena's back.

Felix would remain at home while Arielle and Selena ventured out to the docks.

"Do you really think the gun is necessary?" Felix asked as

he watched Arielle pack her backpack with the camera, pistol, and throwing knives.

"I'm not planning on even getting close enough where I'd need to use it. But I'd rather have it than not. Keep in mind, we'll be outnumbered, but we'll keep a safe distance when trying to take the pictures. That's my primary goal for the night. If we can get clear shots of Landon involved with drugs and weapons dealers, the rest of the mission will be smooth sailing."

Felix laughed. "Smooth sailing. Right. We've heard that one before."

"This can end tonight. Tomorrow at the latest, depending if we can get these pictures printed."

"And what's the plan with the pictures? Drop them off at the police station? Pin them to Michelle's office door?"

Arielle smiled. "No. We'd deliver them to Adam Marshall, of course. Is there any sweeter justice—granted, he has no idea what's awaiting him—then to let him be the one to have those photos when the feds come in to arrest him?"

"That seems just as risky," Selena said. "We don't have evidence that he *isn't* involved, aside from unknowingly signing these contracts on behalf of the company."

"You're right," Arielle said. "And that's why we're going to have one last conversation with him, if we can. We can go to his house and explain what we've been investigating. He has to understand what he's been signing all this time. Maybe he's playing dumb and is getting part of Landon's money under the table, but unlikely. He never spoke up in that meeting in Michelle's office, and I would think for someone putting his name on every transaction, he might have more to say. I think it's a menial task he does. Probably doesn't even read the contracts anymore and just signs away to keep Michelle off his back."

"Do you not fear the risk of telling all this information to Adam?" Felix asked. "What if he really is working behind the scenes, knowingly, and just staying out of the limelight. If so, delivering him this info could do even more harm. If we can't risk calling others on the executive team, I don't see why we're treating Adam any differently."

"We have to tell *someone,* and it should be someone who still has a connection. Handing it off to someone completely random—say my old manager—is even higher risk. They may not take it seriously and nothing ever comes from it, or they blow things out of proportion before it's time. In that case, it's most likely to end up right back with Michelle or someone else on her team."

"We can plant some of these documents somewhere in the office," Selena said. "Even my desk. If I go after hours and leave it in my desk drawer, it will get found soon enough. Once I don't show up on Monday, it would probably be a few days until they realize I'm not coming back and clean out the desk."

"That's actually not a bad idea," Arielle said. "I still want Adam to have all this information. He's ultimately going to be accused of orchestrating this whole thing, so he needs to be equipped with the truth. During the trial, all he had was his word against his own signature on all the documents. And that's how we know he wasn't playing dumb about all this. He couldn't defend himself because he had no idea who was pulling what strings behind the scenes."

"We might as well hit everywhere we can with the proof once we have it," Felix said. "We can deliver it to Adam, the

WonderHome offices, even the local police station. Hell, we can even send it to a news station. Having that many bases covered can only help our cause. Are we planning on leaving as soon as we deliver the evidence, or waiting around to see what happens?"

"Let's see how everything plays out first. I don't want to make any assumptions this close to the finish line. We still have work to do this evening. I expect fireworks—Landon has his back against the wall with nowhere to go. Felix, do you have one of those body cameras I can wear tonight?"

"I should be able to get one before you leave."

Arielle checked her watch. "I'm heading out with Selena in six hours. Get me that camera. I want every single movement recorded tonight. I'm not taking any chances."

Chapter 54

Arielle and Selena arrived at the docks an hour before Landon's scheduled time. They didn't know what to expect—Landon hadn't shown his face at WonderHome since the call with Arielle.

It was entirely possible he wouldn't even show up at the docks tonight, considering the size of the target he perceived to be on his back.

They parked three hundred feet away. Arielle killed the engine and lowered the windows an inch, allowing the cool breeze to seep into the car. Seagulls cried out from the bay, gliding above the water in their search for dinner. Bells gonged on the buoys, swaying with each subtle gust of wind.

"Which one is it?" Selena asked.

Arielle pointed straight ahead to the end of the dock. "Last time, there were four or five guys who showed up on the boat. Landon was the only one who came to meet them. If it's that small of a group again, what do you think about firing some warning shots their direction?"

Selena scrunched her face, glaring at Arielle. "Don't take this the wrong way—I think that's the dumbest thing you've ever said. Fire a warning shot? What is that supposed to do? Aren't you supposed to kill the bad guy?"

Arielle smiled. Hearing Selena voice a strong opposition strengthened the trust she had in her teammate, her sister in this mad world of time travel.

"I only kill people who cause physical harm to others. Murderers don't have a place in this world."

"What do you consider yourself?"

Arielle paused. She could recall every single person she had ever killed. Even in her line of work, the sensation of removing a life from existence never grew numb. Each kill was a reminder of her own mortality, the fragility of life. Each time the guilt of playing executioner would twist her thoughts. A universal trait across all the villainous men and women she had encountered was their self-manipulation to justify their horrid actions. Was she not doing the same thing?

Was there really such a thing as good conquering evil, or was assassinating the wicked of the world simply good wrapped in evil?

"I consider myself an Angel," she finally said. "I don't like it, but I'm one of the few who can shoulder the burden of taking multiple lives. Not only am I numb to death, but I got to witness firsthand how powerfully cruel humanity can be. I guess that makes me the perfect candidate for a job like this, now that I think about it."

"Which is why you're *not* going to fire a warning shot. Doing that won't change anything of substance. You can either kill this guy or not, but don't settle for middle ground."

"It's not middle ground. There *is* a difference. What Landon has fallen into is being driven by greed. Maybe he'll never satisfy his hunger for more, but he deserves a chance at reform. A murderer does not."

"So it's settled. No warning shot—no shot at all. He can

live for another day. Because if you fire that gun, these goons will look all over until they find us."

Arielle had once picked off an entire drug cartel one-by-one without any help. A handful of drug runners hardly posed a threat. "Good point," she said. "Looks like someone is coming."

She caught a glimpse of a car turning onto the road in her rear-view mirror, and lowered her seat back to stay below the windows, prompting Selena to follow suit.

"Is it him?" Selena asked in a whisper.

"Couldn't tell. Could be, since we only have half an hour until the planned meeting time."

They remained low for a minute, waiting as the vehicle took its time cruising by, the engine a gentle hum, gravel crunching beneath the tires as it passed.

Once in the clear, Arielle and Selena nodded at each other before raising their seats to the upright position. They saw the rear of the vehicle, a black Lincoln Continental with windows tinted too dark to see inside. The license plate was a regular tag from Washington state.

"That's not Landon's car," Arielle said, brows narrowed as her eyes followed the SUV rolling down the dock.

"It looks kind of familiar," Selena said. "But I'm not sure from where."

The vehicle had nothing unique to identify it. They could probably stop by the airport and find another dozen that looked just like it.

The Lincoln stopped at the dock they were watching and parked in the same spot Landon had last week. Plumes of smoke puffed out of the exhaust pipe as it remained parked, no one stepping out.

"What's going on?" Selena asked, looking through her binoculars.

Arielle did the same. "I don't know. We've already altered things enough that we can't predict what's going to happen next."

She put the binoculars down and reached under her seat, pulling out a handgun and flicking off the safety.

"Whoa, what the hell?!" Selena cried out, shifting closer toward her door. "I thought you're not going to shoot anyone."

"I don't plan on it. But it's good to be prepared for anything."

They waited another five minutes before a second vehicle appeared on the road, and did their same routine as it passed by. This time it was Landon in his Corvette, and he pulled up right next to the SUV.

Arielle and Selena both returned to their binoculars, watching the two vehicles, still no one stepping outside.

"They probably think they're being watched—well, at least Landon thinks that. Explains why they're hesitant to get out of their cars."

"Do you think they have someone checking the area?"

"If he's that concerned about it, I wouldn't be surprised. But I haven't seen anyone besides the few sailors closing up their boats for the day."

The same blue boat from the prior week finally appeared, carefully drifting up to its anchor point.

"That's the one," Arielle said. "Crates of drugs and guns, and who knows what else. Looks like the same size crew, too."

They watched as a half-dozen men gathered at the center of the boat, waiting for it to dock.

"Shit!" Arielle shouted. "Get down!"

She yanked the lever and snapped her seat all the way back in an abrupt motion. Selena only paused for a second before realizing she needed to do the same.

"Someone's coming from behind," Arielle said. "Walking."

"Shouldn't we get out and fight?"

"We don't even know who it is. Could be an innocent bystander."

"Let's hope."

They braced themselves in the car, the only sounds those from the bay still carrying through the cracked-open windows. They lay flat on their backs for a clear view of the world outside. A long shadow cast over the car, swaying with each step its owner took.

Maybe we should have just gotten out of the car, Arielle thought. *They still wouldn't see us from the dock.*

Something in Arielle's gut, which she was listening to more, told her the person approaching their vehicle was no coincidence. As the shadow grew larger and closer, her stomach tightened to the point she thought she might vomit. She had the gun in her grip, but had never felt in such a defenseless position.

The pace of the walking shadow moved consistently. Confidently. The footsteps became audible, clopping along the road.

Please just keep walking by, Arielle prayed.

The footsteps stopped, and a pistol rapped against the driver-side window.

Chapter 55

"Put the gun down and get out of the fucking car!" the man shouted.

Arielle wasted no time releasing the gun from her grip. The man outside could blast right through the window, and she needed to buy time to find a way out of this situation.

"Both of you OUT!" the man yelled, tapping the gun on the window again, this time with more force. "And don't try anything cute."

"Just keep your hands visible," Arielle whispered to Selena, elevating both hands as she crunched her stomach to sit up straight from the reclined seat.

"Good girls," the man said, keeping the gun pointed at Arielle as he reached down to open the door. "Get out slow and put your hands behind your head—we're going for a walk."

Arielle and Selena both rose from the car, fingers intertwined behind their heads. Selena circled around the front and stood next to Arielle, where the man moved the gun back and forth between them. Arielle saw an opening to kick the gun out of his hand, but didn't want to take such a risk so soon. She hadn't seen where this guy came from, and didn't know who else might be hiding in the distance.

She assumed the man knew Landon. Who else would have

any interest in watching them once they arrived?

They were still far enough where even if Landon saw Arielle take this man down, there wouldn't be much he could do aside from blasting some incredibly long-distance shots. They could be back in the car and out of the docks in a matter of seconds. She had left the keys in the ignition—a detail the man didn't notice.

They continued forward, and both vehicles at the dock now swung their doors open. Landon stepped out of his car, and another man stepped out of the Lincoln. They were too far to make out who it was, but Landon and the other man met in front of the Lincoln, shook hands, and proceeded onto the boat.

They didn't even look back this way.

Could Landon really have been that cocky, to trust one of his thugs to handle whoever was following him? He assumed the FBI was tailing him, so why would he run such a risk as holding a federal agent hostage?

Arielle looked around, scanning the top of the shipping containers. That's where *she* would hide in this scenario, and it appeared the man had no backup. She needed to distract the man. She needed Selena to understand this, but had no way of getting her attention as they continued walking at a gradual pace down the boardwalk. They were side by side, elbows almost touching, while they kept their hands behind their heads.

Over the next couple of steps, Arielle exaggerated her sway from side to side until she nudged Selena's elbow with her own. Selena took it in stride, continuing at the same pace as they continued toward the dock.

Selena didn't draw attention to the intentional contact, but

Arielle could feel her staring at her from the side, begging to know what to do next. She could only imagine Selena's simmering fear, having never been in a situation like this. Fortunately for them both, Arielle remained calm and under control. One of the many lessons drilled into all Angels responsible for carrying out the dirty work was to always find a way out. No matter the situation, setting, or how many people were involved, there was *always* a way out.

She had no way of communicating what she wanted Selena to do. Reading each other's thoughts was a skill that would only come after years of working together. This being only their third mission together, Arielle would have to create the distraction and hope Selena understood what to do next.

Arielle slowed her pace, gauging how far behind the man was. She guessed about four feet. What she couldn't tell was where his gun was precisely located. He could have kept it lower by his hip to not appear so obvious. Or maybe he didn't care who saw what was happening and kept it elevated, level with his shoulders as he aimed directly at Arielle's back. That left Arielle with a two-foot window where she could spin and kick, but she didn't like those odds. Her foot could swing and miss everything. Then he would certainly fire the gun and draw the attention from the drug dealers on the boat.

She needed to guarantee the gun's placement and knew going to the ground was her best option. She slowed more and sensed the man—or rather the gun—now two feet behind her back.

Now.

With her next stride, Arielle drifted her right foot toward the center of her path, much like a model might walk down the runway, and planted it firmly on the ground, forcing all of her body's weight onto it. Her left foot continued forward, where she let the tip of her shoe clip the back of her planted foot, sending her sprawling forward. Her hands flew away from her head as she braced for the landing.

On her way down, she caught a glimpse of Selena's bulging eyes, and saw just enough understanding in them to know this half-baked plan just might work.

"Hey!" the man growled, lowering his pistol to Arielle on the ground, having caught herself in a position resembling a difficult push-up.

Arielle looked over her shoulder and saw a clear shot to kick back and knock the gun out of the man's hand, but she was too slow.

Selena hammered down a fist on the man's wrist, causing his hand to lose all sensation and drop the gun, where it clattered along the concrete. Arielle jumped to her feet just as this happened, the man letting out a howl of pain, so she reared back and punched him square in the teeth to silence him.

The punch knocked him off his feet, sprawling him where he landed square on his back, blood immediately spouting from his nose. Selena leaped for his gun, swiftly turning it on him.

"Don't make another sound," she said, crushing the gun into his cheek. "Or I promise you it will be the last."

The man moaned, rocking his head from side to side, not opening his eyes.

"Easy, Selena," Arielle said in a near murmur.

She had turned around to find the dock. They had only walked about one hundred feet, leaving another two hundred to the boat. Had it been a silent evening, the commotion might have carried toward the drug dealers, but the wind continued to whip and blew the sound of the man's painful whine into the void.

They were still far enough to not appear as anything concrete to the men on the boat.

"We need to get him out of the road," Arielle said. "Help me."

She crouched to grab the man under one shoulder, and Selena joined her as they lugged him twenty feet and lay him against one of the shipping containers. He continued to mumble incoherently, so Arielle kicked him on the side of his head, leaving him completely silent.

"Jesus Christ!" Selena gasped. "You gotta warn me when you're going to do something like that."

"Sorry. We can't take any chances. I'm quite certain this guy is a decoy sent from the past."

"How do you know that?"

"Think about it. If he had any relation to the events taking place on that boat, don't you think they'd be watching what happened to us? Or even helping once they saw trouble?"

"The past can't just create a new person to come impede with our mission. That doesn't fit the reality we know."

"I'm not saying the past *created* this guy. Keep in mind, we have already altered things in this timeline. The ripple is always wider than we can understand. We have no idea why this man was taking a stroll down the docks today, or why he had a gun and wanted to seek us out. But something over the past five months has led him exactly to this point. Clearly, he thought we were someone worth hunting. But none of that matters right now. He's out of the way and we can only hope that was the last big hurdle the past can throw our way."

"So, what are we doing now? Going back to the car?"

"Do you have your cell phone?"

Selena smiled and reached into her pocket to pull it out, waving it in front of Arielle. "Always."

"Good, we're going to need it for pictures. We've already come this far. I want to get closer to the boat. Let's go."

Chapter 56

There were enough obstacles between them and the boat to hide behind, so they hurried from one parked car to another, to a row of oil barrels, and eventually to a stack of empty wooden pallets, placing them a mere seventy-five feet away from the boat full of criminals.

"How well does your camera zoom?" Arielle asked as they crouched behind the pallets.

"Decent enough for a 2014 model," Selena replied. "Let me see what I can get."

Selena pulled out her phone and zoomed in toward the group of men chattering on the boat. Arielle watched as Selena's face pinched into a confused look.

"What is it?" Arielle asked.

"I think that's Raj."

"Raj? The vice president of WonderHome?!"

Selena nodded cautiously, as if she was still trying to convince herself of what she saw. "Here. I took a picture."

She handed over the phone, and Arielle snapped it out of her hands, studying the pixelated photo. She looked up and squinted toward the boat. "Holy shit, I think you're right. I *knew* there had to be more involvement from the executive team. No way in hell Landon was pulling all this off on his own."

"And Adam Marshall is nowhere to be seen. He has to be completely innocent."

"We need to get closer." Arielle took a step forward, just as Selena grabbed her by the arm.

"Are you crazy? There's nothing left between us and the boat. We're sitting ducks if we go any closer."

"Nonsense," Arielle said. She had done far riskier things. "We're going to use their cars to shield us. If it was only one car, then no, we wouldn't be doing this. But there are two, and they're parked in a V-formation. It's literally a wall if we stay low enough. Trust me, missions rarely throw you a bone like this."

Selena shook her head. "I don't think I can do it."

"Don't kid yourself. You saw what you did back there, right? I had no idea if my plan of tripping myself was going to work, but you took care of business. You have nothing more to doubt about yourself. You are *good* at this work. I'd even say *great*, if you had a little more faith in yourself. It's getting darker by the second. The wind is loud. This is our chance. C'mon."

Now Arielle grabbed Selena by the arm and pulled them both out from the pallets, crouched like stealthy burglars ready to escape.

"We don't do all those lunges for nothing," Arielle said, gaining speed as they crossed the road where it curved to the right, leaving them vulnerable out in the open.

The two vehicles provided just enough coverage. They reached the Lincoln in a matter of seconds, Arielle stopping at the rear bumper.

They were now less than twenty feet away from the gathering on the boat, and could clearly hear the voice of a shouting man.

"Raj?" Selena whispered.

Arielle nodded. They couldn't see anything, but it was obviously the vice president's voice, elevated to a pitch they had never heard before, his slight accent growing thicker with his mounting rage.

"You have got to be shitting me, Landon," Raj bellowed. "Two million dollars of product on this boat, and you want to send it back? Do you know how ridiculous that sounds?"

"I'm trying to protect us," Landon shouted right back. "You put me in this role so you could keep your hands clean. *I'm* the one with the real estate team. Everyone knows it's my team and my idea. If only they could know the truth, you weasel."

"Well, I'd say you're doing a real shitty job," Raj fired back. "If nothing is supposed to be tied back to me, then tell me why I am on this fucking boat right now. I was never supposed to meet any of these people. Now they all know who I am and what I look like. You feel some heat and now you want to bring everyone down with you. You're a coward. A pussy!"

"Be that way, Raj. Go crawl back to your office where you can hide and be safe. I'll take care of things like I have been, this *entire time.*"

Raj laughed. "Landon's a funny guy, don't you guys think? Take care of things, you say? Like sending away two million dollars. I don't think you should be involved any more in this project. But I can't take you off, because clearly you're a coward and will bring the entire company down. You weak little man. I told Michelle to not hire someone so young for this job."

"Was that before or after you were sucking her tits? We all know it's true!"

Raj erupted with laughter. "Oh, Landon, you truly are one lost puppy. You're letting your dark thoughts win. You're no longer equipped to do this job, so consider yourself removed from the project. We will shift the real estate team to someone else and make all this go away for you."

"The feds called me on my office phone!" Landon screamed, as if he had mentioned this three dozen times already today. "What are you not understanding about that, you ignorant little fuck?!"

"You really don't trust the plan we set up, do you?" Raj asked, letting out a laugh. "It's fool-proof. Everything goes back to Michelle's assistant. *Everything.* Why do you think we went through so much trouble building a secret server to operate all the real estate transactions? And the fake accounts we made for him. Every single transaction for your team is on that hidden server, and every single one is tied to him. We may get questioned if the feds find out, but once they take a closer look, they'll find Adam Marshall was the brilliant mastermind behind the entire thing, and no one will doubt it. He can swear against it all he wants, but the proof is all on that server. *Thousands* of emails in his name, all related to these real estate purchases. It's his word against his own, and I think they'll believe the written proof over his denial."

"You'd better hope so, because they're getting closer."

Raj laughed again. "Let them look. If they really thought something was going on, they'd be here right now busting up the party. But once again, you're blowing things out of proportion. Typical Landon. All emotion and no substance. It's people like you who cause the downfall of a great thing like what we have going. There were always going to be questions surrounding our business practices. Whether from the feds or our competitors, it doesn't matter. Maybe our competition asked the feds to look at what we're doing. At least we don't have to worry about them speaking to you anymore."

"HEY! WHOA!" Landon screamed, fear slipping into his voice.

This caused Arielle and Selena to stare at each other. Arielle rose just enough to see Raj with a gun aimed at Landon.

She hurried back down. "Take a picture. Now!"

Selena circled around Arielle, hand extended with the phone in her grip.

"I'm sorry, Landon," Raj continued. "But you are currently the most dangerous factor in this entire operation. We still have a chance if you're out of the equation."

"You can't just kill me!" Landon cried, terror and desperation thick in his voice. "If I go—"

The gun fired, a crisp, cracking sound that echoed all around the docks. Seagulls screamed as they flew away in a hurry.

Arielle and Selena instinctively crouched lower to the ground, nearly sitting.

"You all work for me now," Raj said to the men on the boat. "Nothing needs to change in your weekly routine. I'll meet you here at the same time every Thursday. You will not speak of this. Now, help me toss his body into the water. Do we have anything that can weigh him down?"

Arielle and Selena exchanged a glance. Arielle had to force down a gulp to clear her throat before speaking. "We need to get the hell out of here."

Chapter 57

They only waited ten more seconds before Arielle peered around the Lincoln to see the men gathering around Landon's dead body. As much as it tempted her to get even closer for pictures, she knew they had enough to protect Adam.

Dusk had taken hold, turning the sky a bluish-purple tinge.

"Now," Arielle whispered, breaking into a sprint away from their hiding spot, Selena quick to follow.

Their footsteps made plenty of noise, but they had to take the risk. Hiding out any longer would only increase their chances of being caught. The wind had actually picked up in speed, and they could only hope it blew the sound of them running *away* from the boat.

Racing at full speed, they reached the car in thirty seconds, both panting for breath as they sat inside. Arielle hadn't looked back once, and was delighted to find no one following them.

"Oh my God," Selena panted. "What the fuck was *that*?!"

Arielle turned the key and sped out of the parking spot, flipping the car around as smoke spewed from the rear tires. That would surely have gotten the men's attention, but it was too late for them to do anything about it. Arielle blazed down the road.

"Raj was behind it the whole time. Michelle too. I don't think she had much of a role aside from ensuring certain people remained employed at WonderHome."

Selena flipped through the photo gallery on her phone. "I got it all. Pictures of Raj and Landon shouting, their crooks standing around the background. One is even holding a rifle. It might not prove what was on the boat, but it's a picture of the last time Landon was alive. Raj has the gun pointed right at his face, so it shouldn't be too hard for them to piece this all together."

"Excellent work. Text those pictures to Felix so we have them backed up, and he can start sorting them out."

"Where are we going now?"

"Home. We got through the hard part, but we still need to package this all up to deliver something substantial. I'd like to get it done tonight so we can get out of here. Every moment we hang around here now becomes a little more dangerous. As of right now, nothing has changed in Adam Marshall's life, but that's all going to change once they rule Landon as missing. We don't know Raj's next move, either. Will he tell Michelle what happened, or is he taking this to his grave? Either path alters the rest of the future for everyone involved. Tell Felix to print five sets of these pictures."

* * *

Twenty minutes later, they arrived home, jumping out of the car and dashing into the house. Felix was at his post in the dining room, laptop flipped open as a wire ran from his phone to the computer, and another from the computer to a printer.

The printed pictures lay in five stacks on the edge of the table, the top photo on each stack showing Landon getting out of his car when he had arrived at the docks.

Felix sprung out of his seat. "Are you two okay?"

They each gave him a quick hug. They were far from okay.

"We're alive and well," Arielle said. "We need to get these pictures out to the proper channels tonight. I want a set of photos dropped off at the *Seattle Times*, one directly to Adam Marshall, one to the police department, and one to the WonderHome offices. Let's leave it in the desk of Amara Edwards. I'm certain she has no involvement in any of this."

"That's only four copies," Felix said.

"The fifth one's for us. We're not going back without evidence."

"Are we just dropping off the pictures with no context?" Felix asked. "We can't assume anyone will know what to do with them."

"Can you print out a note to include with each? Say 'WonderHome money laundering. Raj Kalan killed Landon Greene. Body in Lake Union. Adam Marshall innocent.'"

Felix nodded and returned to his computer to type.

"It was never our job to piece this together for the authorities, just to clear Adam's name. I think we've done enough to do that."

"Are we going to split this up?" Selena asked.

"I was actually thinking we pack up and all head out together. Everything is close by. The office, newspaper, and a police precinct are all within a two-mile radius of each other. Adam's home is maybe another six miles away from the office. We should stop at his place last."

"You want to go there so late?" Felix asked. "It's already 7:30. It'll be close to nine o'clock, maybe even later, if Selena takes forever to pack all her shit."

Selena crossed her arms. "Hilarious. I may pack heavy, but I can do it all in thirty minutes. Can we say the same for you and all of your tech gear, nerd?"

Felix chuckled. The mood had definitely lightened now that a return home was on the table.

"Let's settle down," Arielle interrupted. "Go pack your things. We still have a lot of work to do."

Selena lowered her hands to place them on her hips, jutting out her head toward Arielle. "You're already packed, aren't you? This was your plan since you woke up this morning, wasn't it?"

Arielle grinned. "I packed last night."

"And you didn't tell us to do the same?" Felix asked.

"Sorry. I didn't want to impede your work today if you knew we might go home. That's how people get rushed and do a poor job. Besides, none of it was guaranteed. Still isn't, but I'd rather be ready to leave right after we drop this stuff at Adam's house because who knows what will happen once he gets it." Arielle checked her watch. "Your thirty minutes starts now. Let's get to it."

Chapter 58

They met by the front door twenty-five minutes later, all with wide, nervous smiles.

"It's not over yet," Arielle reminded them. "I know it feels like it, but we still have to be on our toes. We've altered this timeline beyond recognition."

"Good for the timeline," Selena said. "All I see is *my* bed in *my* house. And it's glamorous."

"Soon enough. This couldn't be a worse time to let our guards down. Shall we?"

They followed Arielle to the car, loading their luggage into the trunk. Felix took shotgun, while Selena settled into the back seat. Arielle started the car and pulled onto the road.

"Where to first?" Selena asked.

"The *Times*," Arielle said. "Then WonderHome, police, and Adam last."

"Have you thought about how you're going to give this to the police?" Felix asked. "You can't just walk in and hand it over."

"I'll tape it to the door, or maybe slip it underneath. We'll see what looks easier once we get there. We need to move quickly everywhere we go, especially once we reach the police station. They won't be able to tie anything back to us. But we can't hang around to see what happens."

"Not like we ever do," Selena mumbled.

"For good reason. Sticking around afterwards has never led to anything good. That's why we have a Futures team to scout things after the fact. The longer we're around, the greater the chances of getting tangled in whatever mess we leave behind. Think about it, by tomorrow morning the WonderHome offices are going to be teeming with police and detectives. As an employee there—and one who was recently seen sneaking into Landon's office—do you really think it's wise to stay? You'll be a suspect, even more once they find out you called out for the entire week Landon goes missing. We may have the proof with the pictures, but your name will come up plenty of times. It's easiest to vanish without a trace. It stirs up the suspicion, sure, but it leaves the authorities with nothing to pursue."

"I see," Selena said as they pulled up to the office for the *Seattle Times.* "And what do you plan on doing here?"

"Easy," Arielle said. "The building is open. They still run their printing press upstairs. I'm not going that far, but I'll be able to get this envelope into the hands of someone. Now, if you'll excuse me."

Arielle grabbed the first envelope from Felix, who held the stack in his lap. She parked along the sidewalk and stopped the engine, stepping out without another word. The downtown skyscrapers blocked most of the wind gusts that had been plaguing the area, making for a rather pleasant night. The block around the newspaper was deserted, save for a handful of cars parked across the street.

The building entrance had glass double doors, and Arielle saw a security desk right inside, an older man sitting behind it as he flipped through a recent edition of *Sports Illustrated* highlighting the Seahawks' Super Bowl victory.

She tried the doors to find them locked, the rumbling sound getting the guard's attention. He looked up, and Arielle smiled and waved.

He tossed aside the magazine and took his time getting out of his seat, Arielle imagining all of his old joints cracking and popping as she interrupted his nightly routine. He shuffled to the door and returned a grin as he pushed it open enough to stick his face through.

"Are you lost, young lady?" he asked, his voice gentle.

"No, sir." She held up the envelope. "I'm a private investigator with an incredible story that needs to be shared. I was hoping you could pass this envelope along to the proper person."

The guard studied the envelope with curious blue eyes. "This isn't really the way this works. You can mail it in, or you can email the editor about your story. Unfortunately, the world is a mad place, and we have protocol for a reason. Lots of sick people out there like to send mail into newspapers laced with poison."

"And I completely respect that. But I can assure you I'm no criminal. In fact, I've caught the criminal. It's all in here."

The guard looked at the envelope again, and Arielle could tell a part of him wanted to take it. He was trying to convince himself.

"Look," Arielle said. "It's not sealed."

They had only tucked the flap into the envelope to keep its contents secure, so Arielle flipped it out and stuck her hand into it. She did this for ten uncomfortable seconds while the guard looked from her to the envelope and back.

"My story is true," Arielle said. "I hope you can take my word for it. A bad thing has happened tonight, and I need to make sure the story gets to the right hands. I'm leaving town tonight—my job here is done. I'm sure the mail room has a procedure to check for poisons. You can even take it straight there. Just make sure it gets addressed to go to the correct person, which I'm assuming is the editor."

"I hope I don't get in any trouble," the guard said, reaching through the door, but not opening it any more. "Hand it over."

Arielle hadn't realized the tension building in her shoulders until the relief flooded over her. "Thank you so much, sir. You're helping make the world a better place tonight."

"Uh-huh, I'm sure."

"It's just some photos with a note about the situation. Front page news story."

"I've heard that one plenty of times. But I'll do this favor just this once."

Arielle clapped her hands together. "Thank you, again, you won't regret it."

The guard chuckled. "Honey, at my age, regret is simply a word. Have a good night. I'll get this sent upstairs for you. Good luck."

He offered one definite smile before closing the door and trudging back to his post. Arielle didn't need to wait around to see what he did with the envelope. He was likely going to open to have a look for himself. That would be all he needed to see before knowing it most definitely had to go upstairs.

Arielle returned to the car, and continued to their next stop at WonderHome.

Chapter 59

The parking garage was practically deserted. Even the workers who prided themselves on staying late had gone by 8:30.

"This one's all you, Selena," Arielle said as she parked by the elevators.

"Excuse me," Selena replied. "How is that smart? What if security sees I'm in the building and comes to find me?"

"Building security won't do anything. WonderHome has questions for you, not the building. They're going to know you're in the building, regardless, since you need to swipe your badge to enter. If me or Felix were to enter with your badge, that would only draw more suspicion."

Selena sighed. "Fine."

"This should take five minutes, most of it riding the elevator. Just put the folder on Amara's desk and come right back. Nothing to it."

"Okay."

Selena grabbed the envelope from Felix. "Good luck," he said, as she opened the door and stepped out.

She drew a deep breath, taking in the musty smell from the garage, before heading for the elevators. Each footstep echoed multiple times, making it sound like someone else was walking nearby. But there was no one.

Selena pushed the button to call the elevator and waited as it hummed. The chime rang out emphatically, and she realized her elevated senses. The slightest tremor shook the envelope in her hands as she stepped into the elevator, throat swelling with tension as she watched the doors close, cutting off her view of Arielle and Felix.

Alone in the elevator as it climbed thirty floors, Selena paced in circles. She wasn't sure if it was stress being back inside the office, or a true gut feeling that something was off.

We didn't even confirm who's in the building. We're just assuming everyone is gone by now. Michelle could be here. Even Amara.

Selena talked herself out of it. Possible, but unlikely. She had never known Amara to stay so late.

"Home by dinnertime with the family," she always said, and encouraged the rest of her team to live by the same rule.

But Michelle didn't have a family. WonderHome was her spouse, so she *might* be around.

The elevator stopped, and the doors parted to the executive level. Selena had been on the floor plenty of times, but never had she seen it so dark. The lights were all off, minus a couple above the backsplash in the kitchen area. The refrigerators purred as the only sound.

Selena looked around to see all the doors closed, figuring there was a new mandate to do just that after the footage had leaked of Selena slipping into Landon's office.

Landon.

His door would remain closed for how long? Likely until tomorrow, once word spread about what had happened.

Selena felt the cameras watching her, capturing her face clear as day as she wandered through the office after hours.

I'm definitely going to be a suspect, she thought, realizing how questionable her actions looked on the surface. Hopefully, the proof in the envelope would clear her name, but people would still speculate on Selena's involvement. Her presence in the office mere hours after Landon's death didn't exactly paint her as innocent.

She passed Landon's office, not so much as looking at it, but feeling the haunting presence that always made her head spin when she thought about death and her own mortality.

She passed Mila's office before arriving at Amara's, reaching out her shaky hand to the door handle.

Damn. Locked.

She wiggled the handle a couple more times to confirm, pissed she didn't think of asking Felix for his lock pick.

Selena squatted, finding a gap of about a quarter inch beneath the door, plenty of space to slide the envelope through.

"It'll have to do," she said, dropping the envelope flat on the floor and sliding it under.

Selena had been so focused on her task that she never heard the elevator chime down the long hallway. Never saw the figure approaching her from behind. All she felt was the cold metal of a gun pressed against the flesh on the back of her neck.

"What do you think you're doing?" Raj asked from behind.

Even in a squatted position, Selena's knees locked. She thought she might have been having a heart attack because she couldn't feel it beating in her chest.

"Please don't shoot me," she said. "It's not what you think."

"I think it's exactly what I think, Selena Nicole. If that's even your real name. Turn around and don't make any sudden movements."

Selena did as instructed, pivoting around on her knees, raising her hands for the second time this evening.

"Stand up, dammit," Raj snarled.

Selena rose, her legs wobbly. Surely they would give out any second.

"Please," she said, scanning the area for anything she could use as a weapon. But she had no options. She was pinned against the wall, twenty inches between the gun and her face.

Staring into the tiny black hole brought a flood of emotions. *I'm going to die,* she thought. Raj had clearly gone off the deep end with blood already on his hands. He had proven he would do anything to keep his scheme alive, but could he go as far as killing someone on camera? Did he have connections to make the tapes disappear? Crazier things had happened with corrupt, greedy men.

"Who are you?" Raj asked.

Selena focused on her breathing, hearing, but not listening to Raj's words. He wanted to talk, and that meant she had time to buy.

"Answer me, dammit!"

Raj reared back and whipped Selena across the face with the gun. Pain erupted in her cheek as a tingling numbness spread across her entire face. She didn't know blood was oozing from her nose until it seeped into her mouth and she tasted the metallic flavor.

"I'm Selena Nicole. Like you said."

Raj cracked his lips into a menacing smile, madness raging behind his eyes. "I looked into your file. No one on your resume has ever heard of you. It's all fake. Tell me who you really are and what you're doing here."

Selena's mind felt like a game of whack-a-mole, one idea popping up after another, unable to nail one down she liked. What could she say that would decrease the chances of Raj pulling the trigger?

"I'm undercover," she finally said. "Undercover with the FBI."

"I knew it," he replied, satisfaction in his voice.

"You can't shoot me. We're on camera."

Raj threw his head back and laughed. Selena stared, wondering how Arielle could ever muster enough courage to throw out a punch toward a gun. Not that Selena currently had the physical strength to attempt such a thing.

"I'm not afraid of the cameras. I can erase the footage before anyone ever knows what happens to you."

"My team will know," she said. "Do you really think I came here by myself?"

Selena saw a sliver of doubt creep into Raj's eyes and knew she had bought even more time for herself.

"Bullshit," he said. "Probably another lie like everything else you've told since you've been here. You're snooping around the money laundering. Why else would you have gone into Landon's office?"

"Of course, that's what I'm here for. My team has been watching you guys for the past six months. I'll admit, we had no idea *you* were involved. We were entirely focused on Landon."

"That's because Landon was the brains behind it, so you were correct there."

Fucking liar, Selena thought, then said. "Okay then. If that's really true, maybe we can work out a deal. Immunity for all the information you know, including Landon's whereabouts. We haven't been able to find him since Monday."

Raj started deep into Selena's eyes, the gun never wavering. He was giving it deep thought.

Selena saw a small motion out of the corner of her eye, accompanied by a whizzing sound, followed by a *thump!* on the wall further down the hallway.

They both looked over to see a sharp object sticking out of the surface like a dart.

"What the—" Raj began, his words cut off.

Selena looked back at him and saw a throwing knife lodged in the side of his neck, blood shooting from the wound.

Raj dropped the gun and flailed for the knife, falling to his knees as his hands scrambled helplessly. Selena watched as all strength fled his body in a matter of seconds. His shirt turned black from all the blood it had already soaked up. He tried speaking, but his words came out in bloody gurgles. His eyes bulged from their sockets, the life slipping out of them.

Selena jumped aside as Raj fell forward, his body smacking the ground with a heavy thud, blood pooling all around his head and seeping into the carpet.

She looked to her left, toward the elevators, and saw both Arielle and Felix panting for breath.

Chapter 60

"Let's go!" Arielle yelled.

Felix lunged toward the elevator and pushed the button.

Thirty seconds ago, Selena thought she was going to die in the middle of the WonderHome office. Now, she looked down at the company's vice president, who had choked to death on his own blood.

Selena turned and sprinted, her legs still weak. She tumbled, even tripped, but held herself along the wall as she whirled toward the elevator lobby. Her face throbbed with excruciating pain, the cheekbone likely fractured. The blood from her nose slowed, but hadn't stopped.

Despite the suffering, she made it to the elevators where Felix was already inside, arm extended to keep the doors open. Arielle wrapped an arm around Selena's waist and helped her into the elevator.

"What happened?" Arielle asked, propping Selena up against the wall. "Your face is smeared with blood. I don't even know where to start."

Selena pointed to her cheek where the gun had struck her. "Pistol whip," she said.

"Jesus Christ," Arielle said, still panting. "You're so lucky. An inch higher and you'd probably have lost your eye. An inch lower and half of your teeth would've been knocked out."

Selena nodded. "Lucky. Yes, that's it." She tried to smile, but winced at the pain burning from her nose to her jawbone.

"Seriously, Selena," Felix said, also panting like a thirsty dog. "This could have gone so much worse."

Selena noticed Arielle had another throwing knife in her hand, a gun tucked into her utility belt.

"How did you know?" Selena asked through closed teeth like a ventriloquist, not wanting to cause herself any more pain.

"We saw him in the parking garage," Arielle said. "He pulled in like a maniac and we knew something was wrong. We knew his office was on the same floor as Amara's and that he'd probably find you."

"How did you get in without a keycard?"

Felix reached into his pocket and pulled out his lock pick. "No keycard needed, but we had to run up thirty-four flights of stairs. That's why we still can't catch our breath."

Selena wanted to question this further, but saved her strength. How the hell could they have run up that many flights of steps? And Arielle still delivered the deadly blow to Raj's neck, even if it took her two tries.

Selena wanted to smile, but knew better than to try. "How do I look?" she asked.

"You look like you just last lasted twelve rounds with Mike Tyson," Arielle said.

"But you should see the other guy," Felix added, laughing at himself.

Despite the throbbing injury and the tension from just surviving a close call with death, Selena broke into tears of gratitude.

"Selena, what's wrong?" Felix asked, the humor in his voice replaced with sudden concern.

She shook her head. "I can't believe I'm alive. You saved my life. Both of you. How can I ever pay you back?"

The elevator stopped, and the doors parted to the garage. Somehow, it had already felt like a lifetime ago when Selena was last here.

"Your legs feeling better?" Arielle asked. "You want to try walking?"

Selena nodded, some resemblance of normalcy returning to her legs during the elevator ride. The adrenaline was fading and her body felt like itself, aside from the piercing pain on the left side of her face.

They got into the car, Arielle moving with urgency. Building security might have not had an initial interest, but if they caught a look at what had just unfolded on the executive floor, a pursuit would surely follow.

Arielle turned on the car and flew out of the garage, driving at a calmer speed once they reached the road and blended in with the rest of society.

"You don't owe us a thing," Arielle said, speaking to Selena in the rear-view mirror at a red light. "Everyone in this car would do the same thing for each other. We sensed danger from the moment we saw Raj show up and knew we had to literally run up those stairs for your life. It's why we put in the work to keep our bodies in tip-top shape. If we had been two steps slower, who knows what might have happened."

"Arielle's right," Felix said. "It was like we both knew exactly what we needed to do. I'm not sure we even said anything to each other. We just got out of the car and figured out how to get to you."

"It's all instincts. We've all gone through the same basic training where they teach survival techniques—you're not allowed to go on missions without it. You retain more than you know. Once you've done so many missions, that sort of thing comes second nature."

"Well, thank you," Selena said. "The margs are on me when we get back."

"Wait," Felix said. "Are we still going to the police station right now?"

"Of course," Arielle replied, nonchalant. "Why wouldn't we?"

"Because you just murdered someone on a live camera feed. The police could already be looking for you, for all we know."

"I'm not worried about it. We'll swing by and see how it looks. If it's a quiet night, I'll slip the envelope under the door and we'll be on our way. We're only two minutes away."

They rode in silence, pulling up to the police station, a two-story building surrounded by towering skyscrapers.

Arielle parked along the curb. The entrance had two sets of glass double doors. A couple of officers walked out of the building, sharing a laugh as they strolled to a patrol car parked across the street.

"See," Arielle said. "Quiet night. Two people have been killed and they don't even know it yet. I think it's your turn, Felix."

Felix laughed. "I don't think so."

"I did the newspaper, Selena just did WonderHome, and now it's your turn. We're all going to approach Adam together. Just open that first door, toss the envelope on the ground, and come right back. Nothing to it, and we're all right here."

Felix shook his head and stepped out of the car without

another word.

They watched as he looked around, then hurried to the door. No one had appeared once he reached the door and pulled it open. He threw the envelope down and pivoted around to run back to the car, jumping into his seat.

"Easy," he said. "Now get me out of here."

Arielle put the car into drive. "We have one last stop."

* * *

They arrived at Adam Marshall's house fifteen minutes later, relieved to be further from the WonderHome office that would soon swarm with police activity.

Selena's face remained in a tolerable pain, but she could speak a little better without wincing on each word.

"Okay," Arielle said. "Game plan. We're a group of private investigators with important information. We don't know how he's going to react, so we'll need to roll with it. At the very least, we need to make sure he's aware of the envelope and that we're leaving it with him for his own protection. The past has removed both people who should take the fall for this, leaving a line of evidence that will point back to Adam. As soon as we deliver the envelope, we don't owe Adam another second. We come back to the car. I'll drive around the block so we're out of his sight, and we'll take our Juice to return home. Does that all sound good?"

"Sounds perfect to me," Selena said.

"Let's do this," Felix said.

"Okay. I don't expect any fireworks from Adam, but let's

still be on our toes, just in case. We're not home yet. Let's go."

Arielle stepped out first, the other two following her up the path to the Marshalls' front door. A light on the upstairs level was on, but Arielle could see another through the narrow window next to the door. It was past nine o'clock, so Arielle knocked instead of ringing the doorbell to not wake the kids.

Arielle took a step back and crossed her arms in front of her waist. Felix and Selena remained a step back, the envelope clutched tightly in Felix's grip.

"Any snooping neighbors?" Selena asked, scanning the area.

It was much too dark to see if anyone was out for a late night walk. The block had a few lampposts stymied by the tall trees.

"I think we're okay," Felix said.

Arielle knocked harder.

"Do we just leave it if he doesn't answer?" Felix asked.

"He'll answer."

On cue, they saw the movement of a shadow appear through the window, growing as it approached the door. When it reached the door, the shadow stopped.

Arielle forced a fake smile, knowing whoever was on the other side was looking through the peephole.

A snap came from the door as the deadbolt was unlocked, and it swung open to reveal Adam Marshall dressed in his pajamas, reading glasses perched on his nose, a John Grisham novel in his grip while a finger held his page location.

His eyes jumped across all three Angels standing on his doorstep, then behind them to study their car.

"Can I help you?" he asked, keeping his free hand on the door.

"Yes, good evening, Mr. Marshall. Do you have a moment to speak with us?" Arielle said.

Adam kept looking back and forth between the three of them, pondering the late-night visit. "May I ask what this is regarding?"

"Your freedom," Arielle said sternly. "Your future is at risk. We just need two minutes of your time, and we don't even need to come inside. Everything you'll need is in my colleague's envelope."

Arielle turned around and Felix handed her the envelope.

"Let me grab a jacket," Adam said, closing the door and re-opening it ten seconds later. He stepped out, looking over his shoulder before closing the door behind him. "Okay, what is this about, exactly?"

"I'm afraid you made a mistake taking a job with Michelle Garrison," Arielle said.

"Michelle?" His voice elevated. He wrapped his arms around himself to keep warm, but unease spread across his face. "What does she have to do with this?"

"As far as Michelle is concerned, we're still not entirely sure. WonderHome has been laundering money from drugs and weapons sales through its real estate program. Landon Greene and Raj Kalan overlooked the operation. Both men are now dead."

"What?!" Adam cried. "Dead?! I just saw Raj this after-noon."

"I'm afraid so," Arielle said. "All the real estate transac-tions are run through you, correct?"

Adam looked past Arielle into the distance, running through his memories. "Yes. Michelle assigned me as a special assistant to the real estate team. My only duty is to sign the purchase agreements on behalf of the company." Adam leaned back against his door. "Oh my God, am I going to jail?"

"No. That's why we're here. You'll definitely be questioned and, like I mentioned, you are meant to look guilty. In this envelope are pictures of Raj and Landon on a boat full of drugs, weapons, and their dealers. Raj shot Landon and dumped his body in the water. The location is noted in there, as well."

"I'm sorry," Adam said. "Who are you? This all sounds made up. I need to make some phone calls."

"I'd advise against that. We're a team of private investigators. We were looking into the laundering scheme and have uncovered a lot about it, including how it's all tied back to you. There are other names involved, sure, but it sounds like Raj and Landon were running a fake email account in your name on a hidden server. We couldn't access the hidden server, but we can only assume it is full of all the information meant to paint you as guilty."

Adam laughed. "You know this is crazy, right? I can't just accept this and move on with my life."

"No one here is laughing, Adam. If you brush this all aside, you're going to prison for a long time. We've already delivered this information to the *Seattle Times*, Seattle PD, and even left a copy in Amara Edwards' desk. We did that in case you really don't believe us, you'll at least have a fighting chance."

"I can't just *believe* you. This is the most absurd thing I've ever heard."

"It's all true," Felix said, stepping forward. "We do this for a living. We see absurd all the time. You're an innocent man, and we saw the opportunity to help you. That's all this is."

Adam stood up tall and nodded to Selena. "And what happened to her?"

Clearly, Selena's face had been morphed out of recognition if Adam didn't recognize her from the office.

"This is Selena Nicole," Arielle said. "From your POPS team. We planted her at the company to help with our investigation."

"Selena?" he asked, jutting his head forward for a closer look. "Can't be. She's . . . wow, it really is you?"

"Hi, Adam," Selena said. "Listen to what we're telling you. It's the best thing you can do."

"We need to go now," Arielle said. "Our work here is done. The rest is in your hands. Let's go."

She turned and started walking.

"Wait!" Adam said. "The envelope?"

Arielle grinned to herself before turning back around. "Apologies." She handed it over.

"How can I get in touch with you?"

"You can't. We're off the grid for a reason. Don't even mention us to anyone, or we'll know, and we can make you pay. If anyone asks, just say this envelope was left on your doorstep. There will be footage of us, and they'll probably print some pictures to ask if you've ever seen us before. You will tell them you have not. Are we clear?"

Adam nodded, eyes wide. "Yes, ma'am."

"Good luck with everything, Mr. Marshall."

Arielle turned back around and started for the car, Felix and Selena hurrying to her side as they returned to their seats. She fired up the engine and drove off, Adam remaining on his doorstep, watching them disappear into the night.

"Do you think he believes us?" Felix asked.

"Once he looks in the envelope, he will," Arielle said. "He just needs to see the faces of Raj and Landon, and then he'll start picking apart every contract he's signed. He'll be fine." Arielle turned to the next block over and parked the car in front of a house with all of its lights off. "Does everyone have their Juice ready?"

"Oh, it's ready," Selena said.

"Got mine," added Felix.

"We still have a long journey back to Denver, but let's just get back to our present time first. Before we do, I want to say how proud I am of this team. This mission took a ton of resilience, and you both showed it. We're going home really banged up. But we're still going home—that's all that matters."

"I can drink to that," Selena said. "Cheers."

They raised their flasks of Juice to the center of the car before taking a swig to return to the present.

Chapter 61

Present Day

The trio's transition to the present passed seamlessly. Thanks to Arielle having access to her own private jet, they didn't need to wait around for a particular flight to leave. They did, however, stop by the Seattle Road Runners' offices for Selena to get checked out. Each office across the continent had a resident doctor, along with a closet of medical equipment.

After an hour at the office, the doctor cleared Selena for their return travel home. X-rays showed no structural damage to Selena's facial bones, but her cheek would remain swollen and bruised for at least a couple of weeks. The doctor gave Selena painkillers and prescribed her a heavy regiment of ice and pressure to the injured area to help bring down the swelling.

They headed to the hangar where Arielle had already arranged their flight home. It was midnight by the time they boarded the jet, leading to the rare instance of all three Angels sleeping during the three-hour flight back to Denver.

They landed at four in the morning, local time, and were back at the Denver headquarters by 4:45, both the city and office nearly vacant.

"Is this a bad omen?" Felix asked once they entered the

basement.

"What do you mean?" Arielle asked.

"Well, the last two missions ended with us having a margarita at D'Corazon. They're not exactly open right now. How are we supposed to cap off another victory?"

They had all regained some energy thanks to the extended nap, the drive to the office rather chatty considering the hour.

"*You* want a margarita right now?" Selena asked.

Felix shrugged. "I believe in tradition. And I suppose if we let it die after only two times, then it isn't actually a tradition, and just something we did on those first missions."

Arielle definitely didn't want a margarita, but she understood Felix's point. Having the margarita wasn't about the drink itself, it was the endcap to a mission. The final stamp of approval. Until the next one.

"Well," Arielle said. "We can alter it. As much as I'd love for it to be D'Corazon each time, that's just not feasible. There will be other instances we come back at weird hours and they're closed. There might even be times we stay overnight in whatever city we're in—I'm strongly giving that some thought after tonight. But we can still have a margarita, no matter where we are."

"Are you suggesting we have one here?" Selena asked coyly.

"We should have everything we need in the kitchen, so why not? We can't just go our separate ways tonight without having our celebratory drink."

"What the hell is going on?" Selena asked. "Felix and Arielle are the ones pushing for a drink at five in the morning. Am I hearing this correctly, or was the doctor wrong about me not having a concussion?"

Felix laughed, the sound echoing around the office. The

three Road Runners who were still awake and working in the bullpen all turned to look at them.

"Trust me," Arielle said. "I don't want a drink, but Felix is right: doing it for the third time will cement it as our tradition. It's our thing. If thinking about that marg pushes us to the finish line on these missions, then so be it. I'm not here to interfere with whatever motivates us."

Selena half-smiled, unable to give a complete grin. "Okay then, let's go find the blender and tequila."

They started across the office, Felix stopping when they approached three men working in the bullpen.

"Hey guys," he greeted them. They were all focused on their computers and spun around to face the three superstar Angels. "This might be an odd request, but are any of you able to do us a favor and find some news articles from the *Seattle Times* in the year 2014? We're looking specifically for the week after February twentieth for a story regarding a company called WonderHome. We know the Futures Report won't be available until tomorrow, but just want to know what happened."

"That's not a problem at all, Mr. Francisco," one of the men said, swiveling back around to face his computer. "Give me five minutes and I'll get something printed out for you."

"Thank you so much, and please, just call me Felix. My dad is Mr. Francisco, and that makes me sound old."

Selena laughed, shaking her head. "You're the one who acts older than your dad."

"Don't sass me," Felix said, pointing a stiff finger at Selena.

"Thank you again," Felix said to the Road Runner. "I look forward to it. We'll be over in the kitchen area."

Arielle led the way and rummaged through the cupboards, piecing together the blender, margarita mix, and tequila, while Felix gathered the ice and orange juice. He also grabbed an ice pack for Selena, who instantly pressed it against her purple cheek.

"I still can't believe my eyes," Selena said. "Arielle Lucila playing bartender and making margaritas. In the middle of the night. Are you sure you know what you're doing?"

Arielle flipped off Selena and continued mixing everything in the blender, her tongue clenched between her teeth as she concentrated on getting the perfect measurements. "Hope no one's sleeping right now," she said before flipping on the switch to start the blender.

Once it fell silent, leaving a smooth and frothy mixture in the blender, Arielle poured the drink into three cups. "I'm afraid they don't have margarita glasses here, but I promise it tastes just as good."

She passed out the glasses, and they all lifted them to the center of their informal circle.

"To another mission in the books," Arielle said. "And to all of us returning home. May we never take that for granted."

They touched glasses and took their first drinks.

"Holy shit, Arielle!" Selena cried. "This is incredible. How do you know how to make these so good?!"

"Well, I am Mexican," Arielle laughed. "Seriously, though, who do you think played bartender at my family parties growing up? Once I was twelve, my dad taught me how to make drinks and never looked back. It was funny because I couldn't drink anything I made, so I had to experiment based on how people reacted. I just kept tweaking things until I got reactions like the one you just had."

"It really is good," Felix said. "So smooth."

The man from the bullpen made his way toward the kitchen

with a sheet of paper in hand. "Excuse me," he said. "I'm sorry to interrupt, but I have what you asked for, Felix."

"Thank you, kind sir," Felix replied, taking the paper. "We really appreciate you doing that."

Felix shook the man's hand and waited for him to return to his desk, walking with his head high and chest puffed out.

"I know you don't read the Futures Reports," Felix said to Arielle. "But this isn't one. Are you okay with me reading it out loud?"

Arielle crossed her arms and considered this. "That's a fair point. I suppose it's fine because I'm not sure how much the Futures Report will even discuss WonderHome, since the mission was about Adam Marshall. Let's hear it."

"Okay, here it is from the *Seattle Times*, dated February 22, 2014. Police have reported several suspicious tips regarding the murder of Raj Kalan, the vice president of the online real estate marketplace, WonderHome. They have a person of interest, and believe the murder to be related to the disappearance of the company's chief financial officer, Landon Greene, who hasn't appeared in the office since the start of the week. The tips officials have received suggest Mr. Greene was also murdered, and that both men were involved in a corporate money laundering scheme together.

"This separate matter is being handed over to the FBI for further investigation. Police are trying to determine the validity of these anonymous tips. Michelle Garrison, the CEO of WonderHome, has not responded to our requests for a comment, nor has the company's legal team. This is an ongoing story. Please check back for updates, and if you have any pertinent information, please contact Seattle PD."

Arielle smiled, nodding to herself. "We did it. No mention

of Adam Marshall, even though I'm sure he's being grilled by the detectives."

"You thought the murders would hurt his case, but I think they're actually helping him," Selena said. "They'll be able to clear him of the murders, and that's only going to allow him the chance to explain his side of the story."

"It's a success," Arielle said. "And that's all that matters. Adam will get to live his life with his family and never have to go through all that pain and suffering."

"Cheers to that," Felix said, raising his glass once more. "I know we're all looking forward to a long rest and recovery after this one, but let's soak it in. We made the world a better place, and *that's* all that matters."

They clinked their glasses one more time and sipped margaritas until the sun came up.

READ THE FUTURES REPORT!

414

Just because Arielle Lucila doesn't want to look at the Futures Report to find out what happens after the mission, doesn't mean you can't!

Enjoy an exclusive look at the official Futures Report for the WonderHome mission that is prepared for the Commander's office following each mission.

All you need to do is join my e-mail Reader Club by signing up at **https://bookhip.com/FMWAMSP**

Author's Note

Thank you for reading Dirty Money. To date, this is the longest book I've written. I planned it that way, too. I wanted to try things differently with this book by diving deeper into the three main characters of Arielle, Felix, and Selena. I also wanted to experiment with writing scenes from the perspective of the troubled Adam Marshall, hoping to bring some humanity to the subject in question, so that it wasn't just another notch in the belt for the team of Angels.

In the next book, I'm looking to add more scenes from the perspective of the potential suspects involved.

This is all part of what I consider the next logical step in my growth as an author. Past books have always revolved around three characters or fewer. I want to expand the universe I have created, and the only way to do that is by bringing in new characters. Who are the Road Runners that make all the arrangements behind the scenes, and deliver them in a simple file for the Angels to begin their mission? I look forward to finding out with you and seeing who else we can bring into the mix.

More on that later.

Dirty Money was inspired by my time in corporate America. No, I've never worked for a company that played along with a money laundering scheme, but a lot of the vibes in the office, the executives, and other employees in this fictional company of WonderHome are all drawn from real-life experience. I imagine you can relate to working under money-hungry executives who will do anything to improve the bottom line, even at the expense of the regular folks.

It was my great pleasure to bring these fictional executives down, along with the company. Too often in our society, we see the filthy rich maneuver out of justice. I couldn't dare let this story end that way.

I hope you enjoyed how it all played out, and that you are growing closer to all three of the Angels as they continue to grow together as a team and learn about each other.

Thank you to everyone who helped with the production of this book. Special thanks to my editor Stephanie Cohen-Perez, my narrator Cynthia Farrell, and to all my fans in the Gonzalez Gang. You've kept me going for nineteen books now, and I look forward to the many more!

Lastly, thank you to my wife Natasha for continuing to support me on this journey. None of this would be here without you.

Andre Gonzalez

August 17, 2022 - February 15, 2023

Enjoy this book?

You can make a difference!

Reviews are the most helpful tools in getting new readers for any books. I don't have the financial backing of a New York publishing house and can't afford to blast my book on billboards or bus stops.

(Not yet!)

That said, your honest review can go a long way in helping me reach new readers. If you've enjoyed this book, I'd be forever grateful if you could spend a couple minutes leaving it a review (it can be as short as you like) on the Amazon page.

Thank you so much!

Also by Andre Gonzalez

Arielle Lucila Series:
  Dirty Money (#3)
  Secrets in the Vault (#2)
  Angel Assassin (#1)

Wealth of Time Series:
  Time of Fate (#6)
  Zero Hour (#5)
  Keeper of Time (#4)
  Bad Faith (#3)
  Warm Souls (#2)
  Wealth of Time (#1)
  Road Runners (Short Story)
  Revolution (Short Story)

Amelia Doss Series:
  Salvation (#3)
  Nightfall (#2)
  Resurrection (#1)

Insanity Series:
  The Insanity Series (Books 1-3)
  Replicate (#3)
  The Burden (#2)

Insanity (#1)
Erased (Prequel Short Story)

The Exalls Attacks:
Followed Away (#3)
Followed East (#2)
<u>Followed Home (#1)</u>
A Poisoned Mind (Short Story)

Standalone books:
Snowball: A Christmas Horror Story

About the Author

Born in Denver, CO, Andre Gonzalez has always had a fascination with horror and the supernatural starting at a young age. He spent many nights wide-eyed and awake, his mind racing with the many images of terror he witnessed in books and movies. Ideas of his own morphed out of movies like *Halloween* and books such as *Pet Sematary* by Stephen King. These thoughts eventually made their way to paper, as he always wrote dark stories for school assignments or just for fun. Followed Home is his debut novel based on a terrifying dream he had many years ago at the age of 12. His reading and writing of horror stories evolved into a pursuit of a career as an author, where Andre hopes to keep others awake at night with his frightening tales. The world we live in today is filled with horror stories, and he looks forward to capturing the raw emotion of these events, twisting them into new tales, and preserving a legacy in between the crisp bindings of novels.

Andre graduated from Metropolitan State University of Denver with a degree in business in 2011. During his free time, he enjoys baseball, poker, golf, and traveling the world with his family. He believes that seeing the world is the only true way to stretch the imagination by experiencing new cultures and meeting new people.

Andre still lives in Denver with his wife, Natasha, and their three kids.